Still Water

CATHERINE MARSHALL

CONTENTS

STILL WATER

CHAPTER ONE

My vision has blown. It's no surprise, in the circumstances, my senses shutting down on me. Lights flash and glare, sound blares and rears like waves. Details jut from the blur - *Information, Toilets, Costa Coffee*; above me, high-pitched nasal announcements in a language I somehow do not speak. My legs begin to fold and I wait for the floor to smack against me because my balance is going as well.

It doesn't happen. I just sway, or I think I do. It's hard to tell. I do know, though, I have to keep going, keep moving, escape, the impulse cold and hard against my spine. I head unsteadily across the concourse towards the cashpoints. There's no queue but my hands are shaking so much it's as though my card has been glued into its slit in my purse, even when I prise it out I can't align it with the slot of the machine. People will think I'm drunk or stoned.

People will think.

It's so late there's hardly anyone around, the occasional dark haze of their presence brushes past me large but unthreatening like the ghosts of bears. I punch in the numbers of my birthday, Enter, and frown hard to read the screen. Another press, on the maximum amount offered, and my heart's thudding in case they already know and have immediately blocked my account. In case they are searching already the CCTV footage, and I've betrayed myself already, because I've watched enough crime shows to know they can track you down every time you access your own money. The machine whirrs and my card ejects an inch. I snatch it back to safety, grab the notes and stuff them into my bag. I'm still shaking. Hot and shivering, slick with sweat inside my canvas jacket. But I can't stop to deal with that because I have to buy a ticket and I don't know when the last train goes I might be missing it even now.

The ticket office is dark and empty. Feverishly I scan the Departures board, its dot matrix information barely discernible. I think I read the word I want, the destination I need, the number of the platform, the departure time five minutes from now.

I can't run. Can't coordinate my legs, the synapses have burned through. I manage a halting stumble towards the platform, jerk myself up into the first carriage, fling inside. Lines of empty seats before me, no reservation tickets this time of night. No passengers, no luggage. The whole train is swinging like a hammock. My ears are ringing and I drop into an airline seat. Too much chance, at a table, of having another face in front of mine, eyes and knees and the smell of their polystyrene coffee.

I crouch rigid. My head hurts, rammed full of spikes from the inside. As I stare sightless ahead, I'm vaguely aware of seats being filled, middle-aged adolescents with lager cans and stubbled scalps, thin dark wisps opening laptops or books. I hear, as if through water, a whistle, feel the jerk of the train beneath me. The platform begins to slide away.

Moments pass. Minutes. "See your ticket, love?" I rummage for the notes I thrust inside my bag, draw out one, tell him where I want to go. I cannot look at his face, speak to him more than necessary, in case he remembers me. I have to blur in his mind with the other women alone on this train. My appearance won't catch at his attention; distressed jeans, cotton khaki jacket, mass of hair. There are a lot of students where I'm going. I could be one of them. I've always looked younger than I am. He hands me my ticket and my change. I thank him and he moves away.

And then it slices through me that I'm making the most dangerous assumption. I've no idea how I look. My reflection in the window throws back nothing, or not enough. I sway to my feet, out into the aisle, hit the 'open door' sign with my palm and lurch into the toilet capsule. Lock it fast behind me.

Already it's a mess. Reeking of pee, the pan stained or worse. Tissues soaked sticking to the floor. Graffiti, buzzing dim light. The usual. Rocking with the motion of the train I can't meet my own eyes, try to examine myself with a cursory glance. My skin is greyish green, my eye sockets bruised, but that could be the light. I could just be ill. A second and final darting glimpse and I'm sure. My face is not marked with

2

blood.

So that's all right then.

The warning I get is a burning in my throat and nostrils, my stomach kicks and abruptly and violently I vomit into the stainless steel basin.

The train cranks to a halt and I fall out onto the tarmac of the platform below. As I stumble upright a handful of shapes blur past me, heading towards the car park and the road up into town; it's the middle of the night and the end of the line.

I hang back, barely breathing. The others shift, slip away, an amorphous whisper and soundless footfall as they disappear ahead of me into the dark. I take the steepening path, walking so fast my chest hurts. Head down, tunnelling blind and deaf through empty streets, hell-bent on the light at their close. Every so often my feet skid from under me and I lurch and falter but I don't stop.

No concrete now, just the grass and the bare ground. Nothing stirs. The house looks shuttered against me and it burns across my mind that I've done the wrong thing. The fatal thing. I might have been protected by the anonymity of the city; having lost everything else, I could have lost myself too. But here is the first place anyone will come. And it's already too late.

Inside I tread over a deluge of mail and the taut thread that's been keeping me going and focussed begins to spin away from me. Though I'm moving as fast as I can locking doors, throwing bolts, drawing curtains it's like slo-mo, and all the time there's a keening, whining noise which I know at some distant rational level is me.

In the bathroom I vomit again. It gets in my hair. I'm crying and shuddering now, pulling blankets from the bed because I need to sleep but not up here, not in a bed, up here there's too much space.

Downstairs I drag cushions from the sofa and stuff them under the kitchen table. Crawl inside with my blanket. Sheltering from the bombs. I pull the blanket around me for suddenly it's cold. So cold. I can make out shapes on the dresser. A pile of books, hardbacks on their sides. I can't quite read the titles but the gold lettering glints at me from their spines. Bottles, squarish ones of oil, taller ones of wine. It calms me for a minute, staring at these things, working to identify them. My heart rate begins to slow though my tears course still. There's a can of something – air freshener? hairspray? – and a cable, an extension lead maybe or a phone charger, I can't tell how thick it is and an old spherical CD player/radio with its mouth open like a Pacman and a photo in a frame.

I'm sick again into my hand. Or I would be, if there were anything left in my stomach to hurl. I jerk up to find something on which to wipe the acid from my palm, hitting my head against the table, gritting my teeth in pain and it's then that it comes

the pounding on the front door

I freeze, though I'm shaking so much I'd be out of the game, clamp my mouth shut to stop the whimpering.

Again. A fist against the wood. Heavy with urgency. My eyes squeeze shut and I draw up my knees, bury my head against them.

Go away go away go away go away

And it does.

It's gone.

At some point I must have stopped breathing because suddenly I have to start again and I gulp at the air, the sound rasping through the silence. And then I leap and splutter because this time the pounding is at the kitchen door, feet away from me, in the room with me, louder and more insistent and it's a death knell.

And then he shouts my name and my unravelling is complete.

It's Gil.

Chapter Two

First light, the sea a silent pale shimmer beneath a vast wash of sky. Gil let his backpack drop with a soft thud into the sand and inhaled deep. Nothing for the remainder of the summer would equal this first dawn, the salt taste of the water, early sun glittering off its surface, the caw of gulls above an empty beach. He felt his muscles loosen as he exhaled, his spirits kick free into swift and glorious ascent. It was like rebirth, he thought it every time, though he'd have said it out loud to no one. In the longed-for collapse of endless sunburned days through endless debauched nights, such an admission had no place, even if it were the truth.

Because it was the truth.

"Hey Gil!"

He turned, smiling already at their voices. Henry and Radar and Buz, shaggy haired and long limbed, tanned and salt and sand encrusted way ahead of the season, all popped out of the same surf dude mould. They originally hailed from Barnstaple and Gloucester and Newport Pagnell yet their intonation rendered every statement a question, every ounce of their energy focussed on the next wave. There were, he knew, worse ways to be.

"Hey guys."

"Where you been, mate?"

"Earning a living." He said it lightly, gestured towards his bag in the sand. "Just got in."

"Staying at Cecily's?"

He grinned, knowing already where this was going. Nothing ever changed. But whose fault was that, exactly? "If it's free."

"She *keeps* it free for you."

"Keeps it *warm* for you."

He cocked an eyebrow, indicated the water. "Like a pond out there."

"S'all you know. Tide's coming in."

And so it was. He hoisted one strap of his backpack over his

5

shoulder. "Patrick's? Around eight?"

Henry smiled. "Sure thing. Good to have you back, Gil."

"Not coming out with us?" Radar, airing the old line. But nothing changed there either. Gil shook his head. "This is the year we'll get you, you know."

He raised a hand. "See you later." Watched them trot across the sand with their boards. He was one of them and he wasn't. It had always been the case and it was kind of the way he liked it. Lingering as they vanished into the grey-blue water, he spotted after a moment their heads bobbing like buoys on the swell. Roll and heave and they were gone. Then rising crouched low, boards higher on the waves, bodies lifting tentatively, legs slowly straightening … and lost again in the crashing tide. He hesitated, sorely tempted to strip and plunge into the water himself, take his inaugural dip of the summer. But another reunion was tugging for his attention and he turned to stroll back along the beach.

Climbing the steepening lanes behind the sea-front rows of tourist tat, whitewashed cottage walls bright with bougainvillea, sunshine already burning off the morning chill, he emerged into the palm-lined square which over the years had become something of an artists' enclave. Gradually evolving from a potters' workshop and makeshift tearoom, it had sprawled to include two seascape galleries and craft studios, a hippie-goth boutique stuffed with fantasies of black leather trenchcoats and black skirted basques, tie-dye shirts and floaty hems skimming the dust. At its centre stood a low-slung seventeenth century pub with ivy clad walls, lawned gardens overlooking the sweep of the bay. Beside it a second-hand bookstore crammed tight with torn and ageing stock. The little glass shop with its intricately formed roses complete with shards of thorns and dolphins riding a crystal surf. And here to his left the bow-fronted café decorated as he had always known it in creams and wedgewood blues, furnished with reclaimed pine settles and stained and splitting tables, the paintings on the walls and the pottery on the Welsh dresser all for sale. They supported each other, the people who lived their lives and ran their businesses in this square. Gil loved it all.

Even the tourists.

Pressing down the brass handle of the café door, he crossed the threshold. The place was empty but for an elderly couple finishing fruitbread toast and a pot of tea. Slipping his rucksack from his shoulders, he stowed it in a corner beside the dresser, dropped his jacket over the top.

"Good morning." He strolled over, smiled. "Everything all right?"

"Oh, it's very good, thank you." The woman had neat grey hair, good clothes, a stern-approval thing going on. Retired school teacher, Gil decided. Maths.

"Beautiful day, isn't it?"

"It's what we come here for, this weather. We've never had it so nice anywhere."

"It isn't so nice anywhere, but then I could be biased. Tell you where would be lovely this morning, the path around the top of the bay. You can pick up the footpath just down the side of the pub here. Easy walk, spectacular views, very peaceful. Now," he smiled again. "Is there anything else I can get you?"

They wanted only their bill, let him clear their cups and plates as though he had been waiting on them all morning and not just stepped in from the street. He carried the crockery through the archway to the kitchen, where a slender woman in denim shorts and a baggy vest, her tawny hair piled into a loose knot, was cutting rounds of pastry and singing along to the radio. His heart mushed a little.

"Table two ready for their bill."

She caught her breath as she recognised his voice. "Gil!"

He grinned. "Cecily."

She flung her arms around him. He hugged her in return, the warmth of baking on her skin. "Every year," she said, "every year I think I'll sense when you're going to turn up. Every year you take me by surprise."

"Yeah that's me. Predictably unpredictable."

She stood back from him, leaning against the cooker, her eyes still dancing with pleasure at seeing him again. "How are you? You look great."

He grinned back. "Well so do you. And I'm fine. And you're

doing breakfasts now?"

"I figure I'm here, I might as well be taking money. It's not like the place is ever over-run at this hour." She was still gazing at him. "God. It is *so* good to see you."

He laughed. "Come here." Hugged her again. Kissed her cheek. "So, there still a place for me here?"

"Gil." She was mock-solemn. "There will always be a place for you here."

The studio room he rented from her every summer lay at the top of an iron staircase attached to the side of the café. From its entrance it stretched south along the rear of the building, three walls of glass giving an uninterrupted view of the sea from emerald shallows to indigo horizon. A view of the sea, Gil admitted, which in his city days he could close his eyes and recall in the minutest of detail; a view which took his breath away even now. Across the floor of bare and creaking boards lay the bed with its tarnishing frame and boot sale quilts, beside it a folding stool holding the book he'd been reading when he'd last been here, under the windows the stained and battered table at which he worked.

Cecily watched him. "It is in fact a shrine to you. I hold guided tours during the winter months – you know, when business gets a bit slow."

He laughed. "Yeah, you'd make a lot of money doing that."

"I'd make a lot of money redecorating and putting in a proper ensuite instead of that germ infested hell-hole you use."

"Hey. I like germ-infested hell-holes. What, tart it up and rent it out to some yuppie couple down from London, you mean?"

"Did you actually use the word 'yuppie' then?"

"Who'd spend all their time complaining about the birdshit and the tourists and the fact there's nowhere to park?" He stopped, realising she was teasing him. "You're not going to, are you?"

"Nope. Can't afford the refit."

"Cecily."

"And anyway." She shrugged.

He sat against the table, the sun already hot through the

glass. Cecily drew a line in the table-top dust, pausing when her finger came within touching distance of his thigh. "Look at this. Appalling housekeeping. You should complain."

"Saw the guys," he told her.

"Patrick's, tonight?"

"I love how nothing changes here." He caught her eye. "You'll come?"

She smiled, rueful about something she might confide to him later. After half a dozen drinks. A midnight walk along the beach. "Sure. Like the man said, nothing changes here."

*

A mile and another world away from the beach, the graveyard stretched some way along the headland, sun-bleached stones jutting among the marram grass under an open sky. Jem, kneeling on the damp soil at the foot of the grave, fitted her handful of wild poppies into a half-empty Evian bottle and placed it carefully before the weathered granite.

Marianne Rae Gregory 1958 - 1996.

Twice a year they came, on the day she had been born and the day she had died, their visits bookending the summer. Jem glanced across to see her father standing apart, his eyes fixed as they often were on distant horizons. After a moment, as if sensing her attention, Alex turned towards her. Smiled his wry smile. "Funny sort of graveyard, I've always thought."

She took in the arcing expanse of sky, the views to left and right of turquoise water. "It's lonely. Peaceful. Nothing between the dead and their God."

He crossed the yard or two of sea grass between them. "When I was a boy, graveyards were about ghosts and ghouls and scary dark places. Full of secrets and places to hide." He smiled, shaking his head.

"What?" She followed his gaze to the Evian bottle. "Would she have minded?"

"No. I think she'd have been surprised we were still coming."

Jem remembered that first summer of anniversaries, her

9

thirteen year old self laying flowers, whispering promises. She saw a slide show montage of every year since, herself growing and changing, Alex ageing by degrees. She said, "Half my life ago."

"Mm."

"You could have had a whole other family by now."

He paused, cleared his throat. His gaze slid away, back to that distant horizon. "No I couldn't."

She looked up at him from where she sat, shielding her eyes against the sun. As a child she had been aware of the bewildering behaviour around him of other children's mothers: a sudden brightness of face; lightness of voice; how close they endeavoured to stand to him; how eager they were to engage his attention. Her university friends, when she had brought them home with her, had been far more direct. Without his shield of good humour and courtesy it might have been embarrassing, their flirting with him, their easy familiarity with this gentle, private man. One of them had commented that he looked like a film star gone to seed. 'Will you stop it?' she had cried. 'He's my *dad*.' But she had seen what they meant. Saw it still.

She dared - "So after Mum … ?"

"After her, nothing." The words were drawn from him as teeth.

"Have you ever wished there had been someone?"

"No." He paused. Added, more lightly, "Anyway, I had you."

Their cottage was the last in a lane which wound from the centre of town to peter exhausted at their doorstep, where it promptly abandoned itself to rocks and the tangle of encroaching grassland. No one – save tourists either adventurous or lost – passed their way by chance, lending them a sense of isolation the half hour walk into town belied. In childhood Jem had understood that her father needed solitude in which to work, to produce the great canvases of sea and sky which put food on the table and assuaged his soul. As she'd grown up she'd realised he needed solitude in which to be. Not that he was, by any means, an unsociable man, but she recognised the need for privacy in him because she knew it in herself. Today, though, today she thought of paths never taken and questions never asked and as he sat at the table in their chaotic kitchen and she flipped pancakes for breakfast she said,

"What you said, about Mum being surprised we still visit?"

"Well, people move on, don't they. Move away."

"We never did."

"*I* never did. You went to university."

"I came back."

He looked at her. "What is it, Puddle? Been bitten by the travel bug?"

She smiled, putting his plate of pancakes and blueberries in front of him, sliding into the seat opposite with her own. The kitchen, tiny enough when empty, was so crammed with essentials and junk and recycling it was never possible to move freely. Its only saving grace was the deep bay of the window seat and its table, onto which in good weather sun streamed most of the day. "Not really," she answered him. "It's just the beginning of summer. Always makes me restless."

"For new places?"

"New anything."

"I know what you mean. At the beginning of every season I always felt the air humming with possibilities."

She gazed at him, her throat clogging suddenly. He covered her hand with his.

"Hey now. Come on. New possibilities, remember?"

She nodded, dumbly.

"Couple of new places opening up in The Walk. Might be worth sounding them out."

"I've already made appointments. For tomorrow afternoon."

He was delighted. "That's my girl. Never let the grass grow. You have to remember when you're in business for yourself, you make your own luck."

"Were you always this full of platitudes or are you making a special effort?"

Alex laughed. "It's my age. I'm entitled."

She smiled. Chased a blueberry round her plate and speared it with her fork.

"You know sometimes," he added, "just when you think you can't take anymore of the same old, same old, the world presents you with something wonderful."

"No all right stop now. You're freaking me out. Help me choose which pieces to take with me tomorrow. Lecture me about tax returns."

"Well I would." He pushed up from the table. "Terrific pancakes, by the way. But I have work to do myself. Cup of coffee, about eleven, would be nice."

She watched him go. Sank her head to the table and closed her eyes, the wood warm against her forehead. In a minute, she would schlep up to the spare room, haul out her cases and spread her jewellery samples around her. She would sort through the lengths of wires and bags of clasps, the beads, the stones, the symbols of silver and pewter, she would select the most impressive and appropriate pieces, pin them to a new black velvet board, attach one of her cards with her name and website address in bold Edwardian Script. She would create such an irresistibly dazzling showcase for her talent that no avant garde jeweller or upmarket gift shop proprietor would think twice about offering her a commission.

In a minute.

The roar of the ocean was as nothing compared with the roar inside Patrick's when the boys were back in town. The bar was packed not just with surf dudes (of both sexes) and their groupies (of both sexes), but with anyone under the age of thirty-five from within a ten mile radius, and vibrated with the base line of indie rock bands, jarred with a hundred shouted conversations. Long before midnight and very long before he'd downed anywhere near enough alcohol to feel it burning up his veins, Gil couldn't hear himself think. Which was a good thing. Life was always so much simpler, he found, when he had only the vaguest handle on his thought processes. As Buz and Henry and Radar embarked upon their third drinking competition of the evening, Cecily edged into their booth, placing her glass on the table and one cheek of her buttocks onto the end of their bench. Gil hutched up to give her space. "Hey," he smiled. She was wearing a faded floral dress under an even more faded denim jacket, her hair loose, earrings the circumference of handcuffs.

"He*llo* Cecily!" Radar whooped.

Buz and Henry raised a deafening toast. "Cess – i- leeee!"

"Hi boys." She murmured to Gil, "I think I'm getting way too old for this place."

"I think *I*'m getting too old for this place. Good day?"

"You know how it is. I give them food, they give me money. Everybody goes away happy. You look kind of comfortable already."

He had to read her lips. "Yeah, I'm Easing Back In. An art form I've developed over the years."

They watched Buz steadily draining a series of shot glasses, Henry and Radar beating a rhythm on the table which grew faster and louder the more he emptied. Cecily raised her eyebrows.

"Have you done this yet?"

"Nope."

"You going to?"

Buz fell at the last fence, vodka streaming back out of his mouth and into the glass as he coughed with a consumptive's vigour. Gil and Cecily exchanged glances.

"Getting kind of hot, in here."

"I thought so."

Making their excuses and shouldering their way through the crowd, they pushed out via the French windows onto the walkway adjoining the pier. She let out a long breath. "Oh Gil, you know I love them but … "

He laughed, slipped his arm around her shoulders as they strolled the boardwalk, the cacophony receding behind them, lights becoming a distant fairy glow. They passed an elderly couple walking their elderly Jack Russell, a gang of kids brandishing alco-pops and larking about. Cecily said, "So how's life, out there in the real world?"

"It's not so bad. I'm a hot young designer, apparently."

13

She grinned. "Are you now? Who told you that?"

"Lady journalist. Came to the workshop to examine my wood."

She snorted with laughter. "So she just meant hot."

"No, no. It was strictly professional. Seriously, a friend of hers had bought one of my tables from the gallery in Clifton and told her about me. For some reason she thought it'd make a good article."

"And was there an accompanying photo of you at work? Planing something wearing a tight sleeveless top with your hair all artistically mussed?"

"Well now you mention it … " He was laughing too. "Hey, it pays the bills." They reached the railing and leaned against it, nothing ahead but the night sky and the dark waters of the Atlantic ocean. The air was cool after the clinging heat of Patrick's, the clamour far away. Gil said softly, "And how about you?"

She was silent.

He took her hand into his. "What do you need me to do? Listen? Shut up?"

"I'm fine." She hesitated, met his eyes briefly. "I wasn't, for a while, but I am now."

"Okay."

"And what I need you to do is just be around."

"I'm here." He took a breath. "I know – "

The scream from one of the alco-pop kids cut him short. Though they had been shrieking the whole time he and Cecily had been out here, he recognised the change in tone instantly. The strident note of terror. And fast upon it, the splash.

In the water below a boy floundered and yelled, submerged and bobbed up again.

"Jesus." Gil strode towards the teenagers, the drunkest of them lunging over the rail in a misguided rescue mission. Gil hauled him back. "Stay where you are, you're too pissed. Can he swim?"

They didn't know, were barely articulate. Gil thought that if the boy were as drunk as the rest it didn't matter whether he could swim or not. He ran a few yards down the pier, pulled off his jacket, kicked off his shoes. Cecily behind him cried, "*Gil what the hell're you doing?*" Swinging through the gap in the railings he grabbed the ladder attached to the pier wall, slid down it, rusting metal burning his hands. The sea pulled cold at his feet, his legs, as he scanned the surface for the thrashing boy.

Nothing.

He cursed. Then a head, a hand, just visible above the churning foam.

Gil jumped.

The water was only twelve, maybe fifteen feet deep but the boy was a leaden weight already and struggling in fear. "Keep still, shut up." Gil seized him under the chin, ploughed backwards through the chill water towards the beach, his own limbs already heavy, eyes stinging. At last his feet hit sand and he rocked, finding his balance, stood and heaved the boy onto the shore. As the other kids and Cecily came running towards them through the dark and the boy choked into consciousness Gil, on his knees in the sand and breathing hard, saw through the crowd and the dripping tangle of his hair a still figure on the promenade, watching.

A little while later he stood soaking wet and barefoot on the prom, the taillights of the ambulance becoming a distant glow as it bore the boy away, Cecily seething in silence beside him. The boy's friends had sobered up fast, one hopping into the ambulance with him, others disappearing into the winding lanes, a couple hanging back to thank him. He had shaken his head, dismissed his deed with a mumble. The paramedics had wanted him to be checked over at the hospital too but he'd insisted he was fine, incensing Cecily still further. Her rage was hard to miss, the clenched jaw, clenched fists, her refusal to utter a single word. He turned to stride back along the pier to fetch his jacket and trainers, aware of her in his wake.

Sitting on one of the benches he rammed his damp feet into his Converses, pulled on his jacket, its aged leather soft and cold against his skin. She stood watching. "*What?*" he exclaimed finally.

She said nothing.

15

"Oh for … " He stood, glanced towards the suddenly very welcoming lights of Patrick's. A drink would be good right now. Several drinks would be excellent. He took a breath. "Look I need to get warm and I need to get a drink. I know you're waiting to tear a strip off me but I just saw him in the water and I didn't think, okay?"

She said tightly, "It's not thinking that gets people killed."

"How was I going to be killed?"

"You've been drinking."

"I'm not drunk. It was twelve feet of water and I can swim."

"You know as well as I do the depth doesn't matter. It's the current."

"It's the pier. We're not in the middle of the fucking ocean."

"Don't swear at me Gil."

"Well cut me some slack! That kid might've died, and because of me he didn't, and generally speaking, that's a good thing. Why're you giving me such a hard time?"

In the fleeting moment that she hesitated he thought she was going to give in, that he might get a smile, or a hug, or even just a few kind words for Christ's sake. But she shook her head.

"It's always about your ego, isn't it."

If he wasn't allowed to swear at her again he was going to have to walk away. But that would mean leaving her with the last word. "It wasn't about my ego," he said furiously. "I didn't think – hey, someone's drowning, here's my chance to be a hero. As I've already said, I didn't think anything. But if you imagine I jumped into that water and heaved that boy out to make myself look good, well fine. I've nothing more to say to you." He did walk away, shoulders tense, head pounding suddenly, emotional when half an hour ago in the thick of it, he hadn't been.

She said, "It was a stupid thing to do."

He turned on his heel, spread his arms. "I *know* it was a stupid thing to do. So I'm stupid. But Cecily, you know what? If someone you loved was drowning, wouldn't you hope there'd be someone around stupid enough to do something about it?"

He saw to his dismay her face slacken the way it did when she was about to cry. He would rather have been wrong and let her have the last word than make her cry. He said quickly, "I'm sorry."

She shook her head. "No. I'm sorry. Take no notice of me, Gil." She walked towards him, squeezed his arm. He held her for a moment, kissed the top of her head.

"Come on. Let's get a drink."

"No, you go. Go and get drunk with the boys – " she smiled – "and I'll see you tomorrow."

"All right. You're sure?"

She pushed him gently in the direction of the bar. "Very."

He watched her go, the evening sea breeze billowing her skirt around her bare legs, then crossed the remaining yards of boardwalk towards Patrick's and was swallowed immediately into the heat and the roar and a resounding and heartwarming cheer from guys who thought it admirable to do stupid things.

Jem switched on the light in the rotting conservatory and stepped out into the dark wilderness of the garden, careless that before long moths the size of sparrows would be fluttering round the smeared glass and battering against the bulb. Her town friends used to shriek and hide when she casually disposed of dead mice and monstrous insects. She had been bemused by their squeamishness just as she was bemused by their neat and gleaming homes; while their pairs of parents and squabbling siblings had meant nothing to her, staying in a house with visible surfaces had been like visiting a foreign country. Her friends, in their turn, had said they envied her freedom. This had puzzled her. It was true that Alex didn't believe in rules but then he had never had to set any; they had always taken care of each other. For thirteen years they'd anchored each others' lives. She had never thought of it as freedom.

Now she sat on the garden wall, a glass of Tempranillo precariously balanced in the rough grass at her feet, planning her trip to The Walk tomorrow with her sample board and price lists, preparing what she would say, how she would be.

17

At the beginning she had been shy of promoting herself and her work, unable to understand why anyone would hand over hard-earned money in return for her trinkets. But she also knew that holiday makers would squander their cash on any old tat, and a friendly smile and a bit of chat went as far to making a sale as the jewellery itself. Watching Alex at the gallery over the years, she had seen him suppressing his natural reticence for an enthusiasm and affability which won him buyers who returned summer after summer. It was neither an act nor a calculated business ploy, but the unleashing of the more outgoing man he might have been.

Suddenly she could smell the sea. There was no view, from any angle of the cottage, of the beach but sometimes the scent – and sense - of the tide was so strong she might have been standing on the shore. Sometimes she could feel the water lapping around her toes even when she stood indoors a mile away.

"It'll be barbecue weather before long." Alex, a glass of the Tempranillo in his hand. "Look at that sky."

She looked. It was clear, pearl dark above the silhouetting trees. She said, "I saw a man rescue someone from drowning."

"Tonight?"

"Down by the pier. I went for a walk after supper."

He sat beside her on the bench. "What happened?"

"I couldn't tell really. I was too far away. A boy fell from the railings. The man jumped in and dragged him out. It was … awe-inspiring."

Alex frowned. "How so?"

"To see someone who could have died, living. Being given a second chance. Imagine doing that, being that person who'd given someone a second chance at living."

"People do that all the time, don't they?"

She looked at him. "You mean doctors? But what if it isn't your job, what if you're just an ordinary person, and you save someone's life."

"Then you've earned your place in heaven." He smiled. "Who was the man?"

"I don't know."

They sipped their wine. She shivered a little. "I just keep thinking, a boy is sleeping in his own bed tonight who maybe shouldn't be."

"But maybe he should, and that was the point."

"That he was meant to be saved?" She thought about it. "It raises all the big questions doesn't it, fate and courage and responsibility. What sort of person does that, do you think? Saves someone else's life? Do you have to be very brave or very stupid to jump into the sea for someone else?"

After a moment Alex replied, "I don't think it's a question of bravery or stupidity. I think it's about humanity."

She considered this. It was true that she hadn't recognised the man, but she had seen that he was young, that he had a mess of dark hair, that he was strong enough to haul a body through the water.

Her father said gently, "It's upset you."

"No. Not really. It's just, it's not often you get to witness an act of real life heroism, is it? And it gives you pause."

"It does."

She shivered again.

"Come on," he said. "It's getting chilly out here."

"Thought you said it was nearly barbecue weather."

"Freezing to death while you're charcoaling the sausages *is* barbecue weather."

She followed him inside, remembering beach parties spent huddled in towels for warmth, goosebumped and searing her fingers in the flames. "I want an idyllic summer," she told him as he stood beating the moths from the conservatory with an old tea-towel.

He cast her a glance. "Don't we all."

Chapter Three

He bangs the door shut behind him, throws the bolt. He's breathing hard, his hair damp and wild, and when he turns towards me his bloodshot eyes are those of a stranger. I gasp on a sob and then I'm lost, shaking and keening as I weep, out of anyone's control. He stares at me, appalled.

"Why here?" he says at last, and the roughness of his voice tears at me. "Why here, of all places?"

I shake my head. I haven't the energy or the will for any sort of fight.

"I mean, I get it, you want to run to the ends of the earth … but not when the ends of the earth is where you *live*."

I gulp, wretched. "I just wanted to feel safe."

And then my face is pressed into the wet leather of his jacket, his arms tight around me. Silence except for my snivelling. There's nothing to say, when we know neither of us will ever be safe again.

"Okay." After a minute he pulls back, his stubble scraping against my forehead. "Stop crying. Look at me." I manage it, just. His eyes are wet and red-rimmed too. "You need money," he says. "And your passport."

I stare at him.

He runs his hand back through his hair, lets out a long breath. "Two choices. And you have to make that choice now. We walk into a police station tonight or we use the time we've got to get as far as we can. Justice or freedom. Which way do you want to go?"

"How long … how long d'you think it'll be … "

"A day? Two, maybe."

"Do we have to go now?"

He looks exasperated, then catches sight of my den under the table. I think he can probably smell my puke as well. He says, more gently, "We do, yes. But you've time to wash, get your stuff together. You can sleep in the car."

I think of the life I've had, everything I've ever known, all of it drifting away from me forever. But it's the wrong image. It's already gone, and it hasn't sailed gently into the sunset; it's burnt to ashes.

Upstairs I stand whimpering and trembling under the shower, clumsily soaping my skin. The water's hot but I can't feel it; my body's clean again but I can't care. I have to snap into action but I just want to crawl back under the table, fall asleep and never wake up. There are ways to make that happen, of course, several of them available to me in this house. The thought has been exploding intermittently in my head like flares in the dark.

Except Gil's here.

I wrap a towel around myself, letting my hair drip, and find him standing desperate in the careless mess of my bedroom, my rucksack empty on my bed. He says, "You need to pack. We won't be able to carry anything more than that." He's watching me, trying to determine what state I'm in, wary and impatient at the same time. I rub myself dry, squeeze the ends of my hair in the towel, pull on clean underwear, jeans, t-shirt and hoodie before cramming half a dozen of the same into my rucksack. My passport is in the bedside drawer as it always is. I fumble with wash stuff in the bathroom, find my bag and twist all the money I took from the station cashpoint into a tight roll, secure it with a hair bobble. I tuck this into my pocket, then let my gaze trawl helplessly round the room. I don't know what else I'm going to need and everything I can see is so familiar and precious my heart contracts with panic and loss.

He sees this in my face. "Don't think about it."

I nod.

"Come on." He pulls the drawstrings of my rucksack tight and hauls it easily over his shoulder. I follow him out onto the landing, pause outside the door at top of the stairs. For a moment I can go no further and my fist closes around the handle.

Gil, halfway down, stops and turns back towards me. "No. No, no. Come on. Don't think about that either." He marches up again, takes my hand. "You said you wanted to be safe?

21

That's what we have to think about now. What's ahead of us, not what's behind."

I waver. "I'm never going to come back here, am I?"

"No," he says.

I let him lead me down the stairs, out into the lane. It's pitch dark and silent but even so he's tucked the car out of sight. We slide in, the thunk of our doors shutting loud in the stillness. He's taken one of the blankets from the kitchen and wraps it around me. "You all right?"

"No."

"No," he says. "No. Me either."

He hesitates for the briefest of moments, both of us staring ahead through the wind-screen at the navy sky and black sea, and then the stench of fear and shame becomes too much, and he starts the engine.

Chapter Four

It was a morning less piercingly beautiful than the last. Cecily pulled on a cardigan as she pottered in her café, wiping down tables and topping up salt and pepper while the first batch of scones was baking, removing furling gerbera heads from the bud vases and replacing them with pale blown peonies. Outside the only movement in a deserted square was a gull on the window sill, snapping at the rain which dripped from the blue and white striped awning. She made herself a coffee from the Gaggia, its whooshing and squirting one of the background noises of her life, and sipped it whilst surveying her realm.

More years ago than she cared to calculate, she and her parents had spent the summer sanding this floor and painting these walls, driving across the county sourcing settles and tables and benches of reclaimed pine, installing industrial appliances in the kitchen she'd thought would never be free of mouse droppings. They'd said it was their investment in their old age, when they'd weighed in with more money than the bank would countenance, and then the minute they retired they'd buggered off to Spain. Not that she resented being able to spend the darkest days of a British winter on the Costa de la Luz, but it had meant that for better or worse the little café, the business, was all hers. She gazed around and wondered for the first time in a long time how much it was worth.

The ting of tubular bells as the door opened and she looked up, saw Henry amble in, push the door closed on the chill draught which had accompanied the tinging. He loped across the room, pulled out the chair opposite hers. "Hey."

"Hey." Groundhog day, she thought. One or more of the surf dudes stumbling in early doors, hung-over but too accustomed to dawn rising to sleep it off. She'd tease them about lack of commitment and they'd complain but not too much. Breakfast at Cecily's was one of the ever-fixèd marks of their day. "Coffee?"

Henry grunted. She fetched him an Americano and he smiled at her from beneath the unwashed blond strands of his hair. "Thanks."

"You're welcome." He was, she thought, an unexpected sort of build for a surfer, tall and heavy-shouldered, more weight on him than you'd imagine would be helpful when you were trying to balance on a strip of board in the middle of a crashing wave. But hey, what did she know. He was also the least chauvenistic of the surf dudes, the most sensitive, least tiresome. It had taken her some while to realise this, to make the effort to distinguish one from another. For a long time she had only seen them as they hung in Gil's wake, Peter Pan and The Lost Boys.

"It was a good night, then?" she prodded.

He sipped his coffee, gestured that the state he was in was evidence of just how good the night had been. "Fine times, Cecily. Fine times." It was a phrase from the old days. She smiled, remembering flames crackling in the dark, Buz playing 70s guitar solos, digging pits in the sand to cool the beers. Laughter and drunken philosophising and someone's hand warm against her skin.

Henry was frowning. "What happened to you?"

"Last night? Oh, I was ... tired." She shrugged. "Gil told you, about his heroics?" He wouldn't have told them, she was sure, of her reaction because Gil had his flaws but he didn't bitch.

"Didn't have to. Couple of guys saw it, bought him drinks all night."

"Ah." She indicated his coffee mug. "You want something to go with that?"

Henry considered. "You know what I'd really like? Waffles. Do you do waffles?"

"I can do waffles." She stood up. "Honey? Maple syrup?"

"With, like, cream?"

"With actual cream." She tripped through to the kitchen, turned on the radio. After a moment Henry joined her, leaning against the arch of the threshold. "How's your year been?" she asked him.

He watched her assembling ingredients, plugging in the waffle iron. "Yeah, it's been good. Have to wonder how much longer I can keep going at the day job though."

"Why? Is the work drying up?" Henry had begun as an Outward Bound instructor, dabbled in the waters of Management Team-Building weekends, taught sailing and wind-surfing at a recreational centre in Falmouth. None of it ever seemed to take up very much of his time.

"No, far from it. It's just, you know, I'm gonna be thirty this year. Maybe it's time I started taking something seriously."

"Well absolutely," she deadpanned. "Because if you pass thirty and you haven't started taking something seriously, who knows what might happen? Floods, earthquakes, governments could topple."

"All that was my fault?"

She laughed. He grinned. "Truthfully?" she said. "I know whereof you speak."

"What, this place? This is grown-up stuff though isn't it. Your own business."

"Mm." She added lightly, "But is it what I want for the rest of my life?"

He looked at her in surprise and she realised this wasn't a conversation she was ready to have yet. She had barely formed the thought in her own head. The tubular bells tinged again. "Ooh," she said. "Customers."

Henry glanced back into the café. "Nah. S'just Gil."

He sauntered in, wearing jeans and a short-sleeved check shirt, his dark curls still damp from the shower. "Hey. We're making waffles."

"We are," Cecily agreed.

Gil glanced from one to the other, unused to finding them alone together and certainly unused, she thought, to the sense that he might be interrupting something. "So how are you two this morning?"

"Henry is hung-over, I am fine and you are … ?"

"Great." He smiled. "Great."

Henry snorted. "You were leathered."

"What can I say? I can hold my drink. Henry have you

worked out how to use that coffee machine yet?"

Gil stood close while Henry played with the Gaggia. "You okay?"

She gave the batter a whip, poured it carefully into the waffle iron. "Yeah. You gave me a scare last night, that's all. Sorry."

"That's really all?" He held her gaze.

She looked back at him levelly. "Believe me."

"Sure." He paused, took a breath, got that mildly embarrassed look he did when he was about to say something tricky and didn't want to lie about it. "Last night?"

"Mmmm."

"Did you notice – on the beach, before the ambulance came – did you notice anyone watching?"

"There were lots of people watching, you attracted quite a crowd. Anyone specific?"

"No, I just … " he shrugged. "Nah. Never mind. Probably just me." He smiled, dropped a fleeting kiss on her forehead. "Need some help?" The bells tingled again and he picked up an apron, tying its strings above his bum as he went. "I'll go."

"Gil." Henry, having beaten him to it, met him under the arch. Cecily and Gil looked past him to the slight redhead waiting in the midst of empty tables and peonies. "Lady from the press for you."

The Walk was a narrow cobbled lane running parallel to the harbour. Here every year in its relentless carousel a trendy bistro or sandal-and-sarong boutique opened and a gallery of driftwood and seascapes closed. In winter a gusty tunnel offering shelter from the lashing rain, it was now a gauntlet of ice-creams, dog-leads, other people's sunburned flesh. Jem shifted her display board beneath her arm and paused to assess the wares in the window of The Joshua Tree. Slouch suede bags in summerfruit colours; scarves of silk and lace and devoré velvet; tribal necklaces of dark and pale wood. She suspected her jewellery might be a bit too Gothic for their implicit target market, but you could never tell. Beyond the display, deep in the recesses of the shop, a woman was sitting at a white wrought-iron table typing into her Notebook, her blonde hair tied thick and blunt as a blusher brush at the nape of her neck, sleeveless cream top draping elegantly from her shoulders. Her appearance distinguished her; most people who lived and worked in this town looked as though the passage of time ground more slowly here than anywhere else on the planet. Jem was tempted to flee, to shut herself in her box room workshop with her wires and her silver. The thought of doing so and having to admit it to Alex propelled her onto the step, through the door and into the centre of the oiled wood floor of The Joshua Tree.

Grace Kelly looked up from her computer. Jem pasted on a broad smile and crossed the space between them. "My name's Jemima Gregory." She held out her hand. "I made an appointment to see you this morning."

The woman glanced down at the open diary beside her keyboard, smiled. "Of course." She rose, briefly took Jem's hand. "Atlanta Fox. Have a seat. Shall I get us some coffee?"

Jem opened her display board and stood it on Atlanta Fox's desk, rows of earrings jangling lightly in their holes as she adjusted the angle of the velvet boards. She unwrapped several silver pendants on leather thongs and a couple of intricately laced cord and pewter cuffs. As a child, she had been fascinated by the sets of plastic beads and acrylic threads she'd been given as presents, poring over the myriad shapes and colours, spending hours rapt in creations for which her parents had duly exchanged small change and milk bottle tops. But she had never quite been able to part from her treasures and had, to her parents' amusement, insisted on collecting them all back in again afterwards. Even now, needing to earn a living, her heart contracted a little when a favourite piece was sold. She ought to loan them out, she sometimes thought, like designer jewels on Oscar night.

Atlanta returned with two white square mugs standing on white rectangular saucers which allowed room for a biscuit or two, in this case chocolate amaretti. "Thank you," Jem smiled. Added bravely, "I love your name, by the way."

Atlanta rolled her eyes. "My mother had a thing about *Gone*

27

With the Wind. I have two sisters called Scarlett and Tara."

"And a brother called Rhett?"

"Thankfully not. I think my father would have drawn the line at that." She smiled, her gaze settling upon Jem's display boards. "Oh. Heavens." She touched the curve of a stylised pendant rose. "May I?"

Jem gestured. "Please do." She watched as Atlanta examined her work, the gentle stroke of her fingers, the sharper appraisal of her eyes, and struggled to down her coffee feeling as if her own skin were under scrutiny. A lifetime ago this had been her normality, pasting on confidence with her smile, peddling her wares. She remembered how it felt as if it were a part she'd once played and she were recalling glimpses of the script.

"Are you local?" Atlanta asked her.

"Mm. I live just off the cliff road. Have done all my life."

"How amazing, to have grown up here. You're so lucky."

"I am," Jem agreed. "I appreciate it every day. My father thought that when I went away to uni he'd lost me to the world, but I felt lost *in* the world."

"I know just what you mean. I've been here a couple of months and it is just such a relief. I don't miss the city at all." She unhooked a pair of earrings, turned them over to check their fastenings. "I must say, it's been terribly easy to settle in. Everyone's been so friendly."

She paused, added lightly, "Is there a high turnover of businesses here?"

"It depends," Jem said. "Your stock should have a pretty broad appeal, for example. End of the summer all the tourists go home but they're plenty of us left still needing to shop."

Atlanta looked at her gratefully. "That's exactly what I was hoping. And it can be a bit of a trek, can't it, into Penzance or Truro. Especially if the weather's bad. Do you have other outlets, by the way? Apart from your website?"

Jem smiled inwardly at the thought of having 'outlets'. "I have a stall, which I trundle onto the pier when the weather's good and into the market when it isn't."

"What about other shops? In town, I mean?"

"There were a couple, but they've closed down over the last

couple of years. That's what today is about for me, raising my profile here. There's a place in St Agnes and one in Porthleven which take a basic range, but I've tended to stay away from the bigger towns." Her lines were coming back to her more readily than she had expected. It felt odd, hearing herself discussing her work as she had used to do, as if it were something that mattered.

Atlanta was nodding with enthusiasm. "You see, I love your pieces. I could buy a dozen of them straight off, just for myself. There're a bit more funky and edgy than I usually sell, but I imagine there's a real market for that here." She replaced the last piece on Jem's board, hesitated a moment. "So when you've been to the other places and heard what they'd like to offer you, come back to me. Because I'd like to talk to you about exclusivity."

"Can I get you anything?" Gil offered. "A drink? Some breakfast? Cecily rustles up a mean waffle."

Eve Callaghan, the Lady from the Press, surveyed him for a moment. "I'm fine, thank you." She sat down. Gil remained standing.

"So," he smiled. "How can I help?"

She gazed up at him. She was wiry with age rather than slender with youth, he noticed, lines criss-crossing faintly above her sallow cheeks, her auburn hair dusty around its parting. "The parents of the boy whose life you saved are very grateful."

He pulled out a chair, sat backwards on it, his arms resting on the toprail. "How is he, do you know?"

"He's fine. Discharged from hospital last night. You did a good deed."

Jeez, Gil thought. Letting the guys buy him drinks all night in the privacy of Patrick's had been one thing. Making this all about him in the local press was another. He shrugged. "Anyone would have done it. "

"Nobody else did."

"No, well, it was kinda quiet."

She narrowed her eyes at him. "Every year someone drowns

out there. Usually, like last night, a stupid kid. Sometimes a child. Sometimes a grown-up who should know better. But every year someone drowns."

"I know."

"What I want to do," she explained, "is write this piece as a cautionary tale. Of course, this time and thank God it will be celebrating someone's rescue, but I want it to sound the warning bell nonetheless. And I want to keep sounding that bell all summer. I know holiday makers don't tend to read the paper and no one ever thinks it's going to happen to them anyway but even so. If a bit of publicity now makes just one idiot teenager think twice we'll both have earned our place in heaven."

Gil thought that in his case it might take rather more than that but nodded anyway. "Right."

"And you'd be happy with that?"

"Sure." For what else could he say? 'No, don't make me part of a campaign which might save lives'?

"All right. So." She uncapped her pen. "You're Gil Hunt?"

"I am."

"Gil short for Gilbert?"

"Gilman. It was my mother's maiden name."

"Like the painter."

"The painter?"

"Gilman Hunt."

He laughed. "You mean Holman Hunt. The Pre-Raphaelite guy. *The Scapegoat*, *Lady of Shalott*."

"Of course," she said dismissively. Clearly she didn't like being corrected. Nor, he thought, had she heard of the paintings. "And you're … ?"

"More a Rossetti man myself."

She frowned. "How *old* are you?"

"Oh. Twenty-eight." She had thick, masculine hands, he noticed and chastised himself for being uncharitable in his own head. What was there to like about her? He considered her while she wrote. Her quest to save lives, of course. The way the khaki silk vest she wore complimented her hair. The … no, he couldn't be bothered to think of anything else.

30

"And not a local?" she continued.

"Nope, I live in Bristol. I come down every summer, stay with my friends, get some work done, chill out."

"Are you an artist?"

"Hardly. I make furniture. Carve stuff."

"That's a kind of art, isn't it?"

"It's knocking cabinets together. It's ... " He shrugged. "I don't know. I guess, if you want to call it that."

She glanced at him. "Tell me what happened last night."

He did so, without melodrama or embellishment. The café had grown busy around them and he wanted to grab some breakfast and head up to the studio, start planning a project for the summer which would remind him that he did this for love as well as to earn money.

She wrote fast, glancing at him now and then as he spoke. "When I told you that every year here someone drowns, you said that you knew."

"Like I said, I'm here every summer. I've heard that particular bell toll too many times."

"And what would you say, to warn people?"

He smiled. " 'Don't be a dick'."

To his surprise, she smiled too. "How about something I could use?"

"Oh, you want a sound-bite?"

"Can you manage that?"

"I can do cheesy and misogynistic. 'The sea is like a woman's wrath: underestimate it at your peril'."

She frowned. "No, I kind of like that."

He laughed. "It's awful. Seriously - you're not going to use it?"

She slipped her notebook and pen into her bag. "Watch this space."

When she'd gone he stepped back up into the kitchen to find Cecily alone and the workbench piled with order slips. "Henry gone to the beach?"

"Yep."

"Surf dudes, eh? Heads up their own arses." He picked up the oldest slip. "Has this gone yet? Table five, two

31

cappuccinos, cinnamon muffin, pancakes."

"Yes, I'm doing table two. Can you look at three for me?"

"Sure." He read the order, swiftly assembled two English Breakfasts from the array on the hob. Cecily glanced across at him.

"You didn't like that woman. The journalist."

"It showed?"

"Body language. All you need to know."

"Oh and mine is so transparent?"

"It is actually."

He grinned. "Aah, she was all right in the end." He whipped two latte mugs under the Gaggia. "Done."

They dealt with the first morning wave of customers with easy efficiency, so familiar were they with each other, with the work. "It's like a dance," Gil said, twirling her round when the café had emptied a little and everyone remaining had been served. She spun away from him at the length of his extended arm, back towards his chest. "Ballet of the Petit Déjeuner."

"Lunchtime Tango and Evening … ?"

"Tarantella." He kissed the top of her head, released her hand. "What *is* the tarantella?"

"Italian folk dance. Bells and tambourines."

"I mean, how do you do it?"

"Not a clue." She smiled. "Coffee? Left-over muffin?"

They ate and drank, stacked the dishwasher, kept a weather eye on the café. A single shaft of sunlight slanted across the workbench. "I sense," he said, "a beach party coming on."

"It's only just stopped raining."

"It'll be fine by tonight."

She cocked an eyebrow at him.

"This week, though? Go on, go on, say yes, you know you want to."

Cecily laughed. "I do. Yes, this week. You going to round up the boys?"

"Rub two sticks together and they'll be there. Right, I am going to nip down into town and pick up a couple of things and then I'm working. Thinking about working. Preparing to think about working."

"Go on," she smiled. "See you later."

He sprang up the iron staircase for his wallet, back down again into the square. Already the sun was beginning to burn off the morning damp, the chill a memory in the air. A few tourists, those not yet ready to brave the beach in their jeans and pac-a-macs, clustered outside the glass shop and the hippie-goth place. He wondered about doing something for Cecily, other than being around and helping out, but he knew that when she was down she often just liked you to let things lie. His father was a man of drama and grand gestures and while his own instinct leaned in that direction too, Gil had learned from his mother and his sisters - and mostly from Cecily - the value of kindness and of listening. So as he crossed the square he promised himself he'd keep an eye on her. He'd organise a beach party, which she'd always loved. He'd drop by with a bottle of wine when the café closed and she was too tired to go out. The usual stuff. Stuff they'd been doing for each other for the best part of the last decade.

He strolled past the pub and the palm trees to the steep descent into town, threading his way through shortcuts of snickets and stone steps, between whitewashed holiday cottages, their hanging baskets trailing luxuriously with lobelia and nasturtiums, chalk board menus appearing on the pavement outside tiny, half-hidden restaurants. Already the sun had grown warmer: the streets were filling with people shrugging out of their jackets and cardigans; he glimpsed between buildings children in swimsuits digging up the harbour beach. The list in his head was comprised of the dullest of essentials but he decided to take a detour, check out what was new, what was happening. He understood that at some point in the last twenty years this little seaside town – always beautiful, always popular - had made the transition from quaint to cool and nowhere was this more in evidence than The Walk. The owners of the upmarket restaurants and expensive little boutiques made him smile with their bid for hip, exclusive nonchalance as though they thought they were in Santa Barbara or Venice Beach. He wanted to slap their shoulders and tell them to get over themselves, to buy them a beer in Patrick's and chill out. Which was probably a Californian expression anyway. No escape, even for him.

The girl stepped out a yard in front of him, a huge board tucked under her arm with which she could do a fair amount of collateral damage if she whipped round too fast. He pulled up, registering long dark hair, purple t-shirt bearing some sort of seventies festival logo, black cargo pants, a great deal of silver jewellery. She turned, joining the slipsteam of holiday-makers and after a minute he lost her in the crowd. He frowned, certain that he had never seen her before in his life and yet equally certain that the chord she had struck in him for that briefest of moments had been one of recognition.

"Dad!" Jem left the back door open to the late afternoon sunshine, moved her right arm a further inch from her body to allow her display board to slide gently down her side to the floor, and dumped her carrier bags on the kitchen table. "Dad!" She leaned the board against the wall, unpacked strawberries and fresh trout and own-brand champagne.

"Well." Alex smiled. "No need for me to ask how it went, then."

She flung her arms round him and kissed his cheek, handed him the bottle. "Open it."

He looked at the label, back at her, dead-pan.

"It's the spirit," she told him. "Pretend it's Bollinger. We're having trout pan-fried with almonds and strawberries for dessert and yes it went well but that's sort of not the point."

He untwisted the wire around the bottle's neck, pressed his thumbs beneath the cork. "The point being?"

"The point being … " she paused as the cork popped, held up the glasses for him to fill. "The point being that I was out there, selling my work and people *liked* it. The woman at The Joshua Tree liked it so much she's talking about exclusivity."

"Is she indeed? And what did you say?"

"Not very much. She's waiting for me to get back to her."

Alex smiled, clinked his glass against hers. "To you. It's good to hear you talking like this again."

Jem smiled too. "It's good to feel like this again."

"Come on." He patted the table. "Sit down and tell me all about it."

She put the fish in the fridge and sat. Alex liked her to give detailed accounts (though only her, he insisted – anyone else's bored him rigid) especially laced with wit and insight and she always enjoyed delivering. She described at length the woman who looked like Grace Kelly and whose family had been named from a great American novel, the bemusingly jolly Sweeney Todd and Mrs Lovett goth shop couple, the teenage girls who'd tried on her samples and declared them 'sick'. Alex listened, discreetly swapped his champage for a bottle of German lager, and discussed with her the pros and cons of an exclusive deal. They shared the cooking; Jersey potatoes and salad with the trout and almonds, dipping the strawberries into melted chocolate from the fondue pot she'd found some years ago grown dusty at the back of a cupboard. Alex drank another lager. Jem dripped the remaining champagne into her glass.

"I've so much to do," she mused. "Stock to build up, my web site to update, publicity to design."

"Busy summer," Alex observed.

"Bring it on."

He laughed. "I've been thinking about work too."

"Oh yes?"

"Mm. I've been thinking I need to start something new. Drive up the coast, find something that inspires me. I've always fancied doing a series on Tintagel."

There was the smallest of silences. She said, "When?"

"Oh I don't know." His expression was more guarded than his words. "Later this month maybe." He paused. "You'd be
…"

"Fine. Absolutely. You go." She smiled. Watched him for a moment. "You're sure?"

He shook his head, amused. "You are daft to be worrying about me."

"So I'm daft. So shoot me." She held up her hands in surrender.

Later, climbing the stairs on her way to bed, she thought of all the ways in which she had worried about him, and he about her, and how all that time had now spiralled away from them. Her past lay dark, furled and heavy somewhere and she stood chilly and poised for flight. A fresh new dawn. She shivered with apprehension, stopped outside the door at the top of the stairs, trailed her finger lightly down its stained and splintering wood.

"Puddle?" Her father, in the hall below, frowning up at her. "You all right?"

"I'm fine, Dad." She smiled, to reassure him, to reassure them both, but it would be invisible to him in the yellow wispy light of the hall, and was invisible to her always.

Cecily weighed scoops of soft, cool sand in her palms then tipped her hands and opened her fingers to let the grains run loose. She did it rhythmically, her eyes fixed on the dusky horizon, on surfers she didn't know riding the last of the day's waves, on a middle-aged couple strolling the white edge of froth. She remembered years ago being told that distant figures were painted as carrots: the indistinct, frondy head; the width of shoulders tapering to the point of feet. Her heart contracted and she blinked hard, scooped sand a shade more compulsively. The beach emptied fast in the evenings when there had been little heat in the day and she could see barely a dozen carrots either way she looked, only the horseshoe of rocks which created this cove and the wide, flat sea ahead.

She drew in her breath.

She had always thought of restlessness as a gentle, meandering sort of state. A luxury, almost. An indulgence. Instead it turned out to be incapacitating and laced with panic. It had her short of breath and sharp of temper and fearful of the years to come. It *unnerved* her, which was ridiculous when her survival strategy had always been rooted in the belief that it was not the hand you were dealt that mattered but the way in which you played it. She had steered herself through life playing her hand as calmly and as stoically as she knew how, with grim resolve when times had been stormy and a bitter awareness that she must shoulder the responsibility for her own sorrows. It had served her well. Would continue to serve her well. She fixed her gaze on the horizon, dark now beyond the lapping shoreline. Could she give up this perfect life she had carved out for herself? Was the gnawing inside her reason enough? She lowered her forehead to her knees for a moment, listened to her stern inner voice. *Get a grip, woman.*

Later she trod softly through the shadows of her empty café and up the wooden staircase to her sanctuary, a sprawling attic with tiny shower room and kitchen built into alcoves, her bed with its faded patchwork quilt tucked beneath the eaves, living space defined by the blue striped sofa, the rug, the television on the whitewashed chest. She kicked off her sandals and stretched out across her bed, switched on her laptop. Google offered several businesses for sale in this corner of the county but none – as far as she could tell – as well situated or as desirable as her own. She searched restaurant businesses in Spain, Italy, the Californian coast. Typed in *volunteering in africa* and *postgraduate certificate in education* and couldn't bring herself to look at any of the responses. Instead she rolled onto her back and stared up into the dusky corners high above white painted beams. Breathed in deep and out long. You're fine, she soothed herself, you're fine. It's all fine.

Alex mixed the precise shade and consistency of turquoise he needed to describe the water filling the rock pools at Clodgy Point and applied it to his canvas. He had left the door to The Wharf on the latch, letting distant voices and footsteps lap at the edge of his tranquillity. In a couple of weeks' time, when the Easter weekend heralded the beginning of the season, he would have that door propped wide, he'd have hung the paintings currently either - depending on Marianne's temper and his point of view - stored in or cluttering up the cottage and the racks for the prints would have arrived. Before which he needed to whitewash the walls, install a dozen spotlights and ink his name in large black italics into the huge window overlooking the harbour. Part of him was intoxicated with the combination of achievement and promise. Even the other part, charged with remaining eternally watchful and sober, felt hopeful this bright spring morning. At his easel, in the centre of this great echoing space which would become his workshop, he was at peace.

The smallest murmur, a bubble of sound released gently into the cool air, and he paused, his focus shifting from the recreation of rock pools to the Moses basket resting on the old apothecary's chest six feet away from him. He waited. His daughter's hand was thrust into the air, the transluscent tips of her fingers briefly visible over the rim of the basket before disappearing again. He smiled, poised to retrieve her, but she sighed and quieted and he returned to his painting. This morning when he'd woken Marianne had been asleep beside him, which after so disturbed a night had been a blessing. He had crept around her, scooped up the baby in her basket and borne her downstairs with him, changed her nappy when she woke and fed her from a bottle of expressed milk, all intervening doors closed to preserve her mother's rest. Afterwards he popped Jemima, all wide-eyed and dribbling, into her sling and walked down into town with her bouncing happily against his chest. He ran errands, stopped to chat now and then, his daughter effortlessly enchanting his friends and neighbours, and finally arrived at the quayside property which he'd bought, along with the cottage, only weeks ago. Two mortgages and two unstable incomes. He was trying not to think about that too much, about where he would be if the current public thirst for his painting became sated, if Marianne – well, he was trying not to think about that too much either. He stared hard at the canvas he'd begun the previous day and, seeing that the baby was asleep again, carefully slid her from the sling into the basket. He picked up a palette, a brush. His work, always his life blood, had become too welcome and necessary a distraction from the troubles which gnawed in his head and his heart.

Hearing the click of the street door, he hastened through before any greeting call woke his daughter. His visitor was Eve, the red-headed teenage girl to whom Marianne had given piano lessons last year and who had since unaccountably become something of a fixture in their lives. He didn't mind; her abrasive edges amused him and masked, Marianne insisted, a touching insecurity and anyway, sympathetic and cheerful friends for Marianne were to be encouraged.

Eve smiled as he appeared and he put a finger to his lips, gestured towards the workshop. She glanced in, tip-toed to the basket and stood watching for a moment. Alex smiled. He had spent hours of her short life watching his daughter sleep.

"She's gorgeous," she whispered, when she had tip-toed back to him.

"Thank you. I think so too, but then I am besotted with her."

Eve grinned. "I came to tell you I've had some good news. I've got a job with the Express & Echo. Just, like, cub reporter stuff but still ... "

"That's great. Eve, I'm so pleased for you. When do you

start?"

"Next month. I wanted to tell Marianne."

"I would leave it for while, she didn't sleep much last night."

"Of course, with the baby."

He hesitated. Sometimes telling the truth seemed like a betrayal of his wife and really, who needed the absolute truth? "I'll get her to give you a ring."

"Thank you." She beamed at him.

She had been gone for quarter of an hour at the most when the door opened again. Once more he put down his brush and went quickly into the gallery. This time his visitor was his wife. Though it was a half hour trek down here from the cottage, she looked as dazed as though she had just woken. He prepared himself for whatever was to come.

"Hello." He went to her, kissed her unbrushed hair. "I thought you needed to sleep."

"I woke up and you weren't there."

"Giving you some peace." He smiled, inviting her to smile back. She regarded him with suspicion.

"I didn't know where you were."

He had noticed, when he kissed her, that she smelled faintly stale and sweaty, that her shirt was stained with breast milk. "I'll get a phone put in here," he told her. "Then if you need me you don't have come all the way down."

She nodded.

"Eve dropped by," he said. "She has some good news."

She began walking around the empty space, rubbing her arm compulsively. He watched her, knowing her distraction to be focused inward, her head full of bewilderment and fear. "Marianne? Shall I go and get you a drink? Some breakfast, maybe?"

She shook her head. The sound of post flapping through onto the wooden floor almost made him jump. He went to pick it up, sorted quickly through circulars and a couple of white window envelopes which couldn't, surely, be bills already. He'd decided to have his business mail delivered here, in the effort to compartmentalise his life which he needed to make but had no confidence was going to work.

When he looked up again she was gone.

He turned towards the workshop, saw that Marianne had taken their daughter from her basket and was holding her in both outstretched hands as though she were a gift, or a sacrifice. "Look what I found!"

He was beside her in a second.

She said, "Where did you get her?"

His heart sank. He said gently, "Well, she's ours."

Marianne frowned, confused. "Ours?"

"She's our daughter. She's six weeks old. Jemima Rae Gregory." With each detail he prayed there would be some flicker of recognition, but she continued only to gaze at the baby in awe. "She knows you," he added. "Talk to her, she'll respond to you."

"But I thought ... our baby ... "

"What?"

She shook her head. "I had ... someone told me she ... " Her eyes filled with tears. "She's beautiful, isn't she."

"Yes," he said. "She is."

Jemima had twisted her head at the sound of his voice and, finding his face, smiled. He smiled into her eyes, said with his usual humorous affection, "Hello Puddle." He lifted her from her mother's hands to hold her safely to him, where she drooled against his neck. Marianne was shivering. He took a breath. Another day in the gallery lost but what choice did he have. "Come on," he said. "We'll go home."

Chapter Five

Gil strides back across the tarmac towards me, the wind whipping his hair across his face as it whips the stink of oil from the ferries across the dock. I've dropped my rucksack to the ground, pulled the cuffs of my hoodie over my fingers. He says, "We're in luck. Sails at six forty-five, arrives Roscoff around one."

"I always thought it sounded Russian, Roscoff."

He looks at me askance. "I got us a cabin. You need to sleep. We can't do this with no sleep."

I don't think I'll ever sleep properly again, but I'm trying not to say anything unhelpful. I had dozed briefly in the car, woken on a scream which had us slewing across the empty road. He braked and I had to get out, stand shaking in the hedgerow, breathing in the dawn. We dumped the car later out of town. Gil wanted to leave it at the airport but the airport closed this month, there were no flights going anywhere anymore. It wouldn't have fooled anyone.

"Anyway," he adds, "there won't be any CCTV in the cabins."

Gradually little knots of other foot passengers have appeared along the quay; a line of cars is forming slowly between the barrier and the road. I turn my face to the grey churning of the Channel – no surfers here, no one paddling, no sun glittering off the water; it might be an entirely different element. I am shivering, for my life is an entirely different element now, divided irrevocably into before and after.

Gil scans the road behind us, traffic increasing as the minutes tick by. He looks intense when he's deliberating over a menu; it's only appropriate now. I wonder what he's expecting, how it will be when it happens: blue light flashing, siren whooping, guns and loudhailers or an unmarked car drawing silently alongside us, a flick of ID, a word in our ear.

He looks back at me, sees my face, squeezes my shoulder. "Hey. It's okay. It's going to take a while, you know."

I nod. "But you're jumpy."

"Cold, is what I am." He rubs his hands together as proof, glances towards the ferry waiting for us at the end of the quay. "You'd think they'd be letting us board by now."

And they do. We head the small crowd, past the duty free and row after row of empty seats, the smell of bacon from the restaurant almost but not quite eradicating the smell of sea and oil. Gil finds our cabin and we swing inside.

It's a tiny white capsule of bunkbed and en-suite, everything a little chipped, a little shabby, but clean nonetheless. He takes off his rucksack, runs his hand through his hair. "I'll get us some food, something to drink. What would you like?"

"Anything." Nothing, actually, but I'm still in helpful mode. Alone, I take off my shoes and hoodie, step into the en-suite and recoil from my reflection as I did hours ago on the train. I look ill. We both do. My make-up's in my bag but there's no point; I don't care and besides, foundation and blusher will conceal nothing. I wash, dry myself with a towel from the rail, weary now. My bones ache. When I sink down onto the lower bunk the duvet is softer than I'd expected, inviting. I want to curl up beneath it and disappear.

Just as I'm wondering where he is, whether I should be panicking, tearing round the ship endlessly searching for him like a mad woman or someone in a nightmare, Gil returns. He crouches on the floor, unloads a bottle of water and a can of Red Bull, sandwiches in plastic triangles, blueberry muffins and coffee, says apologetically, "I couldn't take out any hot food."

"I couldn't eat any hot food."

He snaps the lid from a cardboard beaker of coffee, takes a sip. I unwrap a muffin and break a piece off. "When we get to Roscoff," he says, "I'll hire a car. We'll go inland, minor roads, stay where we feel safe."

"Hiring a car will leave a trail."

He nods. "We won't be able to keep it. We'll go by train sometimes. Buses, whatever. And we'll have to empty our accounts as soon as we can."

I think about this. I've no idea how much money we have.

How much we'll need. "Is France big enough to get lost in? If you have no paperwork and you don't speak French?"

"I don't know," he says. "I've never done this before."

I put down the muffin. I cannot speak. My throat hurts and I reach for the water.

"Hey." He comes over to me on his knees, folds my hand into his. It's the first time he's touched me, the kindest his voice has been, since we were at the house. "One day at a time, you know?"

I struggle not to unravel. "I know."

"We just have to get our heads round it. We're going to have to get used to a different kind of normal. And no looking back." He holds my gaze, tucks a loose hank of my hair back behind my ear. "There's no one left to miss us anyway."

Chapter Six

The garden of the inn overlooking the bay had always been one of Jem's favourite places. Due to its distance from the beach and the precipitous drop beyond the palm trees and flowerbeds, it was one of the few places in town between Easter and September free from the wailing and paraphernalia of small children; a grown-up sanctuary in the midst of bucket and spade mayhem. Jem, arriving early, had taken possession of a picnic bench at the far end of the lawn, allowing the most secluded spot, the prettiest section of palms and lavender blue hibiscus and the best view of the Atlantic Ocean. It was a bit of a stroll to the bar but she had bought a large glass of white wine which she promised herself would last her the length of her stay. She had also brought her sketchpad and a pencil. An idea for a new design had half come to her in a dream, and she was trying to clutch at the dissipating fragments of it now and fix them to paper.

"Thought I might find you here."

Alex. She smiled up at him. "Hey."

"Hey." He sat on the end of the opposite bench, gestured towards her sketchpad. "Inspiration struck?"

"Something like that."

He smiled, gazed out over the greenery and the sea shimmer beyond. "We used to come here a lot."

"We did. I think I'm going to start resurrecting old traditions."

"Not starting new ones?"

"There's room," Jem said, "for both."

He reached for the copy of the local newspaper, which lay folded on the table between them. "May I?"

"I bought it for you."

She glanced at him now and then while she sketched and he read, knowing of old which pages he would read first, and second, and last, the point at which he would fold the paper in half and take out a pencil to attempt the sudoku, that it would

45

be accompanied by much frowning and rubbing-out, the occasional *blast!* and inevitable defeat. She wondered why he bothered when there was a perfectly good crossword on the same page and they were both much better with words than with numbers. But then that was the point after all; rising to small challenges was how her father thought you should live your life, not so much taking the road less travelled by as taking the road which encompassed potholes, a ford and a bit of hanging off a cliff edge. It was as well, she had always thought, that she had inherited his spirit and didn't hanker for routine or security. Or perhaps it was just that he had taught her well.

"So," he said after a while, clearly having reached a point in his sudoku when conversation became preferable, "what are these other traditions you'd like to resurrect?"

"Oh … " She considered. "Fish and chips on a Friday night. Going to the beach on Sunday mornings to watch the sunrise. Listening to the radio in the evening instead of playing spider solitaire on my laptop."

He laughed. "That is a choice you make, you know."

"It isn't a choice, it's a compulsion." She quit the pretence of trying to rescue the Gothic Surfer range of jewellery from the recesses of her sleep and put down her pencil. "Any more thoughts about your trip to Tintagel?"

"I have, in fact. Had a word with Archie Fellows, do you remember him?"

"No. You always ask me if I remember people you were on nodding terms with before I was born."

"He was a good friend and you were in high school. Anyway, I'm going to doss down at his place for a few days. It's just a mile or so up from Port Isaac, it'll be very handy."

"Doss down?" she cocked an eyebrow at him, reached for his abandoned newspaper and began to turn the pages. "What will it be, a mattress on the floor?"

"Very nice spare room, actually. If you don't want me to go … "

"No, no. You should go. I can just see the pair of you reliving your beer and paint stained bachelor days. I … oh my

God."

"What?" He looked over at the page at which she was staring.

"It's that guy." She turned the newspaper at ninety degrees between them. "This is the rescue I saw last week, do you remember?"

"I do." He skim-read the report, laughed. "She doesn't get any more original, does she, old Eve? 'Saturnine good looks' indeed."

Jem looked at the photo of a man called Gil Hunt, read Eve Callaghan's brief account of events and considerably less brief call for action, and returned to the photo. She felt oddly breathless. "Do you recognise him?"

"No. You'd think I would, if he's an artist of sorts and he's here every summer. But then a lot of young people are here every summer and you know me, I don't get out much." He glanced at her. "Why? Do you?"

"No. I mean, from that night, but … " And yet, there was something. She looked hard at the photograph. Gil Hunt, she thought. So that's who you are.

Party-time at Patrick's. Whose party no one knew or cared, its music and energy spilling into the bar, fairy-lit waves of rhythm rolling over guests and customers alike. You didn't have to be too picky if you held your private celebration at Patrick's: as the dance floor divided what passed for a function room from the society of tourists and regulars it became impossible to keep them apart. Cecily had never known anyone to mind. She sat on a bar stool with one leg tucked beneath her, swirling her third drink of the evening and people watching. A young man wearing a straw hat and floral shirt bopping in joyous unself-consciousness while a gaggle of barely clad girls wept with laughter. Radar and Buz cranking up their dumb surf dude double act for the benefit of two wise-beyond-their-years teenagers but also for their own amusement, Radar in knock-off RayBans and Buz having gelled his sunbleached mop into some bizarre kind of quiff. A couple around her own age, sitting in wicker chairs at the edge of the dance floor, watching the kids, turning back now and then to each other. Gil at the other end of the bar paying rapt attention to an elegant blonde, listening, laughing, emanating his fun-yet-honourable vibe. And Henry, beside her. Buying her another drink.

"Jeez, Hen. I'm going to be wasted. I have to get up and fry stuff in the morning."

"D'you care?"

"Hell no."

He smiled, pushed her drink towards her. Her gaze returned to the crowd, reading body language, catching the smallest interactions, singling out the beautiful, the introverted, the careless. We all have our stories, she thought, lifting her glass to her mouth. Every one of us.

"Wanted to tell you something actually." Henry's words filtered into her thoughts and she turned slowly back to him.

"Yeah?"

"What we were saying the other day."

Cecily didn't blink. If he kept talking she'd cotton on.

"You remember?"

"Sure." She kept her face straight while she dredged her memory. "Remind me."

"About taking something seriously."

"I do. Of course I do." She put down her glass, rested her chin in her hand. "So tell me."

He hesitated. "I have this cousin, in Australia. Brisbane. My aunt and uncle emigrated out there when we were kids. Anyway, he has his own watersports business, been going a few years now, doing pretty well. He's asked me if I'd like to go out there, just for a holiday and … " He stopped. "You can see where this is going, can't you?"

"I can. And you know, it sounds great but … Oh Henry, an English guy, teaching Australians how to surf? Really?"

"Listen, I want to bring home the trophy. Show them it's not just cricket we can beat them at. I want people to say – hey, there's this great surf instructor, best I've ever had, and you know what? He's *English*." He grinned. "Truthfully, of course I know. And I'm only going for a trip. But the thought of

Australia … "

Cecily nodded, equally wistful. "Take me with you."

Henry looked at her.

"Take you with him where?" Gil arrived beside them, buzzing with just the right amount of beer inside him and the scent of new woman in the air.

"Australia," Cecily said, watching his reaction.

"No kidding?" Gil looked from one to the other. "You're kidding, right?"

"Who's the blonde?" Henry said.

Gil laughed. "She's stunning, isn't she? New in town, opened a business on The Walk a few months back. *Very* cool, very together, sort of - "

"What's her name?" Cecily asked him.

He took a breath, frowned.

"You know, Gil, if you can't remember her name it all ends here."

Henry shrugged. "Ah, you don't need to remember their names when you have saturnine good looks."

Gil grinned. "Fuck off."

Cecily tensed, her body reacting instinctively to the opening bars of the next dance tune before her brain had registered what it was. *Los Lobos, La Bamba*. Gil heard it too, held out his hand to her. "No," she said, though she was half out of her seat. He waited. "No, no. I can't, I can't. Oh all right then."

He led her into a small space on the dance floor, and as the music rose and the press of other people's bodies closed in on them she remembered how this felt, giving yourself up to the rhythm and the beat, twisting and turning, letting go. Gil twirled her, his hand lightly on her waist, her hip, edging back to give her room. She stretched and clapped, clicked her fingers, shimmied and spun. She wanted the floor to herself, wanted to dance as she had danced twenty years ago but at the same time that didn't matter; this moment was enough.

When it was over Gil smiled, winked at her. Henry, six feet away, was on his feet, applauding. "It was one of her favourites," Gil explained. "Back in the day."

"Cheesy but irresistible," Cecily agreed.

Gil read Henry's admiration and grinned. "She's an amazing dancer, isn't she?"

"Not so bad yourself," Cecily said.

"Oh, I just jig around."

Henry stared at her, remembering. "You were a dancer."

"I was. I told you once, I think."

"Wow."

She hitched back onto her bar stool, reached for her drink. The cool, together blonde had returned to the bar and Cecily met Gil's eyes. "Thank you," she said to him, as Buz and Radar hoved inexorably into view. "See you tomorrow."

Later, walking home through the dark with Henry, their footfall and voices soft in the quiet streets, he said, "Did you train, to dance?"

"I did, in London. For a few years I did all the usual stuff, clubs, a few small shows, the odd cruise. It wasn't as romantic or as glamorous as it sounds. It was exhausting and insecure and painful. But I loved it for a while."

"Why did you give it up?"

"It was hard. I was nothing special and there's such competition and then, well." She shrugged. "Life happens. It was a long time ago."

"And Gil knows all this?"

"Gil knows everything."

They emerged into the square, shops shuttered now, the last drinkers trailing from the pub into the cool still night. She gazed around and her heart contracted with misgiving. "I love this place," she said. Henry nodded. "Love my café." Her voice was louder than she'd intended in the emptiness and she sighed. "I'm a bit drunk, you know."

"I know."

"Are you coming in?"

"Better not." He smiled. "Good night, Cecily."

"Good night." Her hand curled around her key in her pocket, but she stayed on the doorstep, watching him walk away, his lumbering figure slowly swallowed up by the shadows.

Alex's gallery overlooked the harbour, which was great in

terms of inspiring panoramas and tourist traffic and less great in terms of nowhere to park and seagull shit. But then the latter could be said of anywhere in town and you had, Jem knew, to be grateful. She could see as she approached people browsing the paintings he'd hung on the wall, heads tilted, stepping back for a better view. Others turning slowly through the prints in the racks. The air of thoughtfulness and calm characterised not only the space but the paintings themselves. Alex didn't paint to express violent emotions or political agendas or intellectual ideas. He painted to convey beauty in whatever form he found it. What set him apart was that it wasn't always where you might expect.

Jem crossed the sand strewn floor towards him, standing in the doorway from the gallery to his workshop behind. The contrast between the two always amused her – here, ordered airy tranquillity, there a chaos of canvas and acrylics, newspapers and half empty coffee mugs. "Good morning?"

"Excellent morning. Sold two of the Minacks."

"Ooh. Celebration."

"Bills paid." He smiled. "What have you been up to?"

"Oh." She sighed. "Walking. Thinking. I'm trying to come up with something new. I've got people willing to take my stuff now and I want to show them there's always going to be a surprise with me, something a little bit different. As well as the pieces that always sell, of course."

"Of course."

"But it's just … eluding me, at the moment."

"Plenty to do in the meantime."

"Yeah." She sighed. "Okay. I'm going to go home." She kissed his cheek. "See you later."

"See you later, Puddle."

She took the winding road out of town, rising past the fringe of small shops and less prosperous cafés, through streets of guest houses and sugared almond painted terraces, until the spaces between the buildings grew wider and the road became a lane of hedgerows over which, were she tall enough, she could have glimpsed the sea. In her kitchen she poured the dregs of a bottle of white wine into a glass and took it up to her room, slid a CD into the player. *10cc: The Original Soundtrack*. Music from her parents' youth. Music from her own youth seemed manufactured and overblown by comparison, she had never been able to understand her schoolfriends' passions for Robbie and Madonna, for Westlife and Kylie anymore than they had understood her still living a flower power life at the dawn of the new millennium. Many of those friends were wives and mothers now, she saw them sometimes wheeling buggies or Tesco trollies through their ordinary lives as though the world she knew, the world of freedom and creativity, were another dimension. But none of them, she thought wryly, would have been drifting through town half hoping to catch a glimpse of a man they didn't know. A man she'd seen once at a distance on a darkened beach and again in a newspaper photograph. How could the thought of him have her distracted and unsettled? You are behaving, she told herself, like a teenager with a crush on a rock star. Or worse, like some sad stalker. Sad and mad. Mad, bad and dangerous to know.

For God's sake, Jem.

She pulled out her sketchpad, which had yielded nothing helpful since her afternoon in the pub garden, took a sip of wine and listened to 10cc telling her they weren't in love. In 1975 her parents hadn't been in love. They hadn't even known each other. They had been Alex Gregory and Marianne Rae and had met six years later at a music festival. Alex having already decided that painting was the only way he could live his life with any measure of integrity, they had spent their first year together renting a shack in someone's garden and eating beans while the rest of the county embraced shoulder pads, mobile phones and the worst excesses of the Thatcher government. By the time Jem was born, Alex was selling enough of his work to manage a deposit on the cottage and Marianne supplemented her job at the tourist office teaching guitar and piano to anyone who would pay her. Some of Jem's most vivid childhood memories were of sitting on a dusty floor playing with watercolours and thick stubs of pastels while her father painted, of the plinky plonk of keys and discordant twang of guitar strings from the room in which her mother spoke patiently to another ungifted child. She used to think it ironic that her sensible, practical father had hitched his livelihood to the whims of other people's tastes while her mother, given to seasons of melancholia and wild imaginings, held down the nine-to-five. Later she had thought that they were finding some sort of balance, complementing their inner selves as they complemented each other. She recalled her mother's trailing Indian cotton skirts and trailing fair hair, her sudden trips away from which she would return dizzy with excitement, carrying an air of other-worldliness and odd little presents she'd bought them. Alex hadn't liked these trips; he'd be frantic then bad-tempered which Jem had thought unfair of him, but she had minded her mother's absence too. She remembered the way she looked cycling down the lane to and from work, hair flying, body swaying with the rhythm of the bike, the clink of her bangles

the clink of her bangles

Jem sat up, sprung from her reverie.

"I had the best idea," she told Alex later, piling spaghetti onto their plates. "I don't know why it's never occurred to me before. I'm going to design a new range based on Mum's jewellery."

"Hm." He considered. "Her style was very different to yours."

"Oh I know, I was looking at some of her pendants and bracelets this afternoon. She went for more fragile, conventional things than I do. But it's a starting point, isn't it?"

Alex smiled. "It is. And it would be a lovely tribute."

She nodded. "That's what I thought. I was wondering, do you think there's more of her jewellery amongst all the junk in the cupboard? It's so long since we looked through any of it." She spoke lightly, barely looking at him, allowing him to dismiss the notion without it becoming an issue. After her mother's death, Alex had sealed all her belongings away and refused to deal with them. It had taken years and gentle persuasion before he would unpack and make decisions about any of it, and then almost everything had simply been stored unexamined in the landing cupboard.

"Well." He opened the fridge, took out a can of lager. "I'm not sure. We could have a trawl through it together, if you like."

She smiled, kissed his cheek as he passed her. "Before you go off for your wild week with Archie Fellows?"

"Leaving you here to have a wild week of your own." He took their plates of spaghetti from her, put them on the table. "There are other avenues you could be exploring, you know. Not just for promoting your business."

"Yada yada."

"I'm not having you turning into a recluse."

She cocked an eyebrow at him.

"Fair enough." He sat down to eat. "But I am a grizzled old man and you are too young and beautiful to be holed up here morning, noon and night. How long is it since you took your stall onto the pier? We've been having more than ten minutes of sunshine a day for weeks now."

"All right."

"All right what?"

"All right I will take my stall onto the pier and I will talk to people. I might even pop into the bar afterwards and talk to people."

"Steady now."

Jem laughed, despite herself. "D'you know? I can't wait for you to go."

*

Gil knelt back from the fire, watched it for a moment, stuck in a few more pieces of driftwood. The flames were small but burning well; before long there would be enough heat to take the chill off the cool summer evening. It was past eight, the sun casting tall shadows across the beach, and already a couple of the girls had pulled cardigans around their shoulders and were inching closer to the fire. Gil passed round bottles of WKD and Smirnoff Ice, unearthed a Budweiser for himself. Lucy, whom he knew from Patrick's, stood watching the guys kicking a ball around on the wide stretch of flat, hard sand between them and the gently frothing tide. She wore denim micro-shorts and Gil felt his attention drawn to her bronzed and slender legs as by an invisible yet powerful thread. Someone called to her to unpack the coolbag of meat for the barbecue and she bent from the waist in front of him. Gil groaned, dragged his line of vision back to the football, weighing up whether he wanted to jog over there and join in. Not really, was the answer. Instead he pushed to his feet, walked round to the other side of the flames and dropped down beside Cecily.

"Done with ogling Lucy?" she greeted him.

"I was not ogling."

"Yeah yeah." Cecily lifted her sunglasses up onto her head, catching her hair back from her face. She wore jeans rolled to her calf, her toenails painted deep red wine. "How did you get on with the woman at the party? The cool blonde?"

"Oh we got on very well. She was great. Then she told me about her fiancé stationed at Brize Norton and you know, the magic kind of went."

Cecily smiled. "Time was, that wouldn't have mattered. You used to prefer them spoken for. Less responsibility."

"Did I ever actually say that?"

"You didn't have to." She narrowed her eyes at him. "Have you shagged *anyone* since you got here?"

He sighed heavily. "I really wish you wouldn't use that expression. It cheapens the whole … profoundly spiritual … intimacy of … " He gave up. "No."

She drew in her breath, mocking him. "Losing your touch, Gilman."

"Maybe this year I'm looking for something different."

She frowned. "Are you? Seriously?"

He took a long swig from his bottle, fixed his gaze on the guys – and girls too now – and their five-a-side, Radar scooping the ball out of the sea, Henry launching it back across the sand, Lucy and her Barbie doll legs … "Are you seriously interested in Henry?"

She stiffened. "He's a friend. Like he's always been."

"No, sweetheart, not like you think he's always been. He has a massive crush on you. It's tattooed across his forehead every time he looks at you and if you can't see that … "

"I can see it."

"Yet you left with him."

"Jesus, Gil. Yes, I left with him, but I didn't take him to bed. He walked me home. I know it's hard for you to imagine leaving it there but we did. Maybe Henry's just more of a gentleman than you are."

"I'm just saying be careful, that's all."

"It's really none of your business." Her tone was so hard she might have slapped his face.

"Oh right." He swallowed. "Okay." He drained his Budweiser, stood up and sprinted down to the game, the ball rolling his way as he ran. He booted it hard and it flew.

"Fucking hell Gil!" Buz called. "Making an entrance or what?"

As the sun sank they returned to the fire, cooked burgers and sausages to the requisite shade of black, downed bottle after bottle and lay replete in the sand. Buz fetched his guitar and continued to play House of The Rising Sun through universal groans and Radar throwing balls of paper at him. Henry lounged beside Cecily, engaging her in whispered conversation. Gil let alcohol assuage his resentment and Lucy stroke his thigh as he drifted in and out of the talk and the music around him. When he opened his eyes most people had gone, Lucy and Henry were walking together along the water's edge and Cecily was chucking empty bottles into a plastic holdall.

"Jeez," he said. "I went right out."

"Yeah." Though it was dark she had her sunglasses back on and he couldn't read her eyes. "Pissed off or just pissed?"

"Both, I guess." He didn't mind apologising when things weren't his fault if it restored the peace. He preferred continuing as if nothing had happened.

She sat back amidst the remains of their evening. "You going to help me with this?"

"Sure." They cleared the litter, stamped out and disposed of what was left of the fire. After a while he said, inconsequentially, "There's a lot of change in the air, this year."

"There is. You don't like it."

"I don't mind change, but not if it isn't for the better. I was in town today, went to visit this gallery I really liked, down on The Wharf. I'd admired the guy's work for – well, years. Anyway, it was empty, all boarded up. It saddened me."

"Sign of the times," Cecily said. "You come down here every summer like it's a holiday in some sort of frozen-in-time utopia. Well, this town isn't your playground, Gil. It's real lives. And people's real lives are going down the tubes just now."

The asperity was back in her voice and he was stung. "I appreciate that. And I don't behave as if it's my playground. Actually that's pretty offensive. I love it here, it means a lot to me and I'm sad to see it going the way of – well, everywhere else these days. That's all."

"But once a year you swing on by here like you own the place and you party hard and you mess with people's lives and then you just take off again."

"Whose lives do I mess with?"

She was silent, concentrating far harder than she needed on bagging everything up, shaking out beach towels.

He stared at her. "Yours?"

"The girls you come here to fuck. You shag them and break their hearts and leave them with nothing."

He shook his head, anger and disbelief fighting it out for first place. "Great memories, is what I leave them with. Anything else – not that there ever has been anything else – I'd deal with. They always have my number. Why are we even having this conversation? You know that better than anyone. Christ, you know *me* better than anyone."

She said nothing. He watched her, dismayed. "Where has this come from? Why are you saying this stuff?"

"Because you think you have the right to tell me how to behave with someone."

"Henry?" He was incredulous. "Is that what this is? That's

what we're fighting about?"

She shrugged.

He said, "I don't believe you. You were mad at me that first night. The very first night. I must have missed something really big here because we don't get mad at each other."

She paused and he saw the first chink in her rage. "We don't see each other for months and suddenly you're deliberately picking arguments like you want to push me away. Tell me what's going on."

She said bitterly, "It's not actually about you."

There was a long silence.

He said, "I can't read your mind."

"Right now, you wouldn't want to."

The voices of Lucy and Henry became audible as they strolled back up the beach. Gil was at a loss. "Fine," he said quietly. "You know where I am if you want to move on from this."

She turned away from him, gathering up the bags to carry them to the car.

Henry called, "Hey, let me give you a hand." He took the load from her, ambled away with her towards the prom.

Gil closed his eyes, felt a slap on his left buttock. "Come on," Lucy said at his shoulder. "Bar's still open."

Chapter Seven

We have travelled as though blinkered through changing landscapes, from windswept lowland to vineyard valleys, across ancient bridges over flowing rivers. It's beautiful, I know that, in the small part of my mind which still registers such things, but all we see is the road ahead and the space we can continue to put between ourselves and retribution.

It's grown dark along this last stretch, undergrowth encroaching, trees hanging low, miles from the main routes. The car bumps and rolls to a halt. There's a silence. I say, after a moment, "Are we lost?"

"I think you have to be going somewhere to be lost." Gil's been driving for seven hours on the wrong side of the road in a county he doesn't know and his nerves are shot. Even more than they were to begin with. He looks at the dashboard. "Shit. Need to fill up again."

"What do garages look like in France?"

"Not a clue." He opens the door and gets out. "Like they do in England? Is that too much to ask? Did you notice anything on the way?"

"No." I've followed him but hang back.

"I think," he rubs his eyes with his finger and thumb, "there's a village a bit further on. I think I saw a signpost. What's French for petrol?"

"Le pétrol? Le gasoline?"

He stares at me.

"I don't know." I walk away, can hear him ranting –

"I might've paid a little bit more attention in school if they'd told me one day I'd be on the run and the language might come in fucking useful."

"There is a village." I can see, through a gap in the bushes, a distant church steeple, lights. He peers over my shoulder.

"And there is a god."

There is also a garage. He fills the tank, pays with some of the euros we exchanged back in Roscoff. "It's *l'essence*," he says. "Petrol. For future information." He pauses. I'm leaning against the car and neither of us can bear to let the darkness inside it swallow us up again. "Listen, this place might be bigger than it seems. Let's see if there's somewhere we can eat, spend the night." He reaches for my hand. "Come on."

Beyond the garage the road opens onto a sloping cobbled square with a stone monument at its centre. On three sides closed-up shops occupy the ground floors of tall buildings, iron balconies jutting from upper storeys. In the centre of the fourth side is an archway wide enough to take a carriage and at the railings to which horses might once have been tethered bikes are chained. Youths loiter in a corner of parked cars, the glow of their cigarettes and lilt of their voices one of the few signs of life. The building outside which they are gathered bears the words *L'Étable café-bar*.

It's dark and low-ceilinged inside, yellow-green lamps in the booths, bright gold above the long polished sweep of the bar. There are a few glances as we enter but the room doesn't fall silent, no one glares or comments, as far as we can tell. We slide into the nearest booth, the high-backed settles allowing us privacy. Gil picks up the menu and his hands are shaking.

"It's okay," I whisper.

He looks at me as if it is anything but okay, glances out into the café. A huddle of old men stand at the bar, their clothing dark and loose, the rolling grunt of their conversation punctuated by the knock of glass against wood. An overweight man and a sulky looking woman sharing a table eat their meals in silence. A young couple blow in, as we did, from the square, greet the barman with a string of looping, indistinguishable chatter. It is all hopelessly foreign and bizarrely familiar, as if we have strayed onto a film set full of extras from Gallic Central Casting. But Gil doesn't look as if he's distracting himself with desperately whimsical observations. Gil looks as if anyone taps him on the shoulder he will punch them.

He returns his attention to the menu, scans the pages, shakes his head. After a moment he says, "I can't read any of this." He's laughing but there's more hysteria than humour in it. "I don't know what any of it means." His eyes glitter in the lamplight and he stands up – "Give me a minute" – and strides back out through the doors into the square.

My eyes are pricking too and I stare hard at the menu. In the jumble of words some seem familiar and I concentrate on translation because I don't want to think about why he's gone or where or whether he'll come back. A waitress appears and I ask for *une carafe du vin rouge* because even I know what that means. Thankfully she leaves it with me and I pour myself a large glass, knock it back because oblivion feels like a good place to be. Planning, thinking rationally, belong to that other life now. All I can see is an inch or two into the dark.

Halfway down my second glass and my head already thumping, he appears, slides back behind the table. "They have a room for tonight."

"How do you know?"

"The waitress remembers a few words of English." He says it almost apologetically and I wonder what his part in the conversation was. Gil can look at you, touch you a certain way and if he wanted you to, you'd remember you were fluent in Swahili. "Sorry," he adds. "I kind of lost it, for a minute."

"I know." I fill his glass. We order food, receive chicken with potatoes and onions which we chew and swallow as if it were tasteless, grimly finish the wine. When we leave the table my knees buckle and he grips my arm to steady me. We find the staircase at the rear of the café and stumble up onto the narrow landing. Gil unlocks one of the doors and I sway inside. There's a sagging bedstead, a large mahogany wardrobe, an armchair. He draws aside a stained yellow curtain and finds in the recess behind it a toilet and a sink, a shower with a spider lurking in its cobweb above it. I lower myself too quickly onto the bed and it creaks beneath my sudden weight.

"I'll have the chair," Gil says. He takes one of the pillows from the bed, opens the wardrobe and finds below the clanking hangars a spare blanket.

"You can't sleep in the chair."

He almost smiles. "It looks as good a prospect as the bed."

He dumps the pillows and blanket on the floor and kneels before me, unlaces and removes my trainers, kneads the soles of my feet. "I'll be okay."

My spirits sink further still but I'm in no state to argue. We undress to our underwear and he tries to settle into the armchair. The mattress dips in unhelpful places and the sheets are cold. I close my eyes.

It seems a minute later. I wake in a great seizing rush of panic and roaring thirst. In my rucksack there's water and I fall out of bed, unbuckle the flap and search for the bottle. Gil is asleep. I watch him while I drink, the line of his stubbled jaw, one arm loose from the blanket, his fingertips brushing the floor.

And something under the bed yanks at my foot.

I gasp, try to jerk away, but its grip is fast, and hard. As it holds me down it drags me under, so strong the carpet scrapes my knees, my thighs. I scream Gil's name but he doesn't stir. Its claws tear at my calves, my buttocks, and I kick, shrieking in terror, the room disappearing as it pulls me in to its lair of tensile limbs and dripping hair. It hauls me over onto my back, its weight and strength and the underside of the bedframe imprisoning me no matter how I wrestle, my arms flailing, fists falling short as wild-eyed and salivating it rakes lines of blood through my flesh, talons digging deep into my eyes, my throat.

I wake again.

I am wedged into the small space between the toilet and the sink, my knees and arms pressed tight together, my hands covering my ears, rocking.

"Jesus Christ." Gil, horrified in the doorway. He comes to crouch on the floor in front of me, reaches for my hand. "What happened?"

"She came to get me."

He stares at me. Lets out his breath. "It was a nightmare."

I stare back. My heart is racing. He says, "There's no one here. Only us. Come on. Come here."

I uncurl myself, already stiff. He draws me out and up, his arm around my shoulders. "My God." He holds my face in his hands, wipes away my tears.

"I was so scared she was here."

He nods slowly, kisses my forehead, holds me for a moment. I can feel his breath against my hair, his warmth the length of me. When I lie down again he climbs in beside me.

Chapter Eight

Cecily ran barefoot up the iron staircase and knocked at Gil's door. It was *warm*, she thought, waiting for him to answer. She had braced herself against the early morning chill but the sun was shining and the air was actually, properly, warm. She tipped back her head and gazed up into cloudless blue sky. Summer at last.

After a moment she realised there had been no response, not even an irritated grunt at having been woken. She rapped again, on the glass this time, her words of apology running through her head like a ticker-tape message. *I'm sorry*, she read ... *such a cow* ... *don't know what's the matter with me* ... *forgive me?* This last delivered with a rueful smile and a kiss planted on his stubbled cheek. He would hug her and tell her to forget it, probably apologise too. They would go down to the café, grab some breakfast and pretend they didn't both know that something was seriously up and she was choosing not to tell him what it was. The least she could do, she thought, was keep it safely locked inside. It wasn't fair of her to throw her despair in his path like so much acid waste. None of this was remotely Gil's fault.

Still nothing. "Gil!" she called. "You in there?" Maybe he had risen anatomically to her challenge and secured his first shag of the season. Lucy, she imagined, with her enviably long and slender limbs and flawless skin and wheat coloured hair. Not that they were a breed, Gil's women. They were characterised by their differences rather than their similarities, as if he were trying out every possible variation. "Gil!" She gave him another minute, then skipped back down the steps and into the café, where Henry was helping himself to coffee.

"If you're not going to put a shirt on," she told him, "you might stay in the kitchen."

"Oh, sorry. But there's no one here."

"Even so." She glanced across the empty tables – still early yet – and back at him. He had spent last night on her sofa, which given the size of Henry and the size of the sofa was no mean feat. Now, bleary with lack of sleep and excess of drink, he leaned against the counter with one hand wrapped around a striped Cornishware mug, his belly lolling comfortably over the waistband of his shorts. His shoulders had bulk and heft, his smooth skin a carelessly gained golden tan. If she were to go to bed with him at some point in the very near future, was that going to be the answer? Would week after week of mind-blowing, no-strings sex blot out everything else? Would it even be mind-blowing with Henry? She thought of Gil, muscled yet lean, of the spread of dark hair across his chest, a line of it stretching the length of his taut stomach to his navel.

"Was Gil not in?" Henry asked and she wondered were her thoughts visible in bubbles above her head.

"No. Well, there was no answer. Unless he's choosing not to speak to me." The idea came to her suddenly and filled her with dismay.

"Nah, he's not like that." He looked at her. They had spent an hour or two last night skirting round the issue of why she and Gil had been snarling at each other on the sand. Henry hadn't wanted to know any more than she had wanted to tell him but it had been in the air between them nonetheless. "Don't let him get to you. We all fall out with Gil now and then, he'll get over it."

She smiled. "Do we? All fall out with him?"

"You bet. He can be a bit of a twat when he wants."

She laughed. "*Hen*ry."

"Sorry. Any message, if I see him?"

"No, just … I'll catch him later." She heard the tinkle of tubular bells, the voices of her first customers of the day. "Maybe much later."

Gil lifted the apple wood log, which he had driven halfway across Cornwall to buy, from the passenger seat where it had sat companionably beside him for the duration of their journey home, carried it up the staircase, into his studio, set it down with some ceremony on the workbench and examined it from as many angles as were available to him.

"Right," he said to it eventually. "You tell me. What do you want to be?"

Eight or nine months of the year Gil toiled in his Bristol workshop building cabinets, tables, chairs and any other bespoke item of furniture customers could afford to commission. When he applied himself, it paid the bills. Very nicely sometimes, scarcely at others. But three or four months of the year he took to his seaview studio a hunk of wood which had been whispering to him all through the rain and the dark of the city and created something which made his heart sing. This year, the hunks having been either silent or unappealing, he had driven out to a supplier he'd heard of who specialised in reclaimed timber and wood from fallen trees, spent most of the morning waiting for a piece to choose him, and surveyed it now with excitement rolling like incoming waves. He loved beginnings, when everything was still possible, when the mystery of the shape inside the wood was still his to find.

The log looked back at him.

Sometimes it took a while.

Patrick's was no less busy at lunchtime than it was at night; only the clientele differed. Most of the clientele. Gil said it was their responsibility to maintain some sense of continuity and bagged a table overlooking the pier while Henry – freshly surfed – paid for their drinks.

"Great day for it," Gil commented, the heat of the sun burning his shoulders through the glass.

Henry shrugged. "Bit calm out there."

Gil sipped his drink, trying to decide whether he wanted to voice the words in his head when Henry beat him to it.

"Cecily was looking for you this morning."

"She was?"

"Uh-huh."

"When?"

"Around eight. We thought you must've gone out."

We? Gil managed to swallow his mouthful of beer without choking. *We?* "Yeah," he said. "Took a drive out to that reclaimed timber yard near Redruth. Bought a log."

"She asked me to give you a message."

Gil waited.

"She said, she'll catch you later."

He laughed. "That's it, that's the message?"

"What were you expecting?"

"I don't know. 'Fuck off, dickhead'?"

Henry said coolly, "Look, I don't know what you two were arguing about last night – "

"No," Gil agreed. "You don't. And you know what? Neither do I. But you don't have to get all bristly on her behalf. Cecily's quite capable of standing up for herself."

Henry shook his head. "See, that's where I think you're wrong. I think she needs some support at the moment."

And you're the man to give it to her? Gil let his gaze travel to the pier beyond the open French windows. "Yeah," he said after a minute. "I'll drop by later. See how she is."

The scrape of chairs, thunk of glasses. Radar and Buz, in from the beach. "Hey." Gil smiled up at them, relieved. Their good natures combined with their heightened sense of the ridiculous meant acting morose and difficult in their company became laughably adolescent. Which was ironic, he thought. "How's your day going?"

"Just took a turn for the better." Radar grinned. "*Big* party going down Saturday night."

"Oh yeah? Whose?"

"Windsurfing guy we know, Phil. Has this amazing place with his girlfriend down by the cove."

"Everyone's invited." Buz smiled over the rim of his beer glass. "Bring a mate, bring a bottle. Well, two bottles."

"But don't bring the guitar?" Gil suggested.

Buz threw him a glare. "So where's Lucy today? She working?"

Gil shrugged. "I guess."

They looked at him, all three of them. He raised his hands. "Nothing happened. We had a drink, I walked her home." Though he could hardly blame them for their scepticism. On her doorstep she had pulled him close and kissed him with intent, which had been very nice, but he'd felt no inclination whatsoever to take things any further. He didn't understand it himself.

Radar said, with awe, "You're getting old, man."

Buz shook his head. "It's that bust-up with Cecily. Isn't it, Gil?"

Gil opened his mouth to reply, realised he didn't know which way to go with the response, and sighed. "Gonna go for a walk," he said, standing up. "And then I have work to do. I'll see   you   later."

*

Jem was not the only stallholder on the pier. Three of the others were old friends: McDowell, the thin man with the grey ponytail who sold leather belts and purses, bags and wristbands, punching patterns into soft tan hide as he waited with apparent indifference for customers; Annika, her stall fluttering with designs of henna tattoos ranging from flamboyant to barely discernible – Jem had been mesmerised by them one summer and counted fourteen separate works of art lacing her own skin by the end of it; Pavao, the shy Croatian who painted tiny, detailed fantasy worlds and mythical creatures onto slabs of rock and pieces of drift-wood, worlds which had nothing to do with the surrounding sea and sand and everything, she had always thought, to do with Pavao's inner landscape. There were new stalls too, she could see their owners and glimpses of their wares from her customary pitch halfway between the bar above the beach and the lighthouse. She wondered would Annika mind her stall for a little while when it grew quiet so she could check them out. For now, the sun had brought the crowds. Typical that as soon as she'd let Alex bully her into trundling up here again, the day had dawned as close to perfect as she had known it yet this year. "Do you control the weather now?" she'd asked him as she left.

He'd laughed. "Make the right decision and the sun shines. The pathetic fallacy is not such a fallacy as you might think."

Between customers she adjusted cards of earrings and

selections of cuffs, smiling and catching the eyes of potential buyers as they sauntered past, the young women and the teenage girls, the mothers, the lovers. All her other sales were made indirectly, through shops or her website, and she was curious to see the faces of the people who would part with money for the finely wrought treasures into which she poured her soul. The sun grew hot against her shoulder blades as she chatted and explained and slipped the pieces into her signature velvet bags before taking their cash or fitting their cards into her machine. As soon as a lull in traffic allowed, she reached for her bottle of water from beneath her stall and drank deep, though it was repellently warm and the plastic sticky to her touch, observing the stream of holiday-makers, the gulls flying low to steal ice-creams and chips, children bending to watch the sea through the gaps in the boards.

And there he was.

She lowered the bottle slowly, wiping her mouth with the back of her hand. Gil Hunt, strolling this way. A few minutes at a distance on a dark beach, one black and white photo in a newspaper, and she would have known him anywhere. She felt panic stricken, as though her body would not cooperate with anything her brain required it to do. She turned her attention to her rows of earrings, knocking two or three pairs askew and a necklace from its perch, and waited for him to pass.

"Hello."

He was talking to her. Standing the other side of her stall and talking to her.

"Hello," she managed.

He smiled. "Nice stall."

"Thank you."

He lifted a pendant into his hand, examining it. Jem tried to breathe deep, examining him. Jeans, khaki t-shirt, jaw-length dark hair pushed back from his forehead, brown eyes beneath heavy, arching brows. *Be normal*, she told herself.

He picked up one of her engraved pewter rings – he was wearing rings himself, she saw, silver, on the third and fourth fingers of his right hand. "This is impressive stuff."

"Thank you," she said again, like a polite child at a tea party.

"Are they yours?" he asked. "Do you make them?"

"Yes." She gestured toward her card pinned to the board. "That's me."

"Jemima Gregory," he read. "Gil Hunt."

"I know," she said before she could stop herself.

He laughed, "Okay, this is going to sound slightly less cheesy now – seriously, have we met?"

He knew? He *recognised* her? "Um … I saw you, save that boy. I was on the prom when it happened."

"That was you?"

"That was me."

"And I think I saw you in town a week or two ago. You were carrying … well this, I guess." He indicated her board. She thought – he remembered me. He saw me in the street and remembered me. "Small world," he said.

"Small town."

"It is that." He smiled, glanced along the pier. He's bored with me now, she thought. He'll wander off for a chat with McDowell, flirt with Annika. She didn't know why she was attributing to him propensities for boredom, chatting and flirting; what did she know about him beyond a readiness to fish people out of the sea?

His attention swung back to her. "Business looks buzzing."

"It has been," she smiled. "I've been sitting here since half past nine and made a small fortune."

"Really? I guess you're a bit like exhibitions yourselves out here all day."

"Very sunburned exhibitions, at this rate."

He said instantly, "Let me get you a drink."

"Oh, no, it's … I'm … "

"Do you have someone with you?"

"No."

"And you've been sitting in this sun for – what, four, five hours and you wouldn't kill for a cold drink? I'll just nip in to Patrick's, be ten minutes."

"Okay," she capitulated. He grinned, took her order. She wanted to watch him walk away but a woman had appeared beside her stand and was studying a necklace of tiny bronze discs and amber beads with the look of a serious buyer. Jem said, her gaze still following Gil Hunt, "Would you like to try it on? I have a mirror."

She saw him again minutes later, negotiating his way through the crowd, a tray aloft in one hand. She could hear the faint chink of its half dozen glasses and watched as he distributed them to Pavao and Annika and a couple of the newbies. Finally he returned to her with a smile - "There you go" – and handed her a tall glass full of ice with lemon and lime.

"Thank you. This is so kind of you."

He shrugged. "We have to help each other out, don't we."

We? Human beings? Artists, craftspeople? What had the newspaper said he did for a living? A pair of prepubescent girls pushed in front of him to play with her box of rings and she wanted to push them back.

"I'm getting in the way of your profits," he observed with humour. "I'd better give you some space."

No, she thought, no no don't go.

"It's been lovely to meet you," he said as though he meant it. She managed to babble something similar in response and suddenly he was leaving, disappearing by degrees into the crowd, and her disappointment was eclipsed by the knowledge that for a shining, shimmering moment a little of Gil Hunt's light had shone on her.

Cecily ran up the iron staircase and knocked at Gil's door. She hadn't had a table empty for more than five minutes all day. In a burst of frustration and impatience at having no time to go out and breathe in the sunshine, she had abandoned the café at the first opportune moment to Justine, the seventeen year old specialising in lethargic disdain who Cecily employed for as many hours as she could bear to wash dishes and wait on tables. Five minutes with Gil, she had thought. What damage could Justine do in five minutes? So she knocked, and this time she heard his voice.

He was standing in the centre of his room, staring at a three feet by two feet log which squatted on the workbench in front of him. "Is this your project for the summer?" she asked.

"It will be."

She stood beside him and stared at it too. "Not inspired?"

"Yeah. It's just … it isn't speaking to me yet."

The perfect cue. "Gil. Last night … " She paused. He wasn't rushing in with excuses or reassurances as he usually did. Too distracted by the bloody log. "I'm sorry I was such a cow."

He did look at her then. "No, you were right. I was being an arse. It's none of my business."

Somehow that wasn't quite what she'd wanted him to say. Or if it was, not in that tone. But then he was concentrating on a chunk of wood he would hew and chisel and smooth into a work of art. When the intensity of his focus was directed there not parties nor Patrick's nor dancing naked in front of him would be any diversion.

She said, "Friends?"

"Of course." He relented. "Of course, friends."

"Dinner? My place?"

"Yeah, sure. Let me know when."

Well, tonight, she thought. I meant tonight. She watched him walk stealthily around the block as if it were a deer in long grass. "I'd better get back downstairs," she said. "Left Justine in charge."

"Okay." He smiled briefly. "See you later."

I've been dismissed, she thought, clattering back down the staircase.

Or he is seriously obsessed with that piece of wood and will carve it into something so amazing it will make his name and fortune.

Or he is still so pissed off he can barely bring himself to talk to me.

Or all of the above.

She swooped back into her café to find Justine hanging over the boy who delivered the fruit and veg and the floor slippery with the food the last family's children hadn't cared to put in their mouths.

What could I do, she wondered as she went to fetch the broom, in Australia?

Gil stood at his window, distracted not by the prospect of craftsmanship or residual ill-feeling but by his encounter this afternoon with a girl called Jemima Gregory. There was no view of the pier from his studio, he had spoken to her for five minutes at the most, but still all he could see were her kitten green eyes and the long ripples of her dark hair. That the girl watching from the prom that night and the girl who'd struck such a strange chord within him on The Walk and the ethereal beauty selling her jewellery on the pier were all the same person astonished him. He'd wanted to sit down with her and marvel over the coincidence. He'd wanted to hang around, find out a little of who she was. How – why – had he walked away?

All right, he'd been nervous, which if not exactly a first was certainly a rarity and then having wanted to impress and delight her he'd found a deeply prosaic way of doing it and scuttled off. Where was the old charm, the seductive persistence? What was the matter with him?

You talked to her for five minutes, Gil.

You are a madman.

He grabbed his wallet and his keys and set off down the steps and across the square, realising that he had no idea when she was likely to leave the pier or how to find her if she already had. He hurried through the streets, becoming snarled up behind the snail's pace progress of tourists, dodging round interminable trails of families and pensioners and teenagers, vaulting backstreets of bins and crates and cats as if he were freerunning. He could see even from some distance that the pier was emptier than it had been a few hours ago and as he drew closer he saw there were fewer stalls, many fewer customers. *Shit.* He slowed, panting a little, narrowing his eyes against the sun.

She was gone.

His first thought was that they had been burgled. Marianne was at work and yet the kitchen door stood ajar. He lowered Jem from his shoulders, where she had ridden all the way up from the gallery, keeping hold of her hand. "Marianne!" He pushed the door wider, stepped inside. "Marianne?"

Jem joined in, her little voice rising through the empty rooms. "Mamma? Mamma?" She looked up at him. "Gone?"

"Apparently so." He sat her in her high chair with a beaker of milk. "Two seconds."

But she was nowhere in the house, or the garden. She had left without locking the door, which was after all a far more reasonable explanation than burglary. He picked up the

74

phone, rang the Tourist Office. If he had learned anything these last years it was the importance of caution. "Hello, this is Alex Gregory. Could I have a quick word with Marianne?"

"I'm sorry." A voice he didn't recognise. The summer relief, no doubt. "I'm afraid Marianne hasn't been in today."

His heart contracted. "Well ... did she ring in sick?"

"Not as far as I know. She just didn't turn up."

"And you didn't think to call me?"

The summer relief sounded bemused. Which you would, Alex reminded himself. If you didn't know. "I think someone tried ringing your house but there was no reply."

Jem was banging her beaker on the tray of her high chair. "Mamma!" He gave her a biscuit. "Dadda," she said gratefully.

He rang Eve at the Express & Echo, but she knew no more than he did. There were so few people to whom he could turn, he felt it sorely every time: Marianne's parents were dead, his own on the other side of the country, she hadn't many friends and he had never been able to bear to unburden himself to his own. He looked helplessly at his daughter. "Where is she, Puddle? Where's your mum?"

"Gone," Jem said.

Too early yet to be ringing hospitals or the police. He couldn't even say how long she had been missing. An hour? Eight hours? Was she in fact missing, had she perhaps wandered to the shop, to the library? She had periods of reading feverishly, devouring book after book, barely stopping to eat or sleep and he wondered, if he asked her later, would she know what they had been about?

He dealt with yesterday's washing-up, fed Jem and bathed her, all the time anxiety clawing inside him. If she wasn't home by the time it grew dark he would make the calls. But it was midsummer, and darkness still a long way off. He let Jem play while he watched the television news, images sliding away from him, the words a distant buzz. She had been fine lately. Normal, for her. She would be fine.

He tucked Jem into bed, sat beside her reading about Miffy and Spot the Dog and deciding absently to raise her level of bedtime stories to something more intellectually challenging. She traced the pictures as he read, observing their ritual as she always did, with huge seriousness.

Downstairs the kitchen door banged. He froze. Jem said, "Mamma?"

"Let's hope so. Marianne!"

"Hello!" Her voice. Her footsteps on the stairs. The great hard coil of worry in his chest loosened a little.

She came spinning into Jem's room, her fine blonde hair trailing, cheeks pink, eyes bright. Too pink, too bright. He said carefully, "Have you had a nice day?"

"Oh, you wouldn't believe it! It's been such a beautiful day I couldn't resist. I went for such a long walk. The poppies, Alex. Great fields of poppies. You should come with me, we could take Jemima. Tomorrow. It's not supposed to rain tomorrow. I walked right over to the cliffs, the colour of the water there – "

"You didn't go to work."

"Oh."

"Or lock the house."

She frowned. "I was with Eve. We had a picnic in the poppy field but then she went swimming and I didn't see her again after that. Oh and I brought presents!" She dug in the pocket of her skirt, retrieved a handful of shells which she let fall onto Spot the Dog. Jem regarded them solemnly, picked one up and held it between her forefinger and her thumb.

"What is it, Jemmie?" Marianne asked.

"Shell."

Marianne laughed. Alex wanted to say, 'do you know how worried I've been?' and 'what were you thinking?' but there was no point. No reasoning with her when she had the coordination of the drunk and her words spiralled tangled and unstoppable. "Let's all go out tomorrow," she begged him. "All together, for a picnic or to the beach. It'll be exciting."

"Sure." He would never tell her that neither he nor Jem needed this kind of excitement or that of course they would all be together, because he really couldn't trust her alone anymore.

Chapter Nine

I wake before him, unpeel my warmth from his and slide out of bed. The drumming of water into the plastic shower tray barely two yards away is going to disturb him, so instead I make a half turn of the basin tap, hold my soaped flannel beneath the gush, and wash fast and shivering. After I've rubbed myself dry, I scoop yesterday's clothes from the floor and pull them on, stumble into my trainers, and unlock the door. The latch chinks faintly and I hold my breath, watching him. He lies supine, arms flung wide, his chest rising and falling but he does not stir. I open the door and escape.

There are muffled sounds from the café's kitchen but no one in sight. It's dark in the bar, only minimal daylight filtering in through the glass. I expect the door to the square to be locked but to my relief the handle yields beneath the pressure of my hand and I slip outside into the still autumn morning.

The village is cranking into life: shopkeepers around the perimeter of the square lift back their shutters; a woman loads sticks of bread into the basket of an old-fashioned bicycle; a dark grey Mercedes with a yellow smiley face sticker in the rear window glides away beneath the arch. I breathe in the damp air and exhale slowly, queasy with last night's alcohol and the memory of despair. It's hard enough coping with our own, separate, fears but I know my night terrors had appalled Gil and his tension and his tears frighten me. He's as brave and positive as it's possible for a human being to be, and this is what I've done to him.

I sit on the steps at the foot of the stone monument, watching this alien world waking around me and try and fail to find something to give us courage. Last night he held me until I slept, but we'd both lain silent and fearful for a long time first. I don't know whether it's better to delude ourselves that we will survive and everything will be fine or to continue grimly in the knowledge that it won't. For continuing grimly isn't living; I might as well have stayed and surrendered if that's the best we can do.

After a long despondent while I remember we'll be moving on soon and shake myself into action. Opposite me is a boulangerie, its light a small beacon in the barely lifting gloom. I buy rolls and *pains au chocolat*, handing over my euros like toy notes. I still don't know how much we have or how much we need; we're so deep in chaos managing money is beyond us. There are no other customers and the baker – if that's who he is – hardly seems to register me. I want to linger in the warmth of his shop, amid the smell of the bread, but soon someone might be asking him about an English girl passing through here today and I need him to remember as little as possible. I step back out into the square and there is Gil, walking across the cobbles towards me.

"Where the fuck did you go?" he hisses, his voice sharp with anxiety. "Christ, I woke up and you weren't there … "

"I'm sorry. I thought you needed to sleep." It hadn't occurred to me that he might be worried. And anyway where could I go, and how?

He lets out his breath. "I've settled up, at the café. Are you ready to move on?"

I nod, see that he has our rucksacks with him. We trail to the car, beginning the day as querulous and wired as we had ended the last. He chucks the rucksacks in the boot, slams the lid. We get in and I put the bag from the boulangerie into the well between our seats. He ignores it. After a long moment he says, "Where to?"

"Does it matter?"

"Of course it matters! Jesus! We come all this way and now you *want* to be found?"

"I don't know where to hide! We stick out a mile in places like this but who'd think of looking here? In the cities we'd be like any other English couple but it'd be easier to track us down. I don't know where we should go!"

"Neither do I."

Another long silence.

I press the heels of my palms against my eyes and feel her claws gouging my sockets. "Please let's not fight."

78

"No," he agrees. "It doesn't help."

"Is it … " I pause. "Let's be realistic. Is it *if* we're found, or is it *when*?"

He stares ahead. Neither of us can bear to look at the other. "It's when."

We both contemplate the bleakness of this, the futility of everything we have done the last twenty-four hours. I swallow. "Then the best we can hope for is time?"

He nods.

"So … let's enjoy it. Let's go to the south coast, stay somewhere beautiful."

He considers. "We can do that. But you know there's no running from what's in our heads."

"I know. But it has to be better than fighting and being scared all the time. It's like we're punishing each other." My voice trembles and instantly I'm ashamed of myself.

He turns to me and I can see the old Gil in his eyes. "Oh God. I'm sorry. I'm so freaked out I'm all over the place."

"Well me too."

He holds my gaze. "Last night, finding you like that … " He shakes his head, beyond words, touches my hair, my cheek, instead.

"So let's be kind. We can't change what happened, however much we want to." It's like rolling aside the stone which covers the mouth of hell even thinking about that. "All we can do is be kind to each other and live in the moment." How am I saying this? Where has it come from? Is it sense, or am I just intent on delusion? Delusion as coping strategy. It isn't as if I'm not experienced in it after all.

"Okay," he says softly. He squeezes my hand. It feels more intimate, more full of promise and more reassuringly normal than all the hours of the night we'd spent pressed naked against each other. He smiles faintly. "Okay. South coast. Will that be left or right?"

We try to work back from the direction we came yesterday. He helps himself to a *pain au chocolat* from the bag. I suggest buying a map might be a good idea. In Roskoff, which feels like an eternity ago now, we'd been in too much of a hurry.

We both remember a majorish road a few miles back and he starts the engine. As he reverses, looking over his shoulder, and turns the wheel, I catch sight of a smiley face sticker in the window of a dark grey Mercedes parked a few yards in front of us. It's odd, I think fleetingly, that it didn't go very far.

Chapter Ten

He groaned in frustration and disappointment, cursed himself, thought about crossing the pier to Patrick's and getting drunk out of his skull then remembered that she might be here again tomorrow and his crippled-with-hangover look wasn't going to charm anyone. He turned, intending to walk back up to the square via The Wharf and the beach, and suddenly there she was, leaning against the door of the boarded-up gallery, watching him.

"Hey." He laughed in surprise. "How did you do that? I was just thinking about you."

"You were?" She came a step or two towards him. Now she wasn't sitting behind her stall he could see how slender she was, her black jersey harem pants and purple vest allowing glimpses of her small curves. She wore a leather lace tied around her upper arm, metal cuffs on both wrists, earrings glinting through the long darkness of her hair.

"Yeah, I was looking for you."

"Thinking about me *and* looking for me?"

"Mm." He smiled. No playing it cool now. "Was it a good day?"

"A really good day." She was smiling too. "I might do it again. Oh, I took the glasses back to Patrick's, by the way. Didn't want your name to be mud with them."

"I spend way too much money in there for that. But thank you."

"You're welcome." Her eyes were soft and she was standing closer to him than she would if she thought him a complete loser and couldn't wait to escape – but hey, you could never tell.

He said, taking that risk, "So … do you have any plans for this evening?"

"No."

"Can I buy you a drink?"

"Another one?"

"Mm-hm."

"I'd like that."

"Well good." They were both grinning, he thought, as if he were offering more than a drink, which maybe he was, and there was more going on here, which maybe there was. He wanted to laugh out loud. She looked so beautiful when she smiled.

He decided against taking her to Patrick's. He didn't want the guys giving her the once-over or Cecily asking if he knew what her name was and whether he'd shagged her yet. He didn't want to expose her to any of that. Luckily Patrick's was not the only bar in town.

Despite its name, printed in understated italic font, *bluewave* was more urban and sophisticated than anywhere else he frequented, marble floor glittering beneath sapphire lights, baroque glass tables separating navy velvet sofas. "Wow," she murmured as they stepped inside. "This is a surprise."

"They do great cocktails."

"Can't wait." She studied the menu, chalked up on the board above the bar. Gil, already familiar with it, studied her face, flushed with the day's sun, the ends of her hair skimming her nipples, embroidered belt laced around her waist between handfuls of breasts and bum. He swallowed, his libido getting in on the act already. She smiled at him. "What do you recommend?"

He ordered Alabama Slammers. She watched the barman pour quantities of Southern Comfort and sloe gin, amaretto and orange juice into the shaker, fill their glasses with ice. "Why is it called a Slammer?"

Gil said, "You can have it as a shot, slam it on the bar with your hand over the top and drink it while it's still fizzing. Gets you drunk really fast."

"Ah. Well, the night is young."

He smiled, paid for their drinks. "If you've never been in here before, we have to sit upstairs."

A spiral staircase opposite the bar led to an upper floor whose tall windows opened onto wrought-iron balconies. A table at one of them had been recently vacated and Gil deftly cleared the smeared glasses and crumpled napkins onto another. She sat, glancing down into the pedestrian traffic of The Walk. "I must have passed here a thousand times and it never occurred to me it might be like another world inside."

He knew what she meant. "It's unexpected, isn't it."

"And also when you live here your perception of it is different; it's as if it exists in another dimension for you than it does for the tourists."

"You live here?"

"I do. You visit?"

"Every summer for the last nine years." He laughed. "Why haven't we come across each other before?"

"Well ... " She sipped her drink. "We have. Twice in as many weeks."

"I mean, before that." He realised he was talking to her already as if their meeting had significance, assuming she shared his sense of recognition.

She looked at him over the top of her glass. "Maybe we just weren't meant to."

"Fate?"

"You don't believe in fate?"

"I like to think we're in control of our own destinies."

"I don't know which is more comforting. To have control or not to have it."

He smiled. "This is deep."

"Sorry." She smiled too, embarrassed. "I don't do smalltalk very well. I always leap right in there and go for the profound stuff. It's unnerving. I'll shut up."

"No. Don't shut up. I like two o'clock in the morning conversations. And as you say, the night is young."

She rested her chin in her hand, looking at him. "It said in the newspaper you're an artisan."

"Ah." His turn to be embarrassed. It had said in the newspaper he was a lot of things. "You saw that. She has a romantic vocabulary, that woman."

"So you're not?"

"No, I ... " He explained: his love of and apparent talent for turning a lump of wood into an object of use and beauty; his parents' frustration at his lack of interest in academia when he'd been predicted top grades; his years at Goldsmiths and the apprenticeship to a cabinetmaker which he'd wrecked through his own waywardness. He described to her his redemption through work and the business he was building for himself. He spoke with humour and honesty and she listened, rapt, to every word, as though what he was saying was of interest and value. As though she understood.

"It's the same for me," she said. "I couldn't work for anyone else. I don't have much but what I do have is mine, on my terms. It's a kind of freedom."

"It's more than that - in the words of the late, great Freddie Mercury - it's a kind of magic."

"I *love* Freddie Mercury."

"Oh me too, all the old stuff – Queen, the Eagles, Fleetwood Mac."

They both smiled. She looked at their empty Slammer glasses. "These are really good, aren't they?"

He ordered another round. And later, another. They talked seventies rock as the pinnacle of musical achievement, discovered that five years ago they had both been at Glastonbury, their tents pitched possibly minutes from each other. "The guy I was with," she told him, "was a friend from uni. Only that weekend it turned out he didn't want to be just a friend." She wrinkled her nose. "It all got a bit … messy. I thought for ages afterwards it had been my fault, that maybe I'm just not very good at reading people."

Gil decided not to admit that he could understand a man wanting more from her than friendship. "Yeah, but blokes can be a pain like that. At the risk of tarring us all with the same brush, we're not very good at intimacy without sex. You blur the line between friends and lovers and we think we're getting mixed signals."

"And are you? Tarred with that brush?"

He thought of the two serious relationships he'd had in his life and how they'd ended, the one night stands and casual flings, the line between sex and friendship he'd blurred himself. "I think I'm pretty good at reading signals. I have three sisters so no excuse for not being a bit clued-up. But sometimes, yeah, I get it wrong."

"Three sisters?"

"Two older, one younger."

"Are you close?"

"I guess. We were, growing up. We all still like each other." He smiled. "How about you?"

She shook her head. "I'm an only child."

"Close to your parents, then?"

"Very."

A subtle and fleeting shift in her expression, a barely perceptible lift in her voice. But something there, he thought. Something more than she wants to say to a guy she doesn't know, the first time she talks to him. She intrigued him, the rock chick thing she had going on, the connection there seemed to be between them, this hint of something unspoken. And beneath it all, beating through his veins, the steady pulse of desire.

She was looking at him, her head tilted slightly. "Can I ask you something?"

He gestured – anything.

"When you rescued that boy from drowning, what went through your mind?"

He paused. The first time he had discussed this he had been exasperated and defensive. The second time he had felt it sensationalised for someone else's ends. Maybe, this time, it would come out right. He said, "Nothing. Nothing went through my mind. I saw him in the water, I jumped in, dragged him out."

"So it was instinctive?"

He shrugged. "I guess I just I didn't see the danger."

"You weren't thinking of yourself."

"It wasn't like that, exactly. If I thought anything at all, it was that I was doing what needed to be done. But then it gets served up as heroics in the local paper and a friend of mine's furious with me for putting myself at risk."

She gazed at him. "I don't think it's about heroics. I think it's about humanity."

"Humanity?" He smiled. "Yeah, okay, I can live with that."

"But you kind of wish you'd been able to do it without anyone noticing."

"Kind of. But then there you were. And here we are."

"Indeed."

Their eyes held and suddenly he knew for sure that this was going to go beyond a couple of drinks tonight. Beyond great if opportunistic sex and end of summer promises to stay in touch. He knew for sure that this – and what had he said earlier about fate? – could be something special.

They ate – steak sandwich for him, salmon wrap for her – where they were because she said she didn't want to stop drinking cocktails. Afterwards, when she admitted she really couldn't drink any more cocktails, they walked along the beach. The same beach on which, twenty-four hours earlier, he had been arguing with Cecily. It felt a light year ago, and ridiculously unimportant.

Jemima had found a sharp pebble and, like a child, was writing her name in the sand. Half her name. "Jem," he read. "Great name for someone who makes jewellery."

"Yes, I had no choice," she said dryly. "My future was set in stone."

He laughed, groaned.

"Only my mother ever called me Jemima."

"Jem, then."

She straightened, stepped close and, very lightly, kissed his mouth. "Gil." She spun laughing away from him before he could hold her there, walked backwards through the dark across the sand, the tide licking her bare feet. She was quite drunk, he reminded himself, and so was he. Intoxicated in all senses. He caught up with her, took her hand and pulled her towards him, her eyes huge with anticipation, he could feel the tremor of it through the whisper of space between them. He lifted her chin and kissed her, softly. Drew back to meet her eyes. Kissed her again, with intent. She pressed against him and kissed him too, melting into it.

He withdrew a little, his interest having become impossible to disguise.

"Sorry," he laughed.

"No, I want to," she said. "I will." She kissed him again. "But not tonight."

"Oh God, sure – "

"I want to have something to look forward to."

He smiled. She was amazing. "Those words," he said, "will be in my head all night."

"Good." She smiled. "Mine too."

He wanted to walk her home – or rather, he didn't want to leave her at all, but taking her home seemed the best compromise - but she said no, I'll be fine, let's say goodnight in this perfect place. And he said, all right. All right and I will come and find you tomorrow.

He drifted up to the square, his head and his heart and his loins full with her. Then mildly worried that he had agreed to leave her tipsy on the beach, that being a gentleman had come second to doing as she wished. They hadn't exchanged mobile numbers. Bugger, he thought, stopping in the middle of the square.

"Hey Gil."

He recognised the voice before he saw its owner ambling towards him from the pub.

"Hey Henry."

Henry slowed as he approached, his tone more carefully judged than it would, before the last twenty-four hours, have been. "Lovely night." He indicated the clear and starlit sky.

"It has been," Gil admitted.

"Been down at Patrick's?"

He smiled. "You haven't."

"Nah. Fancied a change of scene."

"Right." He refrained from making the observation that the pub was also a hundred feet from Cecily's door. Instead he went for - "Sign of age, you know. When you're tired of Patrick's, you're tired of life."

Henry frowned. "Is that a quote?"

"A misquote." Gil sighed inwardly. He counted Henry as a friend but in the exertion of switching allegiances the guy had lost his sense of humour along with his cool. He took a step away, said amiably, "See you tomorrow."

But Henry had something on his mind. "This party, on Saturday."

Gil had forgotten. "Party?"

"Friend of Radar. He told us about it at lunchtime."

"Ohh. Windsurfing Phil."

"Yeah. You going?"

"Maybe." Probably not. Hopefully not. He already knew where he wanted to be on Saturday night and it wasn't in the company of drunk and sweaty surf dudes. "You?"

"Thought I'd give it a go." He paused. "Thought I'd ask Cecily."

He smiled. "Why not?" And then his memory kicked in properly and he recalled what else Radar had said about that party. *Shit*, he thought. And, *stay out of it Gil. It isn't your business.*

But of course it was his business. He could spare Cecily the question and Henry the answer or himself Henry's pique. And when had he ever been able to stay out of anything? He said, "It's at the cove?"

"Yep. Phil and Nina's house is at the cove."

Gil took a breath.

"What?" Henry said.

"She won't go."

His face stiffened. "She won't go because it's me asking her, not you?"

You are so fucking predictable, Gil thought. "Doesn't matter who's asking. Ask her, if you want. I'm just warning you. She won't go." He raised his hands, took another step away. "But if you care, take her to Patrick's Saturday night. Take her out to dinner."

Henry said, "What gives you the right to tell me where I can and can't take her?"

Gil paused. "Jesus, do what you want." He turned and walked towards the iron stair-case leading to his room.

Henry's voice followed him loud through the darkness. "What is it you know?"

"Nothing." Gil climbed the steps. "I know nothing."

Jem swung through the kitchen, along the hall and into the living room to find Alex sitting reading in his wing chair like the narrator in a Victorian drama. She dropped down onto an empty patch of the chaise longue, the papers beside her tipping to the floor and revealing the worn green velvet beneath. "Hello."

"Hello." He was regarding her with amusement. "Nice evening?"

"A*maz*ing evening."

"Coffee?"

"Coffee would be good."

While he was making it she scooped up the fallen papers and stuffed them into a drawer of the bureau, catching a glimpse of herself in the mirror above the fireplace – bright eyes, flushed cheeks, hair dishevelled from her elated spin home. She thought, this is what Dad has just seen, but then she was, had always been, incapable of hiding anything. Her emotions showed in her face with the same immediacy and clarity as they tumbled from her lips.

"There you go." Alex placed the mug in her hands, returned to his chair. "So what've you been getting up to then?"

"Having cocktails and dinner with Gil Hunt."

"Have you now?" He was smiling. "How did that come about?"

She described the day to him: Gil's first appearance on the pier like a benevolent local celebrity; his return hours later to focus his attention entirely upon her; the evening they had shared at *bluewater* and how talking to and being herself with him had felt not only possible but natural and right; their walk afterwards on the beach, the taste of his mouth, his breath against her skin. These last details she did not share but held in her thoughts to guard and polish like secret jewels. "We have," she finished, "so much in common it's unnerving."

Alex had listened, intent, reacted precisely as she would have wished and foretold. But now he said, "Be careful."

She frowned.

"It's lovely to see you so excited about someone and I'm

sure he's a good man. But dads have to say these things. And I'm saying, be careful. You're vulnerable, remember."

She said nothing.

"Did you tell him?" he persisted.

"No." She felt tears in her throat. "I just want to be normal, for a bit."

"Of course you do."

She waited a moment, until she felt capable of speaking without crumpling. "He's really nice. I really like him."

"I know."

"You'd like him too. You should meet him, actually."

Alex smiled. "Don't frighten the poor man off."

She smiled too, albeit waterily. "I'm scared of frightening him off. I'm scared of seeming needy. I'm delving deep to find the person I was last summer, before … " She let out her breath. "Because that was still me, wasn't it?"

"That is still you."

She thought about it.

"Now," he said, watching her, "when are you wanting to go through that cupboard with me?"

She remembered her plans for her mother's jewellery as if she'd had the idea months rather than days ago. "Soon."

"Before I go?"

"Maybe."

"Ah, listen to you, with your new priorities."

"Shut up." She smiled, uncurled herself from the chaise longue and leaned over to kiss his forehead. "I'm going to bed."

"Good night, Puddle."

She lay awake, reconstructing her evening, Gil's tales of his past, his musical taste, his humour, his perception and intelligence and honesty. The shape of his mouth, the dark arch of his brows, his hands in her hair when he had kissed her. I will come and find you, he had said. She had wanted to reply, you have already found me.

Chapter Eleven

Today has decided it's an Indian summer. We sit on the terrace of the beachside café and the sun is as warm, the sea as blue as it is in Cornwall. If it weren't for the taste of the coffee and the murmur of other tongues, I could be home. "I think I need," I tell Gil, "to be close to the sea."

He nods, with sympathy. We've calmed down a bit this afternoon, the two hundred mile drive quiet and beautiful enough to soothe my fears and his temper. We've even managed to talk a little, the inconsequential commentary which, a lifetime ago, we wouldn't have given a second thought. Now we stretch out and drink our coffee and stare at the sea and my thoughts turn, in survival mode, to possibilities. "This morning," I remind him, "when you said it's when we get caught, not if … " He looks at me, knowing what's coming. " … what if it isn't?"

He sighs. "You want to plan for a future we don't have?"

"What if we do have it?"

"There are extradition laws in France, you know."

"Is there anywhere we can go that there aren't?"

"Oddly enough, it isn't something I've ever had to give any thought." But he says it wryly and without censure. "Go on, then."

"Well … what would we do?"

"I suppose … find some sort of itinerant work that pays cash and doesn't ask any questions. Rent or squat somewhere. Go quietly mad." He almost smiles.

"But if we were left alone, we'd relax into it, wouldn't we? After a while, it'd just become our way of life."

"Wouldn't it just become a different kind of life sentence?"

I gesture towards the view, the tranquil sea and the rocks, the line of restaurants, the hillside mansions. "Does this look like a life sentence to you?"

Gil pauses. "Inside my head there's a horror movie running on an endless loop. There's such rage and terror and grief I want to smash my skull against the wall to make it stop. That's the life sentence."

My eyes fill with tears.

"Oh don't." He takes my hand into his.

But I cannot stop. The tears spill down my cheeks, drip from my jaw onto my t-shirt and the table-top. I try to wipe them away but they're falling too fast. "I love you."

"I know."

"And you loved me."

"I did. I do."

"But – "

He says softly, "We can't have this conversation."

I'm still crying. "I never meant – "

"Shh." He kisses me to shut me up. "Stop now."

After another minute or so I do. He's right; there are things we cannot say because there's the mouth of hell again, waiting for us. He fetches me another drink, strokes my hair. "Okay?"

I nod. "So ... " I swallow. "What sort of itinerant jobs?"

We stay at the café until dusk. Already the days are assuming a pattern: driving for hours through changing countryside; getting hopelessly and irritably lost; trying to find petrol; arriving desperate for food and drink and somewhere to spend the night. All this punctuated by our own alternating kindness and hostility. I think I need to stop for a while, but then maybe he's right again and if we do hole up somewhere we will just go mad more slowly. While he's paying the bill I hop over the low boxes of flowers which divide the café from the promenade and stand at the railings, gazing at the deepening blue of the Mediterranean. Like Dorothy, I want to go home.

"Ready?" He comes up behind me and touches my waist. "No trouble finding somewhere to sleep tonight."

We walk back towards the car park and the long string of hotels. One of the other advantages of being on the coast is that communication is easier; Gil finds us a room in the first hotel he tries. It's on the second floor, sparsely furnished but the bathroom is clean and the bed doesn't creak. There's even a television which he switches on, searching for satellite channels. I step out onto the balcony with its view of the street, of the little shops which are closing up and of the bars lit in anticipation of the night's trade. On the opposite side of the road, parked outside the entrance to a shuttered *droguerie* is a dark grey Mercedes. I would not have registered it at all but for the smiley face sticker in its rear window.

It can't be the same car. Can it? I peer down at the number plate, see that it is British and my insides twist painfully. But it's a coincidence. It has to be. Or I'm imagining it, and the car I saw with the sticker this morning was dark green or navy or black. Surely. I hadn't even noticed its number plate.

I think perhaps I won't tell Gil.

Chapter Twelve

He was close behind her up the iron staircase, grabbed her at the top and pulled her to him, kissed her long and messily. Jem, stretching up to press her body hard against his and kissing back, remembered him dragging someone through the water, how strong he had seemed, how capable. Well now, she thought, he is rescuing me. She slid her fingers between his low-slung jeans and the heat of his groin. He groaned, fumbled at the door and they fell inside.

She was aware of a long, narrow room, of an uncurtained grandstand view of the sea and then Gil was kissing her again, his hands at her bum holding her hips against his, kissing her throat and her neck, lifting her silky camisole over her head, her hair tumbling back down. She unbuckled and unzipped him, both of them pulling out of their clothes until these were pools of cotton on the bare floor, and with deft urgency he rolled her with him onto the bed.

"So I've bought," Gil had explained an hour earlier, laughing at his own madness, "this great hunk of wood." He described its size with his hands. "And I haven't a clue what I'm going to do with it. Inspiration eludes me and it's crouching there, in my room, looking at me like 'you loser'."

Jem smiled. They were sitting at her favourite table in the garden of the inn above the bay, beside the palms and the lavender blue hibiscus, behind her the still evening blue ocean, in front of her Gil. Happiness and anticipation had been rolling and crashing within her since he had turned up at her stall this afternoon and not since left her side. She said, "What do you usually do?"

"Oh, animals, figures, abstract stuff. But it's never enough, you know? I'm never completely satisfied with it when it's finished."

"But isn't that always the way? When you create something, the reality of it never quite measures up to the idea, it's always just as close as you can get. As if the inspiration for it is somehow god-given but we're too mortal to be able to reproduce it."

He was wry. "I think I'm just too fucking lazy to be able to reproduce it."

She looked at him, knowing self-deprecation when she heard it. "How can you be lazy? You have your own business."

"I … " He let out his breath, said honestly, "I'm still easily distracted."

"Is that what your school reports used to say?"

"Pretty much. 'Gilman will never amount to anything until he gets his arse into gear and actually finishes something.' "

"And did you? Get your arse into gear?"

"Hey. A man has to eat." He smiled. "There's this Italian sculptor, Livio De Marchi, and his stuff just blows me away. He did a wooden Ferrari, life-size, and floated it on a canal in Venice. There're pictures on the web. He sculpts clothes and the folds of fabric look so real it's only when you notice the grain of the wood that you realise they're not. Amazing talent. I would love to be able to do that."

Jem, still thinking about his arse getting into gear, wondered whether it was possible and what it would cost to take him to see this Livio De Marchi's sculptures. She sipped her wine. "So could you do that, with your log?"

He laughed. "I wish."

"What, then?"

He considered, held her gaze for a long moment. The mood shifted, perceptibly. He lifted her hand into his, turned it over to trace a slow circle on her palm. She shivered. Every nerve in her body felt connected to that circle. He shook his head, smiled. "I'm trying but I've got to tell you, I've been having trouble thinking about anything but you."

She swallowed. It had taken a beat, this step over the precipice. "Me too."

They lay, heart rates subsiding, panting and sticky. She said, "I want to do that again."

Gil laughed. "Give me a minute."

"A minute?"

He laughed again, cuddled her to him. She could see now, across his chest and through the semi-darkness, beyond a book and a lamp on the stool beside the bed, a monstrous shape squatting on the table in front of the window. "Oh my God. Is that the log you were talking about?"

He turned his head, as though it might be possible she were referring to something else. "That's it."

Jem raised herself to give it proper attention. "And how long would it take you to make something from it?"

His finger travelled lightly over her breast, across her stomach. "Well that depends." He kissed her navel.

She slid back down to him. "You could do something amazing."

"I just did."

"Something … " She frowned while he continued to caress her, to whisper a line of kisses from her ear to her shoulder. "Something almost spiritual."

"Mm." He paused. "You didn't … "

"It's okay."

"Let me." He shifted her onto her back, knelt above her.

"Something," she suggested, suspecting conversation was soon going to be beyond her again, "like the Tree of Life."

Cecily bid the last of her customers goodnight and turned the sign on her door to *Closed*. She thought it rude to shut up the café around people and always settled for subtle background clatter instead. It meant more to do when they were gone, but she would rather that than give them the you-are-outstaying-your-welcome vibe most other places were happy to promote. Tonight, though, the floor looked as though it needed no more than a swift mop and brush, the tables clearing and wiping and the dishwasher would take care of the rest. An hour at most, she reckoned. Then bath with a glass of wine and bed with a book.

The tubular doorbells jangled before she had finished stacking the dishwasher. Her heart lifted a little and she called out – "Hello?"

"Hi!" It was Henry.

"Oh. Hi."

He appeared beneath the arch. "Bad day?"

"No, no." Guiltily she injected some enthusiasm into her voice. "Sorry, just a bit tired."

"Ah. I wondered if you wanted to come out for a drink."

"Well … " She made the 'not really' face.

"Have you eaten?"

She paused, knowing that admitting to being hungry would be allowing him to provide a solution. But what the hell. She'd always been good at settling for less and oh God, that was a truly awful way to think of Henry. She said, "No."

He beamed. "Chinese or Indian?"

"Surprise me."

While he was away she finished loading the dishwasher, set it running, then nipped upstairs to shower and change into pyjama trousers and a t-shirt. She unpinned her hair from its day-time knot and shook it out, noticing that it seemed to have grown since she had tied it up there this morning, making her look less free spirit than ageing hippie. She sighed, regarding herself with dissatisfaction. You need, she thought, to be a bit more realistic.

Down in the café Henry was dishing tikka marsala onto her best square white plates and had set a table with candles and a posy of flowers which wasn't hers. "Thank you," she said, touched and guilty all over again.

He said solemnly, "You are very welcome."

"Music?" She slid a James Brown CD into the player, scooped a bottle of wine from her rack. They sat at a corner table with the blinds lowered, one leg tucked beneath her on the wooden settle, her fork in her right hand. "So tell me about your day at the beach."

He swallowed, took a mouthful of wine, described to her the morning's surf, the further combined idiocies of Radar'n'Buz, the parents who'd had wanted him to instruct their small sons in the art of surfing before they returned to Hampstead on Saturday. His observations were revealing, his humour dry. He was so much better, she thought, without his friends'

CATHERINE MARSHALL

competing sexual magnetism or entertaining lunacy. Better
when he was alone and his good sense and his kindness could
shine. She said, "Have you run the Australia plan by your
parents?"

"It wouldn't surprise them."

"They'd miss you though."

"Same as your parents miss you."

"Except they were the ones who went away." She tore off a
piece of naan bread, aware of him watching her.

He frowned. "Are you completely alone?"

"I have a brother in Orpington. Much use he is to me there.
He's older than me, an accountant, married, grown-up kids.
We're like strangers."

"I didn't know you had a brother. It's funny isn't it," Henry
said. "All the years we've known each other, we've known
nothing."

She shook her head. "We haven't appraised each other of all
the biographical facts. It's not the same as not knowing each
other."

"Isn't it?"

"Oh Henry. I spend more time with you than I do with my
own family. What do you think?"

He smiled, topped up their glasses. "What's your life like,
September through till March?"

She looked at him. How much honesty did he want? She
decided to put him to the test. "Quiet. Empty. The tourists
disappear from these tables, you guys all melt back to your
real lives. The weather changes. Everything becomes colder,
in all senses. Cold and grey and a lot less fun." He looked
surprised and more concerned than he needed to be so she
added, "Which isn't to say I spend the winter steeped in lonely
melancholy."

"But it's a hibernation of a kind?"

"Yes." She laughed. "Yes, it is. Hibernation of the spirit."
But this year not even that. This year she had been knocked so
far off kilter she was still staggering with the shock of it. Don't
go there, she told herself. Don't so much as twitch the curtain.

Henry said, "Then we should make the most of the

summer."

"I do. Every single year."

He hesitated. "With that in mind, there's a party on Saturday night."

"There is?"

"Phil, windsurfer bloke and his girlfriend."

"Whose name is? And she does what?"

"I don't know. I do know it's building up to be a great night."

She said wistfully, "I could do with a great night."

"Then you'll come?"

"Why not?"

Henry grinned.

The night slipped in around them, the café lit only by the candle flame and the distant glow from the kitchen. Cecily, tired of listening to the same tracks on endless repeat, went to change the CD. Thought of something and walked back to the archway. "Coffee upstairs?" she suggested.

Henry sat in the middle of the sofa on which he sometimes slept. She put his coffee mug on the table and handed him an envelope. "Look what I found."

He opened the flap, pulled out a handful of photographs of them all, photos of beach parties, of nights at Patrick's, posed shots of them laughing and clowning in the square, unexpected unframed shots of elbows and blurred features. "When were these taken?"

She had knelt beside him on the floor and was looking through them with him. "I'd guess about seven, eight years ago."

"God," he said. "I was thin."

"I was young."

"We were all young. And it isn't so long ago."

"Scary, huh?"

He went through them again, more slowly this time. "We have history, the five of us."

"We do."

"And you know, you haven't changed. You've always been gorgeous."

She understood that he was trying to say it in a throwaway fashion, as a less self-conscious man might have done. But there was nothing throwaway about Henry, and his attempt made the comment more touching still. "Oh Henry. Thank you." She rubbed his thigh briefly, a casual, friendly gesture, as no doubt she had rubbed it a hundred times before. But this time he turned his face towards her upturned one, and kissed her.

Just as she was thinking, I don't know if I want this to happen, she realised that his kiss was in fact unexpectedly agreeable, and that it was happening because she was returning it, reaching up to him, unwinding herself from the floor to slide into his lap. He murmured, "Are you sure?" and she unbuttoned his shirt. A little while later she climbed from his knees and led him towards her bed under the eaves.

It was comfortable, having sex with Henry. He was strong and warm and she felt protected, which wasn't something that had ever occurred to her before when pinioned beneath a man with her legs splayed and his body heaving against her. He was more considerate than skilled but actually a pleasant surprise. She could do this again, she told herself in the affectionate if not orgasmic afterglow. He would take care of her. She kissed his shoulder. "You're a lovely man."

He smiled. "You are gorgeous. I meant it."

"I know." She sat up. "Back in a minute."

He rolled onto his side to watch her bum as she walked to the bathroom. The bedside drawer from which she had earlier plucked the condom was still wide open and he leaned over to push it closed, was at the wrong angle and had to half rise from the mattress, gaining a view of the drawer's contents. He glimpsed a couple of books, her passport, a vibrator, a jar of face or hand cream, a receipt and a small ring of transparent plastic. He frowned, dimly under-standing what this last object was and picked it up. It was soft and would have fitted over one of his fingers. Inside it a narrow slip of paper read 'Male infant of Cecily Ward'.

"So tell me," Cecily's voice preceded her out of the bathroom, "about this party."

He dropped the identity bracelet back into the drawer and pushed it shut.

"Um … it's … "

She walked back to the bed, wondering was it the sight of her upright and naked body provoking his confusion. "Where do they live?"

He replied, after a moment, "Overlooking the cove."

"Oh." She tried to formulate a reasonable response but he beat her to it.

"We don't have to go. We could go out for dinner instead"

"Now that," she climbed back beneath the quilt, "sounds like a plan."

"We don't even have to stay around here. The new Thai place in Penzance is supposed to be good." He was watching her closely and she smiled. He said after a moment, "Did you know that tonight was going happen?"

"Oh yes. I've known it for weeks. Haven't you?"

He said slowly, "I wouldn't have dared to hope for it. You were always … " He paused, and she knew he was trying not to say the name they'd both been successfully avoiding all evening " … an enigma."

She laughed, surprised; it was not how she'd thought he was going to end that sentence, not a word she'd thought was in his vocabulary. "Sounds almost glamorous."

"But you are glamorous."

"Hardly. I'm the harassed and knackered lush you've known the last ten years. Tonight doesn't change that."

He wound a tendril of her hair around his finger. "It changes everything."

A warm summer evening, the sea beneath the rose and orange glow of the setting sun as still as Alex had ever seen it. On the far horizon the outline of a ship was just visible against the deepening sky. Marianne, who had been walking a little way ahead collecting shells and pebbles, her long white skirt trailing in the sand, stopped and followed his gaze. "Where will that be going?"

"I don't know. The Scilly Isles, perhaps? France?" Despite living on the coast for the last five years his interest in ships was limited to whether they formed a detail in or the focus of a scene he was painting; he had no knowledge of their destination or provenance in real life.

She said, "We should take a trip, when the season's over. This year, before Jemima starts school and we can only go anywhere exactly when we need to be at home."

"We should," he agreed. She reached for his hand, curling her finger around his thumb. It was their wedding anniversary; Eve was babysitting and they had wandered through the sunlit evening to eat a leisurely meal at a new restaurant in town, were ambling home now along the beach. Just as if, he thought, they were any other couple. For months

102

Marianne had been rational, almost serene. He tried to appreciate it but he honestly didn't know that these sustained periods of peace weren't more painful than the storms, taunting him as they did with the reappearance of the girl he'd had fallen in love with, the marriage they should have had. He clasped her hand more firmly in his own.

"We should do more of this too," she said presently.

"Walking on the beach?" He smiled. "Literally or figuratively?"

"Both. You come with Jem though, don't you." She was quiet for a moment. "She's yours, isn't she, Jem? Completely. She looks like you, she already thinks like you. I want someone who's mine."

"I'm yours."

"I mean, a baby. I would love to have another baby."

"Oh Marianne." Here it was, the conversation he had been expecting and dreading. If he'd had any kind, reasonable arguments rehearsed they deserted him now. "We can't. "

"We could."

"No."

She swallowed. "Who are you thinking of, when you make that decision for us?"

"I'm thinking of you. And of Jem."

"Not of yourself, then?"

He took a breath. "Yes all right. I'm thinking of me too. Life's enough of a struggle already, isn't it? Most of the time?"

"Jem'd love a brother or sister."

"Not if it cost her you."

"I've been so well."

"I know. That's why I don't want to take that risk." He looked at her, saw her tears. "Come here." He slipped his arm around her shoulders, drew her close.

"I hate this," she said. "It's so unfair. Because of who I am I can't have a normal marriage, or another child."

"It isn't because of who you are. Or if it is, it's only one small part of who you are."

"Is it?" She wiped her eyes. "It seems it's more and more of

who I am, and there's less and less of me."

He could say nothing. It was such a painfully accurate summary of what was happening he couldn't immediately think how to contradict her. He kissed her. "You're still you. I still love you."

"You must." She looked at him. "You must, to still be here."

"Shh." He held her. "Anyway, tell me who you think has a 'normal' marriage? We've made our own normality, the same as everyone."

"No Alex. Not the same as everyone." But she squeezed his hand, and after a while they spoke of other things, of the season ahead, a September holiday. Planning the future was always so much more comforting than dissecting the present.

Back at home, edging their way round the charity shops boxes blocking the hall, they found Eve watching a television chat show, Jemima fast asleep in her bed. He drove Eve the short distance to her parents' house, listened to her talk about a man she'd just met and how he fitted, absolutely, into the spaces around her social life and her work. She was twenty-one, bright and already brittle with certainty. Alex felt the ten years between them to be a generation. He remembered being twenty-one, filled with belief in himself and in the opportunities the world was just waiting to offer him. He held onto the knowledge that it had offered him the triumph of growing success in a career which so often yielded nothing, a daughter for whom he would lay down his life. He had become very good at, indeed to rely upon, counting blessings.

When he returned Marianne was sitting in bed, writing her diary. He smiled. "Has it been a day worth recording?"

"It has."

He sat down on the edge of the bed. "I'm sorry. About ... "

She shook her head. "You're right. I don't want you to be, and everything in me is railing against it, but you are."

"Sometimes," he said, "there's no pleasure in being right."

She put her diary aside, leaned forward to kiss him. "I don't know where I would be without you."

Chapter Thirteen

So I have two lives now.

Three lives.

I have the Life Before, and the Life After, and I've just begun to get my head around that. I know my Life Before has gone, and I will never have any of it back, and the grief and the guilt are overwhelming. Will always be overwhelming. Life After is like floundering through shark infested waters punctuated by moments of being washed up on small islands of safety, where it is warm and the sun shines, but the water and the sharks are waiting.

The third life?

The third life happens when I sleep.

We have good days now, me and Gil. We don't argue too often. He's calm and attentive. Most of the time. We live in hotels, we move slowly, inexorably, on. We don't talk, very much, about anything because there is nothing to say. Nothing from Before. We've put it all in a box and closed the lid and locked the box away. It's with us, all the time, but we can't think about it. It's a survival strategy and that's what we're doing; learning to survive.

At night for me it's a different story.

I am afraid to sleep.

The beach at night is lit by the moon, by streetlamps along the prom, by the yellow windows of the hotels and the distant crackling glow of fire. The laughter and voices from the party carry in the air as the surf washes around my feet. I inhale, deep. It's always felt cleansing, the beach at night, its peace restorative. It's why I come down here. What I was doing here the night I first saw Gil. I watch as the tide pulls the sand from beneath my toes, dragging lines beneath the frothing waters.

And then it hits me. She hits me. Her claw twists my hair as her body slams me to the ground, sand and saltwater and seaweed in my mouth and my eyes. Blows to my back and my stomach have me screaming, curling up in pain. She spits in my face, in my ear, and I scream again in rage. I kick out but she's everywhere, stronger than I am, an unnatural force, wrenching my arms from my sockets as she hauls me deeper into the water, kicking me until I collapse face down, her weight on my shoulders and the back of my neck until the sea is in my throat and my nose and I can't move, can't breathe.

I wake on a shuddering cry. The hotel room asserts itself around me while I gulp and choke as if I have indeed been drowning. The dreams are so vivid the transitional phase between them and reality is too blurred for comfort.

"Ssh. It's okay." Gil, beside me.

"It's every night," I whimper.

"I know."

"It's real. It feels real."

"But it's not."

Slowly, I calm. He fetches me a glass of water. "We need to get you some sleeping pills."

"Will they help?" I can't imagine any drug powerful enough to quell my nightmares. I can't believe it could be that easy.

"I don't know. It's worth a try, isn't it?" He touches my cheek. "Jesus. You're burning up."

We stand on the balcony, where the night air drifts cool around me. The town is subdued below us, only an occasional car passes, a soft quick patter of footsteps. I can smell the sea. "What's French for 'sleeping pills'?"

He smiles. "I don't know."

"What about sedatives? Tranquilisers? What if I have to live doped to the eyeballs?"

"Ssh." He strokes my hair. "We'll find a way. I don't want you ill with not sleeping."

I say nothing. I can't begin to answer his concern because I don't deserve it. I don't deserve a minute of his sympathy or compassion. It's more than I can bear.

"I thought of somewhere we could go." My voice sounds shaky even to my own ears.

"Oh yes?"

"That sculptor you really like. The Italian guy?"

"Livio De Marchi."

"Where is he based?"

"Venice, I think." He frowns. "We could go to Venice?"

"We can go anywhere."

He smiles faintly. "We can."

So I have three lives now.

Four lives.

I have the Life Before, and the Life After. I know my Life Before has gone, and I will never have any of it back, and the grief and the guilt are overwhelming. Life After divides itself in two - the Waking Life, through which I steer us with desperation and common sense and the occasional moment of relief, and the Sleeping Life, which is full of violence and terror and from which no one can save me.

The fourth life?

The fourth life lies ahead.

Chapter Fourteen

Cecily heard the raised voices from the kitchen, the aggrieved male rumble and the familiar piercing response. She strode through the café packed with holiday makers and out into the sunshine to find Justine, tiny and explosive as a Roman candle, arguing with a large muscle-bound biker demanding the cheese baguette he had ordered and not the garlic mushrooms Justine had delivered to him. "I'm terribly sorry," Cecily said to the biker. "As you can see, we're extremely busy but nevertheless that's no excuse – "

"But he ordered the fucking mushrooms!"

"Justine." Cecily kept a vice-like grip on her composure. "Please go inside."

"Oh for God's sake!"

"I'm sorry," she repeated as Justine flounced back into the café. "I will fetch your order. Which is now on the house."

"Thanks pet," said the biker with a thick Geordie accent and surprising goodwill. "I'm allergic to mushrooms, like."

She returned to her kitchen, where Justine was wielding a breadknife and a fresh baguette. "Thanks for that," Cecily said.

"Sorry," Justine muttered. "Being a bit crap today."

"Yes. You are."

"Are you gonna sack me?"

"I should." She was tempted. Justine had arrived an hour and a half late this morning and knocked three plated meals onto the floor before her confrontation with man mountain.

"He was dead rude before you turned up. You think the customer's always right."

"I don't, actually. I think the customer always pays me. Take him his lunch, smile, apologise, and get on with your job. All right?"

"Yeah. Sorry."

Cecily judiciously removed herself from Justine's company to tend the till. The day had begun with more covers than she could comfortably handle and had not quietened for a minute since. Customers filled the dining room and spilled out into her al fresco brink of the square, wanted breakfast, brunch, mid-morning tea, coffee, cakes, lunch, ice-cream, afternoon tea, cream teas, everything hotter, colder, vegetarian, gluten-free. They brought children who would not sit down, elderly relatives with wheelchairs and zimmer frames, dogs on long and winding leashes. They left their tables littered and their tips negligible. Cecily cooked and wiped and pacified and longed – *longed* – for Gil to saunter in, to release her tension with a grin and a kiss, to clear and serve with his customary speed and charm the customers and Justine into submission. To do, in fact, what he had been doing every summer for the last nine years.

But Gil had been conspicuous by his absence for more than a fortnight now. She missed him more than she would admit out loud to anyone and blamed herself, in part. She blamed him too. She was afraid the silence between them might freeze into permanence but at the same time that was ridiculous. Unthinkable. This was *Gil*, for God's sake. Gil, who …

Her eyes filled with unexpected tears.

She clenched her jaw and concentrated on the bill in front of her, clocking Justine sidling past with a cheese baguette and extra chips as a penance. Cecily considered the likelihood of finding someone to take Justine's place at a day's notice. Considered the wisdom of doubling her staff instead.

Later, having subsided into a frazzled heap in a corner of Patrick's, she drank enough Southern Comfort to take the edges off and detailed her day to Henry. He said, "You should have rung me."

She looked at him. "I've run the place on my own for years."

"You and an endless succession of useless assistants."

"It was just a bad day." She corrected herself. "A very busy day. You have to make the most of those and not fritter all your takings away on another pair of hands."

"But if the economy doesn't pick up and more people holiday in this country more regularly, most of your days could be like today. Another pair of hands would make you more efficient and more profitable."

She looked at him through narrowed eyes. "Who do you vote for, Henry?"

"Tell me I'm wrong."

She sighed. "No, you're not wrong. It's just … change, you know?"

"But you want change."

She opened her mouth. Closed it again.

Henry said, after a moment, "What happened last summer?"

She looked at him. "What do you mean?"

"That makes it different from this one? Last year you weren't talking about selling up, moving on. "

"I don't know. I guess I'm just restless this year. Wondering what else is out there. Maybe it's a natural conclusion - were we all really going to be doing this the rest of our lives?" She swallowed the last of her drink. "Anyway, it's this summer that's different. Last year I wasn't sleeping with you."

He smiled. "Well this is true. Last year I wasn't with anyone."

"Really?"

"No one special." He paused. "Were you?"

"Oh." She shrugged. "The usual."

He looked at her for a long moment. Appeared to make a decision. "Another drink?"

"Would be lovely." She beamed at him. She couldn't tell whether he believed her or whether he was just going to let it go. After this drink she would take him home to her bed, because it would make him happy and the sex would be comforting and because she had known for a very long time that the easiest way to side-step the past was to make the present count.

Jem was a genius, no question. Not only was her own artistry beautiful and original and expertly done, she understood how he worked best and what would work for him without his having needed to explain it. He had shown her pictures of his sculptures and a few bits he had lying around the studio – a bowl, an otter, a symbolic piece he'd called

Grace – but her instinct had come before that and she was absolutely right. And she was not just a genius, she was intuitive and lovely and he ached for her all the time they were apart and, to be fair, pretty much all the time they were together.

Except for this minute, when he was standing in the centre of his room glaring at the log.

"So what are you going for?" she asked. "A symbolic tree or a realistic one?"

"A real one." It was the most important – the only – decision he had made about it yet. "I mean, I want it to be recognisable as a tree."

"What sort of tree?"

"Well, it's apple wood, so ... "

"It's going to have apples on it?"

He turned to look at her, lying naked in his bed, entwined with the fraying quilt, her hair still tousled from sleep, her skin warm and sweaty from the sex they'd had on waking.

He smiled. "Are you making fun of me?"

"Just a bit." She laughed and stretched, the silver pendant she wore sliding on its leather thong between her breasts. "Will you make a start on it today?"

"With you here?"

"Why wait?"

He cleared his throat. "Jem, I really want you to stay ... " She stilled in instant alarm, and he saw again in her the thin shaft of vulnerability which revealed itself sometimes, like a mask shifting briefly out of place. He sat down on the bed to reassure her. "You are so tempting. And you know what I'm like with temptation."

"You're not saying you don't want me here?"

"No. I'm saying I do want you here. Too much."

"I want you here too."

Their eyes held.

"Oh God," he breathed as she swung up into his lap.

"We will have," he told her afterwards, murmuring the words into her hair, "lunch and a walk on the beach and then I will do my work and you will do yours but separately, because clearly I cannot resist you."

She laughed. "It's the same for me."

"Jesus. We're going to be so bad for each other."

They showered and dressed, descended the iron staircase into the sunshine of the square. "What about this place?" She gestured towards Cecily's, where the pavement tables swarmed with families. Gil managed a casual shrug.

"I don't know. Looks pretty busy." His once simmering resentment towards Cecily had been tempered now by guilt and distance, none of which he felt comfortable with, having never been much of a grudge bearer. They needed an air-clearing conversation, and they needed to have it alone. Besides which, he wanted to hold Jem close, not to expose her to the inevitable mockery of Cecily and the guys. Not to expose himself.

"Okay." Jem was happily dissuaded. "There's a great little place I know down in town."

They walked, hand-in-hand, through the crowded streets and along the promenade, avoiding the beach's minefield of windbreaks and sandcastles and games of Frisbee. "I try to come down here first thing in the morning," Jem said. "Or when it's beginning to get dark. Just me and the surfers."

"You know them?"

"No." She laughed. "Do you?"

"Some."

"Do you surf?"

"Badly." He laughed too. "So, no."

"There's something you do badly?"

"God, a million things."

She was smiling at him, her beautiful, light-up-the-world smile. How quickly, he wondered, could you know you'd lost your heart to someone? Could it take just a meeting of eyes, the moment they spoke your thoughts? A kiss, an orgasm, an exhalation of their breath against your skin? How fast could you fall?

As fast as he was falling.

"Hello Gil."

There, on the promenade, as if their lives were so closely

aligned there were certain points every day when they would inevitably find themselves in the same space, was Henry.

"Hey," Gil smiled, recalling the mood in which they had last spoken and unsure whether Henry would yet have recovered from it.

"Hey." Henry was ambivalent.

Jem smiled brightly, pointedly. "Hey."

"Sorry. This is Henry. Henry, this is Jem."

"Hello," Jem said demurely.

"Nice to meet you."

Gil watched Henry's appraising glance and felt a prickle of irritation. "So. How's life?"

"It's good."

"Yeah? Mine too."

"Clearly. Haven't seen you around."

He shrugged. Hesitated. "Sorry, if I was a bit out of order the other night."

"No." Henry looked at him askance. "It wasn't you. Not just you."

Fuck, Gil thought. The *weight* of what we're not saying. "You up for a sesh at Patrick's?"

"I was there last night. Life goes on you know, Gil, without you."

Slightly stunned, Gil bit back a response. They were standing beside a grey Mercedes. Henry pressed a button on his key fob and the locks shot up. He opened the driver's door. "See you around."

Gil watched him pull away, disappear slowly through the crawling traffic. The smiley face stuck in the rear window watched him back. Jem said, "Am I reading too much into that or does he really not like you very much?"

"Yeah. I've become the kind of guy whose friends don't like him very much." He shook his head. "We had words. Something and nothing."

She looked up at him, waiting for the explanation.

"Ah. Forget it." He smiled, kissed her nose. "Where's this great little place?"

For a small town, Cecily knew, this one could be very good at hanging on to its secrets. Sometimes a whisper of gossip breathed into the air at dawn, which anyone might reasonably expect to have infected a willing population by lunchtime, dissipated like sea mist. Sometimes she wondered whether people were too immersed in their businesses during the summer and exhausted during the winter to pay much attention to the petty dramas and scandals of their neighbours. Sometimes she had thought, thankfully, that they were all too dim or insular to care.

She wished that this time just one of those had been the case. She hadn't wanted to know that Gil had been seen walking on the north beach with a girl called Gemma or Jenny, that he had looked happy and well. She hadn't wanted that to be all the information available because no one quite knew who Jenny or Gemma was and Gil remained removed from her. She let Henry take her out to dinner – their third since she had succeeded in steering him away from anything involving the cove – and told herself repeatedly that Gil had never before abandoned friends for lovers, anymore than she was abandoning him for Henry. It didn't mean she was never going to dance with him, or get drunk with him, or put the world to rights with him again. Except it had been almost a month now, which was unprecedented.

Henry was talking about Brisbane. She watched his mouth moving and let some of the words register in her head while she drank. He seemed to have been engaged in lengthy email conversations with his cousin, resulting in definite arrangements to fly out in October. She let her eyes glaze while he told her more than she had any interest in hearing about the watersports business and the standard of living in Australia and why Britain was financially, educationally and socially going down the toilet. She thought about where she would be in October, the prospect of a long and empty Cornish winter ahead of her without the most fleeting glimmer of hope or human warmth. Her head hurt and she closed her eyes for a moment.

" ... all right?" Henry's pale blue eyes were fixed on her

again, instead of on a new life on the other side of the world.

"I'm fine. Just tired and a bit pissed. My status quo," she added wryly.

"I think," he said, "you need a break."

"I would agree with you, except you don't ever get a break from what's inside your own head." Jesus, she thought, listen to yourself. Carry on like this and even Henry won't want to know you anymore. "Sorry," she said. "Don't pay any attention to me. What did you have in mind?"

"A holiday, maybe? At the end of the season?"

"Where?"

"I don't know. South of France? Italy?"

Cecily smiled wistfully. "I love Italy."

"So are we on?"

She looked at him across the table, across the remains of their meal and their wine glasses (hers empty, his half full), tea lights flickering in amber votives, and she thought, does he realise I'm with him by default? Am I prolonging false hope, agreeing to go away with him? But then he will be gone too, and I'll be alone again, and where's the harm. She felt that she could no longer tell wrong from right.

She heard herself say, "Why not?"

He paid their bill, which he always insisted on doing even though she felt she ate and drank far more than he did despite the size of him, and they wandered back through the dusky streets towards the square. He said after a while, "Did you ever see that film, *Sliding Doors*?"

She nodded. "Gwyneth Paltrow and John Hannah."

"The story's told in two time-frames – "

"Yes."

" – and in one she gets on a tube and in the other she doesn't because the doors slide shut – "

"Yes."

" – and it's about how you life can change in an instant, forever."

"Yes! Jeez. I know the film. I understand the concept."

He laughed at her impatience. "It's sort of what's happened with us, isn't it."

Shit. She heard herself, say, *I love Italy*, and, *why not?* and she thought, I'm regretting it already. She took a breath. "Henry ... "

"It's what happens to us all, all the time, every decision we make."

Okay. He was getting general. General was good. She wondered had he drunk more of the wine than she'd thought. "I guess," she said. "We all have our roads not taken."

"This time next year I could be living a life on another continent. It's weird to think a choice which will make such a difference is just down to me." He paused. "Like when you gave up dancing to come here."

"London is a foreign country," she admitted.

"How long ago was that?"

"Sixteen years."

"Do you miss it?"

"Yeah." I'm sure, she thought, we have had this conversation. "But like I said, dancing kind of gave me up."

"So why Cornwall? Why *here*?"

She remembered another set of questions not so very long ago, questions about last summer and who she had been with, and her spine prickled. He couldn't know, she thought in dismay. Had she said something, given herself away somehow? He couldn't possibly know. She said, "Because it's beautiful."

"Oh sure. But it's such a life change."

"It was."

"A really brave choice."

"It wasn't about being brave." Enough, she thought. Enough already. "Do you think going to Brisbane is about being brave?"

"Oh definitely. Much easier to stay here and stagnate."

She imagined him in ten years' time on the brink of English middle-age, more ponderous and grumbling and larger still. Life on an antipodean beach might be the making of him. On her doorstep she kissed him goodnight and reminded him she was tired and a bit drunk and he was, as always and thankfully, a gentleman. She thought as she climbed into bed alone how persuasion and passion from one man could arouse and from another repel. She lay awake a little while, thinking of Gil and his mystery woman, of Henry and his questions. Was his intent as innocent as his tone had been? Was she, hyper-sensitive, reading too much into it? Henry didn't do manipulation or artifice and how could he have the faintest inkling? No matter how things were between them, she would trust Gil to the ends of the earth.

She lay awake.

"Dad!" Jem pushed the back door shut behind her and called into the empty rooms. From somewhere above her she heard a bump, a clunk. "Dad?" She laid down her display board and her takings and went into the hall.

"Hello." He was at the top of the stairs, the cupboard doors open wide, her mother's trunk lying across the landing.

"Hey." She smiled. "I guess we're doing this now."

They sat, mugs of tea beside them, Alex on the edge of the old-rose slipper chair, Jem cross-legged on the floor, the trunk before them, unopened. "It's a kind of treasure, isn't it?" she said.

"Kind of." A key hung on a length of string from the handle and he turned it in the locks on either side. Neither of them made any move to lift the lid. There was a sobriety in his manner which she knew well, a constraint which she didn't. She touched his knee.

"Are you okay with this?"

"Yeah." He sighed. "Shouldn't make such a big deal of it."

"Then we won't." She opened the lid.

It might have been treasure, for the colours inside were as rich as jewels. Piles of soft fabrics in emerald velvet, scarlet satin, sapphire silk. Jem lifted them reverently out. "She used to scour the charity shops," Alex said. "If the clothes were no good she'd keep the material. She was going to make cushions and bedspreads, sell them at the market, keep some of them for us. For you."

"But she never did?"

"There was so much. She hoarded it all, boxes and

cupboards full of the stuff. In the end I only kept the best."

She had a dim recollection of the spare room inhabited by supermarket boxes, boxes which overflowed onto the landing, stood stacked in the hallway, boxes packed with other people's cast-offs. As a child she had believed her home crammed with the clothes of the dead. "I thought it was weird."

"It was weird."

She was aware of his gaze on her as she reached deeper into the trunk, her hand closing on a series of small books tied together with raffia. Diaries, it transpired, from her mother's teenage years to a year or two after Jem was born. "Can I read them?"

"If you want to."

Jem slipped one from beneath its binding, flicked through the pages, weeks of blank sheets followed by screeds dark with tiny, slanted handwriting. "Were there any more?"

"None that I've ever found." He took a suede patchwork bag from the trunk. "This is where she kept her jewellery."

They spread the contents onto a square of scarlet satin, the tangled chains of necklaces, bracelets on over-stretched elastic, odd earrings. Jem trawled through them, sadness rolling inside her. "Did you give her any of these?"

"A couple of things. This … " He separated a string of malachite beads from the chaos. "Again, most of it's charity shop. We never had the money for good stuff."

"What about her wedding ring?"

"It went with her."

He hadn't wanted to keep it. She couldn't meet his eyes. After a moment she said, "I was twelve when she died but I might have been three or four, for all I remember. Why doesn't any of this mean anything to me?"

He frowned. "You have memories of her, though?"

"Distant ones. I remember her music lessons, and watching her ride her bike down the lane. Fragments of memories like … I don't know. Like a *sense* of her more than a solid reality."

He was silent for a minute, rubbed his eyes. "You did spend more time with me."

She lifted a trailing knot of chains into her lap, began to try to unpick them. After a long moment she said, "When was the last time we did this?"

"When you came home from uni. We opened the trunk, and we looked inside, and we talked a little, and then we put it all away again." He paused. "You know we've only done this two or three times since she died."

She nodded.

He said, "Until you were about fourteen you wouldn't look at any of it, wouldn't speak about her. I thought – I think – it's how you've managed losing her."

She looked at him. "But it was always you. You never wanted to talk about her. You packed all her things away. You couldn't bear it."

"I still can't." He gestured, helpless. "It wasn't easy when when she died – it wasn't easy when she was alive - and God knows I wasn't much use to you. Neither of us has been very good at coping."

She understood. "We shut it out."

"We did. I'm sorry."

"Don't be sorry. We just coped with it in the same way, that's all." She fingered a brooch she'd picked up from the jumble on the satin, clipping and unclipping its pin.

He watched her. "So what now? Do you want to carry on, or put it all away?"

She rubbed her palm across her forehead, back and forth. "I'm a grown-up now. I should be able to deal with it."

"She was still your mum, no matter how old you are. The relationship and all the feelings that go with it don't change."

"It's the same for you."

He said nothing.

She looked over the edge of the trunk at a selection of records, an orange triangle of stained glass, a miscellany of china ornaments. After a little while she scooped up the corners of the satin, making a hammock for the jewellery. The rest of the material and the suede bag she put back into the trunk. "I'd like to keep these," she told him, the hammock in one hand, the diaries in her other.

Alex nodded, his concern undimmed. "All right."

119

I could measure out my life, Cecily thought, with parties at Patrick's. At least this time she knew whose it was: a couple who had met two years ago at a beach barbecue she and Gil had thrown together and who were tonight celebrating their engagement. They had festooned Patrick's with streamers and created champagne glass fountains as though it were already their wedding. People were making speeches. Cecily groaned audibly into her drink and allowed herself to be entertained by the Buz'n'Radar show. She hitched up onto a bar stool and flirted for a while with the bar guy. Chatted with Lucy. She watched with amusement Henry attempting to disentangle himself with chivalry from a skinny and very inebriated girl possibly half his age. And she danced. The music rescued her from the boredom and irritation she could see fast becoming her default setting. It filled her heart and freed her mind. She danced alone and she danced with strangers and when finally she returned to her table she felt as though all her aching, mean-spirited thoughts had been exorcised from her.

It didn't last.

Radar and Buz drummed their hands on the table to welcome her back. "Way to go Cecily!"

"You should go on one of those shows."

She laughed. "I was in shows."

Henry said, "She likes dancing with strange men."

His resentment-concealed-as-humour hit a bum note. She cocked an eyebrow at him. "Who was the child attaching herself to your crotch, Henry?"

"*She* came on to *me*, all right?"

"All right. I was only teasing you. I didn't seriously think the two of you'd be sneaking off into the sand dunes." She realised as the words left her mouth that her tone made them less than complimentary, that Buz and Radar were laughing and that it was already too late to retract.

Henry, insulted into a u-turn, said, "Why wouldn't you think that?"

"Well … " Unforgivably she began to laugh too. Oh *God*, she thought.

"Because I don't look like fucking Gil?"

"No," Buz snorted, "because you don't act like fucking Gil."

"Or like Gil fucking." Radar was inspired.

Cecily said, "Because you have integrity."

"Shit," Henry said. "I'm sorry. I'm pissed."

"No really?" She smiled, rubbed his back. "Lighten up."

Another round of drinks arrived on their table. Buz's head swivelled. "Christ, where did they come from?"

Henry looked glum. "I think I might have ordered them in a previous life."

Cecily laughed. The bar was packed, as ever, and being friends with the staff their only advantage. The heat today had been British summer at its best. The heat in here tonight was almost unbearable. Dancing like a whirling dervish for the best part of an hour hadn't helped. She fanned herself with a beermat.

"Do you want to sit outside?" Henry asked.

She turned her head in the general direction of the pier. "There won't be any tables. It's okay."

"Can you believe," Buz was saying, "Karl and Lauren are getting married?"

"No kidding?"

"No, but they're like, what, twenty-two?"

"But they're in luuurve," Radar drawled. "Can't put an age tag on luuurve."

Buz tipped his glass towards his mouth and missed. An inch or so of beer spilled down his chin and onto his t-shirt. Radar and Henry cackled.

Well here's a turn-up for the books, Cecily thought. Everyone's drunk except me. She said, "Does the thought of marriage scare the shit out of you, Buz?"

"Sure." He wiped his chin on the back of his hand. "All that having to – wash up, and have sex with the same person for, like, ever."

"Wash up?"

"Yeah and shelves and stuff."

"Washing-up, shelves, sex. Anatomy of marriage."

Radar said, "You ever been married, Cecily?"

"*No*. Have you?"

More laughter. "Fucking hell," Buz roared. "Who'd marry him?"

"I don't know. Can he do shelves?" She grinned. "Have you ever been close to it, any of you?"

They looked blank.

"There was this girl," Henry said unexpectedly, "in my oboe class … "

Anything he might have added was lost in the immediate hysteria. "In your *oboe* class?" Cecily wiped her eyes. "Oh Henry."

He said, "Have you?"

"No."

"No?" He was frowning at her, Buz and Radar distracted by spilt beer and helpless laughter and someone mooning outside on the pier.

She said quietly, "Not been close to marriage, no."

"Why?"

"I've just never been in that kind of relationship."

"But that's not true, is it?"

She thought she must have misheard him. "What?"

"I've given you a lot of opportunities to tell me over the last few weeks. And now I'm asking you directly you're actually lying to me."

"Lying to you? Jesus, Henry." She didn't know whether to be more incredulous or offended. "What is it you think you're accusing me of?" And then suddenly she could see it coming. Her skin was clammy. Suddenly she understood what all the questions this last week had been about.

"You had … "

She stared at him. She was going to be sick. "I had … ?"

He said, "You had a baby."

She felt very cold. "How do you know that?"

"I saw the bracelet in your drawer." That he recognised he was making a terrible mistake was visible in his face. She didn't care.

"You went through my things?"

"No! It was open. You left it open. I saw the … *shit*."

122

She had to escape. The bar was so packed there was barely standing room; they were fenced in by the thighs and hips of sweaty bodies. She rose, felt a rushing in her ears, swayed. Henry said, "I'm sorry. Cecily, don't, wait. I didn't mean … " She shoved her way through the crowd, pushing, slopping drinks, ignoring protests, ignoring Henry, at her heels.

Outside, in the crush of smokers and the cooler air, he caught her dress. She lifted her hands – don't touch me – and yanked away. He was contrite. They walked a few yards. She was shaking.

"What happened?"

"He died," she said coldly. "My baby died."

"Oh Christ. I'm so sorry."

"I can't talk about it."

"Well no – I … " She was walking away fast now and he hurried to draw level with her. "Does Gil know?"

She turned on him. "Oh my God. I tell you that and that's all you care about – "

"It isn't – "

"Of course Gil knows." She held his gaze for a minute, her own steely with rage and withheld tears. "And even we don't talk about it. But of course he knows."

Chapter Fifteen

We are in a small coastal town between Toulon and Cannes, on our way to Nice. So much has changed in our fugitive flight and knowing where we are isn't the least of it. Gil's driving echoes his mood – less frantic, less angry. He's slowed our pace: we linger over meals; while away hours in bars. I'm itchy to press on but he's easier to be with when he's chilled, like the old Gil, and he doesn't know, he has no idea, about the car with the smiley face.

We're sitting in a bar now, the cool autumn sunshine slanting across polished table-tops, hitting the rows of coloured glass bottles, the gold handles of the pumps. Gil is talking to the barman and a young English couple. I can hear their French and Home Counties accented voices, his peal of laughter. I sit alone, running my finger around the edge of my glass, sour and sick inside. Thoughts of home, and my father, hack away at my peace.

Gil returns, his smile the residue of lively conversation with normal people. "We've been invited out tonight."

I stare at him. "Are you mad?"

He looks irritated. "It's called hiding in plain sight. When are we more suspicious, chatting and clubbing with people our own age or skulking in dark corners glowering at each other?"

"Clubbing?"

"A little place over the road, apparently. Indie music, cheap drinks."

I lower my forehead to the table with a thud.

"Fine," he says.

After a minute I look up again. He's still there. "What'll happen to the house?"

"What house?"

"My house. Dad's house."

"I don't know. Why are you thinking about that now?"

"I think about it all the time. I think about all of it, all the time."

He sighs, relents. "It might be good for us, you know, to have a night off from thinking."

"You said we can't escape from what's in our heads."

"I didn't say we couldn't try." He smiles, conciliatory. "Then tomorrow we can drive on to Nice. And after that – "

"To infinity and beyond."

He frowns, recognising the phrase. "What's that from?"

"*Toy Story*. Buzz Lightyear."

"Ah yes." He starts to laugh. I do too, and we laugh like we do these days, on the edge of hysteria. It's better than crying.

By the time we descend into the black pit of the club, we're both pretty well-oiled. Me because I know it's how I'll survive the night, Gil because … well, it's one way of escaping what's in your head. The Indie music he promised me pumps through the dark, ricocheting from floor to ceiling, bouncing off the neon lights behind the bar. Helen and Craig, the English couple he befriended earlier, are already here, cool and sophisticated like they're in a Martini advert. Gil and I look as if we've spent the last six months hitching round the third world. No one seems to mind. The boys order drinks while Helen and I claim one of the booths. They have curtained entrances, u-shaped sofas with woven cushions which make me think of Moroccan harems; I half expect to see a hookah in the middle of the table. Helen asks me questions and I lie to her, fantasies spilling from me as readily as facts. Gil and I have had this conversation and he will be lying too. It's heady and liberating, pretending a different truth. She tells me she works in London in PR and Craig is an IT consultant, that they have a tiny flat right at the end of the Central Line but that when they want to start a family, which they will in the next couple of years, they'll move out to a proper house in the countryside and Craig will commute. I can't believe she's giving me so many details of her life so fast. They could be lies too of course but somehow I doubt it.

When Craig and Gil breeze through the curtains with a pitcher of what turns out to be a lethal cocktail, some edge returns to the proceedings. It takes me a while to identify it.

Gil is all effusive charm, his voice a little louder, his gestures more expansive than I have seen for oh God, so long. And Craig matches him shout for shout, his stories as rambling, his humour as infectious. His hand rests while he talks on the inside of Helen's thigh. She strokes the back of his neck and when she leans across him in her diaphanous silk top we are all aware of her tits swinging free. Gil's knee presses against mine. It doesn't need to; there's enough room on the sofas for us all to stretch full-length. Which Helen does, her feet in Craig's lap. He takes off her shoes and massages her soles, her calves, his hand sliding beneath the hem of her skirt. Later it's me stretched out, in the u bend of the sofa while she is somehow sitting beside Gil and I watch the way she touches his arm while she's talking, the crinkling around his eyes when he smiles in response. He's mine, I think, wanting him. I imagine myself getting up, pushing her away from him, lowering myself into his lap. I can feel his heat, taste his mouth. The pulse of desire is so strong it must surely be visible through my skin.

When Helen goes to the loo and Craig is at the bar buying another pitcher of Death By Alcohol, Gil comes to sit beside me. Wordlessly he lifts back my hair, tilts my chin, kisses me with an urgency and passion I had thought belonged to another time. I'm so drunk, so greedy, I want to unzip him there and then and he, well he's more than ready to be unzipped. Then simultaneously we remember where we are and break apart, breathing hard. Craig and Helen are on the dance floor, his hands squeezing her bum, her breasts. We stare. Gil says, "You all right?"

"Mm-hm."

"You want to go somewhere and fuck?"

Outside we slam up against the deserted terrace wall behind the club, between baskets of still sweet smelling flowers and vines of clematis. "Do you think it's okay? Out here?"

"It's France," he mutters. "It's probably compulsory." His hand is inside my pants, his jeans around his knees. He licks my throat, nips my neck. I suppress a cry, his hair in my fist, my back scraping against the plaster. It's fast and hard and

fierce and as soon as the world spirals away from me we're
done, clinging to each other, his breath harsh, chest heaving.
"Ah God." He kisses me.

"We should – "

"Mm."

We make ourselves decent, lurch out into the street. Music
vibrates still from the club but beneath the periodic glow of
streetlamps no one passes, nothing stirs. Gil's arm is around
my shoulders as we stumble in the direction of our hotel.
"There's another way to survive," I tell him. "Drinking and
screwing till we can hardly stand."

He laughs. "Gotta tell you, it's working for me."

I laugh too, while I can, because tomorrow we might be
teetering again on the brink. He kisses my temple, cuddling
me to him as we walk. I burble about our journey to Nice
tomorrow, longing just to fall into bed with him, to fall asleep
with him, now that the taboo of sex, or lack of it, has been
broken.

He has stopped, so suddenly I almost trip. "What?"

He's staring ahead, at the road in front of the hotel. At a car
parked a dozen yards away.

The car.

"Shit," he says under his breath.

"Gil … "

The taillights come on.

He belts towards it, as if he would heave the door from its
hinges and haul the driver into the road. The car reverses fast
with a screech and I cry out, sure it will hit him, but then as
soon as he's leapt out of the way it's speeding forward, a
shadowy squealing rush between the rows of parked cars and
palm trees, disappearing into the night.

He gives a great yell of frustration, spins back towards me.
"You know who that was?"

I nod.

"*Fuck*." He claps his hands to his head. "They've found us."

Chapter Sixteen

Gil walked along the rocks high above the north beach, stepping over pools and seaweed, treading easily from sharp ridge to slanting plane. The light was fading and soon it would be foolish to remain up here alone, watching the sea grow blacker than the sky, risking a slip and skid in the dark. He and Jem had spent the day apart in order to work, their first whole day without each other since their meeting on the pier. It had been her suggestion and he had reluctantly agreed, reminding himself that she did not have another source of income; it was unfair to expect her to spend her every waking minute with him. Besides, he had wanted her to be surprised and impressed by the progress he made in her absence; proof of his industry and vision. But instead he found himself bored and uninspired, frustrated and mocked by a block of wood. He turned his back on it, sent her a series of increasingly erotic texts, to which she had replied with such tantalising promises he had been unable to think about anything else. As dusk fell he had broken out of his self-imposed cage and walked to the beach, striding up onto the jagged rocks, standing so close to their edge that the crashing and swirling tide seemed to crash and swirl against him. And he saw, as though it had risen from the depths of the sea itself and were hovering on the horizon, his perfect tree, dark and bare and reaching its stark branches into the skies.

It was always the case that when an idea finally seized it took up residence within him, growing stronger and more focussed until his final commitment of it to material was done. He hurried back to the square, keen to face the hunk of wood with some degree of triumph, to call Jem and describe to her his Eureka moment before describing to her, in precise detail, what he would like to do to her. Though it was late now lights and customers spilled from pubs and restaurants, the square was still buzzing and he saw, as he approached and through the knots of holiday makers, Cecily at her door.

Well this was good timing, he thought. Both of them alone,

the night not yet over. An opportunity maybe to put things right. "Hey," he called softly, closing the distance between them, and she turned towards him and he saw to his dismay that she was crying. "What is it?"

She shook her head, her hand trembling badly at the lock. He took the key from her and opened the door, moved her gently inside. "What?" he said again.

"Henry knows about Sam."

"Oh Jesus." He drew her into his arms and held her for a long moment. Her shoulders racked as she wept and he stroked her hair, kissed the top of her head. "Oh sweet-heart. How?"

She pulled back, wiped her face with her hand. "He found his identity tag."

Gil, knowing where the identity tag was kept, made all the connections and his spirits sank a little further.

She watched him. "Do you have to be somewhere now? Can you stay for a while?"

"Of course I can stay." When life was good or when they were annoying the hell out of each other it was easy to forget all the things that only he and Cecily knew; that there were times when no one else's comfort or company was enough. She plucked a bottle of wine from the kitchen and he followed her upstairs.

He smiled as they entered her rooms. Nothing much had changed. He remembered the summers he had spent more time here than at his own place, all the confidences and intimacies they'd exchanged, all the times they'd peeled each other out of their clothes and fallen together onto her patchwork bed under the eaves. It seemed like yesterday. It seemed like a lifetime ago.

They sat on the stripy sofa and Gil poured her a large glass of wine. "Tell me."

She did, describing the evening and the earlier conversations when Henry's questions had seemed determined and too close to the bone. He listened, silently furious with Henry's insensitivity, with his own failure to protect her. "How much did you tell him?"

"Only that he died." She hesitated. He squeezed her hand.

129

"After that I didn't want to be around him. It's all always been so private and I couldn't believe firstly that he knew and then that he thought it was okay just to blunder in with it."

"But that's what Henry does."

"He was upset."

"You're upset." And so was he, but he wasn't going to make it any worse for her by saying so. "Do you want to talk, about Sam?"

She shook her head. "There's nothing to say."

He nodded. "When I first came back you were upset about something. Was it this? Had you been thinking about him?"

She was quiet for a moment. "Kind of. Sometimes the force of not having what I thought I was going to have – what I did have, for such a short time – hits me all over again and it leaves me reeling."

"I know. God. Why wouldn't it?"

"I think I coped amazingly well and that I came to terms and all that crap and then one person says one thing and … " She gestured. "It brings everything back. You know Henry wanted to take me to that party at the cove?"

He nodded. "What did you say?"

"We went out for dinner instead. Was that your suggestion?"

He was uncomfortable, that it seemed as though he had been interfering. "I was just trying to look out for you."

She sighed. "I'm sorry, Gil. I didn't mean to offload this onto you."

"Jesus, don't say that. Who else can you offload it onto? I know it hasn't seemed like it much these last few weeks but I'm on your side. Always and forever, on your side."

She hesitated. "We've … "

"Been stupid."

"Yeah." She gazed at him. "I'm sorry."

"I'm sorry too."

She touched his wrist. He smiled.

She said, "I hear you're … seeing someone."

"Yeah." He swallowed a mouthful of wine, recognising the need for a skilful blend of honesty and tact which he hoped wasn't beyond him. "I am."

Cecily watched him. "What's she like?"

"She's lovely."

"Are you smitten?"

He paused.

"Oh God. You are, aren't you? It's all right, don't think you can't tell me."

"It's not that. It's ... all happened so fast."

"Well sometimes," she said, "that's what it's like. You meet someone and you know instantly that you have to be with them, no matter what. It doesn't even feel like love, or lust. It feels more uncompromising than that. As if it's ... elemental."

He considered. "It does feel a lot like love and lust though."

She laughed. "It is you." She added, "And then there's the other kind, when it isn't fast at all, when you've known someone for years and then one day the thought of being without them is a knife to your heart."

He looked away. Hearing her say this about Henry was more unexpected, more painful, than realising she was sleeping with him. And how bloody mean and unreasonable of him to feel that when he had just admitted to falling in love with someone else. He said, "Is he still talking about going to Australia?"

She shifted on the sofa, topped up their glasses. "He is. I think it's pretty likely to happen. He wants me to go on holiday with him first. Italy, in the autumn.."

"And will you?"

"I already seem to have said yes."

He smiled, at her tone of surprise and because she was no longer distraught. "I think another beach party is in order."

She looked at him. "After the last one?"

"Hey. No more fighting. Life is too short."

"It is," Cecily agreed soberly. "It really is."

She stood up to put on some music and he listened to the opening chords of *Second Hand News* from Fleetwood Mac's Rumours album – his own, he seemed to recall – lilting through the familiar space. They were all at the tipping point of change. Henry moving away, maybe Cecily with him. His own life headed in who knew what direction. At the beginning of the summer he would have railed against this prospect but

131

tonight, beginning to make peace with Cecily and thoughts of Jem pulling at his heart, he could contemplate with some serenity – excitement, even – the scent of change like danger in the air.

*

Every summer Henry and the boys rented the same flat above a souvenir shop two minutes from the beach. From April to October a track of sand led from one to the other even through the rain. Cecily, following the track up the slope to their doorstep, selected *henry* on her mobile's contact list. "I'm outside," she said to his voicemail. "Five minutes then I'm gone." She waited. She had on flip-flops and shorts, a pink zip-up hoodie intended to shield her from the early chill. Yet this midsummer morning the air was already warm, blue skies promising another idyllic day ahead. She had left Justine on breakfast duty and was already questioning her own wisdom, but there had been no customers when she left and what she had to say to Henry would not take long. Better to let a few words fill a short space of time than wait until evening and let the silence draw on.

She heard heavy footfall down the stairs on the other side of the door, and then there was Henry, looking as hung-over as he smelled. "Hey," he said warily.

"Hey. Come for a walk?"

He was uncertain. He was also wearing nothing but a pair of boxers. "Give me a sec."

She waited again. He returned after a minute or so, in jeans and a t-shirt which also whiffed of booze. She said as they started down the slope, "I just wanted to talk to you before we get any further into the day."

"Okay."

She led him to the first bench at the end of the prom with its views of the beach huts and the empty sands, the tide a quiet shimmer under the gentle sun. She sat with her knees drawn to her chest, her heels resting on the wood beneath. Henry sank down beside her, put his head in his hands for a minute.

"I've blown it, haven't I?"

"No."

He looked at her. "Really?"

"Listen. I couldn't talk to you last night but I shouldn't have run away. You deserved more than that - "

"I didn't. "

"Ssh. Listen. You can't ask any questions and I can't tell you more than this because - well, because it's too hard." She gathered her courage. "I had a baby. A little boy. His name was Sam and he was perfect. He had blue eyes, like me, and light brown hair, like me. He was inquisitive – fascinated by the world, even though he was so little - and he smiled all the time. He used to jig about in his bouncy chair when I sang to him and fall asleep when I played him all my eighties New Romantics slush. He put his fingers in my mouth when I talked to him. He liked sleeping on my chest with his ear pressed to my heart. One morning when he was four months old I went to his cot and he was dead. There was nothing wrong with him. They said it was Sudden Infant Death Syndrome. But I thought it was me, judgement on me for having believed, and dreamed, and hoped. For having been happy." She swallowed. "I couldn't bear to think of him in the ground, so I scattered his ashes at the cove. I used to go there with him all the time. Afterwards it turned out I could hardly go there at all."

There was a long silence. Henry said, "I'm so sorry."

She shook her head, wiped away her tears. "You should also know that I saw Gil last night – I didn't go to him, he found me in the square – and I told him that you know. You have to stop being jealous of him. He's my best friend but anything more than that is over. He's seeing someone else. I'm with you."

He nodded. "All right." He paused "Is he fucked off with me?"

"I think he was more concerned for me."

"Of course."

She rubbed her eyes. "Oh God. I have to go back now. I've left Justine in charge of the croissants." She smiled wryly, stood up.

Henry said, "I was scared – "

"Don't. Don't be scared. We're still here."

He hugged her, at a loss, she knew, because she had told him he couldn't say anything and because finding the right words at the best of times wasn't his forte. He murmured against her hair, "I love you."

Well there was that, she thought. She hadn't forbidden him that.

Chapter Seventeen

"Okay." Gil turns from his curtained surveillance of the street below. "Here's what we're going to do."

I pause. We'd come straight up here, silent with shock, Gil instantly to the window while I packed our rucksacks, hands trembling, desperately occupied. We've both sobered up so fast it's as if the last few hours never happened.

He looks at me properly for the first time since the car with the smiley face nearly crushed him beneath its wheels. "Listen," he says.

I do. It's a nice hotel and the glazing muffles external noise, the air-con whooshes gently like some background lullaby. On the floor above a toilet flushes. There's nothing more.

He says, "It's been this quiet since we got in. It's a good sign."

"Why?"

"Would you feel better if someone were trying to break down the door?" His tone is one of soothing reason and I understand that fear must be emanating from me like a scent.

"You're very calm," I tell him, almost reproachfully.

"Yeah." He takes a breath. "Yeah. Well, now I know what I'm dealing with."

"How can you know that? It was just the car. We didn't even see who was driving, we just recognised – " I'm becoming shrill with terror and he shushes me.

"If the police were involved they'd have burst in here waving their guns at us and we'd be locked up by now."

This makes some sense. I shut up, watching him pull the strings of his rucksack together, buckle the top flap. I do the same with mine but I can't stay quiet for long, however much it'll annoy him. "Why aren't you scared?"

"I am scared. But when you're waiting for the worst to happen, and then it happens, it's almost a relief. And it turns out maybe it's not the worst after all."

"It's something you can deal with."

He looks grim.

"You haven't told me yet what we're going to do."

He swings his bag onto his shoulder. "We're going to drive to Nice. It should only take a couple of hours. Then we'll ditch the car and take the train to Venice. The car's a liability now anyway and we won't need one once we're there." He meets my eyes, ready to meet my inevitable wailings or objections with intransigence.

I say meekly, "All right."

"Okay." He rubs my arm. I think of us against the wall outside the club an hour or so ago, lost in passion. Something in his eyes tells me he's thinking of it too but the moment is long past. "Let's go."

We step furtively out into an empty corridor and take the back stairs to the ground floor. It's the early hours of the morning and there is neither sight nor sound of anyone but ourselves. We're in a bare concrete lobby containing bins and cleaners' trollies, one door leading to a carpeted passage, another to the yard outside. Gil tentatively presses its central bar. No alarm sounds and the catch gives.

The yard too is deserted. Something – a fox? a rat? – shoots from the pile of rubbish sacks across the pavement in front of us. We move carefully through the dark, hurrying softly along the network of alleys behind the hotels and find the car where we'd parked it, half-hidden behind the bushes from an overgrown garden. We climb in, trying to limit the thunk-thunk of our doors as we close them behind us. Gil starts the engine and we crawl out of the side streets, gaining speed as the main road opens up ahead of us. He is quiet, and I catch him checking the rear mirror more than maybe he needs.

"Are we okay?"

"So far."

I lean back in my seat. "Can I stay stuff or will you lose it with me?"

"Give it a go."

"What if we're followed to Venice?"

"Well, like I said, we'll be better without the car. Nice'll be busy, even this time of year. Then we'll probably have to

136

change trains a couple of times, which gives us more opportunity for confusion."

"Venice isn't a big city."

"No, but it's a good place for hiding dark deeds."

I start to say, isn't that the last thing we want, and then I realise that he doesn't mean someone else's dark deeds. He means his own. "Gil … "

"I won't be hunted down." His voice is tense in the dark enclosed bubble of the car. "If he wants to back me into a corner, fine. But I can't answer for the consequences if he does."

I swallow. He's scaring me. "He was your friend."

"Oh I think anything any of us were to each other went up in flames a long time ago, don't you?"

I have a vision of us all, charred remains on a scorched and blackened land and I don't know which frightens me more - its accuracy or the deadness in Gil's eyes.

Chapter Eighteen

Jem sat on the wall clutching her lunchbox and her bookbag, swinging her legs and scuffing her heels against the bricks. Everyone had gone. She'd watched them scrambling into their parents' cars or loping away holding one of the handles of their babies' buggies or running and swooping with their friends. Now she could see all the way up the street into town and down the street to the beach. The teachers would be coming out soon, unloading armfuls of books into the boots of their cars, asking her questions. She hopped down from the wall and began walking home.

It wasn't really so very far, and she had taken the same route with her mother or her father every school day since she had been in Reception. She knew she had to turn right out of the playground, along the road past the vets' and the supermarket, across the big road with its double zebra crossing. She was afraid of the crossing; it seemed too big, to invite traffic from too many directions, to provide too much opportunity for terrible disaster. But the cars had all stopped for a lady ahead of her and Jem scuttled in her wake, her heart thumping and her throat making little whimpering noises until she was safely on the other side.

Then a left turn, past the rows of houses whose walls were painted pastel colours like flavours. They had tiny front gardens, filled with flowers or enormous pebbles; in one of them lived a white plastic stork whom she had secretly named Clarence, in another a tabby cat which lay on the pavement in front of her with its paws in the air whenever she passed. The road climbed now, the houses becoming larger and further apart, fields behind them and the sea winking in the distance. She was growing hot and thirsty, but drinks came with whichever of her parents arrived to collect her and she knew she would have to manage until she was home. Why hadn't one of them come?

After the double zebra crossing, the scariest part was the

lane. The hedgerows on either side were taller than her father and there was no pavement; cars sometimes came whizzing round the corners before you heard them. Sometimes in the early morning there was a rabbit flattened into the tarmac and though she tried not to look a glimpse of white fluff of tail or soft length of ear made her want to cry. She kept to the edge, one foot directly in front of the other as though the grass were a tightrope, balanced by her lunchbox in one hand and her bookbag in the other. An older boy who lived in one of the big white houses cycled past her. A car rolled slowly by.

The further along the lane she trudged the quieter it became until it was her own stretch of road with her house at the end of it. So few people passed this way, so few visitors came, it always felt safe, like time and space outside the world. She pushed through the gate and followed the path round to the kitchen door, which stood open, but before she crossed the threshold she caught sight of something, some unexpected colour and shape further down the garden.

"Mummy?" Jem dumped her bags in the doorway and tramped across the lawn. Her mother was kneeling beside what yesterday had been a small flower bed and was now an empty patch of ground, its blooms uprooted and tossed aside. "You forgot to collect me from school."

Her mother looked at her as though she had also forgotten who she was.

Jem said, "Mummy?" And saw that her mother was raking up the soil with her bare hands. Next to her was a pile of shredded material, a faded sleeve, a trouser leg, a piece of pleated skirt. "Why are you burying the dead people's clothes?"

Her mother continued to dig, scooping up the dirt and dropping it to one side, making a series of little molehills where the flowers had once grown. "You have to bury them to set them free."

"How can they be free if they're buried?"

"Their souls become free."

Jem felt a frown beginning inside. "Do clothes have souls?"

"They have the souls of the people who wore them."

"What would happen if you didn't bury them?"

"Well then their souls would haunt the land."

"And the house?"

"Of course the house."

Jem's throat felt sore and her eyes hurt. She was too hot, standing scratchy in her school uniform in the garden, watching her mother's soiled hands clawing at the earth. She wanted to cry.

And then – "Marianne!" Her father's voice, angry and growing louder as he came through the house. "Marianne!"

Jem wanted to run to him. Her mother paused, momentarily, in her digging. "Oh good," she said under her breath. "Daddy's home."

Gil stood in the cat-swinging space between the table and the dresser and gazed around. "So this is it."

"It is." Jem felt ridiculously nervous, as if he were going to judge her not on the last weeks of great sex and intense emotional connection but on the cleanliness of her kitchen. It felt distinctly odd, having him here. He seemed taller, in her crammed cramped house. More exotic than he already was. She watched his eyes travel across the framed sketches on the walls, the miscellany of junk piled on the dresser, collections of mismatched crockery stacked haphazardly along the shelves. She had tried all afternoon to impose some sort of order on the natural chaos but there was just so much of it.

He smiled. "It's an Aladdin's cave."

"Oh don't say that. I spent ages tidying up."

He laughed, hugging her. "I didn't mean like that. It feels like home. A proper home."

"It feels like a tip."

"You should see my place, in Bristol. I have nothing. Minimum furniture, clothes, CDs, TV, that's about it. I can't get interested in it so it never feels like somewhere I want to be."

"You could change that."

"I think I've needed someone to change it for me. Someone to change it for." He smiled. "What time will your dad be

140

home?"

"In about an hour." She took wine glasses from a cupboard, lifted a bottle of Cabernet Sauvignon from the rack. "Open that. Talk to me while I cook."

"I could help." He twisted the cap, half-filled their glasses.

"Do you cook?"

"Bloke cooking. Flinging things in a pan and chucking in a few spices. That sort of cooking."

"And does it work?"

"Well, you know, it's edible. Usually."

She started to laugh.

"What?" he said, laughing too, drawing her towards him. "What?" He kissed her. Put down his wine glass and kissed her properly. "Every time I touch you I want to take you to bed."

"Every time you touch me I want you to take me to bed."

He groaned, releasing her. "I need distracting. Give me something to do. What are we eating?"

They cooked and drank and she listened to the lilt of his voice, watched his hands as he peeled and chopped, acutely aware of his changing expression as he talked, the line of his body beside her. His sheer physical presence had her breathless that he existed in the world, astonished that every day he chose to be with her. She wanted him to be the person who understood her better than anyone, her lover, best friend, guardian angel. She wanted to say, *I love you* but was terrified of the tumbleweed pause which might follow.

"So tell me," he was saying, "about your dad."

"What do you want to know?"

"What to expect."

"Oh he won't give you the third degree. He isn't like that. He's too wry and laid-back. He's pretty cool actually." She smiled, heard the sounds – click of the gate, footfall on the stone step outside the door – that she'd been hearing all her life. "And he's here."

Gil straightened immediately, as though it were a terrible faux pas to be caught lounging in the kitchen of the man whose daughter you were screwing. She saw the flicker of nervousness in his eyes, and as he came through the door the same in her father's, dissipated in the next moment by his smile.

"Gil, isn't it?" He held out his hand. "Sorry, still a bit paint-streaked. How are you? It's good to meet you."

"It's good to meet you too." Gil's handshake was firm. "I'm fine, thank you. How was your day?"

"Busy, so I can't complain."

Jem watched them pretending not to weigh each other up. "Glass of wine, Dad?"

"Thanks, Puddle. I just want to get a wash first, won't be long."

There was a small silence after he'd gone. Gil said, "Puddle?"

"Beatrix Potter."

He looked mystified.

"Jemima. Puddle…duck."

"*Oh*." He began laughing.

"Shut up."

"Puddle. I love it." He hugged her. "God, you *look* like him though, don't you?"

They ate at the kitchen table, cosy with three of them around it, the atmosphere quickly becoming companionable. Jem thought how strange it was to see her father's attention divided, to see Gil respectful and deferential. He asked all the right interested, perceptive questions about Alex's painting, making her realise that she hadn't seen him around other people before, that she didn't know how he was with anyone but her.

"Have you always painted for a living?" he was asking.

"I have. Though for years there wasn't much in the way of a living being made. It's something of a curse, isn't it, the need to be an artist."

"*Dad*." Jem was horrified.

"Oh it is. And if you're not making any money it's a terrible self-indulgence."

Gil raised an eyebrow. "But the minute you do you become the poster boy."

Alex smiled. "Well you might."

"You were too," Jem said. She had only understood it as she grew older, the news-paper and magazine articles which concentrated on his looks and romanticised his widowed single-parent status as much as they celebrated his talent. She was going to say, it's only a terrible self-indulgence if it affects other people, but decided not to go down that road; she knew where it would lead. Instead she said, "But people need things of beauty in their lives."

Gil said, "They don't need to pay a small fortune for my tables when they could buy one from Ikea for twenty quid."

"I'd rather eat off a tray on my lap than buy a flat-pack."

"That," Alex said, "is because you are my daughter. And with the world as it is these days, Gil and I are lucky still to be in business."

"Oh I know. But when things are bad we all need something to make us feel better, don't we? Something beautiful to heal our souls and make us feel life is worth living. I'd rather buy the cheapest thing either of you made than the most expensive from somewhere like Ikea."

Gil smiled. "It is a bit of a curse, though. I know what you mean. You have to set more store by freedom than security and sometimes that just looks like perversity and ego."

Jem said, "I can't imagine you not walking to the beat of your own drum."

"No," he agreed. "Kind of not who I am. Not who you are either."

"True." She liked that he had a pretty accurate image formed of her in his head, that it meant he listened to and thought about her.

"I hear you're sculpting a Tree of Life," Alex said. "How's that coming along?"

While Gil told him she cleared the table and brought dessert, opened another bottle of wine. "I struggled with it at first," he admitted. "I loved the concept straight off, but all I had in my head was a sort of Disney monstrosity. I was having trouble reconciling it looking like a tree with being – I don't know – dark and powerful, representing that deep pulse of life, the kind of life that can't be suppressed or … eradicated."

"So now it's more of a Tim Burton tree," she said.

He held her gaze, amused but challenging, would have grabbed her had they been alone, kissed her into submission. Instead he laughed. "Yeah, okay."

Alex smiled. "Where do you exhibit your sculptures?"

"There's a gallery in Bristol that takes my stuff, not far from my workshop. And there's the website, though really that's just promotional."

"I'd like to see the gallery and your workshop," she said without thinking, and caught her breath. But -

"Come up with me at the end of the summer," he suggested.

"Really?"

"Sure." He grinned. "You can tell me what to do with my flat."

"There you go," Alex said. "An offer you can't refuse."

Later she walked with him along the lane. He kissed her against the bindweed-threaded hedgerow, moths fluttering in the moonlight. "Thank you, for a lovely evening. Great food, by the way."

"You're welcome."

"And you're right, your dad is cool."

"He is, isn't he?"

Gil smiled. "I liked him a lot."

"Good. I like him too."

They made promises to find each other in the morning, to share breakfast before addressing the day ahead. She watched for a little while as he walked away down the lane, before he was swallowed up into the darkness.

Back in the kitchen Alex was clearing away their coffee cups. She danced over and hugged him. "Well?" she said.

"Well, he seems a very charming, capable young man and we have a lot in common and I expect we'd get on very well and he's clearly entranced by you. So yes, I approve. Completely."

She beamed. "He likes you too."

"Excellent." He smiled. "I haven't seen you so happy for a long, long time. And I can't tell you how relieved that makes me." He added soberly, "You know this is it now, don't you? That I'll be gone in the morning?"

Her elation shrank away. She nodded.

"I'll ring you when I get to Archie's."

"Okay." She was tearful. "I don't want you to go."

"Oh Puddle – " He embraced her. "Come on. You'll be fine. You have Gil."

"I know. But - "

"And anyway." He drew back, put his hands on her shoulders and held her gaze. "It's time. Isn't it."

She nodded. "It's time."

*

Her father strode across the lawn towards them. She didn't want to run to him anymore. His eyes were narrow and his voice was doing that loud raspy thing. "The school rang. They said they hadn't seen either of us pick her up and there was no sign of Jem either. Mrs Thompson was beside herself."

"Mummy forgot," Jem murmured. "I walked all the way home."

"Well you shouldn't! You know you're not allowed to cross that road by yourself."

"There was a lady."

"Marianne! For God's sake." He stared at her and Jem saw his anger change into something more complicated. "What the *hell* are you doing?"

"She's burying the dead people's clothes," Jem said helpfully.

They both watched her folding the scraps of material into the hole, adding a layer of soil, more clothes, more soil. Like making lasagne, Jem thought. Her father said quietly, "Come on, Puddle. Let's get you some tea."

She followed him back inside, sat obediently at the kitchen table while he fetched her a glass of milk and a shortcake biscuit. "Thank you."

He sat down opposite her. "I know you thought you were doing the right thing, and I'm really sorry neither Mum nor I came to pick you up, but you must promise me you won't walk home on your own again."

"Okay."

"I'm not cross with you."

"Okay." She sipped her milk.

"So." He cleared his throat. "What did you do at school today?"

"Reading. I'm on a new book."

"Good. Do you want to read it to me later?"

"Yes please. And we did Numeracy. I don't think I'm very good at Numeracy."

Her father smiled. "You want to know something? Neither am I."

"And Art. I did a sunflower. Mrs Thompson said it was like Vangolf."

"Did she? I'll pick you up tomorrow, I might ask her if I can see it."

Jem was delighted. She swung her legs while her father got up to run water into the kettle and switch it on. Mrs Thompson liked her father. She wondered what he'd meant when he said she was beside herself. How could you be beside yourself?

The kitchen door crashed back against the vegetable rack, sending carrots and potatoes bumping and rolling across the floor, her mother moving so fast she was a streak of blonde hair and flapping skirt, her hand raised then coming down hard across her father's face.

He gasped. She wheeled out, into the hall, through the front door and into the lane, leaving the door standing open.

Jem stared at him. He wiped his mouth. His hand was shaking a little bit. Blood trickled from the corner of his lip.

She burst into tears.

Chapter Nineteen

We drive fast through the night. It's quiet but I can't sleep and if there's a speed limit on the main road to Nice, Gil doesn't care. He's foot to the floor all the way. We don't speak of course because there's nothing to say. I remember hours, days, when all I did was talk to him, spilling out every single detail to try to make some sort of sense of it all. And he listened. He's good at listening, though you wouldn't expect it when you first meet him. You'd expect him to be dismissive and self-absorbed, to have an ego which didn't take anyone else into account. But he isn't like that. He's sensitive and perceptive and he involves himself in other people's lives. He was involving himself in someone else's life the night I first saw him, diving into the water to save a boy from drowning. He didn't know anyone was watching.

There was a time, too, when he talked endlessly to me, pouring out the story of his life. I remember all the connections we discovered, to our delight and surprise, as though they meant something. I remember saying it was fate.

My God I was naïve.

So I eventually told him everything, the whole truth as I knew it then, which turned out not to be even half the truth, because that had been hidden from me all my life. And he helped me piece it all together, except all the while he was doing so he was withholding his own truth – the Big Truth. And that's why we're here.

I still can't quite keep it all in my head. Some of it I understand and I can read it like a picture. But then the rest snags and crinkles and rolls away into dark corners. It won't all hang together. Maybe I just can't bear it to. Maybe the whole thing, unfurled before me, would just be too much. Because this is where my nightmares come from, I'm well aware. Everything I now know, everything I've done, crawling towards me like some monster bent on revenge.

I'd just like some little bit of it to go away.

We drive fast through the night and this is what's in my head. I sneak glances at Gil and it might be what's in his too. He's paler than usual, eyes darker than usual, though that could be an effect of the streetlights above us, of the headlights which glare and wash over us. In the end I can't take any more of the silence.

"How will we know," I say, my voice dry with disuse, "when the trains are to Venice?"

"There might be a timetable," he replies sarcastically. "At the station."

"We'll need to stop before then."

"You'll have to hold on."

"It's not me. It's the petrol."

His eyes flick to the gauge. "Fuck."

There's a garage a few more miles down the road. I stay in the car while he fills the tank. It's dark out there, cold. I close my eyes; easier to relax without him rigid with tension beside me. I know I have a few minutes – it isn't Pay at the Pump and there's a dim yellow light on in the kiosk across the way. I think of dumping the car like we did back in Plymouth, of the anonymity of Nice, of a long train journey to another country. On and on. Further and further. Travelling without end. I want somewhere safe to stop now. A squat, a cave, a hole in the ground. I just want to sleep.

When I open my eyes he still isn't back and I don't know how long it's been. There's no sign of him anywhere – at the pumps, over by the kiosk. My heart's thumping. I clamber out of the car on stiffened limbs. "Gil?" My voice quavers in the empty darkness. "Gil?"

And there it is, parked in the bushes a dozen yards away.

The car with the smiley face.

Chapter Twenty

Gil stood in the centre of his room and contemplated the tree. It contemplated him right back. It was now a don't-mess-with-me tree, Jem had said. A kick-ass, Quentin Tarantino tree. He saw what she meant but it wasn't quite what he'd been aiming for. He'd wanted something mystical and powerful, something you would be awed by, not something that if it came to life might sock you in the jaw with one of its branches. And maybe mystical and powerful were still possible. He wanted to recreate it enough that when she saw it this evening she would be impressed, but the precise alterations to make eluded him and he had done this before, rushed a change he hadn't been sure how to effect, hacked away too much, shaped something badly, ruined it beyond rescue. So he stood staring at it, thinking instead of Jem and her dry, off-the-wall observations and New Age sensibilities, of her common sense and flights of fancy; she too was a mass of contradictions. It was one of their work days and they had therefore spent last night apart: they had agreed to work and play alternate days but when they woke tangled together in his bed neither had any inclination to go anywhere else. Lunches were lingered over into late afternoon. Early evening cocktails became dinner and an easy surrender to the distraction of the night. The balance to his days now was of loving being with her, working, being with her, the worst excesses of summers past having dropped away and been replaced by such elation he didn't miss a minute of them. He did, however, miss Cecily and beach parties and nights at Patrick's, and he wondered would it be a terrible mistake to begin gently introducing Jem to what had been his life, despite her showing no sign of introducing him to hers.

He took his phone from his jeans pocket and texted her. *Got sculptor's block. Want to be with you.*

No reply. No doubt she had a queue of customers. He texted a heart and a kiss and looked afresh at the tree.

Come on then, it said. You know what to do. What are you waiting for?

By late afternoon, when the shadows of the window frame were lengthening across his workbench and the heat through the glass had him perspiring from the day's exertions, he knew the transformation had begun. Minute changes to direction and form were altering the whole sense of the piece, its menace only a whisper now, its implicit life a force for potential good. Or, he reminded himself, it was a skilfully honed bit of wood with some nice turns and appropriate texturing. No point getting pretentious about it. He was, though, slightly more satisfied, slightly less disappointed in himself. He had done some worthwhile work and it was, happily, time to stroll down to the pier and into Jem's arms.

He walked along the beach, enjoying the sun, the sands still filled with parents draped into deckchairs and lounging behind windbreaks, teenagers decorously arranged on strips of towel, toddlers running full pelt towards the water, a father assiduously helping his son to dig what was clearly going to be The Biggest Sandcastle In The World. One day, Gil thought, that will be me, digging that hole, shaping those turrets. But from being the person he was now to father of a small child required a leap of faith so great he could hardly encompass it. He would have to become someone else, someone less selfish, less hedonistic. Someone more patient and reliable. Someone, God forbid, like Henry.

He couldn't distinguish, from this distance, Jem's stall on the pier. He climbed the steps back up onto the prom, turned past Patrick's and onto the boardwalk. Pavao, immersed in his miniature rock painting, was oblivious to the small crowd gathering to watch him; McDowell whistled as he hung belts and bag straps from the rail above his trays of purses and wristbands. Gil greeted them as he passed. There was no sign of her. He walked the length of the pier and back again, but there was no blue-handled stall glittering with jewellery. No Jem. He frowned, took out his phone and touched her number. She didn't pick up. He texted – *Am on pier, where are you?* and a few unresponsive minutes later – *are you ok?* Where

150

else would she be? He realised he had no idea. Shit. She turns off her phone and she disappears. Neither Pavao nor McDowell could enlighten him and he tried to remember whether she had said that today she would work at home (wherever that was), which seemed the most likely answer and, deciding to try her again in a little while and resisting the siren call of Patrick's, he turned to walk back into town.

"Gilman Hunt!"

He recognised the voice before he recalled her name, scanned the busy pavement for the Lady from the Press. And there she was, Eve Callaghan, just as she had been weeks ago when she had interviewed him. Possibly even wearing the same clothes. He folded his arms, caught as he had been that day between curiosity and instinctive distrust. "Hey," he smiled. "How're you?"

"Oh, not so bad. Yourself?"

"Great. How's the campaign going?"

She looked at him. "Can I buy you a quick coffee?"

He let her distract him, for now, from the mystery of Jem's whereabouts and take him to a vegetarian place further down the street, all smoothies and bran muffins and décor the colour of hangover vomit. He ordered strong black coffee as an instinctive reaction and hitched up onto a bar stool at the counter in the window. Eve Callaghan tore open a sachet of sugar and tipped the contents into her drink. "I widened my base," she told him. "Your story was in every paper in Cornwall."

His eyebrows went up. "It was?"

"No use pretending it isn't a county-wide issue. A national issue, this time of year."

"Sure. It's been pretty quiet lately though, maybe that's a good sign."

She shook her head. "It's still early. The madness of August is only just hitting us. People think they can take risks when they're on holiday that they wouldn't dream of taking at home, and August is the silly season. A couple of my colleagues have taken up the baton too, we're all raising consciousness. Running your story in every newspaper was just the beginning."

"That's great. But you know, it really isn't my story."

She frowned at him over her coffee. "You said something like that last time. You can't commit an act of heroism and not expect it to be commented upon, or remembered."

Or exploited. "I just don't think of it, of myself, in those terms." Jesus, this was going to haunt him the rest of the summer.

She put down her cup. "You should be proud of yourself."

"It wasn't – "

"Listen. You don't get to do the job I do in the place I do it and not see things. Not make connections. There's a discrepancy between who you think you are and how other people see you and I think you might need to be careful."

He laughed in disbelief.

"Seriously," she said.

He didn't know whether he was annoyed or amused. "I haven't a clue what you're talking about."

"Well neither do I really. And I probably shouldn't have said it. But what the hell." She paused. "I haven't undertaken this campaign lightly, you know. I have my reasons." He waited, his interest piqued, but she closed the door. "Sometimes when there's nothing you can do you just have to do what you can."

She was a bit loopy, he realised. Trying to carve a career for herself in this peninsula community of frenzied hot summers and desolate winters had driven her round the twist. He said helpfully, "And sometimes what you can do makes enough of a difference."

"Let's hope so."

He stayed long enough to finish his coffee and feign an interest in the details of just how she and her colleagues were raising consciousness, then beat a retreat back to the square. A swarm of customers was leaving Cecily's café and he saw her standing there amid the chaos of crumbs and crockery, wearing her faded shorts and vest, her hair pinned in its messy knot. His heart warmed and he smiled. "Need a hand?"

She smiled back, gratefully.

"I talked to Henry," she told him when they were alone in

the kitchen and Justine was out front mopping spills and wiping menus. "He's okay."

Gil, looking up from checking his phone (still nothing), barely managed to refrain from saying that Henry had no business not being okay.

She said, "You should talk to him too."

"And say what, exactly?" He knew what he wanted to say. He wanted to lecture him about bullying someone into telling you their secrets, to point out that it wasn't about Henry, or himself and Cecily, but about truths being too painful to tell, the need for sensitivity. He knew there was a danger he might be provoked into blabbing that he didn't understand why Cecily was shagging him or why she thought there was any sort of future at all for the pair of them. That it was beyond him and he had no right to any sort of opinion about it and he could put Henry's face through the wall for making her cry. None of this was going to help. He said, "I saw him down on the prom the other day. He didn't seem very keen on talking to me about anything."

Cecily glanced over the orders on the workbench. "Gil, the pair of you have been friends for years. Don't let this change things."

He thought that while they were both behaving as if it were not the first time he had helped out in the café for weeks, things had already changed, possibly irrevocably. He couldn't find a way to say this which didn't make him sound like a complete shit.

She added, "You're lucky, you know. You can talk about feelings. You almost always say the right thing. Henry can't, he struggles with that."

"Jesus, he is a grown-up." He looked at her. "Sorry. Not the right thing."

She smiled. "You've always been able to be the better man. It's one of the things I love about you."

He looked at her, wanted to say – and do you love him? Really? But he already knew the answer. She was fond of Henry. Maybe he was even what she needed just now, kind and loyal and possessive and dull. And what am I? he thought.

Do I really have anything better to offer? He said suddenly, "Do you know Eve Callaghan?"

"The reporter who came here to talk to you? I know who she is. I've never had a conversation with her. Never made the headlines, myself." She smiled. "Why?"

He told her. "It was weird. I mean, she doesn't know me. Why would she say that?"

"Well. Because she's Eve Callaghan. And you know, maybe she has a point. Looking like you do, being as charming as you are, people think one thing about you, and then it turns out you're actually perceptive and trustworthy, and then you go and spoil it all by thinking with your dick. You're a conundrum, Gil Hunt."

"Shit. You know me too well."

She laughed. "Oh, let's not fall out again. I've missed you so much."

He smiled, said with sincerity, "Missed you too."

Jem sat at the kitchen table with her head in her hands. Her mobile rang. She ignored it.

It buzzed twice. She glanced across.

Am on pier, where are you?
are you ok?

She slowly transferred her gaze to the dresser in front of her, its shelves holding books and crockery in a civilised manner but also spilling over with junk: a clay dish she had made in primary school full of old batteries; an aerosol room spray she couldn't imagine they'd ever used; stacks of unopened mail; a ceramic pen holder of paintbrushes stiff with disuse. *What were we thinking?* There was a fine line between comforting and claustrophobic and she was aware she was inching towards it day by day. But the thought of the effort required to do anything about it left her numb.

She picked up her phone, scrolled back to the heart and the kiss he had texted her earlier. *Got sculptor's block. Want to be with you.* The tears which had been falling for hours now brimmed afresh. You won't, she thought. You won't want to be with me.

Of course it was ridiculous to be worried. She was twenty-six years old, this was her home town, and she'd - what? Lost her phone, track of time? Missed a bus? Besides, he wasn't the worrying kind. Gil reminded himself of all this several times as late afternoon expanded into evening and she might as well have fallen off the planet. It didn't help.

And gnawing away at his unease was the knowledge that he had no idea how to find her. She had never taken him home, even alluded to where home might be, or described her family, much less introduced him to any of them. She could just be found at more or less the same time, more or less every day on the pier, or she materialised wherever and whenever they agreed to meet. It was odd. He had known it was odd, he had just been too enchanted by her to care. But here he was, fretting over her absence and helpless in the realisation that the only thing he knew for sure about her was her name.

For fuck's sake Gil. She's just lost her bloody phone.

Impatient with so much impotent waiting, he walked fast down the precipitously narrow streets into town. Somebody – if not, gallingly, her lover – must know something more about her. The other stallholders, shopkeepers, *someone*.

Someone, perhaps, like Eve Callaghan.

Her card was creased in his pocket.

He stopped. Tried to think about this properly, about the possible consequences of calling Eve Callaghan for information on Jem. As he took out his phone it rang.

"Jesus," he said, relief pouring through him. "Where are you?"

"I'm … " Jem's voice faltered. She was crying.

"Are you okay?"

"Not really."

"Are you hurt?"

"I'm at the gallery on The Wharf. Will you come?"

Gil said, "I'm almost there."

He sprinted the remaining hundred yards of the way past bollards, the prom, the sea, holiday-makers, seagulls, to the boarded-up gallery he'd mentioned to Cecily before she'd told him he messed with people's lives, *Alex Gregory* inked in large black italics on the sign above the door.

Alex Gregory.

Alex Gregory, whose work he'd admired, whose company he'd shared over a pint or two up at the inn, long conversations down here in his gallery. Gil could picture him now, greying dark hair, olive green eyes, something about the bone structure, their humour, the way they both spoke. His heart was hammering and not because of the run. The door to the gallery was open an inch. He gave it a push. "Jem!" Went inside. "Jem?"

She was sitting on the floor of the abandoned workshop, the shadows of paintings visible on the walls even in the dim light which filtered around the edges of the boarded windows, her back against the whitewashed stone. She struggled upright as he came towards her only to be almost knocked her off her feet again in the strength of his embrace. "Are you all right? Jesus. What's wrong?"

"I'm sorry. I'm sorry, Gil. I just needed to hide away. I couldn't talk to you before because … Oh God. I have to tell you something." She took a breath, her eyelids pink and swollen. "I should have told you weeks ago … and now you'll think … " She stopped.

He said, "Is it to do with this being your dad's place?"

She stared at him. "How did you know?"

"Finally made the connection. Not too quick on the uptake, I'm afraid."

She nodded, swallowed.

"What happened?" He gestured into the echoing space of the room. "Has he had to sell up?"

She shook her head. "He died."

Of course. Of course this was the answer. Horror and understanding and compassion swept through him. "Oh God." He enfolded again her in his arms and she cried against him. "Oh Jem. I'm so sorry."

After a long while she drew back from him, wiping her face with her hands, tears dripping from her chin. She opened a drawer of the paint-stained chest beside them, took out an old box of tissues. Gil stayed where he was, giving her space. "When did it happen?" he asked gently.

"April." She wiped her cheeks. "It was so stupid. Such a *pointless* end to … If he'd been ill … I don't know … there would have been time to say everything we needed to say, to get used to the idea of him not being here, but … He'd had an idea for some paintings of Tintagel castle. He wanted to take photos, do a few sketches, you know. So he went up there and it was wet and misty and the sea was wild and … he fell. Somehow he fell. They didn't find him until the next day, and I didn't know. I was at home, when he died, watching some stupid TV programme, and I didn't know."

She was crying again. Gil reached for her hand.

"It was just me and him. For more than half my life, just me and him. And I can't – I can't begin to … He's still with me, all the time. It's like I'm still talking to him. All the conversations we had, or I imagine we'd have. I even imagined him meeting you." She took a long moment, battling to recover. "I'm sorry. I'm sorry."

"Don't – "

"I would've loved you to have met. You'd have really liked him."

"I did like him."

She looked at him. "What?"

"I knew him," Gil said. "I liked his work. I used to come in here and have long chats with him. I have one of his paintings back at home."

"Oh my God. You *knew* him."

"Yeah." He smiled. "Not well, but enough." He paused. Said, with feeling, "I can't believe he's dead."

"I can't either. Sometimes I can go almost a whole day and then something new reminds me of him and I just start crying again. I can't bear to be in here without him. Being at home is driving me mad."

He nodded. "I'm sorry," she said. "I should've told you before. But I can't – couldn't - talk about him. And I wanted to be my best for you. I didn't want you to know what you might be getting into, that I was so needy and pathetic – "

"Shush, come here." He drew her against him again, held her for a minute. "It's okay." He kissed her forehead, smoothed a strand of her hair from clinging damply to her cheek. "You can tell me anything, you know. You don't have to pretend with me. What you said, about not wanting me to know what I was getting in to? It's too late. I'm already in way too deep."

"I love you," she told him through her tears.

"I love you too."

Henry arrived in Patrick's with an hour to spare before meeting Cecily for dinner and a longing for a beer, solitude and the Telegraph crossword. The guys mocked him endlessly for being the only surf dude on the planet with a penchant for crosswords but Cecily had said once that it was unexpected and therefore made him more interesting and less predictable, and he had loved her for it. He knew well enough that his admiration of Cecily had been a long time coming. He had always thought her smart and cool and sexy. It was just that until now Gil had always been standing in his way.

The more he thought about it now, the more elements of the whole situation with Cecily and Gil troubled him. This summer's tension between them was unprecedented. But had their shared and secret tragedy resulted in little more than a bit of virulent public squabbling? That aside, they had been as casually affectionate with each other as ever. And almost simultaneously they had both turned to someone else, were now dabbling in real relationships with someone else. He couldn't square it with the death of their child. Unless Gil had spent time with her when it had happened, and in their grief they had come to this conclusion. Henry knew that he had no experience of his own on which to draw, that he had so far lived a tranquil and sheltered life, that he knew none of the details, couldn't bring himself to ask Cecily and certainly wasn't going near the subject with Gil. But even so, it bothered him.

"Hello."

He looked up. A middle-aged woman, ginger hair, gym-addict lean in a splodgy vest top and khaki jeans. She seemed familiar somehow. "Hello," he said.

She ignored the question in his voice. "Can we have a quick chat?"

"Well … "

She was already sitting down, placing her glass on the beermat opposite his. "My name's Eve Callaghan. We met briefly when I came to talk to Gil Hunt at the café up in the square."

"Of course." The reporter. He recalled her brusque manner, Gil's wary response.

"I'm mounting a campaign – Gil might have told you - to raise awareness of the dangers of the sea. I've lived here a long time and I've seen too many accidents, too many deaths as a result of carelessness or stupidity out there, not to want to try to do something about it. It's why I spoke to Gil in the first place."

"Sure. I remember."

"And I noticed that you run a surf school down in the bay."

"That's right." She hadn't noticed it at all, he thought. She had checked him out.

"Parents are one of my target audiences, as you might imagine, and I'd like to do a reassuring and informative piece on the kind of health and safety precautions you have to take in your business – the same sort of health and safety precautions they might take themselves."

"Okay." He knew every risk assessment measure he took could not be faulted, that the children he taught were probably safer under his guidance than anywhere else on the beach. And if it helped, and maybe gained him a little incidental attention, where was the harm? So he gave her a comprehensive run-down of everything he was required by law and commonsense to do and watched her pencil fly over her notebook while he spoke.

"This is really," she said, "exemplary practice."

"I should hope so. It has to be."

She paused, drank from her glass. "And what about as a surfer yourself?" she asked him. "Do you feel you and your friends have any responsibility to warn against the dangers there?"

"Only in our capacity as casual instructors."

"Which you do?"

"Naturally."

She nodded, scribbled a few more shorthand hieroglyphics. "So that's you – Henry Muller – and your friends are … ?"

He struggled to remember their real names. "Richard Parker and James Buzzard."

"Radar and Buz, right?"

He was impressed. "You're in Patrick's a lot, I take it?"

"How else would I find anything out?" She smiled. "And what about Gil Hunt?"

Henry laughed. "Gil doesn't surf."

"Too cool?"

"Too uncoordinated."

She laughed. "He's just there at the right time?"

"Well, I wouldn't say he makes a habit of pulling kids out of the sea but yeah, generally, he does have a talent for being in the right place at the right time."

"Have you known him long?"

"Nine years. The guys and I were friends at uni. Gil we know through this place."

"Where were you at university?"

"Exeter."

"Gil too?"

"No. He was in London. Goldsmiths, I think. Why?"

"Oh, just background colour." She flipped shut her notebook. "Thanks, for talking to me. Can I come back to you, if I have any follow-up questions?"

"Yes, no problem."

She picked up her drink. "It must be nice, meeting up here every summer. Like some sort of extended student vacation."

"Well it is, and I admit we're all getting a little bit old for that. Time to start taking life seriously, I suppose."

"Oh don't do that. Life gets serious enough all by itself without any help from you."

He nodded, thinking of Cecily. "I know. We come here to escape our real lives but for the people who live here, this is real life. It's easy to forget that sometimes."

She looked at him with interest. "Have you become friendly with the locals?"

"As if you were real people, you mean?"

She acknowledged his point. "Sometimes it does feel as if we're just one big service industry. Backstage crew, you know."

"Then that's the advantage of longevity. Yes, we have friends who live and work here. Good friends."

She was watching him. "All of you?"

"Of course," Henry said. He finished his beer, put down his glass decisively. "And I'm afraid I'm going to be late for one of those friends if I don't leave now."

She nodded. "Thank you," she said, "for your time. You've been a great help."

"You're welcome." As he walked away, out of Patrick's and up the sloping streets towards the square, he wondered was it an advantage that people often thought him stupider than he was. For she might have pretended curiosity about his Junior Watersports Club, she might have asked relevant and pointed questions about safety and moral obligations, but Eve Callaghan had not succeeded in disguising from him that what she was really interested in was Gil.

Alex and Jem returned from their customary Sunday morning walk along the beach. They had been buffeted all the way by the wind, their faces barely warmed by the February sunshine. Alex could feel his cheeks stinging, still taste the salt spray on his lips. "Hot chocolate?" he said, hanging up his coat in the hall, taking Jem's from her, her red woollen scarf, her hat with its earflaps and bobble.

"Yay!" she cried, as if it were a rare treat and not an essential part of their ritual. He called up the stairs –

"Marianne? Hot chocolate?"

A murmured assent.

The kitchen was warm from the oven and full of the smell of the beef he'd placed inside it before they'd left. Jem had hopped onto her stool at the table and taken out her drawing pad and felt tipped pens. He was trying to encourage her to sketch in pencil, then use crayons or watercolours, but who was he to deny her the craze for felt tips and gel pens currently sweeping the classroom. He made a point of not denying her any of the habits and desires and preoccupations of a normal childhood. He placed their drinks on the table, called up again to Marianne, and fetched the chopping board so he could prepare the vegetables for lunch at the same time as admiring his daughter's artwork. She was drawing people; not the distant, hazy figures which populated his landscapes but finely detailed faces and complicated clothing, perfectly shaped hands, eyes which regarded you solemnly from the paper. He had taught summer school and evening art classes to adults who paid him considerable sums of money and saw more real talent in his eight year old daughter than he had in many of them in years. It was possible, of course, that he was biased.

Marianne wafted in from the hall, folded herself silently onto the chair at the head of the table and wrapped her hands around her mug. She had been withdrawn for weeks but

162

withdrawn was the least exhausting of her humours and he had learned simply to treat her calmly and with great care. Years ago he had felt he was pretending or being patronising and now it was only the daily currency of their communication. Of his communication with her. At best her response was a sliding glance, a murmur. To preserve his own sanity, to present a cheerful face to the rest of the world, he had had to grow over his hopes and dreams and deepest feelings a hide of horn.

Jem was drawing her mother. He saw it in the peeks she sneaked across the table, her frowning concentration recreating Marianne's oval face and narrow blue eyes. Alex peeled potatoes and smiled. "Tell your mum about our walk," he suggested.

"Oh, it was so windy!" Jem said obediently as she coloured. "There was this little dog – was it a Yorkshire terrier, Dad?"

"It was."

"This little Yorkshire terrier on the beach and the wind was so strong it nearly blew over! Its little face was all scrunched up against the wind."

"So was mine," Alex said. Jem laughed.

Marianne said nothing, but he knew that no attempt to include her was ever wasted; it made it so much easier to pick up the reins of normal life when she could.

"And there was this place," Jem continued, "behind the rocks where you could stand and it was like someone had turned off the wind. Then you stepped back out again and whoosh! they'd turned it back on again. You should come with us, it's really cool."

"It is really cool." Alex finished peeling and chopping potatoes and carried the saucepan of water into which he had put them to the cooker. Marianne slid away. Jem looked thoughtfully at her drawings.

"I'm going to do you now. You have to come here and sit still."

He laughed. "Can't you draw me from memory?"

"It's not the same."

"How will you draw yourself, then?"

163

"Oh I just make myself up." She shifted on the stool. "Actually I have to go to the toilet first."

He cleared away their empty hot chocolate mugs and the potato peelings, was wondering absently what else he needed to do before he had to sit still for twenty minutes being Jem's model, and more pressingly where had the vegetable knife gone, when he heard his daughter scream.

After the horrific scene in the bathroom and the hours at the hospital and the further hours it had taken to soothe Jem to sleep, he sat in the dark of the living room with a glass of Jack Daniels and the phone in his lap. But there was no one to call; no one he needed to tell, no one he could talk to. It was not the first time Marianne had been hospitalised. It was the first time Jem had found her with her wrists pulsing blood onto the floor tiles. His head ached with tears he had not, until now, been able to shed.

He couldn't go on like this.

He didn't have any choice.

Chapter Twenty-one

"Gil?" My voice sounds small and lonely in the dark of the petrol station, its volume dwarfed by the silence. I hear myself whimper. It's been minutes. A few minutes. He filled the tank, went to the kiosk …

I turn towards it. There is no light there now. No figure hunched over a till. It's just an empty booth. It looks as though it hasn't been used in years. *How is this possible?* I wasn't asleep. I'm sure I wasn't asleep. Only minutes have passed. But now there is no Gil, and no attendant, and a car parked in the bushes that wasn't there before.

I'm shivering. I sprint over to the kiosk, but it is locked and too dark inside for any-thing to be visible through the glass. Nothing stirs on the forecourt. The road, stretching out of and into the night, is lined by tall trees, their tops shifting slightly in the breeze. I'm as certain as I can be that no other car has passed while we've been here.

But clearly one other car has.

It still sits, its nose pushed into the shrubbery, and it too is silent. I clench my fists at my side and walk slowly towards it, covering the fifty yards between me and it as though in its boot is an unexploded bomb and that bomb is meant for me. Which, who knows, could be the case. Gil has vanished. Maybe a bomb has come for him too. Maybe he has left me, on this deserted country road in the middle of the night, taken off across the fields because he can't bear another moment.

I wouldn't blame him.

The smiley face grins at me through the dark.

I am within two feet of the car now and no one has leapt out to grab me. The window has not wound slowly down. The car has not gone up in flames. I reach out my hand to the door, half-expecting my touch to be the trigger which explodes the bomb. And maybe that would be for the best after all. But nothing happens. When I press the catch the door clicks open and I hold my breath.

It is empty.

On the passenger seat is a map, in the back a couple of plastic bottles and the remains of what smells like fast food. The keys hang in the ignition. The driver was expecting to return. I am torn between searching the pockets and glove box and running –

Where?

Where am I going to go?

I can't drive. Our hire car is useless to me. I will have to haul my rucksack over my shoulder and walk to wherever is the nearest town, catch a bus, a train. By myself.

Where is he?

Heart thumping, I draw back from the driver's seat and walk round to the rear of the car. I press the catch of the boot. It's locked. I walk back, take the keys, go back to the boot.

Do I really want to know what's in here?

Can I honestly just walk away?

I slide the key into the slot, make a quarter turn to the left. Nothing. I take the key out and press the catch. The lid is released an inch or so. I want to be sick.

"What the *fuck* are you doing?"

I shriek.

"Jesus," Gil says, beside me.

I stare at him in disbelief. "Where *were* you?"

He looks wild. Wilder. "Went for a piss."

"But it's been – "

"Minutes. It's been a few minutes." He takes my arm above my elbow and starts to lead me away. "Come on."

My head's spinning, I want to resist but don't. "The car, Gil."

"Yeah. I know."

"It's empty."

He opens our passenger door, bundles me inside. Walks round. Gets in. I'm shaking again, with relief and residual terror and awful, unspeakable, suspicion. He sits, doing the staring grimly through the windscreen thing we've been doing a lot of lately. Then he cries out, with what sounds like frustration and rage and pain, thumps the steering wheel, sinks his head into his hands.

"Gil," I whisper. He doesn't move. I touch his shoulder.

"Shit," he mutters. He sits up again. His eyes are glittering and he swallows hard. "Jesus fucking Christ." He gives a long, shuddering sigh.

"You're scaring me," I tell him.

He nods. "You should be scared." His voice is ragged.

After a long moment I say, "Shall we get some sleep?"

"No, we need to move on." He starts the engine, jerks the gear stick into first. I look at his hands. It's dark, so dark, inside the car, but I know that he was crying, and I look at his hands.

Chapter Twenty-two

They had reached the end of the lane, a circle of weed strewn tarmac and a stile in a fence allowing access to this part of the cliff walk. Jem had stopped in front of a wooden gate, long ago painted red, which opened onto an undisciplined garden of trailing, spindly flowers and louring bushes. "We're here," she said. Gil nodded, her apprehension infectious. He was still digesting the knowledge that Alex Gregory was her father, and that he was dead. He raged inwardly at himself for having accepted her silence about her family without question, for not having seen that she was stricken with grief. He was supposed to be good at this stuff, for Christ's sake. But then she hadn't wanted him to see. She had wanted, with him, to hide from the horror. He understood that, could imagine doing the same thing. But the thought of her trying to cling on to the pretence that everything was all right made his heart ache. He tightened his hand around hers and her fingers squeezed in response.

He rallied. Said approvingly, "So this is home."

"It is." Letting go of his hand, she pushed open the gate. He followed her along the path which led around the side of the house through an arch of overgrown purple buddleia to the back door. She took her keyring from her bag and unlocked it. She paused. "It's a mess," she warned him.

"That's okay." He touched her arm. She opened the door.

The kitchen into which he stepped was so overcrowded with furniture he couldn't move more than a few feet in any direction without hitting something. The units and appliances looked as though belonged to the seventies; the dresser dominating the room might even be turn of the last century. Every available surface was cluttered, not so much in a scary obsessive-compulsive way but simply because there was just too much stuff for the amount of available space. He said, "It's clean."

She made a sound which in other circumstances might have

been a laugh. "Apparently it's hereditary. He couldn't throw all of her things away and now I can't throw away any of his."

"Her?"

"My mum. She died when I was twelve."

Another bombshell, this one casually tossed. "Oh." He assimilated the information, said with sympathy, "Right." Opposite the dresser was a bay window seat and an old pine table, morning sun already creeping across its scars and stains. The walls were hung with little sketches he recognised as her father's, on the dresser among the crockery and beside an old CD player stood a photograph of Alex with Jem as a child. True, the level of domestic chaos, even just in this room, was greater than he'd ever known but the trail of possessions told the story of a life. Two, maybe three lives. He said, "This is nice, you know? It feels like home."

She shook her head. "The heart's gone out of it. It's just a damp old house filled with junk."

"Hey." He hugged her.

She half-smiled, in spite of herself. "Do you want to see the rest?"

The kitchen proved a decent indication of what was to come. Off the long and chilly hall a small square sitting-room contained a wall of bookcases, a wing chair and a green velvet chaise longue, a small sofa beneath the window. Newspapers and more books were stacked in corners, old paintings propped against walls. She said, "It's partly because it's such a little house. It's hard to contain all those years of acquiring things you love, and things you don't love but you can't part with because they're so steeped in memories."

He squeezed her shoulder. "What do you want to do?"

"I know what I don't want to do. I don't want to live like this and turn into some sort of Miss Havisham. But my dad's things, Gil. I'm never going to see him again. How can I throw out all his things?"

"You don't have to throw out all his things. You just have to start making a series of decisions. Maybe think about what he would have wanted you to keep."

"Well look at it. Clearly he wanted to keep it all."

Gil was beginning to form a theory about that, which it was far too early to voice. Upstairs he glanced into a bathroom in which supermarket brand aftershave took up window-sill space alongside Sugar Crush body scrub. A pair of worn men's slippers sat on the landing. He had understood last night that she was frozen in grief but seeing the physical evidence of it everywhere in the house was disturbing. His gut reaction was to flee.

She opened the door to her own room, luminous stars painted on a navy ceiling, fairy lights strung around the bedposts, the bed itself a nest of cushions and threadbare purple velvet. Transparent boxes on her desk were filled with necklace chains and cords, earring posts and wires, beads and semi-precious stones and various pieces of pewter and copper. He said, "It's calm, in here. A kind of sanctuary."

"It always has been."

But a teenager's sanctuary, he was thinking. She was mired here as much as any-where in the swamp of the past. "Let me show you," she said, "the worst." She stepped back out onto the landing, took the handle of the floor-to-ceiling cupboard doors. Inside each shelf was packed with boxes. At the bottom stood a large trunk, its key hanging from a length of string attached to the handle. "It's their marriage," she said. "Seventeen years of their life together crammed in a cupboard."

Everyone, Gil told himself, had cupboards like this. Attics, cellars, spare rooms. This was no eerier than those. He shivered suddenly.

Jem looked at him. "Let's have a drink."

They sat at the kitchen table with mugs of tea. "Every time," she told him, "I've gathered bin bags and recycling boxes and the moment I pick something up and try to make a decision about it I start to cry. Or I feel sick. It's too much. Too … final."

"But," he reminded her gently, "you said you don't want to live like this."

"No."

"So we need a battle plan."

"We?"

"I'll help. We can't do it all at once and we need to do it alongside work and being together and all the normal things, so it doesn't seem too overwhelming." He added, "You might have to be a bit ruthless."

"Gil. Why are you doing this for me?"

He hesitated. If there was ever a time to speak from the heart, it was now. "Because I love you and I can't bear to see you so upset and I wish I could turn back time for you, but I can't. Because it's all I can do."

Her tears fell.

"Oh come here." He shifted round the window seat to take her into his arms. "Your dad was an amazing guy and maybe we can find something to do in his honour. Something to … commemorate him."

"Like what?"

"I don't know." Speaking off the top of his head again without thinking it through, but perhaps it was an inspired idea after all. He said, "I guess we'll find out."

Cecily, waiting to buy the glass of Southern Comfort she'd been promising herself all day, asked herself why it was she'd allowed habit victory over imagination. There were enough pubs and bars within walking distance of home that she could drink in a different one every night of the month, but during the summer months and whether she was meeting anyone here or not, she was drawn irresistibly to Patrick's.

Back in the day, of course, and she had never admitted this out loud to anyone, she had come, indulging her inner Mrs Robinson, to look at Gil. She had thought him sexy and beautiful and when, to her astonishment one night after a great deal of alcohol-fuelled flirting, he had said he felt the same they had begun a relationship which had fluctuated between so casual it barely existed and as serious as it gets. Nine years down the line, he was her best friend. An unlikely consequence, perhaps, but she was grateful for it. And if she found him sexier and even more beautiful in his present maturity than he had been in youth and no one would or could ever replace him in her heart, well maybe that was how it was meant to be.

She bought her drink, knocked back half of it immediately, and ordered another. The barman – Lucy's squeeze, Mark – laughed and said he would have to keep an eye on her tonight and as she was agreeing with him and glancing round for somewhere to sit, there he was. Gil. Alone in a corner with his saturnine face on. She picked up her glasses and wended her way towards him.

"Hello." She perched on the only other stool at his table.

"Hi." His smile was wry. He spotted her drinks. "Been that sort of day?"

"It has. For you too?"

He nodded.

"Do you want to talk?"

He sighed. "I can't, really. It's not my shit."

"It's hers? Your lovely lady's?"

"Yeah." He paused, settled for – "She's going through a really horrible time."

"And you're doing your Gil thing and being there for her?"

"Isn't that what everyone does?"

Cecily smiled. "No, it isn't." So where is she now? she wanted to ask. Have you abandoned her to her really horrible time to come to Patrick's and get leathered? She decided she didn't care. Time alone with him was a rarity these days. Questioning it and maybe annoying him wasn't the way she wanted to spend it. She said, "Oh, I know what I was going to tell you."

He smiled. "Go on."

"Eve Callaghan accosted Henry in here yesterday, and under the guise of her saving the world gig, she was asking him about you."

"About *me*? More about that kid I yanked out of the water?"

"No, in fact. It sounds as if she wanted Henry to spill the beans, but you know what he's like. Garrulous and indiscreet are not his middle names."

"What beans?"

"Any beans."

172

He raised an eyebrow. "Jeez."

"Maybe she fancies you."

He laughed.

"Why not? It has been known."

"Believe me. Eve Callaghan does not fancy me. Are we really using the word fancy here?"

"So why," Cecily said, "would she be asking questions about you?"

"I dunno." He drained his glass. "D'you want another?"

"Oh go on then."

When he returned from the bar she said, "So what do you want me to tell old Eve? When she comes asking me The Truth About The Real Gil Hunt?"

He grinned. "We could invent something, couldn't we? What could I have done that she'd really go for? Espionage? Murder? Grand larceny?"

"You could be leading a double life. We could lay a fake trail to make her think she's unearthed some momentous crime. You could be Lord Lucan."

"Yeah, how old would he be now?"

"Well you know. Something equally scandalous."

They both considered. Gil said eventually, "We must have really boring lives."

She laughed. "They're the best kind, I sometimes think. Interesting tends to be synonymous with tragic."

She wished she hadn't said it, for he was plunged back into gloom. "It's moving on from the tragedy though, isn't it? That's what defines who we are."

"Yes," she said soberly. "Like, not the hand you're dealt but how you play it." He nodded. She watched his face. "*Are* you all right? I know it's not my business, but if you're not … "

"Thanks. I'm fine. Really. It's just it's sometimes harder to see someone you care about in pain than to deal with your own, isn't it?"

"It's always harder." She frowned, feeling her way. "Do you think she won't cope?"

He sighed. "I don't know. I'd like to say, sure she will. A week ago – yesterday - that's what I'd have said. But now … "

He shook his head. "Ah, take no notice of me. I just kind of didn't see this coming."

It sounded to Cecily like a tangled mass of riddles and sadness and if it wasn't hers to unravel, that didn't stop her wanting Gil clear of it. "She's lucky to have you to help her through it," she said. He smiled ruefully. Later, when they were saying goodnight, he hugged her hard. "If you need a break," she said, "from being a tower of strength, you know where I am."

"I do. Thank you." He kissed her forehead. "It means a lot."

She watched him go. Maybe, she told herself again and with a heavier heart, this is how it's meant to be. Her mobile buzzed with a text. *On my way*, Henry said. *With wine chocs & dvd xxx*. She raised her eyes to the spot where a moment ago Gil had been standing and wondered who would've thought that one day and with such huge regret he would be her road not taken.

Jem began with the newspapers in the sitting-room and the unopened circulars. Off the floor and the bureau and into the black bin liner. Easy. After that she stopped. What else was there that didn't matter? Her courage quailed a little. Anything relating to his work she had boxed up into storage when the gallery had been cleared; now only his sketches and a couple of sets of paints and pastels remained. Her father had always been very good at separating work and home once he had acquired the gallery and her mother, she recalled, had been delighted at the space this freed up and which she had immediately filled with her boxes of the dead. She cast around for something else to dispose of which wouldn't cost her too much in the way of composure. When Gil arrived she wanted him to see that she had made a start, that his promise of support yesterday had inspired her with the confidence to begin.

It had been so much more, of course, than a promise of support.

He said he loved her.

She felt shell-shocked, by the release of her own emotions

after having guarded them so carefully for so long, by his compassion and the admission which she had wanted so desperately and which changed everything. Because if he loved her, he might be around for longer than she had dared hope and she had a responsibility to him: shackling him to her own distress wasn't it. So she had suggested that she spend last night here alone, releasing him to a world where no one was crying or making demands of him or needing comfort. She was grieving but she wasn't stupid. Why should he stay, when what had begun as summer passion had darkened and twisted into something depressing and exhausting? She could see quite clearly that she had suddenly become a very different proposition.

But he said he loved her. And he had offered to help without being asked. And if she could show him how much that meant, maybe he would be able to see the old spirited and amorous Jem in the new weepy and feeble one and he wouldn't want to run screaming for the hills.

It was one thing though, reasoning this out in her head. The reality of decades of her parents' belongings was quite another. She went into her father's bedroom and opened the windows, sat on the bed and looked hopelessly at his wardrobe and chest of drawers. I can't do it, she panicked. I can't open them and take out his clothes.

"Oh for God's sake," Alex said. "Just bin the lot."

She looked at him, standing by the window, the curtain shifting behind him in the breeze. "What are you *doing* here? You're supposed to have gone."

"Well I have. I thought you needed a bit of encouragement."

"You didn't tell me you knew Gil."

"How could I tell you that? You hadn't met him yet." He looked at her fondly. "You need to get a grip with all this, Puddle."

"I know. I am."

"These things … " He gestured. "That cupboard out there. It all has to go. Take it to the tip. Incinerate it. You need to be free of it all."

She nodded. "I know that too."

175

He smiled.

The doorbell rang. *Gil.* She ran down the stairs to let him in.

"Hey." He embraced her. "You okay?"

"I am, I think. Look." She showed him the bin liner she'd filled. "I made a start."

"You did." He smiled. She took him up to Alex's room. "I need to bite the bullet in here. And I was thinking about what you said, about just keeping the things he'd want me to keep."

"Okay." He helped her to systematically empty the wardrobe and drawers. If it was creeping him out, he didn't show it. Silently she began to take from the growing piles of wool and denim a couple of shirts, a few jumpers. They talked, with paper-thin conviction, of other things.

"Oh he was hopeless!" she cried suddenly. Gil stopped emptying and looked at her. "He only ever wore the same dozen things. Everything else is like it was new. How can I bin it all? What do people usually do?"

"Well ... I guess they take it to charity shops."

The clothes of the dead. She stared at him, at the holey fishermen's jumpers and corduroy trousers thin at the knees, at a pristine white dress shirt and black dinner jacket she'd never seen her father wear.

"Or not," Gil said, watching her.

She swallowed. "I need some air."

In the garden she took deep breaths, pressed the heels of her hands against her eyes. *I can't do it. Can't do it can't do it.* Gil, behind her, touched her shoulder. "Do you want me to go?"

She shook her head. "Sorry. *Sorry.* It's my mum."

He waited.

"She used to buy charity shop clothes by the ton and store them all in the house. She told us she was going to make things with the material but she never did. One day I came home from school and found her burying them out here. She said it was to free their souls." She watched his frown of concern deepen into disbelief.

"Was she - ?"

"Fragile." She nodded. "For – well, forever really. I didn't understand, when I was little, and there were times when she was fine and times when she hid it well and then there were times when it was just very frightening." She shrugged. "We didn't talk about it, me and Dad. It was as if it was too much for us to deal with. And time passed and … " She stopped, gazing at the flower beds her father had, fourteen years ago, excavated again and again until they were no longer a burial ground

Gil said, "What happened to her?"

She was quiet for a minute, gathering courage. She could see her father now, coming down the garden towards her in his old t-shirt and painty jeans, to sit with her and talk about barbecues and humanity. "I didn't know, for such a long time. When she died I thought maybe she'd had something like cancer and they hadn't told me, or there'd been an accident, and it was so terrible Dad couldn't talk about it. It was like a door had suddenly closed, and it was just me and him, and everything was calm. But what happened, what actually happened, was that she walked into the sea."

Chapter Twenty-three

We don't dump the car, in the end. We return it to the Nice branch of the car hire company like we were normal people. They smile and thank us and give Gil his deposit back, like we were normal people. No sirens start whooping, no one rushes at us with guns. We step back out into the noise and traffic of a city we do not know, vulnerable without the carapace of the car to shield us. We've hardly spoken.

I follow him, since he seems somehow to know where he's going, across roads and down long palm tree lined walks of hotels and shops. It's warmer here, though it's still early, the sky pale and clear, only a handful of tourists strolling in the sunshine. I'm desperately hungry but daren't say so. Daren't say anything. I want an alternative to trailing miserably at his heels but I can't now imagine a world in which I have options.

After a while the signs for Nice Ville seem closer together and there it is, a huge grand pillared building with a curving roof, as if the French rail network were something to be proud of. I think of the Victorian stations at home and their squat modern concrete counterparts. Nothing at all to celebrate there. Gil heads towards the ticket office and I leave him to it, sit down on the edge of a bench. The station is busier than anywhere I've seen since we arrived in France, but we've mainly stuck to the countryside and the emptying holiday resorts. It feels lonelier here, lost in the rush and clamour of people who are at home, in the assaulting babble of a foreign language. I feel lonelier here.

Gil is heading back to me, tucking his wallet into the inside pocket of his canvas jacket. "The train leaves at five to eleven," he informs me. "We have to change twice, at Ventimiglia and Milan."

Ventimiglia and Milan. The names should fill me with excitement. It should be a glamorous adventure, not a grubby and frightening flight from hell. Through hell. I have no idea what we're going to do when we arrive in Venice, apart from search for the gallery of Livio De Marchi and even that has lost its appeal now. I want to crawl under the bench and sleep forever. He says, with barely concealed impatience, "Do you want to get some break-fast?"

I shrug and suddenly if he could hit me with impunity in front of all these people I think he would. He grabs my arm and jerks me to my feet, makes me walk fast with him to a quiet corner. I wilt against a pillar. "Now. You tell me," he says furiously, "you tell me what the fuck you think happened back there."

"At the petrol station?"

"No. In Disneyland. Yes, at the petrol station. Jesus!"

"I don't know." I rub my arm, which is sore from his grip. "You disappeared. I was scared something had happened to you. Then I saw the car with the smiley face and it was empty."

"And you assumed I had – what?"

"I don't know," I repeat. "What did happen?"

He sighs. "I paid for the petrol. I saw the car. It was empty, like you found it. I took a look around. Nothing. Which was weird. I got back to the car and the rest you know." He glares at me. "Why? What did you think?"

I swallow. He knows this anyway. He's just bullying it out of me. "You said you wouldn't be hunted down. You said you couldn't answer for the consequences. I thought maybe you'd … maybe he'd … attacked you and … "

"You thought I'd killed him."

"No! Hurt him. Put him out of action."

He laughs, disbelief tinged with hysteria. "Put him out of action?"

"You could do that."

"I could." He looks at me. "What I couldn't do is kill someone."

"You were crying."

"I'm knackered and scared and I can't honestly see a way out of this. Tell me in the circumstances crying is a strange reaction." His eyes are still holding mine. "You have to trust me. We have to trust each other."

179

I nod, dumbly. Once upon a time he'd have held me now. He doesn't.

"Because, you know, we can't lose sight of the fact that the car was there and it was empty. It didn't get there all by itself."

I think about this, but I'm tired. So tired. "If he was there and he was waiting and he followed us to Nice – we have to change trains twice today. I think that's a good thing."

"Yeah. So do I." His face relaxes a little and he almost smiles. "Come on. Coffee. Food. It'll help."

"All right."

I go with him to the buffet and watch him order breakfast. Even now he does a good job of being charming, sounding normal. I should be grateful for it. And I want to trust him. I do. But when the civilised masks have been ripped away and the madness behind them unleashed it's hard to trust even the people you love.

I don't trust myself anymore.

I just want it to be over.

Chapter Twenty-four

His instinct had been to get her away from the house, as though the horror had been not lodged in her mother's instability and her father's appalling accident but emanated yet from stone and slate and wood. The nearest café was shabby without being chic; he bought pastries and strong coffee and returning to their table found her looking so much better, so much less likely to be on the point of complete meltdown, that it seemed his instinct was proved right.

She was watching him, said anxiously, "I'm sorry. I'm *so* sorry. We were having such a lovely time and I've ruined it – "

"Jem – "

" - but not telling you was like lying to you, all the time, and I couldn't – "

"Stop, now."

"I'd understand, you know, if you wanted to run a mile."

"I'm not going anywhere."

She shut up. He watched her face, stroked her hand across the table. "Tell me what happened, with your mum."

She took a breath. "Well of course no one knows exactly what happened. Like with Dad." Her voice wavered briefly. "There was no note, there'd been no warning. Dad said that she hadn't even seemed particularly low. She disappeared … and then they found her. And then there was this endless, terrible silence, which we had to learn to live with." She paused. "I always thought I'd accepted her death but that he had a really hard time with it. Then the last time we talked about her, I realised we'd coped, or not coped, the same way. We both shut it out. It feels so heartless now, when I can't think about Dad, or the way he died, or what he meant to me, without … "

Crying. Which she was on the brink of doing. Gil held her hand. "Don't be so hard on yourself. You were a child when she died."

She nodded. "And it was her choice, if you believe taking your own life is a choice. But Dad ... it feels vicious. Like he was torn from the world. He was my hero, Gil. I don't know how to live my life without him."

He squeezed her hand. He was without words. For what did he know about coping with grief? She drank her coffee, picked at the pastry. He watched her slowly, determinedly, regaining some degree of composure. After a moment she began, "Have you ... ?"

"What?"

"Told anyone? Your friends?"

"Only one, and only that you're having a rough time."

"Will you keep this between us?"

"Of course. It's private, I get that."

"Okay. Thank you." She paused. "So here's what I think I should do, today. I'm going to pick up my stall and get out there on the pier and sell my stuff like Dad was always nagging me to do. Afterwards I'll go home and pack up the rest of his clothes and then I'll meet you and we'll do something nice."

It was a close call, he thought, but her courage wrenched at him almost more than her tears.

Business slowed, as it always did, around six. Cecily closed the café at seven but before then most of her customers had returned to wash the beach from their skin and their swimsuits before dining at their hotels and guesthouses or eating out in town. At this hour she was always occupied with filling the dishwasher, clearing tables, separating food which would last until tomorrow from food which wouldn't, emptying the dishwasher, feeding last minute customers, gradually winding down the cycle until the door had jangled for the last time and the café itself seemed to sigh with the silence. Today as she cling-filmed cakes and pies and dishes of salad she remembered that a couple of hours back she had seen Gil heading to his studio alone. She lifted the receiver from the wall and dialled. "Hi," she said in response to his grunt. "Free food downstairs if you're hungry."

"Free stale food?"

"If you're quick. It's like the Harrod's sale in here."

"Five minutes."

Half an hour later he appeared. Brooding again, she saw immediately. "Help your-self," she gestured towards the various platters on the counter. He looked at them without interest.

"Got any scotch?"

"Sure." She frowned, poured him some from her secret stash which she kept meaning to move as Justine was bound to discover and plunder it before long.

"Thanks." Gil sat down on the stool beside the counter and knocked back a mouthful.

She tilted the last two inches of Sauvignon Blanc into a glass for herself. "How're you?"

"Don't ask."

"Okay." She regarded him with sympathy.

"What about you?" He looked at her beseechingly. "Tell me something funny or annoying or just fucking *normal*, for Christ's sake."

"Still not asking."

He groaned. "Ah, Cecily. Come here."

She went, and he hugged her, hard, for a long moment. She tried not, given his distress, to enjoy it too much.

"Thanks." He swallowed some more scotch. "It's just, I feel such an arsehole. Jem's going through such horrors, she's distraught and trying to be brave, and there was a minute today when I thought – shit, I don't know if I can deal with this."

"That's not being an arsehole, that's being human."

"You think?"

"Oh Gil, no one's strong all the time. Does she expect that of you?"

"No."

"But you expect it of yourself."

He put his head in his hands for a minute, then looked back up at her. "I expect as a grown man to be able to handle the shit life throws at us without wanting to do a runner. I know I can be all shallow charm when it suits but … " He paused, said with difficulty, "I can generally see what is the right thing to say or do in a situation, and in times of need I can usually pull it out of the bag. I'm starting to wonder if that makes me a good person or if it just makes me a fucking opportunist."

She said, "It isn't opportunism. Even if it makes you feel better about yourself, and through helping her you get your lovely girlfriend back, that's only the self-interest we all have in performing apparently unselfish acts."

"Kind of a by-product."

"Yes. Or a reward."

He shook his head. "There're no rewards here. Nothing's ever going to make it all right. It's about doing what has to be done and then living with it."

"I understand about that," she said.

"Yes, of course you do. I'm sorry. Bit blinkered at the moment."

He looked so dispirited her heart went out to him. "Another hug?"

"Please."

She did register the tinkle of the door chimes, in a part of her head which wasn't focussed on Gil's arms around her and the smell of his skin, so when Henry said, in tones of forced jocularity, "Not interrupting anything, am I?" she wasn't entirely surprised.

They moved apart. Gil said, "Hey, Henry."

He looked, expectant, from one to the other. No explanation was forthcoming. Gil cleared his throat. "I need to get going. Thanks, Cecily."

"Any time. Let me know, how things are."

He nodded, his eyes more eloquent than his words. "I will."

Henry cut himself a slice of pie from one of the platters and said, when Gil had gone, "What's the matter with him?"

"Oh, he's just really down at the moment."

"Has he split up with whatsherface?"

"No." She decided to open another bottle of wine.

"So what's he thanking you for?"

"For listening," she said crisply, "and giving him a hug when he needed one." Don't, she thought. Don't take that tone and make me voice any of the thoughts churning through my head at the moment. Just don't.

He said, "Right."

She glanced at him but he was preoccupied with the pie and some of the bean salad. "Fancy a drink later?" he said. "Down at Patrick's?"

"Yes all right." Her heart sank a little. He will move to Brisbane, she thought, and he will join his cousin's watersports business and find a bar he likes and recreate the life he has here and *nothing will change*. Except the accent. And the sunshine. If she had ever been tempted she knew at that moment and with absolute certainty that she would not be going with him.

Jem folded away the last of her father's clothes and sat back on her heels. That's it, she told him in her head. It's done now. He didn't reply. She pushed to her feet, padded through to the kitchen and made herself a mug of tea, which she took upstairs to her room. More than an hour until Gil would be here and she felt strangely empty. No great gulping sobs. No edge-of-hysteria rambling. Only drained and tired and a little bit calm. It has taken nearly four months, she thought. Four months and Gil, to get me to this point. Maybe tonight I'll be able to talk to him rationally about something other than me. Maybe he'll look at me with desire again instead of a mixture of pity and panic.

On her desk, beside the tubs of jewellery paraphernalia, sat the raffia-tied pile of books. She trailed her finger down their various spines. Her mother had recorded her thoughts in a range of formal five year diaries, flowery notepads and school exercise books. Jem took a deep breath. She knew they had been erratically kept, months of blank pages followed by tiny illegible scrawl. She knew that deciphering it would reveal to her things she would rather not know. She tugged one at random from the pile and opened it in the middle. The year was 1988. Jem had been four years old.

To her surprise there were entries in handwriting she remembered, her mother's round cursive script from birthday cards and shopping lists, detailing here the progress of her pupils' piano lessons, her pride in or exasperation with their efforts. Jem recalled the plinky plonky sounds from the living room, the children trooping in and out while she sat at the kitchen table with her school reading books and a tray of plastic beads. Later that year, Marianne had written of a trip to London, Easter holidays, the domestic events and trivia anyone might reasonably expect from their mother's diary. She sounded by turns content, excited, bored. Jem raced on, speeding through the snowfields of empty pages in search of further instalments. I never had a grip of who she was, Jem thought, when she wasn't at one of her extremes. I was too young and I didn't know her well enough. Maybe these diaries, if she only read the rational extracts, might give her that, an insight into the woman her mother had been. She looked at the pile which now represented to her the truth. And the question, suddenly, was no longer how could she bear to read them, but how could she not?

For the first time since the beginning of the season they had arrived at the opportune moment and some of the wicker seating on the boardwalk outside Patrick's was free. Cecily curled into one of the wide Colonial style chairs and threw her shawl over another while Henry queued in the growing tumult of the bar for their drinks. As usual he could glance around and see a dozen or more people he knew; a dozen or more people who knew him. Henry was tired of people who knew him, knew what he thought, what he wanted, which way he'd jump. Tired of being judged on the way he looked, and spoke. Tired of being judged on what he wasn't. He flipped a beermat over while he waited. Over again. And again. It was time for a fresh start. Not that he imagined the Australians applied a policy of non-judgement to their immigrants but by then he would be three stone lighter, dynamic, positive and full of self-belief. He would be a different person.

For now, though, he was still inescapably himself. So when he sat down crushing Cecily's shawl his first words were, "So what's going on between Gil and the new woman, then?"

Cecily said, "I don't know."

"He didn't tell you?"

"I didn't ask him." She had that don't-diss-Gil look in her eyes which drove him insane. When he'd come into the café to find them in each other's arms he'd wanted to knock Gil to the floor. She added, "Much as I would love to know, it's none of my business. It's hard, isn't it, when your friends start seeing someone and suddenly there're whole areas of their life which're off-limits."

He chose not to say that it hadn't looked as though there was much between them which was off-limits. "He still talks to you though."

"Sure. We haven't vanished from each other's lives. But Henry, it works both ways. He doesn't tell me private things about her, I don't tell him about you."

"But he knows me. There's nothing to tell."

"If there were, and it was something you didn't want him to know, he wouldn't hear it from me." He could hear the deliberate patience in her voice. She thought he was being tiresome. Perhaps he was. He couldn't help it. She said, "You promised you'd stop being jealous of him."

He had. He had promised her that. She uncurled her legs to rest her bare feet on his thighs and he smiled. "I'm sorry. I let him get to me."

"You were friends before we started seeing each other."

"Well we were, but he always got under my skin."

"Why?" She smiled too. He was massaging the ball of her right foot hard with his thumb, just the way she liked.

"Oh you know. The way he looks. The way he acts. The way he is with you, as if he owns you."

"Nobody owns anybody, Henry." She sipped her drink. "Nobody gives a massage like you do, either."

He wished they could spend all their time together free of the impingements of other people, of Gil and Buz and Radar, of her customers and his watersports kids. If he could transport her with him to a hospitable desert island for the rest of their lives he wouldn't want for much. They talked, of other things, the music and voices from the bar muffled behind them, the fairy lights strung around the wooden frame bright in the evening sky. In so many ways, he thought, this final summer had been the best he'd ever spent here and he could see its numbered days dwindling too quickly into autumn. The thought of anything spoiling them was more than he could bear.

It was the third or fourth time he'd waded back into Patrick's for more drinks that he saw her. She was sitting at the bar, as Cecily did sometimes, chatting to Mark and Lucy as they filled glasses and returned change. Observing the crowd. As the man beside her moved steadily away, precariously balancing three drinks in the triangle of his hands, Henry jostled his left arm and half his chest into the small space left behind. "Eve Callaghan," he greeted her.

She smiled. "Hello Henry." She had yellow teeth.

He indicated her nearly empty glass. "What can I get you?"

"Oh, thank you. G and T."

"Ice and a slice?"

She laughed. "Please. You having a good evening?"

"I am. Just sitting out on the boardwalk."

"I know. With Cecily Ward. I spotted you earlier."

There couldn't be much, he thought, that she missed. There couldn't be many people in this town whose names she didn't know, with whose lives she wasn't at least passingly familiar. He thought of the conversation they'd had in here a few days ago, of the interest in someone she'd pretended not to be taking. Of the way he had felt tonight and for weeks now. He said, "You were asking me the other day about Gil Hunt."

"I was," she agreed.

Henry smiled. "What would you like to know?"

Alex had taken down every painting from the north-facing wall of the gallery and stood surrounded by canvases old and new, kneading the muscles in his shoulders as they loosened for the first time in he didn't know how long. Jem was away for three days on a school camping trip. Eve Callaghan had swooped into town and plucked Marianne from the house, bearing her away for the weekend to listen to the sorry details of Eve's divorce proceedings. Alex felt some sympathy for Eve, but if she would insist on marrying a man who was quite clearly the biggest toe-rag this side of the Tamar valley, what could she expect? Marianne had been far more partisan, providing hours of patient listening, pots of tea and a succession of gin and tonics. Her excitement at the prospect of a girls' weekend away had only been equalled by Alex's relief and unspoken gratitude that she wanted to go. He knew Jem was safe, trusted Eve, and never got time off. He wasn't sure he'd know how to conduct himself.

So here he was, somewhat predictably, playing to his heart's content in his gallery. Later he might amble up to the inn on the square and sink a couple of pints. Steady on, he smiled. Living on the edge there. Was he too old, at thirty-eight, for wild behaviour? He didn't know. He had barely had any practice. He frowned at the whitewashed stone in front of him, different arrangements of paintings appearing in his mind's eye. Large seascapes tended to draw the tourists, great washes of endless ocean and empty skies. He wondered sometimes where they put these pictures when they took them home. Were they hung on the chimney breasts of narrow terraces? In the darkened halls of suburban semis? He couldn't envisage his paintings being viewed in anything but the space and clarity of light in which he had painted them. Perhaps they were imbued with some of that space and clarity of light and took it with them into the terraces and semis. Perhaps they were hung to cover a stain on the wallpaper.

The door opened and he pivoted towards the young woman who'd stepped into the gallery. Younger than he was, anyway, and wearing a fitted rose-patterned dress, curls the colour of liquid honey tumbling to her waist. "Good afternoon," he smiled.

"Hello." She sounded exhilarated, as if something exciting had just happened outside in the street. He glanced past her into an ordinary June day, post Whitsun, pre-summer, the sunshine warm but not to be relied upon. He shifted some of the paintings to give her room.

"Oh sorry, are you open?" she said.

"I am, just having a bit of a reshuffle."

She smiled, gestured vaguely. "Can I ... ?"

"Help yourself." He returned to the older canvases, began carrying them one at a time into his workshop, sliding them carefully into the rack he had built for just this purpose. The only other furniture in the room was the chest, littered with Jem's drawings and the pastels she'd been trying out last time she was here, a couple of stools, and his easel bearing a half-finished painting. He looked at it, decided he would stay here this evening and paint until the light faded, make the most of this gift of freedom. After a few minutes he heard the lilt of the voice of the woman in the rose-patterned dress and he stepped back into the gallery. "Sorry?"

"Oh. I was wondering, are they all yours?"

"Most of them. The ones on this wall – " He indicated the

relevant corner " – are the work of a couple of friends of mine, also local artists. But yeah, I'm responsible for everything else, I'm afraid."

She smiled at his self-deprecating tone and turned, flatteringly, away from his friends' art to inspect his. "Technically?" she said. "I know nothing. If I were try to sound clever I'd probably say all the wrong things and expose myself as a hopeless ingénue. But I think these are beautiful."

"That really isn't the wrong thing to say."

She laughed, strolling from one picture to another, her head slightly on one side, eyes narrowed. "What I love is the way you capture atmosphere, the way you convey a sense of a place through – well – paint. It's magical."

"Thank you."

She grinned. "So that's the opinion of the uneducated."

"What can I say? Even ingénues know what they like."

"I do know what I like. And I'm going to buy one."

"Really?"

"Of course really. Don't I look like a serious buyer to you?" She was teasing him. He couldn't remember the last time he'd had a conversation like this. Couldn't remember the last time he'd felt this precise stirring in his veins. He allowed himself to watch her while she prowled in front of his paintings. She was lovely, the sharpness of her features softened by her hair and her smile, her vitality. Finally she selected a scene set at Clodgy Point in winter, the smack of the sea against the rocks, darkened skies, blue-black waves, an energy and intimation of danger which he felt he'd almost caught. "You can taste the spray," she said.

"Sometimes," he lifted the painting from it hook, "I try to represent the Cornwall the tourists don't see."

"The drama and the isolation?"

"Exactly." He wrapped the picture for her. She picked up one of the promotional leaflets he'd had printed from the counter.

"Can I take one of these?"

"Of course."

She wrote him a cheque. He watched her hand holding the

pen, the loose curling tendrils of her hair, the shape of her mouth. "There!" She smiled. "Thank you. It will take pride of place."

Nothing had happened, he reminded himself, after she'd gone and he was alone again among his canvases and empty space, feeling as guilty and as aroused as if he had lifted her hair and kissed the tanned skin where her shoulder curved towards her neck.

Nothing had happened.

Chapter Twenty-five

The train is surprisingly quiet, late-morning, mid-week, out-of-season, and Gil and I have an area of the carriage all to ourselves. It's in pristine condition and the seats are huge: Utopian train travel. "I can't believe," I tell him, "you bought first class tickets."

"I didn't realise, I was too stressed. I thought they were expensive." He bundles our rucksacks into the compartments above our heads and sits down. We are going to be sitting opposite each other, on three different trains, all the way to Venice. I remember when seeing his black and white image in a newspaper made my heart race, when he could arouse me without touching me. Now we can't even look each other in the face.

"There is no escape, is there, on a train?" I observe. "You're trapped, unless you jump off or climb onto the roof like in *Indiana Jones*. Now you're going to tell me there's no escape anyway."

He gestures – you got it. He's bought a copy of The Times, which he would never read at home, from the station and put it on the table between us. We gaze at headline news of climate change and war in oil-rich countries and global economic recession. I wish it had the power to depress me. The train jerks and begins to slide, soundlessly, along the platform. I watch Nice Ville disappear into the distance. "You should sleep," he tells me.

"It's only an hour to Ventimiglia."

He closes his eyes.

"We could play I-Spy."

"Jesus," he says without opening them. "It's like being with a fucking child."

I study the folded newspaper. There will be a crossword in it, but it'll be too hard for me. I think of Dad and his wretched sudoko puzzles and my vision blurs for a moment. I say, tremulously, "When we get to Venice, do you think we should go our separate ways?"

That opens his eyes. "Is that what you want?"

"Is it what you want?"

We stare at each other, the glove thrown down. He says, "What would you do?"

"I don't know. Find … somewhere."

"And do what?"

"Well what would you do?"

"Disappear, Jem." He rubs his eyes. "Just disappear."

We gaze at each other. "Shit," I say.

"Yeah."

It's a beautiful September day outside, the sun shining on the Provençal countryside, and I'm shivering. "I don't … " I begin, "I don't want … " A tear falls fast down my cheek and he looks at me with less hostility. "Do you wish," I ask him, "that I hadn't told you? That I'd never told you my dad was dead?"

He says nothing.

"Do you wish we'd never met?"

He glances away. "Kind of. Yeah."

I swallow hard. "I don't know where I'd be, now, if … "

"Well you wouldn't be here."

This is true. I lean back against the curved headrest of my seat, tears still trickling. I'd be at home, still mad with grief, as I am now. I would still, somehow, have discovered the truth. I'm fairly sure of that. I say, "It might not have been very different."

"It would have been different for Cecily, and Henry. It would have been different for me."

I remember a different train, cold and dirty, rattling through the night, skinheads with beercans, silent shapes behind laptops. I remember being dazed with shock, hardly able to walk, vomiting in the toilet basin. I say, "What if they're there, when we get to Venice? What if they're waiting for us?"

Gil surveys me. "It doesn't matter."

"But – "

"It doesn't matter because it's not really them we have to worry about, is it? We have each other forever, you know that.

194

I'll never leave you. But you thought I murdered someone out there at that garage last night. If all we have left between us is fear and distrust … " He lets the sentence hang for a minute. "Well maybe that's all we deserve."

Chapter Twenty-six

Gil had been itching with suggestions for the gallery since the moment he'd last stepped inside, had so far held off voicing them because he wasn't sure Jem was ready to hear it. Checking on the place for her while she spent the morning at the house wading through memories, he found the building was safe – no broken windows or forced locks – but noticed how quickly a sense of neglect had crept in; four months since Alex's death and the airy, low-ceilinged rooms seemed damp and forlorn. Gil longed to tear down the boards and throw open the windows, to sweep the floors and repaint the walls. His workshop in Bristol was nowhere near as large or light or well located and he could see the difference this place could make to Jem's peace of mind as well as to her business. Plus, of course, it had been her father's. It would be a natural progression for her to reopen it as her own. But then the house on the cliff road had been her father's too and the change in ambience couldn't be greater.

He had woken suddenly there this morning, jerking into consciousness as though someone in another room had called his name. For the second before his brain engaged he'd had no idea where he was, and while in summers past waking in unfamiliar bedrooms had been the norm, this time the instant of confusion had him panicked. Purple cushions, patchwork quilt and – his heartrate had slowed again – a bare shoulder tattooed with the tiniest black star, a mass of dark hair across the pillow. He'd watched her for a minute while she slept, the shape of her mouth, the tilt of her cheekbones. Jem was beautiful, no question. Beautiful and sexy and talented and vulnerable; an irresistible combination. He just wished the baggage yoked to the vulnerable part didn't make him so deeply uneasy. Last night, after too much wine and drowsy sex, he'd fallen swiftly asleep but otherwise being here he was too spooked to relax. He got up, grabbed his jeans from the floor, went to the bathroom and paused afterwards on the landing at the open cupboard doors. Yesterday after dinner at *bluewave* and a long walk on the beach, she had seemed a little better. She'd been thoughtful and composed and hadn't cried once. Far, far too early to describe it as progress but all the same he didn't want this – he'd glanced the length and breadth of the cupboard – setting her back. It wasn't only her mother's life boxed up in here, it was Alex's too, and if it were Gil's choice he would keep it that way. He'd close the doors on it all.

Now he found himself wanting to linger in the great echoing space of the gallery, to draw up plans on Jem's behalf. Would she like him thinking of her future or would he appear insensitive, rushing her into decisions she wasn't yet ready to make? He let out his breath, ran his hand across the stained surface of the chest Alex had used to store paints and brushes, and remembered the man who had almost been his friend, thought of him all fired up about capturing the spirit of Tintagel, the ideas he must have had, the hopes. Such a terrible waste, Gil thought, stricken. An appalling, tragic waste.

He needed to return to his own work, to the Tree of Life which Jem seemed convinced would make his name. Scooping up the key, he heard the squeak and shove of the external door and walked back to the threshold between gallery and workshop to find Eve Callaghan, waiting.

"Hello," he said, imbuing the single word with – *and you're here why?*

"I saw you come in," she replied.

"You wanted me?"

"I did." She dropped her bag to the floor, stuck her hands in the pockets of her jeans. There was nothing on which to sit, no source of distraction. Nowhere to hide, Gil thought. She said, "I have to say something to you which might … " She corrected herself. "Which *will* seem out of order."

He frowned, intrigued despite himself. Already this wasn't the Eve Callaghan who'd banged on about heroes and campaigns, who'd talked to him as though he were interesting and stupid at the same time. "Go on."

"You're involved with Jemima Gregory."

He and Jem could be seen together most days, on the pier, the beach, in *bluewave*. He was mildly surprised she had noticed, but then noticing people was her job. "I am."

"You do know who she is?"

"I know this was her father's place. I know he died recently. Is that what you mean?"

"You know about her mother?"

Gil, distrustful, said nothing.

Eve sighed. "They were … well, I knew them both, Alex and Marianne. They were my friends. Marianne was my piano teacher when I was a teenager, a decade later she helped me through my divorce." She looked at him. "I'm not here in any professional capacity today. I've come because I've known Jemima since she was a little girl."

"Okay," he said warily.

"Marianne … she wasn't solely responsible, you know, for being unhappy. For what she did."

Gil shook his head. "I don't think you should be telling me this."

"But I should. Because Jemima worshipped her dad and when she finds out she'll need someone there for her. Assuming she hasn't already, of course."

"Found out what? You're saying that Alex was partly responsible?"

She held his gaze.

He was impatient suddenly. "We all affect what happens to other people. You have a row with someone, they crash the car. It doesn't make you responsible for their death."

Eve said quietly, "There was more to it than that."

"Well don't hold back now."

"I suppose," she said, visibly reconsidering, "I feel guilty. I've always felt guilty. She was my friend and I didn't … I wasn't there for her. I didn't realise how desperate she was. Alex was a very attractive man, you know." She stopped. "Don't let her down, Gil."

He frowned, trying to make some sort of sense of her hints and fragments. "Why would I let her down?"

She cocked her head, and he knew that here it came. The

part that was out of order. "Jemima needs stability and protection and I'm afraid you won't give her that."

"You think I need telling how to treat her?"

"I think your history goes before you."

"Jesus." He reeled, decided he wasn't going to defend or explain. Instead he walked to the door, held it open. "You know what? You were right. You're bang out of order."

She took the hint, paused in the doorway. "I'm concerned for her, that's all. Do you honestly think you're capable of being there for someone when all your adult life you've been selfish and irresponsible?"

He stared at her, disbelieving. "Who do you think you are? Who the hell have you been talking to?"

She was rueful. "You know the saying – 'Keep your friends close and your enemies closer'? That's what you've been doing."

His head was spinning. Who the fuck ... ? But he knew who. He knew exactly who.

Marianne's diaries were giving Jem a headache. They were also telling her nothing. Nothing except that Marianne had been clever and kind and a bit dippy and spent much of her life see-sawing between lawless elation and numb misery. Nothing Jem had not already known, or at least sensed. Her boxes contained fabrics and musical scores, family photos, recipes she'd never used. Jem pushed up from the floor in front of the cupboard and hobbled downstairs on pins-and-needles feet. In the kitchen she poured herself a glass of apple juice and took it out to the garden. Maybe she'd been wrong, after all. Maybe the deconstructing of her parents' lives was going to be unbearably sad but not the bomb beneath her she had imagined. She sat on the wall and thought about texting Gil.

"How's it going?" Alex asked.

"Not bad, actually." She looked at him, paying close attention because there would be one day when she wouldn't be able to recreate him in such high definition detail anymore. She would remember his thinning dark hair, Celtic green eyes, the cleft in his chin, but it would never be as if he were sitting beside her again. *Dad*, she thought. She said, "Mum was ordinary really, wasn't she?"

"I never thought of her as ordinary."

"I mean, normal. Happy and sad, bored and excited."

"Sure."

"I wish I'd known her better, known her properly."

"You did. You knew her as well as you could possible have done."

She said, "Why did you never have another child?"

A beat. "You know why."

"But the thought that I could have had a brother or sister … "

He squeezed her hand. "I'm sorry. She was struggling to cope as it was, I was afraid that another child might … well. And then it happened anyway."

"But what if it was not having one that made her worse?"

He looked away. "I lived with that, with never knowing the answer to that. With never knowing the answer to a lot of things."

"And now," Jem said, "I have to live with it too."

The air shimmered and he was gone. She drank her apple juice, thought that if Gil were here he would be urging her to do something else now, something practical that she understood. Make some jewellery, update her website. She left her glass on the kitchen worktop and climbed the stairs.

Cecily traditionally opened the café later on a Sunday. Partly as a gift to herself after the inevitable excesses of Saturday nights, partly as due to everyone else's excesses on Saturday nights the café was pretty much empty before lunchtime anyway. Today, woken at dawn by Henry's snoring, she padded barefoot to her kitchen and began scone making with a large cappuccino beside her and Steve Wright's Sunday Love Songs filling the sun-warmed air. A few moments of peace all to myself, she thought contentedly. How lovely. How rare.

How short-lived. The door to the yard, which she had unlocked minutes ago to take out the rubbish, flung open as if the wrath of God were behind it. She jumped, cried out. "Gil!

What on earth … ?"

His eyes were like stone. "Is he here?"

"Henry? Yes, he's asleep. What … ?"

He strode past her towards the foot of the stairs. "I'm going to tear his fucking head off."

"What's the *matter*?" She grabbed his arm and he shook free.

"This isn't about you."

"You're in my house!"

The thunder of Henry, crashing and stumbling down the stairs. Gil flew at him, his fist connecting hard with Henry's nose, sending him staggering back against the wall then rebounding to lunge at Gil's face.

"Stop it!" Cecily shrieked. Gil had the advantage of speed and rage but Henry's weight lent him force. Blows fell. Blood was streaming from Henry's nose, trickled from Gil's cheek. Gil swung for Henry's jaw, catching him off-balance again. Henry toppled against the counter, knocking the radio into the scone mixture before slumping heavily to the floor. Gil stood above him, panting hard.

"Will you stop, now?" She was almost in tears, torn between them. "What's the matter with the pair of you?"

Henry struggled to sit, eyeing Gil with wary anger. "I'm just defending myself." He was sulky, like a small boy after a playground spat. The savagery in Gil's face hadn't waned.

"Do you want to tell her?"

"Nothing to tell."

Gil stared at him. "He sold me to the press."

"She didn't *pay* me."

"Not that kind of selling."

Cecily looked from one to the other, filling in the blanks, appalled. She said, "You did what?"

Henry hauled himself onto a chair. "It was Eve Callaghan not the fucking red-tops."

"Even so." Gil's voice held no less steel.

"And she's not stupid, you know. She knows who everyone is in this town. She's probably been watching you in Patrick's for years – "

"I'm hardly in Patrick's any more - "

" – shagging anything that moves."

"I don't *do* that now."

Cecily said, "Thanks Henry."

"Shit. I didn't mean – "

"I think you should go."

He gaped at her. "He attacked me."

"Sounds as if you attacked him first."

"Oh I might have known whose side – "

"Shut up!" she cried. "It was horrible, witnessing that just now. Apparently I can't talk to you both about it at the same time. And I have a café to open in – oh, look, less than an hour. Just *go*."

He began to say something, changed his mind. The door to the yard shut smartly behind him. Gil, leaning against the sink now, said, "I'm sorry."

"Does your hand hurt?"

"Yeah. Haven't hit anyone for years."

"Sit down."

She fetched her first aid kit, tended to his cheek and bloodied knuckles. "You might have a black eye later."

He caught her wrist. "I am sorry. I shouldn't have involved you."

"Oh Gil, I am involved. He did it because of me, because he's jealous of you. Of us. What did he say to Eve Callaghan, exactly?"

"Told her tales of my sordid past. She now thinks I'm a shallow, untrustworthy bastard and should have my cock amputated as a warning to all other shallow, untrustworthy bastards."

"Is she going to print that?"

"Fuck knows. Who'd care?"

"Well … Gem."

He groaned. "Oh Jesus. And that's not all. I mean, obviously being shat on by Henry is bad enough, but because of it Eve told me something – *implied* something – that … " He stopped. "I can't. Can't tell you. Can't tell her. Keeping a secret's a kind of betrayal though, isn't it."

She gazed at him. He looked awful, she thought. Upset. Beaten. She said softly, "I don't know what you're talking about."

"No." He shook his head. "This just gets worse. And it isn't even my grief."

"But you've taken it on." She smiled wryly. "You don't look as if it isn't your grief."

He touched the already swelling wound beneath his eye and winced. "What will you do about Henry?"

"I don't know." The thought of being in the same room as him chilled her yet she couldn't precisely identify her reaction. Disappointed? Shocked? Disgusted? Not even remotely surprised? She said, "Just at the moment I'm finding it hard to come up with the right words."

Jem gazed at him across the kitchen table. "Okay. Can I ask questions?"

"Sure." He had told her the truth – almost all of the truth – enough of the truth – and she had listened in silence. He was knackered and his face hurt and trying to skirt around the implications of Eve's words had required more dexterity than he felt he possessed just now. But maybe he'd misinterpreted. For what had Eve said, exactly? That she felt guilty. That Marianne had been her friend and that Alex was an attractive man. Where else was he supposed to go with that? She must have known what conclusion he would draw. Then again, quite possibly he was too exhausted and too fraught to see anything but the most traumatic explanation. Because seriously, Alex and Eve? Alex and *Eve*? It didn't square with the man Jem described to him – but then he was her father. It didn't square with his own construction of Alex – but then he'd hardly known him. And what about me? he thought. Would someone knowing me as I am with Jem be shocked to learn of the man I was? Still am? Aren't we all more complex and less predictable than we think?

Jem said, "So Henry is the guy we met on the prom."

"Yes." He was almost relieved. Questions about Henry he could deal with.

"And when did you last sleep with this woman?"

"Cecily. She's called Cecily. I don't know. A year ago."

"A *year* ago? And Henry can't handle that?"

"Apparently not."

"But you're just friends now."

"Yes."

"Right." She nodded. "What did he think Eve was going to do? Write an exposé in the local paper?"

"I guess. 'Pier Hero Sex Addict Unmasked'."

"But that's why he did it. He wasn't to know that Eve was a friend of my parents and would never publish anything that'd hurt me. He thought it'd mean you'd have to come clean to me and it'd wreck what we have. Like he thinks you're capable of wrecking what he and Cecily have. And that's why you hit him."

She was right. He hadn't fully grasped any of that himself, but she was right. "Yeah. That maybe wasn't such a good idea. I was just so fucking angry with him. I completely lost it. The whole red mist thing. I'm sorry."

"Don't be sorry. He deserved it. You trusted him and when someone you trust lets you down it's a terrible, painful thing. It shouldn't be underestimated. And for the record? I don't care what you have been to other people. I just care what you are to me."

He was moved, briefly, beyond words.

She gazed at him. "Your poor face." Thought about it. "Actually you know, it's quite sexy."

He laughed. Painfully. "Great."

She kissed his bruised knuckles, his temple. "It's strange about Eve. She was Mum's friend, she obviously cared enough to read you the riot act, yet I hardly remember her being around after Mum died. Maybe I should talk to her."

He hesitated. "I don't know. What is there to say?"

"I could reassure her she needn't worry about me because you're doing a fantastic job."

"Am I?" He remembered getting drunk with Cecily in Patrick's, sitting in her kitchen with his head in his hands. The truth was, Eve had a point.

"Come on," she said. "I need to shake myself free of all this. Let's go out."

"Sure you want to be seen with me looking like I went ten rounds with Amir Khan?"

"Ten?"

"One." He smiled. She smiled too.

"We could wait until it's dark," she said.

Cecily was sitting on her sofa, her laptop open at an Expedia search for winter flights to Spain, when her mobile buzzed. She frowned at it as it jiggled across the table. HENRY, it said. She ignored it. A moment later her landline chirruped. She ignored that too, as she compared costs and dates and timings. Escaping the intense and tangled world in which she appeared to be living had suddenly become a pressing need.

Five minutes later the pounding on the kitchen door was so hard it was vibrating into the attic. Setting her laptop aside she went downstairs and threw back the bolt, turned the key. Henry stared at her. "You weren't answering your phone."

She folded her arms. "No."

He took a step into the room, closed the door behind him. She didn't move, effectively barring his entrance. He looked pathetic, in all senses. Swollen nose. Self-pitying expression. "I just want to talk to you."

"I've nothing to say to you. And there's nothing you can say that I want to hear."

"Not even that I'm sorry?"

She sighed. "Sometimes 'sorry' doesn't cut it, Henry. Sometimes what you've done is too big for 'sorry' even to come close."

He shifted, uncomfortably. Usually by now she was pouring him a glass of wine and feeding him leftovers. She could tell he was thinking that if he managed to hit upon the right words in the right order that might still happen.

"I didn't think - "

"No." Her gaze was cold. "You didn't. And before you say his name with your usual contempt, this isn't about Gil. I'd feel the same if you'd betrayed Radar, or Buz, or me. Oh no, wait a minute, it was me, wasn't it, by association. Because if you're going to drag Gil through the mud, you're dragging me too."

He said, "You're not remotely interested in listening to my side of the story."

The thoughts which had been fermenting in her head all day were a trip switch away from spewing out of her and souring everything. Which presumed everything hadn't been soured already. She said, "You should go home. We could both do with some distance from this. Some sleep. I only opened the door to you just now to stop you waking up the whole square."

"No. That's not fair. You sent me away before and I went. I'm not going again."

She looked at him, standing there trying to be reasonable whilst tipping towards belligerence. Perhaps detailing precisely how she felt wouldn't sour everything. Perhaps it would bring him to his senses. "All right. If you really want to have this conversation." She indicated a stool. "Sit there." He obeyed. She picked up the bottle of scotch she'd last opened for Gil and poured them both a shot. "I can't see," she began, "that you *have* a side of the story. And you know, this is what I find so disturbing about what you did. Because what has Gil ever done to you?" She gave him a second or two to reply, forged on. "Nothing. He's always just been himself. And then yesterday he turned to me when he was stressed. He hadn't wronged you, or insulted you. And for reasons entirely of your own, you decided to make him look cheap."

"She already knew," Henry said heavily. "Eve. She'd noticed him around Patrick's for years, she'd seen what sort of man he is."

"So you betrayed him for nothing."

"I just filled in some of the details."

"Oh great." She shook her head. "How can any of us ever trust you again?"

He looked appalled. "I'd never do that to you."

"But how do I know that? What if I really pissed you off, would you go spilling my secrets to someone? What if I did something worse than that, what would you do to me then?"

"Cecily, no." He reached towards her and she drew back. "I'd never hurt you. I've never hurt anyone. It's just him. I'd had enough, I … reacted badly. He did respond by doing this to my face."

"Oh that's right, you didn't fight back. It really disturbs me, Henry. I understand that when he was sleeping around everything was fine because you could be morally superior. But now he's not doing that any more you don't even have that over him. That's why you threw it in Eve's lap. It was all the ammunition you had." He was nodding slowly. Sorrowfully. She pressed on. "But jealousy can create a self-fulfilling prophecy. And it kind of has."

He stared at her. "What do you mean?"

"I can't keep doing this. Everytime you go off in a sulk because of Gil I have a little less respect for you. Everytime I find I'm a little less willing to talk you round."

"But this is an end to it, this time."

She said, with genuine regret, "I think it might be an end to something else."

His jaw sagged. "Are you saying this is over?"

She was on the brink of pointing out that 'this' had been a few months' sex, not a ten year marriage. She didn't say it because one of the realisations crowding her mind all day was that Gil had been right. He had understood back at the beginning that if she embarked upon a relationship with Henry it would mean far more to him than it would to her. He had said as much, and she had been furious with him. I didn't listen, she thought. I didn't want to hear him being right, because I was caught up in my own pain, and annoyed with him for leering at other girls on the beach. I was jealous too.

"Henry, I'm sorry." She saw dismay in his eyes and was smitten with guilt twice over, that she didn't care for him enough to accept and forgive him for what he had done and move on from it, and that she was using it as an excuse. She was being dishonest. But then I've been dishonest from the beginning, she thought. And maybe now it's just time to stop.

Chapter Twenty-seven

We have an hour to spare at the station in Milan. It's a beautiful place, vast vaulted roof, stone sculptures, but Gil rushes us along the platform as if through a crack den. I lift my arm out of his grasp and he looks at me, exasperated. "*What*?"

"Why are you in such a hurry?"

"Well fine, you admire the scenery. I need a drink."

I let him go, watch him heading into the bar as I slow my pace, craning my neck to the steel arcs and coloured glass of the roof, the great stone staircases leading to the ticket hall, long red scrolls attached to pillars advertising some sort of festival. I tell myself how lovely it is, how interesting, but I'm only pretending. My heart is fluttering as it always does when he's out of sight and I can't quite catch my breath. The flow of our fellow passengers from the Ventimiglia train has ebbed now and I am one of a half dozen people remaining on the platform. There are thousands, millions, of places in the world I could be. Who would know, who would guess, I would be here?

My phone buzzes. "Sorry," Gil says.

"It's okay."

"It isn't. But I bought you a drink."

"What is it?" I begin to walk up the stairs and across the ticket hall towards the bar, fifty, maybe sixty yards away.

"I thought I'd ordered brandy and soda but Jesus, it could be anything."

I laugh. It's in my head to say, "Your Italian's up there with your French then, is it?" but it's then that I see him.

He's just a flicker in my peripheral vision, but my body reacts before my brain has chance to register what it's seen, my stomach twisting, nausea rising into my throat. I speed up, clammy with sweat.

And of course when I look back, over my shoulder, almost losing my balance and falling to the glittering concourse, he isn't there.

He's in front of me.

I cry out but he grabs me, moves me aside fast. He's just the same, blond, paunchy, cargo shorts, polo shirt. Except his face is a mess. Bruised and bloodied. I can hear my heart.

"Where is he?" he demands.

"I don't … he isn't … " I can barely speak.

He shakes me, hard. I wonder can nobody see this, doesn't it look to anyone like an assault? "Is he with you?"

"No."

"So he's dumped you?" He stares at me, trying to read the truth in my eyes. "Left you on your own? Yeah, well he always was a bastard."

"Let go of me," I hiss, "or I will start screaming." I'm thinking of a knee to the groin, but he's big, Henry. Bigger than Gil. He could do me damage in an instant.

"Let you go?" His face darkens, his meaty hand tightening around my arm. "Have you any idea how long or how much fucking trouble it's taken to track you down?"

So I do it. My kneecap to his scrotum. As hard as I can. He shouts and as he's doubling over in pain releases me so abruptly I jerk away from him and spin, sprinting through the crowd, knocking against bags, suitcases, small children. Inside the bar I draw up short, panting. There he is, at a window table, visible to anyone.

"I used to think," Gil greets me, "that I knew what it was to need a drink. Now I know that was just wanting one. Shit. What? What's happened?"

I heave on his name.

He storms out to the ticket hall. I knock back the brandy and soda and follow. We aren't doing a very good job of not drawing attention to ourselves. And of course Henry has gone. Gil whirls back to me. "Where was he?"

I show him.

"Fuck." He marches the length and breadth of the concourse, as if the fury of God were in him. I wait out of the way, leaning against the wall so no one can come up behind me, clamp their hand over my mouth, drag me away. After a few minutes Gil returns, still scowling. "Nothing."

"You didn't expect him to hang around?"

"It's what he wants, isn't it? To find us?" He looks at me. "Are you all right? Did he hurt you?"

"No. He didn't get the chance. I kneed him in the balls."

He looks at me. "You did what?"

I tell him, and he laughs in disbelief, and kind of in admiration. "You see now why we have to stay together?"

I nod.

"I'll be better at this. I will."

"Gil." I hesitate. "He looked like he'd been beaten up."

"Well." He takes a breath and I realise at this point that there isn't a mark on him. "It'd be no more than he deserves."

Chapter Twenty-eight

For the first time since her father's death, Jem stood in a space he had owned and experienced it in the present tense. She gazed upon peeling walls with damp corners and surface of uneven whitewashed stone, at the floor sporadically littered with scraps of paper and curled paint tubes, at the mdf boards nailed to the window frames. Those need to be taken down, she thought. It's time.

"Maybe," she said, "I could set up an art student scholarship in his name. The Alex Gregory Award. What d'you think?"

Gil appeared on the threshold between the gallery and the workshop. He wore jeans and a rock band t-shirt, his eye not so much black as purple and yellow and red, puffy beneath the socket and swollen above it. She could take a baseball bat to this Henry, but then Gil had pointed out he'd possibly broken the guy's nose.

He said, "Is there enough money for that?"

"There's this place. And the house. And his bank account."

"You want to sell up?"

"I don't know. I don't know what I want to do."

He came up behind her, sliding his arms around her waist and kissing her ear. "This would be great for your business, you know. Perfect location, no more hauling your stall up to the pier and back."

"I like my stall." She tried to imagine this space of light and air filled with her work. "It's awfully big. Jewellery really doesn't take up much room." She paused. "It'd be perfect for you." He was silent and she turned around in the circle of his arms to find him looking shocked.

"For me?"

"Was that the wrong thing to say?"

"It's a very generous thing to say."

But it was tied up in other issues, she saw that. Issues of what she wanted to do and where she wanted to go now. The issue of what was to become of them at the end of the summer.

Although she had not doubted him for a minute all the time they'd been together, and although he couldn't possibly have been more loving or more supportive, she was afraid of asking the question.

"Will you think about it?"

"Of course I will."

She walked away from him, to sit on the low window-ledge. She could see the thoughts she'd had filling the space between them like holograms. Without giving it any further consideration she said, "Actually whatever happens, I'd like you to have the gallery. You deserve it and it's really too big for me and you know, maybe Dad would have approved."

He looked astonished. "Jem – "

"Really."

He came to sit beside her. "I can't."

"Why can't you? I don't know how I would have coped, these last months, without you."

He stroked her arm. "Listen, I really appreciate you wanting to give me this place. I do. It's a breathtaking idea and I'm half tempted to let you do it. But you should think about it. You have the money and the freedom to do anything now. Anything you like. Move to another house, another town."

"But this is my home."

"Take off travelling for a while."

She said, "The thing with travelling is that it's great if you have somewhere to come back to. Someone to come back to. I only have myself now, there's nothing to anchor me. Travelling would be like cutting myself loose in the world." She paused. "Come with me."

He looked at her. "Seriously?"

"Why not? I'd pay for everything. It'd be like giving you back the holiday I've stolen from you."

"Ah, Jem, you haven't - "

"Unless it's your business … "

"No, no. That would stand me taking a little time off. A little more time off."

"Are you saying yes?"

"I don't know. I don't know what I'm saying." He laughed.

"Are you?"

"God, no."

He took her hand, lacing their fingers. She felt she was about to leap terrified and exhilarated into the wind and empty sky, holding his hand, trusting in him. After having spent so long alone and closeted in the dark the possibility of a different kind of life was shocking. She said, "We should both think about this."

"Yeah, we should." He kissed her hand. "We will."

Her hologram thoughts dispersed into the ether, leaving behind them the memories of this room as it had been for so many years and until so recently, filled with paintings in varying stages of completion. Her father had never worked methodically on anything in his life. The workbench next door would be covered in a sliding pile of sketches. Canvases washed with grey or pale blue had stood beside similar canvases blank but for the faintest of pencilled lines. Others had borne precise and detailed images of one or two sections and nothing else. And then there were those that were finished, or almost finished, and the first glimpse of them would take your breath away. She could see him now, as if the dimensions of past and present existed side by side, standing at an easel, the way he held the brush, his absent-minded reach for the ever-present mug of coffee, the moment he would sense her presence and turn towards her. His smile. The very words he would speak.

It had been a long day. Throughout it Cecily's head had been pounding with a whisky hangover and she had wanted to send her customers away and lock the door. Now they were gone and she was alone with her thoughts, she wished them back, distracting and maddening her with their picky orders and screaming children. Oh God, she thought, I need a break. She thought of Patrick's, which would be noisy and crowded, of staying here, in the great pressing silence of the café. She thought of a bath and pyjamas and a glass of wine and a DVD and it almost appealed.

After going wearily through her nightly routine of clearing

up and closing down and locking doors, she climbed the stairs to her attic, slid an Alison Moyet album into the CD player and ran the hottest and bubbliest of baths. She closed her eyes, letting the water and the music eclipse all else, stayed there, weightless, thoughtless, until the water cooled and the final notes of the final track ended. Afterwards she massaged her most expensive body lotion into her pink and boiled skin, pulled on soft pyjama trousers and a vest top and knelt down on her rug in front of her DVD collection.

Her mobile buzzed.

She looked over, contemplated ignoring it, then reached across to read the display.

GIL

"Hi," she said.

"Can I come up?"

In the kitchen she slid back the bolts and he stepped inside. The light above the staircase cast an eerie glow across his bruised eye, the other half of his face in shadow. She drew in her breath. "My God. Is that painful?"

"A bit sore. Still, I guess I did some damage too." He paused, closed the door behind him. He looked wrecked even beneath the bruises. "Are you busy?"

She thought, it's the third time. Something is making him miserable and stressed and this is the third time he's turned to me. "No. I was just going to have a glass of wine and watch a film. You can join me, if you want."

"Thanks."

She led the way upstairs. "Wine? Beer?"

He groaned, sank down onto the sofa. "I've been trying to drink myself into a coma in Patrick's."

"Unsuccessfully, I see." She sloshed generous measures of merlot into two glasses. "It might hit you later. Or tomorrow morning, the hangover from hell." She put their glasses on the coffee table, returned to the rug and the DVD pile. "*Casablanca* or … um … *The Shining*? *Annie Hall*? *The Way We Were*? I really need to spend more time on Amazon."

He rubbed his eyes with the heels of his hands. "Can we just talk?"

She pushed to her feet and went to sit beside him, curled her legs beneath her. "Sure."

He took a mouthful of wine. "Not about me."

"Okay."

"Yet."

"Okay."

"So how're things with Henry?"

"Ah." She reached for her own glass. "We split up."

"Really? Shit. Are you all right?"

"Yeah. Depressed. Disappointed. But all right."

"And he's … ?"

"As you might expect. Are you surprised?"

"Why wouldn't I be?"

"Because you never thought we should be together in the first place."

He sighed. "I'm sorry. I was being an arse. I had no right to say that."

"But you did, and you were right, and I should have listened." She drank. "It wasn't just that I wanted a fling and he wanted – I don't know – a silver wedding. He was so jealous of you."

He shook his head. "I don't get that. Why would any man who has you be jealous of someone who doesn't?"

"Oh Gil." Her heart contracted.

"It's true."

"He was jealous of us being close. Of us having been close in a way he and I weren't, I guess." She didn't add that Henry had been absolutely right to be jealous, that his instinct regarding her feelings for Gil had been on the nail. She trapped the bubble of thought inside her, where it couldn't do any harm.

He said, "It wasn't the fight, then?"

"It was the cause of the fight. How do you trust someone who can do something like that? I looked at him and I should have felt sympathy or understanding and I didn't. I wasn't sure I even liked him anymore." Gil was listening, his eyes fixed on hers. She straightened her legs a little, her toes brushing his thigh, said, "So what about you? Why are you trying to drink yourself into a coma?"

He frowned, took a breath. A long drink. "I can't tell you."

She was torn between applauding his loyalty and wanting to kick him. "You came up here from Patrick's not to tell me?"

"I came up here from Patrick's to be with you. Because you always make me feel … better."

Her eyes pricked. Don't cry. She clenched her jaw. Do not cry.

"I want to tell you. I do. But I can't, I'm sorry." He considered. "What it means, though, is that I feel like I'm halfway down a road that minutes ago I didn't know was there."

She understood. "It's all moving too fast."

He looked wretched.

"Do you love her?"

"I do. I think I do. She's beautiful and kind of mesmerising and funny and sweet … "

Much as the words tore at her, she could hear the 'but'. And she could see now how upset and how drunk he really was. "Hey." She rubbed his back, soothing. "Shh. It's ok."

"It's not." He swallowed. "It's really not ok. It's got very intense, claustrophobic. And I hate myself for even thinking that but she's promised me things, amazing things. She wants me to go travelling with her."

She wanted to tell him she couldn't bear hearing him talk about his feelings for someone else, but if she did that, she might see even less of him. If he went travelling she wouldn't see him at all. "Do you want to go?"

"Yeah. I don't know. I can't abandon her, I don't *want* to abandon her, but … " His eyes were wet by now, and reddened. Longing to draw him into her arms, she remembered too well how it felt to be on a sofa in his arms, naked in his lap, his hands at her waist guiding their rhythm. Desire pulsed through her. She kissed his temple.

He stilled, turned his head to meet her gaze, and kissed her. Not with his usual breezy affection but softly, with intent. When he spoke she felt his breath against her skin. "What have we done?"

She could say nothing. They were thinking the same thoughts.

"If we hadn't had that row … "

"Gil." The effort it required to pull away from him was agonising. "Stop. This is in danger of being a terrible mess."

He sighed. "I'm sorry. I'm sorry. Jesus! What's the matter with me?"

"I don't know," she said truthfully. "I've never seen you like this. Maybe you've fallen in love for the first time and it's a shock."

"No," he said. "I've been in love before." He held her gaze and she burned with understanding. Her throat hurt.

"Don't say that to me now. It's not fair."

"Come here." He tried to embrace her but she disentangled herself, sat back from him.

"Don't."

"Don't hug you?"

"It feels as if everything's over." Her voice broke.

"Ah Cecily, don't cry. I'm sorry. I'm pissed and selfish and you don't deserve to have to put up with me. Don't cry."

"I'm not," she said, despite the tear sliding down her face. "You need to get your head sorted out."

"I know."

"I can't do it for you."

"I know that too." He rubbed his eyes hard. She watched him. The urge to let him hug her, to yield to a moment of yearned for but ill-judged passion, was so strong she got up from the sofa to sit in the basket chair a yard or so away. He looked at her, at the physical distance between them gaping with their inability to trust themselves. "I should go."

She nodded. Neither of them moved.

In summer most businesses stayed open till dusk, catching the trail of holiday makers as they strolled through town after dinner, picking up souvenirs, on their way to a pub or for a walk on the cooling sands. Alex had frequently been surprised by how much he could sell in the fading light of evening before he'd come to realise that these were the buyers who browsed and hovered during the basking sun or spattering rain of the day. It had become a source of pride to him that his work spoke for itself; that he never had to employ the wheedling tactics of salesmanship which would have gone so much against the grain. Marianne had laughed – "Paint it and they will come." Which was just as well, since she had lost her job in the tourist office a couple of years since and the music tuition had petered out as whisperings of her bouts of illness had spread. The proceeds of his paintings were all they had to live on these days.

It was quite dark by the time he reached home. As he entered the house he was alert, as always, for a sound which might freeze his blood, or a silence deeper than it should have been. Instead he heard the murmur of his wife's voice from upstairs, the responding chirrup of his daughter. Softly he climbed the treads, the amorphous sounds above him shaping themselves into words and becoming, as he stepped onto the landing, a conversation.

" ... your favourite?" Marianne was asking.

"Jo!"

He could see them through the open doorway, Marianne sitting on the bed with an open book in her lap, Jem leaning against her, twirling a dark strand of her hair round her finger. He paused, caught by the painful normality of the scene and briefly unwilling to disturb them.

"Very wise," Marianne agreed. "Jo's the only one who feels real. Meg's annoying, Beth's wet and Amy's a brat."

Jem giggled. "Mum!"

"Well they are, aren't they? And when I read this when I was your age – maybe a bit older - I was so disappointed that Jo doesn't marry Laurie. How could he settle for Amy, what was the matter with him? And Jo's palmed off with some ancient professor." She gestured despair and Jem laughed again.

"It's just a story."

Marianne ruffled her hair. "But the best stories enter your heart and live there forever."

Alex cleared his throat.

"Dad!" Jem cried.

Marianne smiled. "How was the day?"

"Yeah. Pretty good."

"I'll make us a drink." She stood up, squeezed his shoulder as they swapped places on Jem's bed.

"Thanks." He kissed his daughter's forehead, laying the book on the bedside table. "So what's next?"

She shook her head. "I think it's too early for next. I want them all to live in my heart for a little bit longer." She snuggled down into her bed, pulling the sheets up around her. "Why was it a pretty good day?"

"I sold a few paintings. Talked to some nice people."

She was watching his face. "I've hardly seen you for ages."

"It's Saturday tomorrow, you can spend the whole day in the gallery with me if you want."

She nodded happily. His heart contracted. "Okay Puddle, time for sleep."

In the kitchen Marianne was making Irish coffee, with more emphasis on the former than the latter. "Suddenly," she said, voicing her thoughts before he was in the room with her, "she seems to have grown up so much, as if she's gone from eight to nearly twelve in an instant."

"I know just what you mean."

She handed him his glass, complete with the long plastic stirrers which Jem had sneaked out of what she called the Knickerbocker Glory café in town. "I think we should start taking her to places. London, at the very least."

He smiled. "Paris. Rome."

"Well why not? It would be exciting, wouldn't it? For her and for us."

She often strained at whatever leash she thought it was tying her here, to him. He imagined her dancing at the most distant stretch of it almost, but not quite, out of his sight. Better than the weeks she spent withdrawn so far into herself there was no reaching her, but still he found the short times they lived side by side more unbearable than months of knife-edge extremes. Especially now.

She smiled at him. "You don't like leaving your beloved Cornwall, do you?"

"It isn't that."

"What then?" She was teasing him.

"Nothing. You're right. We should take her."

She said, "It isn't that you don't trust me?"

He saw the flicker of insecurity in her eyes and was stricken. "No, no."

"Because we manage that all right now, don't we?"

"Of course we do." He looked at her levelly, watched her anxiety dissipate as swiftly as it had gathered. She nodded, believing him.

"Did you eat, tonight?"

"I forgot."

"You're hopeless," she smiled. "Are you hungry? Let me make you a sandwich at least."

"Marianne, I'm fine." His chest hurt. He couldn't bear to stay in the same room with her being just ordinarily caring.

"You are fine," she said softly.

"I'm going to go and have a shower."

"Okay." She kissed his cheek as he passed her and he went

quickly into the hall to hide the tears in his eyes.

Chapter Twenty-nine

In different ways, Venice undoes us. On the vaporetto, sailing through the lilting waters towards the vast open space of St Mark's Square, I look up at Gil and there are tears in his eyes. Though my heart contracts I resist the temptation to take his hand. He doesn't deserve me beside him fretting and clinging. We are here at last. This is his time now.

It's also of course a travesty of everything it should have been. Venice was supposed to have been the pinnacle of an exhausting, exhilarating tour; we should be crazed with elation. Instead he is in tears and I am just crazed. I clench my jaw and try to appreciate the scene ahead: the domes and the palaces; the bridges, the elegant black curves of the gondolas; the basilica towering against a clear blue sky. It is so beautiful, and so wrong, there are tears in my eyes too.

We step off into the sunshine at San Samuele. Gil tips back his head to gaze up at the huge white marble edifice of the Palazzo Grassi and I read his awed expression. He would love to while away days, weeks, visiting every art gallery, every museum, and how can I deny him that. How can I deny him anything. "Which way?" I ask.

"Calle delle Carrozze."

"You know that?"

"I looked it up." He almost smiles.

The street is narrow and, after the first fifty yards of gift shops and tourists, unnervingly empty. We follow the chill grey alleys between towering buildings of flat fronts and iron-grilled windows, light and space reduced to distant sky. I say presently, predictably, "It's like a film set."

"*Don't Look Now*. Julie Christie and Donald Sutherland," he explains when I look blank. "He thinks he's being pursued round Venice by the ghost of his dead daughter but it turns out to be a psychotic dwarf."

"Right."

"Which stabs him to death. It's a really good film." He

laughs, because I am clearly unconvinced, and the echo of his laughter, low as it is, ricochets around the stone walls. I shudder. If there is a place for hauntings and paranoia, this is it.

Barely a few minutes more and he stops abruptly. "Oh my God." For here we are. It is a tiny place, the ground floor of another high stone building, a single central door, a window either side, its inner lit with halogen lights reflecting off golden walls.

"Wow," I say. "Is this it? I was expecting something … bigger."

"Me too."

"Are you disappointed?"

"Not at all." He's awed again. "It's like a treasure trove."

We step inside. A woman wreathed in black hovers in the doorway to a rear room. Gil smiles and says, "*Buon giorno*."

I glance at him, murmur, "Did you look that up too?"

"Mm-hm."

She says something neither of us understands, but we are already mesmerised by Livio de Marchi's treasure, and it doesn't seem to matter.

Apart from a stunning display of glass balloons, everything is wood. It doesn't look like wood. The clothes hanging on the walls appear at first glance to be silk, cotton, leather. The folds of fabric, teeth of zips, the stitching are all just as you would expect. Only the grain of the wood tells a different visual story. Gil touches the furled lapel of a jacket and draws in his breath. "My God."

There's what seems to be a paper carrier bag with a folded shirt sticking over its rim, a curled umbrella leaning against them. The creases in the bag and folds of the umbrella look so real I too have to trust my fingertips rather than my eyes. There's underwear, knickers with frilled edging and a little bow, a slip with moulded cups and little points, oddly, for the nipples. The detail is astonishing. Gil's jaw is slack with wonder. "Is your mind blown?" I ask him.

"Totally. I think of what I can do and I look at this … " He shakes his head. "It's so beautiful, isn't it?"

"It is," I say softly. He returns to what I understand is going to be minute and pains-taking examination of every piece and I slide away towards the colourful glass balloons near the doorway. I want to buy him something, whatever the cost, but how will I be able to come back here without his noticing? I could leave him in an art gallery perhaps, whisk away under the pretence of ... what? It isn't as if we'll be buying souvenirs to take home.

It happens so fast, so obliquely, I don't know what it is I've seen. I only know that suddenly I'm cold with sweat and can hardly breathe. Something passed the window, the doorway, and registered with my peripheral vision if not my brain.

I bolt out into the street, which is empty.

I'm breathing hard.

Shit.

No one. And a car with a smiley face is no use in Venice.

I look back into the gallery, where Gil is intent upon a wooden trilby, considering the texture of the crown, the unlikely curve of its brim. I take in the tilt of his head, the pleasure and concentration in his face, the dark curl of his hair, the tight fit of his jeans across his bum and I recall my encounter with Henry at the station in Milan, his girth, his smell, the bruises and the blood. His threats. I won't let him do this, won't have the fear of him hanging over me any longer, won't let him spoil Venice for Gil.

It's time to stop running.

Chapter Thirty

Every time he left the square for Jem's house, Gil found himself taking the same shoreline route. Found himself, no matter how lost in thought he had been until that point, pausing on the sand and surveying the water just as he had done that first morning, when he had been filled with happy anticipation of the summer to come. Today he knew neither peace nor elation. In the distance the sea rolled, a long wave steadily gaining height and speed as it headed inexorably towards him. Today guilt and misgiving sat in his gut like a rock.

"Hey Gil!"

He turned. The dudes, wetsuited and board-carrying, jogging across the beach towards him.

"Hey."

Buz and Radar stopped a yard or two away, upending their boards in the sand.

"So what's the deal with you and Henry?"

He would have laughed at their lack of tact, but he was monstrously hungover and just raising his eyebrows made his head hurt. "You know what the deal is. He gave Eve Callaghan the low-down on my sex life. I punched him."

Radar shook his head. "Why'd he do it?"

"I wish I knew. Have you talked to him?"

"He's not saying much." Buz shrugged. "What's she going to do? Is she going to use it?"

"Not a clue."

"Because, like, no offence Gil, but who gives a shit?"

He did laugh, despite himself. "Well exactly." But Eve Callaghan had given a shit. Eve Callaghan had come to see him twelve hours later to warn him off Jem. In spilling gossip which was of no interest to anyone, except him, and Jem, and Cecily, Henry had found the one other person to whom it had been of interest. He had struck lucky. "So," he said, "what's been going on with you guys? Any parties I've missed?"

Radar laughed. "That's the first thing you've said in months that's sounded like you. Thought we had a case of the body-snatchers on our hands."

"You've hardly seen me in months."

"Yeah, at least when you were shagging half the town you still hung out with us."

Buz grinned. "It's his new woman keeping him busy."

"Word is she's hot."

"She is," Gil agreed.

"You should bring her down to Patrick's."

He was about to trot out some weary half-truth as an excuse when it occurred to him that a night in Patrick's might do him good. Might do them both good. He smiled. "Maybe I will."

Radar whooped. "Tonight, yeah?"

"Maybe."

"Tonight. See you there. Gonna hold you to it, man."

He watched as they scampered towards the tide. They were around his own age yet he thought of them as kids. Kid brothers. But give them a year or so and they too might be thinking long-term, of moving on. It was all going to end anyway, whatever he did. He turned to walk back towards town.

When he arrived at her house, Jem was at the foot of the stairs with her mother's belongings packed into cardboard boxes bearing the words Heinz and Nescafé Gold. "I've finished," she greeted him. He kissed her cheek. "I thought it would take weeks and – I don't know, *huge* emotional turmoil. I thought all these skeletons would come crashing down on me. But they haven't."

He looked past her, up the stairs towards the cupboard. Its doors stood open wide, the shelves half empty now. He shivered. "What will you do with it all?"

"I've kept a few things. The rest ... I don't know. A bonfire?"

"Is that what you want?"

"Why? What else should I do?"

"No, whatever you think best."

She looked at him. "What's the matter?"

"Nothing."

"It's this house, isn't it?"

Gil paused. It was the thought of the reality of abandoning his flat and his business for months on end. It was the idea of rootless travelling with a girl for whom his feelings were genuine but increasingly complicated. It was the look in Cecily's eyes when she had said it felt as if everything were over. And yes, it was the house.

He said helplessly, "It's always felt full of ghosts."

"It has been," Jem admitted. "But not any more." She sat down on one of the bottom steps. "I know it must have been awful for her. For him. But somehow it's so much less than I was imagining. I was always so frightened of looking at her things. I was frightened of her."

"Oh Jem."

"Well, she was violent and unpredictable. Her death was violent and unpredictable." She shook her head. "But she was also kind and normal and terribly sad and I didn't appreciate that. I was too young."

Gil watched her, concerned. She had come a long way these last couple of weeks but there were times he didn't trust it. It had been too swift, too easy and he could see her surface composure as brittle as ice. She said, "Anyway. I've been thinking about what we discussed, about travelling."

"Oh yes?" He tried to rustle up some wholehearted enthusiasm.

"What about starting in France and heading out across Europe? I've only ever been on a school trip to Paris. And there's that sculptor you like, Livio De Marchi? He has a gallery in Venice, we could visit there."

"How do you know that?"

"I googled him."

He smiled, touched and guilty and yes, all right, a little enthused after all. "That'd be amazing."

"It would, wouldn't it?" She smiled, her mood on an upward swing again. "Let's go out." She stood up, took his hand. He looked back towards the cupboard at the top of the stairs, its remaining folders and boxes lurking behind the rims of the shelves.

"Do you want to leave the rest of it for now?"

"Oh, that's fine," she said. "That's just Dad's stuff."

*

Cecily had always known herself to be skilled in the art of manipulation. She knew it with neither pride nor shame but as a simple fact. She was good at charm and the seduction of men generally and Gil specifically. He was equally good at charming and seducing her but last night she had had the upper hand. Last night, for a few sweet hours, she could have stolen him. The virtue in having resisted was no comfort to her now when she was aching with the memory of his kiss and strung tight with wanting him. It was a painful truth that she had been aching with the memory of his kiss and strung tight with wanting him since he had first returned, and she'd persisted in pushing him away. He'd known very well what she was doing and been at a loss to understand it – for why would he? - and now here she was, on the brink of losing him forever. All day her throat ached and tears pricked at the corners of her eyes. She banged about in the kitchen, pinned on a tight smile for her customers, was more than usually impatient with Justine. She wanted to scream and throw things. She wanted his arms around her.

When she was locking up, Henry rang. "Come for a drink," he said.

She wilted against the counter. "No."

"Why not?"

It was a good question. She tried to find an answer.

He said, "It's all right, I'm not going to try to persuade you to change your mind about us. I just thought it'd be nice to be friends again. If you want to."

She nodded. She needed friends, and since delusion would be a much more comfortable way of spending the evening than immersed in heartbreak, she could delude herself that Henry had the slightest chance of being one of them again. "Yes. I'd like that."

"Good. Patrick's? Around nine?"

"Where else?"

She decided too that she needed to make some sort of effort. No one at Patrick's thought her anything other than wry and dry and willing to party. She didn't want to frighten them by revealing her inner emotional train wreck. So she blow dried her hair and applied her glamorous-yet-available face and zipped herself into her brightest sundress. Remember, she told her reflection before she left, that you can be whoever you like because no one – *no one* – knows what's going on inside your head.

Henry and a Southern Comfort with ice were waiting for her on the pier. He smiled, "Hello."

"Hi." She kissed his cheek.

"I was afraid you wouldn't come."

"Here I am." She took a sip from her glass, watching him over its rim. He seemed like the old Henry, gentlemanly and at ease, all the petulant aggression dispersed into the ether.

But - "Let me say this – "

"Henry."

"Just once, just to clear the air, and then it's all forgotten. I promise."

She sighed inwardly. "Go on."

"I'm sorry. I'm sorry I wrecked things between us. I know where your heart lies but the weeks we were together meant a lot to me. I think you're an amazing woman and I'm honoured to be your friend."

She gazed at him. "You're pretty eloquent, for a surf dude."

He smiled. "I try. I didn't want the summer to end on a bad note."

"Neither do I."

"Especially if it's the last summer I'll be here."

She swallowed. "Winds of change, hey?"

"Yep."

She looked out across the darkening water. They were standing at the precise point at which, months ago, a boy had fallen and been close to drowning. She shivered.

Henry said, "The nights're already drawing in."

"They are." She couldn't help herself. "Like a metaphor for my life."

He looked at her. "What will you do?"

"Shut up the café for the winter, get a flight out to Spain, spend time with my parents. Try to figure out what to do next."

"Is carrying on here out of the question?"

"Oh I think so. I've known that for a while now. I've just been fighting against it."

He looked at her for a long moment. She thought that if he asked her why, she might just tell him. But he said, "There are worse places to wash up than Spain."

"I know. And having any options at all is a luxury."

"But still."

"Yeah. But still." She smiled ruefully. "In the meantime, don't you think we kind of owe it to ourselves – to each other – to go out on a high?"

"Which I guess means," Henry smiled, "another drink."

Jem said, "Are you sure?"

He kissed her forehead. "Of course. Why wouldn't I be?" She lay in his arms. They'd walked for an hour or two along the cliffs, which he had said helped to clear his head, then staggered back into the glasshouse heat of his studio. He'd thrown open the windows and gone for a shower, where she had joined him, her back sliding against the tiles while he thrust inside her. Afterwards, collapsing together onto his bed, he mentioned the evening at Patrick's. She tried to think of a way of saying that he hadn't wanted her to meet his friends before which wouldn't sound pathetic.

"You're still hungover and you want to go to a bar?" Which sounded, God help her, as if she were his mother.

"I am *much* better now." He smiled. "And I will drink coke all night if it makes you happy."

"It's not that." She paused. "It's, I just wonder, why you were so drunk."

"You don't always need a reason. Sometimes it's just fun,

you know."

She rolled onto her stomach so she could see his face. "And was it?"

He said nothing for a moment.

"Gil?" She watched his Adam's apple move as he swallowed. She could estimate the precise length of his stubble, count his eyelashes. "Tell me."

"You don't – " He stopped. "I'm a complete shit. I … *Jesus.*" He rubbed his eyes with the palms of his hands. She felt cold, in the sticky, baking heat of his room. He had been quiet all day; she'd told herself it was the hangover.

"What did you do?"

"I – nothing. Nothing."

"Be honest with me."

He took a breath. "I got scared. At the thought of leaving everything behind and going off travelling – "

"With a girl you hardly know."

He looked at her. "I feel like we've got ahead of ourselves. We're much more intense than we would have been if … Christ, I'm sorry, it's a fucking awful thing even to think."

"Than we would have been if my dad hadn't died."

"I'm sorry."

"But it's true. And I asked you to be honest. And actually," she admitted, "I kind of agree."

"You do?"

"Of course. We've poured a year's worth of feelings and – expectations into a couple of months and you were having a wobble. I understand that. Is that all it is?" She heard the catch in her voice. "Do you want us to finish?"

"No. Jesus. No, no." He pulled her close again, kissed her. "But can we put the brakes on, enjoy the scenery? Do normal things for a bit?"

"Like meet your friends for a drink."

"Yeah."

She nodded. "Do you remember that I didn't tell you about my dad because normal was what I wanted?"

He looked ashamed. "God, I'm so *useless.*"

"No you're not. I understand. I do." She kissed him, ran her

231

hand across his groin. His penis twitched obediently back to life.

She had only ever visited Patrick's out of season. During the summer it always seemed too full of visiting glitterati. She and Alex had stayed loyal to the inn on the square; with erstwhile friends or the occasional lover she frequented the pubs on the edge of town, country-comfortable and full of locals. On the threshold of Patrick's she hesitated, not only conscious of her hick status but also keenly aware that tonight Gil would be not just hers but theirs. She had never seen him with people he knew before, save for five minutes on the prom with Henry. She had never had to share his attention. It was going to require an adjustment.

It began the moment they approached the bar through the noise and the heat, shouts of *Hey Gil!* and *where the bloody hell've you been hiding?* and *Christ, what happened to your face?* Gil grinned, still holding her hand, and said *hey* and *I've been around* and *ah, just acting like a dick* and finally, pointedly, *this is Jem.* Too many faces, too many voices, for her to take in but the greetings were friendly, the smiles wide. She wanted a drink, swallowed her first like water. Gil cocked an eyebrow - "Catching me up?" – and led her though the crowd to a table on the far side of the dance floor.

"You okay?" he asked her as they sat down.

"Yeah. It's – loud, isn't it?"

"You don't like loud?"

"No, I can do loud. Do you dance?"

"Badly." He laughed.

"Hi Gil." A tall blonde girl leant down between them, her hair brushing Jem's shoulder as she bent to kiss Gil's cheek. "It's *so* good to see you. It hasn't been the same round here without you."

He smiled. "Lucy, this is Jem. Jem – Lucy."

"Hello," Jem said equably, aware she was being assessed, written off. Lucy's mouth seemed to be saying *Hi* but in her eyes Jem read *Back off he's ours.* She watched as Gil and Lucy chatted, the shorthand of their conversation, the casual intimacy of their body language, and wondered how many times this was going to happen tonight.

"Sorry," Gil said when Lucy finally prowled away. "She can be a bit … "

"Can't she, though? I take it she's one of yours?"

"No, in fact."

"But she wants to be."

He shrugged, as if he were forever helpless in the path of predatory women. "Come on," he said. "Dance with me."

He had lied, or been unduly modest: he was a very good dancer, instinctive and inventive and fun. If she hadn't already known, she would have been wondering what he was like in bed. As he twirled her to the fast beats and held her to the slow ones, she thought of all the women who looked at him and wondered that and would never know, and she almost felt sorry for them. Even Lucy.

When they returned to their table it seemed they had been usurped, as it held replacement drinks and two young men, both lean and tanned, one with sunbleached straggles for hair, his sleeveless t-shirt revealing upper arms emblazoned with New Age tattoos, the other close cropped and chiselled of features, like an advertisement for the US marines. Gil was smiling and saying, "Hey guys" and she understood. They were his surf dudes.

The marine was called Radar and Tattoo Man was Buz and they gazed at her with open interest.

"Got the drinks in," Buz pointed out.

"Yeah thanks. Next one's mine." Gil grinned. "So what's the story?"

Jem knew guys like Buz and Radar as if they were in her blood. She had been to school with them, worked in bars with them, hung out at uni with them. Their humour and priorities – in so far as they had any – and their chilled, fatalistic philosophy of life were like the air she breathed. As she laughed and talked she could see the rapport was mutual. I just *get* them, she said to Gil later. It's like we know who we are.

"What do you do?" she asked Radar, when Gil and Buz were engaged in some good-natured, rambling argument. "When you're not surfing the waves?"

"Part-time chef at The Anchor. Sunday lunch, couple of evenings - it's more of a hobby."

She smiled. "And Buz?"

"Oh Buz has it all his own way, puts in a shift at his parents' hotel when he can be arsed. They were real hippies, way back when, jazzed to have a surfer for a son."

"But we're all like that, aren't we," she said. "None of us could do the nine-to-five because *living* here is what we do, it's the single most important thing. Earning money comes second."

"You're a local, then?"

"I am." She hesitated, decided to go for it. "My dad was Alex Gregory, the artist."

"Oh right, the gallery on The Wharf?"

"You knew who he was?"

"Sure." His expression morphed into the wary-sympathetic one people had been using around her for a while. "I heard he died. I'm sorry."

"Thank you." It should have been a moment of triumph. Someone had heard, in the natural way of things, that her father had died. She had been able to confirm it without unravelling. It should have been another small step along the path towards acceptance but instead it felt like another small step away from him. He was disappearing like smoke in the air and she couldn't bear it.

Radar nodded. "He was a good bloke, your dad."

She tried to picture him chatting, in the gallery, in the pub, with Gil and Radar and a whole host of people who had been, were still, strangers to her. At his funeral the church had been filled with people she had known since childhood. Only now, friends and acquaintances swept in on the summer tide, did she see that there had been a strand to his life of which she'd known nothing.

Dad.

Radar said, "Come and dance."

She looked at him, at Gil who laughed and gestured – *feel free* – and she stood, edging her way between the table and his knees, after Radar and onto the dance floor. It was far busier now, a challenge to carve out your own square foot of space and she had to stand closer to Radar, closer to anyone, than she would have chosen. He bopped and dipped, not quite in time to the music, and she dipped and bopped in return. "See, my take on dancing," he told her above the clashing chords and press of the crowd, "is you don't have to be any good at it. You just have to enjoy yourself."

"Oh, sure." Like sex? she wanted to say, but didn't. On the plus side, dancing with someone worse at it than you was liberating and no one else here cared. She swayed and swung, feeling the rhythm as if it were part of her, dizzied by the lights and the drinks she'd downed. Through brief gaps between shoulders, over heads, she glimpsed their empty table, Gil at the bar, Buz holding forth to a group of teenage girls. The music changed to a slower number, Take That's *Rule The World*. Radar lifted his hands. "You want to stop?"

"No." She smiled, stepped closer. He held her loosely as they rocked from one foot to the other. "I'm having such a nice evening," she told him. "Why hasn't Gil brought me down here before?"

"I guess he wanted you all to himself. Can't say I blame him."

"But he's a sociable guy."

"He is. Different with you, though."

"Different how?"

He shrugged. "More serious."

It was what she wanted to hear. She thought she should stop now, before she heard something she didn't. Beyond him bodies parted to allow a view clear across the room. The beefy blond man called Henry was entering from the pier with a woman Jem felt was familiar. Tousled light brown hair, curves accentuated by a flowered dress. Who was she? Why couldn't she place her, out of context? And then she had it. She was the woman who ran the café on the square.

And Radar said, "Hey, there's Henry and Cecily."

She frowned. "Cecily? Gil's friend Cecily?"

"*Our* friend Cecily but yeah, okay."

She felt as though she had been asked to do a complicated

sum which didn't make sense. Gil's close friend and former lover, was the woman from the café in the square?

She had stopped dancing. Radar said, "You all right?"

"Yeah, I … just a bit dizzy."

"Come here." He steered her towards the bar, their table having been engulfed now by a fresh wave of revellers. "Sit down." He propped her against a bar stool. "Gil!"

He was there in a moment. "Are you okay? What happened?"

"Nothing. Nothing, I'm fine."

"Do you want to go for a walk?"

She nodded.

"I was going to … introduce you to … " He scanned the bar. "Where did she go?"

Radar said, "Cecily?"

"Yeah. She was here a minute ago. Where did she go?"

"Don't know. Henry's there, d'you want to ask him?"

Gil laughed wryly. "Maybe not. Come on." He slipped his arm around Jem's shoulders. "Let's get some air."

Chapter Thirty-One

Gil opened his eyes to see, as he had somehow intuited from sleep, that beside him lay nothing more than a tangle of duvet and a dented pillow and the lingering scent of her where warmth of bed met morning air. He contemplated the empty space for a moment, unmoving, then saw that within the dent of the pillow was a sheet of paper.

Gone to start my day. You look so beautiful when you're asleep I couldn't bear to disturb you. See you later. I love you. J xxxxx ☺

He smiled, put the note back on the pillow, rolled over and let himself drift back into unconsciousness.

The pounding on his door had him bolt upright, heart racing, before he was properly awake. "Jesus! Did you forget to leave it on the latch?" But even in his confused and stumbling state he realised she wouldn't be banging on the door, she'd be texting him, and even if she were banging, it wouldn't be as if the hounds of hell were after her.

"It's Justine!" cried the blurred figure on the other side of the frosted panes.

Justine? He pulled on his jeans. Justine … ?

"From the café," she called, as if reading his thoughts. "Is Cecily with you?"

He flung open the door. "What?"

"She isn't there." The girl looked entirely different, her habitual sulk replaced with anxiety. "I've just got here to do my shift and the café's all locked up."

"Have you phoned her?"

"Er – *duh*."

"What time is it?"

"Nearly ten."

She should have opened up hours ago. He scooped up his own phone with his key to the café and hurried down the iron staircase, which clanged beneath his weight and speed, calling up her number as he went. No answer. He frowned. The Closed sign was still showing through the glass of the café door, the room beyond dim and deserted. Justine, at his heels, said, "It isn't like her, is it?"

"No. It isn't." He looked up to the attic windows. "Cecily!"

Nothing. Not a sound, not a glimpse. Aware of the trail of families and teenagers beginning to filter across the square, and the attention he would draw if he continued to stand there shouting, Gil walked round to unlock the kitchen door.

"What if she's there?" Justine squeaked. "Won't she be mad at you?"

"I hope she is there and mad at me." He stood in the centre of the silent sunlit kitchen, surfaces scrubbed and bare, gleaming implements awaiting use. He called her name again, then climbed the stairs.

Her attic room was as peaceful and as comfortable as he had ever known it: the smoothed patchwork quilt beneath whitewashed beams; her jacket swinging from its hook on the back of the door; the DVDs from the other night still scattered across the coffee table; a pair of red high heeled shoes abandoned beside the sofa.

But Cecily herself was gone.

Jem strolled along The Walk to the pleasing sound of her flip-flops flapping against the pavement, the early sun warm on her bare legs. She wore shorts and a grey Stone Roses vest top which she had found to her surprise on the floor of Gil's room, as if her wardrobe were steadily migrating there without consulting her. The smell of coffee and baking emanated from a café as she passed, shops opening their doors and raising their grilles for business. She was toying with the idea of picking up a croissant en route when she heard, from somewhere above her, "Jemima!"

Firstly, who used her full name and secondly what were they doing in the air? She frowned, then saw a pair of long tanned legs descending a stepladder outside The Joshua Tree and there was Atlanta Fox, brandishing a Cath Kidston watering can, her hanging basket of orange petunias swaying and dripping in her wake.

"Hi," Jem smiled.

"Hello! How serendipitous! I was going to call you today."

"You were?"

Atlanta was beaming. "I need more stock."

Jem was taken aback. She had supplied Atlanta with as much stock as would fill her little stall for a glorious summer. "More?"

"I know! Isn't it fabulous? I can't believe what a runaway success you've been."

"It's amazing," Jem deadpanned.

"It's made such a difference to my first season. I was so clever to find you."

She wanted to laugh, wanted to remember and repeat this conversation word for word to Alex. The morning darkened around her, her delight shrivelling. She swallowed.

Atlanta said, "Have you got a minute? I could show you the figures."

"Actually, I'm on a bit of a mission."

"Oh okay. Tomorrow, perhaps? I'll give you a bell."

"Sure. Thanks, that's really good news." She took a step away.

"Oh wait!" Atlanta put her little watering can down on the pavement, reached to fold the ladders. "I saw you last night, at that bar on the pier. You were dancing with Gil Hunt."

"You know Gil?"

"Heavens, everyone knows him. He's a local celebrity isn't he? I had a bit of a flirt with him myself once."

"Did you?" Jem said.

"Yes, when would that have been? Ages ago, beginning of the summer. Gorgeous man."

"Mm," Jem said.

"So, are you two … ?"

"Yes."

"Gosh." Atlanta looked impressed, as though dating Gil Hunt *and* making jewellery that people actually wanted to buy raised Jem to the level of celebrity herself. Oh Dad, she thought. You wouldn't believe it.

Jem was too young to remember a time when the fishermen's cottages at the other end of town had been occupied by fishermen. For as long as she could recall the smarter houses with the sea views had been holiday homes while those on the shadier side of the street belonged to the old and the poor. Eve Callaghan was neither of these; she had simply inherited the place from her parents and never done anything with it. The house had always reminded Jem of her own: small, cramped and wholly unpretentious. But she knew her own home to be crammed with precious, much-loved belongings and nothing about Eve's house felt loved. It was just the base from which she ran the military campaign of her career and while Alex had said there was at least an honesty about that, Jem had always felt defiant indifference was the defence Eve mounted against the world.

"Jemima." Eve looked harassed, impatient. "Come in."

On a huge wooden table in the dining room were reams of newspapers, printed papers, scrawled notes, a laptop and a large, old-fashioned radio whose voices reverberated around the yellowed walls and ceiling. Eve turned the volume down to a background babble. Despite the open windows the room stank of smoke. She said, "How're you doing?"

"Okay." The last time Jem had seen her was at the funeral. Eve hadn't, unlike most others, hugged Jem or told her what a great man Alex was and how his death was a terrible, terrible tragedy. She had been grim and silent and said, right at the end, that Jem knew where she was. Well I do, Jem thought now. And here I am. And I notice you are not at all surprised to see me. She said, "This is a bad time, isn't it?"

"Just on my way out. But go on."

"I've been sorting through some of Mum and Dad's things, and I've realised there's so much I don't know, so many questions neither of them will ever be able to answer and I wondered, well, if I could ask you."

"Now?"

"I thought one night, over a bottle of wine."

Eve frowned. "I was away a lot, you know."

Her tone was distinctly unhelpful. Jem tried again. "Sure. But you have a perspective and … an insight into them which I don't – can't – have. You could tell me things from an adult point of view. From a *friend's* point of view."

Eve was packing items fast from the table into a scarred satchel, pens, a dictaphone, a notebook. "You mean, sharing my memories of them?"

"Yes. What else would I mean?"

Eve glanced at her sharply, said nothing.

"What's the matter?" Jem asked. "Have I said the wrong thing?"

"I'm not sure it's such a good idea."

"Oh. Right. But it was a good idea for you to tell Gil he was selfish and irresponsible and no good for me?"

"Ah." She folded over the lid of the satchel. "I knew that was why you'd come."

"I came," Jem said furiously, "about my parents, your friends, but if you won't talk to me about them at least you can tell me why other people in my life are suddenly your business."

Eve paused, took a breath. "I'm sorry," she said. "You've caught me at a bad moment. Of course I will talk to you about Alex and Marianne. We'll go for a drink sometime soon. As for Gil Hunt … " She shook her head. "I'm looking out for you, that's all."

"You don't need to look out for me. You don't *know* him."

"I know his type."

"He's not a type, he's a person!"

"And you know it too, and that's why you're upset. Because the truth is bloody pain-ful." She hesitated again. "You're as vulnerable, in your way, as your mother was. I don't want to be responsible for anything happening to you the way it did to her."

Jem stared at her. "What do you mean?"

"That I don't want," Eve said carefully, "history repeating itself."

The only good thing, in Gil's opinion, about someone being

as predictable as Henry was that you always knew where to find them. At this hour with this tide he would have completed his first surf of the day and be back at the flat over the souvenir shop. Gil arrived on the doorstep minutes between when he calculated Henry would have stepped out of the shower and before he left for the Junior Watersports club he ran down in the bay.

Henry opened the door, hair dripping, towel tucked around his stomach. In the half-second it took him to recognise Gil his features calcified from their default benign-bovine setting into hostility. "What?"

"Have you seen Cecily?"

The implication of his question hit Henry instantly. "Shit. Come up." Gil followed him up the stairs to the flat. Henry indicated his towel. "I'll just go and – "

"Yeah." Gil entered the living-room, its usual inhospitable jumble of wetsuits and boxer shorts, beer cans and take-away cartons, and sat down on the edge of the sofa. He thought fleetingly of his place back in Bristol, the first floor of a crumbling Georgian terrace in what had been, when he'd bought it, an undesirable part of town. Over those first months he'd sanded and waxed the floorboards and stripped back the shutters, painted the walls from someone's Heritage range, thrown down tapestry rugs rescued from skips, installed an old leather sofa and an oak table inherited from his parents. He refused to live like a student when it cost relatively little in all but effort to live with some sort of style. And it was rare, for him to be in his beloved Cornwall at the height of the summer and to be thinking nostalgically of home. It was unprecedented, for him to be in this level of emotional turmoil.

Henry returned, dry and dressed. "What's happened?"

"Don't know. No sign of her anywhere. No answer from her mobile."

Henry sighed. "This is your fault, you know."

"Yeah?" Gil was sarcastic. "I had a feeling it might be."

"Well for fuck's sake, what were you thinking bringing that girl to Patrick's?"

Gil's insides churned. He didn't want to hear this, that he'd been insensitive, hurt Cecily, that the kind of complications he'd spent years avoiding surrounded him now like barbed wire. That he was as entangled in it as anyone. "What did she say?"

"She didn't *say* anything. The look on her face was enough." Henry shook his head. "You are unbelievable. God knows it pains me to say this but you know how she feels about you. Yet you still have to rub her nose in your shagging someone young enough to be her daughter."

"It isn't … I didn't … *Jesus*."

"Then again, you're nearly always shagging someone young enough to be her daughter." Henry looked at him levelly. "Fucking hell Gil, I could punch your lights out but we're not going there again. What happened last night?"

"Nothing. Jem was dancing with Radar, I was getting the drinks in, you and Cecily turned up from the pier and then suddenly Jem looked like she was going to pass out and Cecily'd disappeared. You didn't see her again after that?"

"No. I should've … " He let out his breath. "Maybe it's my fault too."

Gil said thoughtfully, "She's been different, this year."

"Well yes, what with the baby … "

Gil frowned at him. "The baby? You mean Sam?"

"There's more than one?"

"No, but – "

"See, this is another thing I don't get. It's like you have nothing in the way of feelings about this. You have a child together and he dies and – "

"He wasn't mine! That was years ago. I would've been, what, fourteen when she had Sam."

Henry stared at him, the truth he'd thought he'd known fragmenting in his head. "So whose was he?"

"I don't know. Some guy who was the love of her life and who she's never got over."

"I thought that was you."

"No." Gil shook his head. "No."

There was a short silence. "Right. Okay." Henry cleared his throat. "We need to find her."

Gil elected to return to the square. Henry would take a drive around town. Were they over-reacting? Gil asked himself, striding back through the sunny streets. She was a grown woman. He didn't doubt he held some responsibility for whatever had happened, whatever she was feeling, but at the same time to withdraw when hurt was Cecily's way. It didn't mean she was likely to do something stupid. It meant she needed peace and solitude in which to recover. He understood that. He also understood that the other night they had come breath-lessly, perilously close to making love. Though now he didn't so much understand it as have it burning at the forefront of his mind.

Jesus.

His phone buzzed. In the moment it took him to dig it out of his pocket he heard Cecily saying *I'm fine*, Henry saying *it's not good* so he was slightly taken aback, and relieved, to see that the display read Jem. "Hey."

Silence. Then the rasping, snuffling sound he recognised because he had so often heard her make it. Oh Christ. He said, "Where are you?"

A gasp, her voice shrill and broken. "At the house."

She was in the garden, when he arrived, pacing the lawn beside the flowerbeds which had been the burial place of the clothes of the dead. Her face was swollen with crying. He held her.

When she had calmed a little, he took her to sit with him on the low wall at the foot of the garden. "Tell me."

"My dad … " Tears again. She couldn't speak. He stroked her hair, long soothing caresses. She swallowed. "He was having an affair."

He nodded.

"My mum had discovered it just before she died."

"Oh Jem."

"She needed him so much and he … how could he, Gil? How could he do that to her? She found out he was being unfaithful and she died. She killed herself because he was screwing around." She sobbed, bitterly.

"Screwing around?"

244

"Oh I don't know, I don't know the details. She wouldn't tell me, she said she didn't know. Eve," she added, unnecessarily. "I went to see her."

"And she just came out and told you that?" He wanted to wring Eve Callaghan's neck.

"She said – she didn't want history repeating itself."

"Meaning?"

"I don't know." She wept. "I don't know who he was any more."

"Jem."

"I can't believe he could – "

"Jem listen. You know what he went through with your mum. You know better than anyone what life was like for him. If someone else was kind, offered him - I don't know – sanctuary from the way things were at home, can you really not understand him taking it?"

She stared at him. "Are you *defending* him?"

He held her gaze. "Yes." He took her hand into his. She let him. "He was an amazing guy, but we all need to feel wanted and loved and – "

"She was *ill*. He had me."

He slipped his arm around her, kissed her forehead. "It's a shock."

She nodded. After a while she got up and went into the house. He sat for a few minutes then followed her, could hear from the bottom of the stairs the sound of her crying. It was a very high pedestal Alex had been on. He had a long way to fall.

Gil, casting around for something to do, tidied the kitchen, shoved the boxes of discarded belongings into a neater pile. Stood regarding them. Presumably, then, Alex's affair had not been with Eve after all. That had not been what she'd meant when she'd said she felt guilty. Had she thought she should have seen that he was likely to stray and warned Marianne? Did she think she could have prevented Marianne's death? Bloody woman. Jem hadn't needed to know. Not now, not like this. And no one had been better placed than Eve to find out whether it had been a single affair or a series of sexual

245

encounters and with whom. Was she withholding these details or had she refrained from doing any digging, out of – what? Respect? Compassion? Could it possibly be that Marianne had believed Alex was having an affair, jumped in her fragile state to a conclusion for which there was no evidence? The thought struck him with some force. For in all their sorting and boxing away, they had found no evidence.

A sound from the landing. Jem came halfway down the stairs and sat. He smiled. "Can I get you anything?"

"A hug?"

He sat beside her, drew her into a close embrace.

She said, "I can't get my head round it."

"I know."

"It's as if he's someone else. I feel … wild. I want to scream, run, hit someone." She shook her head. "I can't bear to be here. I thought it was full of too many memories. Now I know it was full of lies."

He saw, with perfect clarity, what he must do. "Come to Bristol with me. You need a break from this place, I have to get back there in a couple of weeks anyway. It might help, you know, for you to get some distance."

"Really?"

"Really."

She nodded, her eyes huge and sombre. "I'd like that."

"Okay."

She rubbed her hands across her face. "I'm exhausted. I just want to sleep."

"Sure. Here? My place?"

"Haven't you got stuff to do?"

"Well." He smiled wryly. "I still haven't finished that bloody tree."

She almost laughed. "Will you do something for me?"

"Anything."

"Will you check on the gallery for me? I haven't been down there for a couple of days."

And maybe she needed some space and time alone, space and time away from some-one so ready to minimise her grief and suggest solutions, so quick to excuse her father's betrayal.

He saw that. "Of course I will."

Chapter Thirty-Two

I step back into Livio de Marchi's magical cave for a moment. Gil is barely aware of me. "I won't be a minute," I tell him.

"Sure." He half smiles - because I only have half his attention, less than half, a sliver -before he turns back to the carvings. As I reach the doorway a group of Scandinavian-sounding tourists blocks my exit and I negotiate their maps and oversized rucksacks with care, sliding past them, head down as they enter the store. I don't want anyone remembering me.

The street is as empty as it was before. High, high above me the sky is a clear, cool blue. There's a smell, a damp, sewagey smell I hadn't noticed earlier and I see that the painted plaster of some of the buildings is flaking, missing entirely in places. There's no sign anywhere of an overweight Englishman, but this street is trickier than it looks. It has tributary alleyways and recesses, sunken door frames. Easy for me to tuck myself away into these, less so for him. But seconds ago he had passed the window and where is he now.

He saw us, I am certain of that. He saw us and having tracked us from Cornwall across France to Italy, he isn't going anywhere. He will be here, waiting. I feel slightly nauseous at the thought. I tread softly along the paving, giving him plenty of chance to leap out in front of me, to declare himself in broad daylight, to give me chance to run. But he has done this already, at the station in Milan, and maybe he will be cleverer this time, stealthier. Maybe he won't waste time with conversation. I take a deep breath. Think. He is waiting, out of sight somewhere, for me to pass. His advantages are surprise and bulk. My advantage will be speed and … well, what? Exactly?

I stop.

These narrow lanes, I realise, thread into each other. There's a network through which maybe only cats and children can pass but possibly, just possibly … I slip into a gap between the buildings. I might get lost, never find my way back. Gil might walk blithely out into the street and it could all be over. I shudder. Slowly, silently, I creep along the path, over bins and junk, washing hung on lines out of windows above my head. It's so dank and shadowed, I wonder how does it ever get dry. My head is full of dead daughters and psychotic dwarves.

I don't know how long I've been doing this, occupied in hopeless pursuit of someone who might have turned right out of Livio de Marchi's instead of left, who might now be far away. Watching, waiting. Calling the police.

But there. A flash of yellow at the end of an alley. The same yellow I'd glimpsed through the window. The same yellow grabbing and shaking me at Milan station. I almost retch. He's standing, twenty, thirty feet away, leaning against a wall, looking out into the street. I creep forward. He doesn't move. Another half dozen feet. Still he doesn't move. He's not very good at this, I think. And then I hear the rumble of his voice, see that his right arm is bent, his hand to his ear. He's phoning someone. Telling them. *They're here. I've found them.*

Now.

It has to be now.

I take the knife which has been in my pocket since Bristol and move at such speed I don't even hear myself. At least, not my feet. I can hear the blood in my ears and my silent scream as my rage and grief channel down my arm, into the knife, into his back.

He doesn't even turn. The phone hits the slabs. He slumps a little more against the wall. I back up, breathing hard. His legs buckle and he sits, as if he's drunk too much and walked too far in the heat. I wait. For another longer time neither of us moves. I vomit against the bins, hot and cold now, shaking violently. After another minute I reach forward and extract the knife from the mass of his flesh. It's harder coming out than going in, which is weird, but my energy has gone. Blood jets from him, dark and fast. I pick up the phone.

Chapter Thirty-Three

Jem had sought refuge in sleep after Alex had died, spending as many hours as safely comatose as she could, aided by gradually increasing amounts of alcohol, of pills. It was when she was barely conscious for most of the day that he had begun appearing to her, just as he had been, wry, sensible, gently chiding. Except in reality he had clearly been both more and less than that. He had been selfish and duplicitous and her memories now were not to be trusted. Everything she had believed about him had been a lie.

She thought of her mother, walking slowly but steadily into the sea, and she under-stood.

Sitting on the purple bedspread of her teenage years, she listened to the silence. Gil hadn't wanted to leave her alone in her parents' house, but then he had never liked the place. She wasn't sure she liked it anymore either, but she knew she wouldn't sleep in Gil's bright, sunlit room with its grandstand view of the sea. She thought of sleeping here with him, his arms around her, and wished she hadn't sent him away, but he needed to believe her capable of coping, of behaving rationally. She didn't want him to regret offering to take her home with him. She could scarcely believe that despite everything, he was still trying to rescue her. If she were going to go a little bit mad she had to do it all by herself, here, steeped in the past she'd believed she had.

She locked the doors and drew her curtains, returned to the bed. Beside her sat the little pile of Marianne's diaries. She picked up a spiral bound book with curved corners, its cover decorated in orange and white flowers looking, like everything Marianne had owned, as though it belonged to the 70s. But it was dated 1996. The year of her death. *You knew*, Jem thought. He was betraying you – betraying us – and in the end you knew. The handwriting swam and her throat hurt. She blinked, flipping the pages mechanically. Marianne had died at the end of May. Most of the pages before then were empty.

She never had been able to communicate her misery.

Jem had been twelve years old. Why hadn't she sensed something? How could he not have let anything slip? How could *her dad*, whom she'd worshipped, whom she'd believed so loving and so full of integrity, have been such a traitor? Or maybe the loving integrity bit had been the charade. For all those years. Why hadn't she *known*? She lay back, tears sliding into her ears and her hair, and tried to search her slideshow of memories of her twelfth year.

It was a dull blur, as it had always been.

She won't be there, Jem had told him, reluctantly giving the details of Eve's address. She was going out when I arrived. Such was Gil's rage with the woman and his need to take action he stormed down there nonetheless, glaring up at the house and banging his fist on the door as if he could make her appear through sheer force of will. But as with Cecily earlier today, there was nothing. He shouted, giving the door a final thump, and stood in the overgrown grass, fury unassuaged, the beginning of a tirade running through his head. *If you are so concerned for Jem's welfare, why, why, would you tell her something so fucking painful when she never needed to know? Why is the truth more important than her feelings? Why would you do that to her?*

He called Eve's mobile. No reply. Of course. Tried Cecily's number. No reply there either. Jesus! He strode back into town, along the sea front, towards The Wharf, his mind churning. He needed to spirit Jem away from here, take care of her until she was no longer careering out of control with grief. They could do normal, restorative things – work, watch TV, go to the pub. He could heal her again with real life. Before that he needed, for his own sanity, to find out what was going on with Cecily and restore some equilibrium there too. He had been brought up to believe that life's shit was best dealt with swiftly and decisively and procrastinating or brooding did no good at all. Not that he didn't indulge in procrastination and brooding sometimes, but he usually managed to haul himself out of it. Not so easy, to haul someone else. Especially if they didn't want to be hauled.

He unlocked the door of Alex Gregory's gallery and stepped across the threshold, breathed in the musty air. No matter how often he and Jem checked the place, opening windows, tidying up, the sense of neglect and disuse wasn't getting any better. He could see this room as it had been when Alex was alive, the walls full of the deep blues and turquoise greens of his seascapes, the hum of customers stirring the airy tranquillity. He could see Alex himself, mug of coffee in his hand, explaining some element of a painting, wrapping one with deft care before he took payment. Gil could understand, recognising temptation on a regular basis as he did, why life with someone as unstable as Marianne would drive you into the arms of someone else. It made complete sense to him. That it hadn't detracted in any way from Alex's love for his daughter was something he suspected Jem was going to take a very long time to accept.

If any of it were true.

The gallery and workshop had been cleared shortly after Alex had died, his paintings now stored away somewhere – as carefully, Gil hoped, as he would have done so himself – and his acrylics and watercolours and pastels boxed up in the house. She couldn't bear, Jem had told him, to walk in here and see everything as he had left it. She could hardly bear, those first few weeks, even to walk past. So the walls and the racks and the cupboards were empty and anything they might have revealed long gone. Gil checked the windows and back door on auto, his mind whirring on illicit affairs and how you would conceal one when you were well-known in a town as small as this. It occurred to him that if it had taken place when Marianne died, it had started at least fourteen years ago, and how did they know when it had ended, other than four months ago at the foot of Tintagel?

He stopped. Ahead of him, in a whitewashed tongue and grooved corner of the workshop in which he was now standing, was a door. It was also whitewashed tongue and groove and thus camouflaged in the general run of appallingly badly constructed panelling. Unless you were looking for it, you wouldn't notice. He had noticed, as he would, and Jem had said it led to the upstairs room her father had always said he was going to rent out and then never did. At the time Gil had been too preoccupied with wanting to take her to bed to pay much attention, but now his curiosity was piqued. He lifted the latch. The door swung open. Behind it a wooden staircase rose up into the light. He smiled faintly, thinking of stairways to heaven, and took the dozen steps to the top.

The room reminded him of his own, except the windows here were in the pitch of the roof with a view of nothing but sky. Against one wall was a brass bedstead with a striped mattress, opposite it an apothecary's chest like the one down in the workshop, but this was neither scuffed nor paint-stained. A faded blue and cream rug covered most of the floor. It was a nice room. A bit small, maybe, for renting out, but nice. He gazed at the apothecary's chest. Walked towards it and pulled out a drawer. It was as empty as everything else today. He realised he had been holding his breath and laughed.

What were you expecting, exactly?

Another drawer held a grey t-shirt, probably Alex's. In another a couple of paper-backs: *The Thorn Birds; Zen and the Art of Motorcycle Maintenance*. Further down, a black frilly g-string. All right, he told himself. You need to stop this now.

Except beneath the g-string was a sheet of paper. Several sheets of paper. He frowned. Hesitated. Lifted them out. Several sheets of thick white drawing paper, a dozen or so pencil sketches of the same woman. Gil raised an eyebrow, for in some she lay naked on a bed, in others half-naked sitting on a stool, a chair, the observed curves and lines of her body as beautiful and as true as though she were there beside him.

As she had been beside him.

His mouth dried. "Oh God." His temperature soared and plummeted as he sifted through them. Alex was primarily a landscape artist but Gil had seen from the drawings of Jem at the house that he could capture a likeness precisely.

As he had captured this one.

He spread the sketches across the top of the chest, his hand shaking. Fourteen years ago. Fourteen years ago she had lost her baby, whose father had been the love of her life. This summer she was angry, restless. She had seen Jem in Patrick's last night and disappeared. He shook his head to dispel this madness. For surely it was madness. It couldn't possibly be real. But the drawings, the specific shape of her hands, her lips, the uptilt of her breasts, the long sweep of her waist into her hips, where his own body had lain.

"Gil."

He spun towards her voice as she stepped into the room. She was pale, this woman he had loved since he was nineteen years old and suddenly barely recognised. "Where have you been?" he cried.

"The cove."

Of course, the cove. It should have been his first thought.

Cceily came towards him, saw the sketches laid out over the chest. "Oh God." She touched them, shifting them about a little. "Oh my God."

"Why didn't you tell me?" His voice sounded thick, even to his own ears.

"I didn't know. I didn't know you were seeing Alex's daughter. I thought it was someone here for the summer. I thought she was called Jenny or Gemma. I didn't make the connection."

"Until last night."

"Mm."

He walked away from her to sit on the bed.

"Can I tell you about him? Do you want to hear it?"

He looked at her, furious, reeling. "Yeah. You tell me."

There was a silence. "I was twenty-seven," she said after a moment. "I'd just finished a long stint on tour and I was here on holiday. One day I walked into the gallery and it was … elemental. He was *so* attractive but also … something in him spoke to me. I just *knew*. We both knew. And we both resisted, for a long time. I went back to work. Nothing happened. And then … he called me." She paused, remembering. "He came to London. It was October, dark, rainy. We went for a drink in a pub off Covent Garden. He told me all about Marianne – you know about Marianne?"

Gil nodded. "I know."

"And Jem. He called her Puddle."

"I know that too."

"And it didn't matter. I had to be with him. I came down to Cornwall and bought the café and we – well, we were very careful. This was our room." She gazed round and he could see her imagining it as it had been then, maybe imagining Alex sitting where he was now. "It wasn't easy. Most of the time he was wracked with guilt. Marianne was ... she'd go missing for days and he'd be mad with worry, she'd lash out at him, at Jem, and then she'd be calm again. She hurt herself. She did bizarre things. His life with her was a nightmare. He needed me." She held his gaze. "Gil, I wanted to give him everything she couldn't. I loved him so much. I wanted to make him happy."

"Yeah. I see that."

"But you're angry."

"I'm not angry, I'm ... Jesus, Cecily. I can't believe it."

She came to sit beside him, crossing her legs beneath her on the mattress. "I can't believe you're with Jem."

"I don't know, maybe it was inevitable. I'd kind of worked my way through everyone else." He glanced at her. "So what happened?"

"Sam happened. Alex was thrilled and distraught. We were happy, for a little while. And then Marianne found out, and she drowned herself. Can you imagine what that was like for him? What it must have been like for her?" She was stricken, even now, but he could only imagine what it must have been like for Cecily, and was appalled. She said, "We thought maybe we could salvage something from it all, atone somehow by becoming a family. But then ... " She swallowed. Gil watched her eyes slowly redden, her tears spill. "Then Sam died and I thought it was judgement on me. It tore us apart. We could barely look at each other in the end. I didn't think I would ever get over it. It was a long, long time before I felt I deserved to have things again. Alex and I, we hardly spoke after we split up. There was so much lost between us. And now he's dead too."

He massaged her palm, trying to get his head round all of this, to feel something other than the tight ball of pain inside him.

She said, "I don't know what I'm doing anymore. It's as though his death has cut me loose from this place but it's fourteen years since we were together, Gil. And since then … Since him … " She stopped. He gazed at her and the air between them became tense as a wire.

He said softly, "I knew."

She stared at him.

"I knew there'd been someone. Some amazing guy, your true love. When you first told me about Sam, I realised that was who he was. And it was like he was away fighting a war or climbing a mountain or something. Something heroic. And I was your affair. The kid you were dallying with."

She shook her head. "That's not how it was. After Alex, I thought I'd never love any-one again. But five years went by, and I immersed myself in the café, and gradually it all began to hurt less. And then one summer night I was in Patrick's and I looked across the bar and there you were. And yes, you were a kid, but … "

"But it didn't matter."

She swallowed. She was crying; so was he.

He said, "You were the real thing for me."

"Gil – "

"You still are."

"Don't." She touched his cheek. He caught her hand.

"You don't feel the same?"

"I do. You know I do."

He kissed her, drawing her closer until she was in his lap, holding back her hair, his other hand travelling up her thigh. He kissed her throat.

She broke away. "Gil, we can't."

"*Christ.*" How could he be governed by such desire and filled with such guilt? *She said she didn't want history repeating itself* . Jesus! He got up, cried out in frustration. "What are we going to do?"

A thought struck her. "Does she *know*?"

256

"That Alex was having an affair, that's all. Eve told her." He gestured his despair.

"Eve didn't know. She must have heard it from Marianne. We were especially careful because Eve had a massive crush on Alex when she was a teenager. Her antennae would've picked me up at a hundred miles if we'd let her." She paused. "Is she devastated?"

"Just about." He gazed at her, his chest rising and falling. "I can't let her down."

Cecily nodded. "I know."

"I can't lose you." His voice cracked.

"I think you might have to."

"No." He came back to her, gathered her to him. "No, no."

"We could carry on just being friends."

He groaned. "Even when we were sleeping with other people, we were never just friends." He could feel her crying against him and drew back to wipe away her tears. "Don't. I'll think of something."

"Gil. There isn't anything."

"There has to be."

*

Jem had run up from town and along the lane so fast her breathing was ragged in her chest. She flung into the house, dropping her bag, kicking off her shoes. "Jemima?" Her mother's voice, lilting from upstairs as if from another dimension. "Is that you?"

By the time the stitch in her side had gone, Marianne was in the kitchen with her. "Oh my goodness. What's happened to you?"

Jem shook her head fiercely. Marianne placed her finger beneath her daughter's chin and lifted it, scrutinising her face. "You've run home."

Jem nodded.

"Were you running away from someone?"

She shook her head again.

"Were you frightened?"

"No," she muttered.

Her mother frowned. "All right then. Glass of milk? Biscuit?"

Jem slid onto a chair at the table, watching her as she drifted soothingly around the kitchen, fetching milk and shortbread, making tea for herself. It was almost winter and dark already outside. There were no lampposts in the lane and any other evening that alone would have had her running towards home. When she was little she'd thought that at night all the animals that had been run over and killed there lifted their grisly corpses from the tarmac to limp mangled and threatening through the dark.

Marianne put the glass down in front of her. "There you go."

"Thank you." She sipped some milk. Nibbled a corner of biscuit. After a few minutes she unbuttoned her coat and shrugged her arms out of the sleeves. Marianne switched on the radio, leaving the volume low, as she liked it, so the background babble of voices and music took the edge off the silence whilst barely impinging on their consciousness. The terrible thing Jem had seen without fully knowing what it was began to blur and fragment like a dream on waking. Only the feeling remained, the feeling which hardly made any sense but had been as real and shocking as a physical blow. She felt it in her chest, half expected there would be a bruise.

Marianne said, "Have you got any homework?"

"French vocab."

"Do you want to do it now, before we eat? I could help you." She smiled. " I was quite good at French."

Jem slipped down from the chair, fetched her bag, dragging it across the floor and heaving it up onto the table. Marianne was making onion soup, the smell and the sound of the wooden spoon against the pan reassuringly familiar. Jem opened her exercise book at the words she had copied down from the board. She let them dance in front of her eyes for a while.

"Right," Marianne said. "I'll read them to you and you write them down." She took away the exercise book. Jem found a pen and a scrap of paper. "La maison," Marianne

said. "Write down what it means as well."

Jem wrote, la maison – house.

"Le jardin."

Le jardin – garden.

"Le chat."

Le chat – cat.

"This is so boring. Why do we have to learn French?"

"So you can speak to French people. You might go to France when you're grown up, Jem. How would you feel if you couldn't communicate with anyone?"

She didn't know how she would feel. She couldn't imagine it. Marianne continued to recite the words but her concentration had skidded away from her. She said suddenly, "Are we still going to let people stay in that room when they're on holiday?"

Marianne was puzzled. "Which room?"

"The one on top of the gallery."

"Oh, that. Possibly. In the summer. Why?"

"There was somebody looking at it today." She shouldn't be saying this. She knew she shouldn't be saying it. Her skin was beginning to burn.

"When were you at the gallery today?"

"On my way home. I mean, not on my way, but – "

"Was Dad there?"

"Yes," she said faintly.

"So who was looking at the room?"

"A lady."

"Oh, not anyone we know, then?"

Jem shook her head. Marianne had given up with the French vocabulary and returned to the soup. Jem saw, in her head, her father's workshop, a large painting on the easel half obscuring her view. She'd been looking at the painting when she'd heard her father say, "Puddle! How lovely! I wasn't expecting to see you." His voice had sounded oddly loud and he was coming towards her from the door which led up to the attic room. The lady followed a moment later. She was pretty, Jem had thought. Smiling. And it was then that she'd seen something so quick she wasn't sure she'd seen it at all. Maybe

259

the lady had looked at her dad, maybe he'd looked at her. Had she touched him? Had he said some-thing? She just knew, beyond all reason, that there was something out of kilter, something she didn't understand yet was seriously wrong.

Marianne said, "Strange though, looking at the room at this time of year."

Jem said nothing.

Chapter Thirty-Four

The sun cannot reach into these chill and shadowed alleys so when I unclench my fingers above a narrow green gully no light dances on the surface or dazzles off the blade. The bloodied knife drops silently into the water and I hurry away.

What I think is going to happen now is that I will return to the gallery, where Gil will still be immersed in the sculptures. I will suggest we go to a bar, where we will sit for hours while he talks endlessly about the genius of Livio de Marchi and I drink until I can no longer think, or see, or remember.

What actually happens is that I return to the gallery and Gil is hanging out of the door, his face creased with worry. "Where the hell've you been?"

I frame a reply – *just for a walk* – but my mouth won't work and I realise what is obvious to him: I'm shaking and crying so hard I cannot speak.

"Jesus, what now?" He moves me aside, into a recess between Livio de Marchi's building and the next. "What happened?" I shake my head. I can't tell him. Can't tell him. He looks at me as I gulp and hiccup and wipe my face with the heels of my hands. "What?"

I draw in a long, shuddering breath. "Henry."

"He's *here*?"

I shake my head, weeping again. "I killed him."

Gil's face is slack with disbelief. "You killed him."

I nod, miserably.

"How?"

"With a knife."

"What knife? You have a knife?"

"I threw it in the canal."

"Jesus Christ. Show me." Her grabs my arm again. "Come on."

"But I don't know … "

"Yes you do."

I stumble beside him as he strides along the street and I

remember the point at which I'd stepped into the maze of alleys and lanes behind the buildings. "Down here." My voice rasps. He looks at me. The passage isn't wide enough for us to enter together.

"Go on," he says. I step ahead of him, edging between the stone walls, past the bins and beneath the same lines of damp, limp washing. He is silent but I can feel him at my back, rigid with tension. A cat darts in front of me. I swallow. The last time I did this – five minutes ago? ten minutes ago? – is imprinted upon the present as if time has doubled back on itself. I half expect to glance down the next alleyway and see him standing there in his yellow polo shirt, holding his phone, peering out into the street.

At the thought at what I *will* see down the next alleyway the world tilts around me and I put my hand to a wall to steady myself, nausea rising again in my throat. Gil waits. "I can't," I whisper. He frowns. Looks into the entrance of the alley. "Down there?"

I nod. I can't look.

"Don't move."

Still trembling, I turn my face to the wall, and wait.

He is gone for such a short time. I hear his footsteps, nothing more. He doesn't shout out, run, try to raise the alarm. I see Henry slumping down the rough corner of the building, his legs buckled beneath him, and my head aches, my tears are hot.

"Jem."

I shake my head. "I can't."

"Jem, come here."

Something in his voice makes me turn slowly towards the entrance to the alley. I gaze the length of it. There is nothing but Gil, standing in the light from the street. I draw in my breath. "Where is he?"

"You're sure it was here?"

"Yes."

"You're sure he was dead?"

"I … Maybe he staggered away. Maybe he's … " I look wildly round, expecting him lurch out at us.

"You stabbed him."

I nod.

"And you took the knife."

"I told you."

"So where's the blood?"

I stare at him. I remember the blood.

"Because you plunge a knife into someone, Jem, and you take it out again, there's going to be blood."

But there's nothing. The ground where Henry fell is dry, unmarked. The alley walls feel closer than they did before, the pavement soft like glue beneath my feet and I want to vomit again. I was sick before, I recall. Over some bins. Is that gone too? Gil's looking at me like I'm scaring him. I decide not to tell him I don't know what's real anymore and try to rally. But it isn't easy coming back from telling someone you murdered their friend and then it turns out maybe you didn't.

He says, "It's all got too much for you, hasn't it?"

I nod, grateful for this excuse which is also the truth. I'm still trying to tell myself maybe he's crouched wounded somewhere, and his blood got soaked up in his clothes and never hit the floor.

"We'll go and get a drink, find somewhere quiet." It's like he's talking me down from a roof. "Let's go back to the hotel, you can get some rest."

I let him take my arm, gently this time. "I'm sorry."

"Shh. It's fine. You'll be fine."

There's a buzzing sound I can't immediately identify. My hip seems to be juddering.

Then I remember again and take the mobile phone from my pocket. Gil watches me in disbelief. No one calls us any more.

"It's Henry's," I explain.

He says slowly, "What are you doing with Henry's phone?"

"He dropped it when … "

The significance of this sinks in, flooding us both with renewed horror. I glance at the display. There's a number one next to the envelope icon. A message. I look up at him. "Should I open it?"

Chapter Thirty-Five

By the spring of 1996, Marianne had ceased to keep a diary at all. Jem, sleep eluding her, flicked restlessly back through the pages, distracting herself from the great black boulder of reality pressing on the edges of her consciousness. How did you tell the difference, she was thinking, between memories and dreams? Were her memories of her parents any more accurate than her dreams of them, which came every night and with increasing ferocity? How could she know whether her memories represented the people they had been or whether they were nothing more than hopes and fictions? *Even you*, she thought bitterly, trying to conjure Alex before her so she could rant and wail and demand answers. But he would not come.

As with all her mother's diaries – as with all the diaries in the world, she thought - the January entries were detailed and regular. She had paid them little attention and anyway she could tell by now what the legibility of the handwriting and terseness of the recording signalled. Weeks of empty pages passed. And then, 20th May, so brief an entry she had missed it first time. So brief it was only two unsteady words.

A boy

Jem frowned. What boy? She flicked back and forth but nothing. It was the final entry. What boy? She lay the diary aside on the bed. Two words, and yet their significance seemed momentous. She shouted aloud – "What boy, Dad? Who was he?" But only the shimmering silence where Alex had once been. There was no one left to ask. No one knows, she thought. I could fabricate my entire background because there's no one left alive who knows what really happened.

But of course there was, as today had proved.

She shoved her feet into trainers, grabbed her keys from the hall. Eve had been going out but there was a chance now she might be back, and even if she wasn't Jem would sit on her doorstep and not move until the truth lay tattered and bloody between them. She careered down the lane, onto the road which would take her into town, her feet bumping over the tarmac. Hours ago she had wanted to put as much distance between herself and the terrible things Eve was saying as possible. Running away was what she did. Now she needed every last, tiny agonising detail. Questions filled her head like darts. And in between them, Gil's voice - *we all need to feel wanted and loved ... if someone else offered him sanctuary can you really not understand him taking it?*

She stopped, leaning forward, panting, her hair in her face and a stitch in her side. Gil understood this stuff better than anyone. He was sympathetic and broad-minded, could always see the bigger picture. *But they weren't your parents*, she thought. *This hasn't happened to you.*

She was aware of a car drawing slowly along the road in front of her. It was large, grey, a yellow smiley face sticker in the rear window. A flicker of memory, gone before she could identify it, and then the car stopped, its window sliding down.

"Jem?" the driver said.

She met his gaze. Blond, chunky, the guy from the prom. The guy who'd betrayed Gil to Eve and blacked his eye. She said nothing.

"Bloody hell," he observed. "What's happened to you?"

It seemed to Jem that whenever her mother came home from hospital she was frailer than when she had gone in. Today she had climbed out of the car as if she were nothing but moving bones. Alex had helped her up the path and into the sitting room, where their tea was now cooling in their cups, the scones Jem had made while he was away untouched on their plates. Marianne sat silent and pale, her fingers twitching in her lap. Jem could hardly bear to look at her.

"So," Alex said. His voice sounded as artificial as this felt. They never used the sitting room. They never all sat down together in the same place any more. "What news have you got for your mum, Puddle?"

She didn't know what he meant. Her mother was the most dramatic and eventful aspect of her life, and she already knew all about that. Or did she? It was hard to tell. But she could see her father was desperate for some ordinary conversation to fill the silence so she said, "School?"

"Sure."

"Um ... " She was invisible at school. It kept her safe. On parents' nights her teachers looked at her as if they had never seen her before. "I passed my French test. You had to get ten out of twenty and I got eleven."

"Well done," Alex said. Marianne lifted her hand, let it fall back into her lap.

Jem could no longer bear it. "I just ... I have ... " She stood up and edged out of the room. Once in the hall she ran, through the kitchen and down across the garden, prevented only by the height of the wall at its end from leaping into the fields and sprinting towards the sea, which was out of sight but a drawing presence always. She gulped in the air, which tasted of salt and summer and seemed to be a different thing entirely to the air inside the house.

After a few minutes her father came to join her. He sat beside her on the wall and for a moment they did not speak. Jem picked a daisy out of the lawn and gave it to him. He accepted it solemnly. She cleared her throat. "I don't think Mum should go back to hospital. It doesn't make her better."

Alex paused. "She won't ever be better, you do know that."

Fear clutched at her. "She'll always be like she is now?"

"No, no. That's the medication. She'll have good days and bad days, as she always has. But there's no cure, you know, Puddle. She'll never be ... "

"Normal?"

"Well that depends," he said, "on whether you think there's only one kind of normal."

Jem thought about this.

"Come on. We can't leave her sitting on her own, what sort of welcome home is that? I'll make some fresh tea, you butter your scones for us."

She returned meekly to the sitting room, knelt on the carpet to slice and butter the scones at the coffee table, sneaked a glance at her mother who looked only tired, and a little confused. "Do you want jam or honey?" Jem said, her voice shaking a little.

"Honey would be lovely."

Jem turned the knife in the honey jar, spread a thick layer on each half of the scone, and took them on a plate to Marianne. "There you go." She ventured a smile. Marianne's smile in return was watery but a reward nonetheless. Jem sat down again to pile damson jam onto her father's scones. She tried to think of something cheerful to say. "We could go for a walk, when you're feeling better. We could go down to the beach and collect shells. Some of my shells are all cracked and horrible now, I need some new ones."

Marianne nodded, as if she thought this a real possibility.

"There's a new shop on the square," Jem added, as Alex came in with another pot of tea. "It has all the sort of things you like. I went in with Miranda after school. All those floaty clothes and candles and patchwork bags."

"Skulls, black leather, alarming jewellery. The usual mix," Alex agreed. "There's a new gallery in town too, which shouldn't worry me too much, their work's very different to mine, much more in the way of technicolour landscapes and miniature detail. But you know, competition can be a double-edged sword."

Marianne nodded again. If their efforts sounded too hearty she didn't seem to notice. Jem prepared a scone for herself, one half honey, the other jam, watching her mother's slender fingers pleating the material of her skirt, the weightless twirl of her pale hair. There were photographs of her parents, in an album in the cupboard at the top of the stairs, taken before all joy had leached from their lives. They barely looked like the same people. She remembered something else she'd seen whilst outside the hippy-goth shop with Miranda after school and in this new spirit of excavating for good news said, "Oh, you know that lady who has the café on the square? She's had a baby. A little boy."

She glanced up, expecting some sort of confirmation from her father, who knew the lady who had the café on the square, or subdued interest from her mother, who on her better days delighted in babies. But Alex looked as if someone had hit him, hard, and her mother was staring at him with tears in her eyes.

"What's the matter?" Jem said uneasily. Marianne's tears spilled and streamed, dripping from her jaw onto her clothes, while Marianne made no attempt to wipe them away. She bowed her head into her arms and sobbed, rocking back and forth in her chair.

"Dad!" Jem cried. But he only stood, frozen. "Is it the medication?" she whispered.

He took a step towards her, bent over her. "Marianne."

She howled, beating him off with her fists, swiping at his face. He reeled back, his arm raised in defence, while she shrieked and screamed and drew blood.

"Stop it!" Jem wept. "Mum! Stop it." She pulled at Marianne's arm, wanting only to stop her from hitting him, from making that awful noise, but Marianne swung, knocking Jem into the table and crashing to the floor with the scalding tea and plates and scones.

Alex grabbed his wife's wrists, holding her off. "Are you all right?"

Jem nodded, but she'd caught her head and her arm when she'd fallen and she didn't know which was worse, her terror or the pain. Alex bundled Marianne roughly towards the door. "I'll be back in a minute."

She sat alone, among the ruins of the tea, and cried.

"What do you mean, what happened to me?"

"You look like shit."

"Thanks."

"Sorry," Henry said, "but … " He pushed open the passenger door. "Where're you going? D'you want a lift?"

"I was going to see Eve Callaghan." She shivered. "But actually I need Gil."

"Get in."

She slid into the warm interior of Henry's car. The sky had clouded since this morning and she was still wearing only shorts and the Stone Roses vest top she'd plucked from Gil's floor a million years ago. Since then she'd cried for hours, tried to sleep, then sped from the house without so much as brushing her hair. She probably did look like shit. She said, "I don't know why I'm getting into your car. You're one of the bad guys."

Henry sighed. "I'm not. Really I'm not. We all do bloody stupid things when we're threatened, don't we?"

She thought about it. He said, "Have you heard from Gil today?"

"He was with me, a couple of hours ago."

"He was *with* you?"

"What's wrong with that?"

He shook his head. His mobile, perched plugged into the car's music system, buzzed and he snatched it up. "Yeah? ... Thank God. Is she all right? ... And you've waited till *now* to tell me ... ? All right. See you there." He dropped it back down. "Gil. He found her, she's fine. They're on their way back to the square now."

"Found who?"

He glanced at her as he turned the car around, snail's-pacing it through the tourists using the road as their pavement. "Cecily. She went missing this morning. He didn't tell you?"

"No. I guess I distracted him."

"We were worried about her. She's ... " He paused. "She hasn't been herself lately."

"Who has?" Jem murmured.

Henry drove in silence for a minute or two. Then he said, "You know Cecily, right?"

"Not really."

"But you live here."

"Doesn't mean I know everybody."

"You were around here fourteen, fifteen years ago?"

"Yes. I was a child."

Henry paused. He said, giving up, "Right, okay."

"Why?"

"Just ... " He shook his head. "Doesn't matter." Reconsidered. "Something happened back then and I want to get to the bottom of it and – "

"Well my mum killed herself."

269

"I'm sorry."

"No, it was fourteen years ago which is a long time and … " Her voice wavered. *Oh for heaven's sake don't do this now, not here, not in front of him.*

They had reached the square. Henry parked the car. He said, after a minute during which they both tried to pretend she wasn't upset, "No, I am sorry. Sometimes you get caught up in something and you lose all sense of other people and their lives – their tragedies – and you just bulldoze ahead. I'm sorry."

Jem swallowed. "Four and a half months ago my dad died."

"Oh God."

"Eve Callaghan told me this morning that my dad had an affair. My mum was always fragile but Eve thinks that finding out about the affair pushed her over the edge. She told me that because of what you said to her about Gil. She doesn't trust him and she doesn't want me being pushed over the edge too."

He was appalled. "So if it weren't for me, you wouldn't know. You would have been spared that."

"Maybe. So actually, yes, you are one of the bad guys"

"Jem … "

"Don't. Don't say you're sorry. It's just consequences, you know? You lose your temper and you say one thing to one person and the ripple effect is … devastating."

He was silent. Then - "But Gil isn't having an affair with anyone but you."

"No. He isn't. Eve is wrong. Oh God." She shuddered. "Why have I said all this to you? I don't even know you." She pulled her hands back through her hair. "What did you want to ask me?"

"It really, really doesn't matter."

She opened the door. "Then thanks for the lift – "

"Cecily had a child."

She closed the door again. "Yes. I remember."

"And I need – I want – I'd like to know whose it was."

"Why don't you just ask her?"

"Because he - the baby - died and it's too painful."

Jem nodded. "Maybe it's also none of your business."

270

"It isn't," he agreed. "It isn't my business. That's it, anyway. I shouldn't have mentioned it."

"Well I don't know who it would have been. How would I know? How long did Gil say they'd be?"

"As long as it takes to walk up here from town."

She kicked off her trainers and put her feet up on the dashboard. Henry shot her an annoyed glance. She ignored him. "I'm going to get a drink," he said. "You coming?"

"Can I stay here?"

He could hardly refuse her anything. She watched his back as he crossed the grass to the pub, stared back ahead through the windscreen.

May 2oth 1996.

A boy

She remembered: arriving at her father's gallery one day after school, Alex and the lady from the café – Cecily – coming down from the attic room; Cecily's presence forever afterwards like a phantom in her peripheral vision, whisking away if she turned her head to see her straight on; Alex becoming less attentive and more patient at the same time; her mother screaming at him and beating him with her fists, a day or two before she died.

And there she was, Cecily, entering the square from the lower corner, Gil beside her. Jem watched them, saw them recognise the car, recognise her. Gil smiled and raised his hand. She waited until he had begun walking up the slope to the driver's side of the car, until Cecily was right in front of her. And then she released the handbrake.

Chapter Thirty-Six

"Move!" Gil yelled, lunging for the car. The slope was shallow but the Mercedes was heavy and as he wrenched at the door and flung inside he felt his own weight lend it propulsion. He cursed, grabbed at the wheel, found the brake. The car tilted, skidding diagonally to a halt. "*Christ*." As it stopped Jem was out the other side, sprinting across the grass. He yanked on the handbrake and chased after her. She headed straight for Cecily, slapping down her outstretched arm with force, pushing her so that she stumbled and fell to the ground, Jem's fists flailing at her head, her face. Gil seized her shoulders, dragging her away, his arms pinioning hers as she sobbed. "Stop it now," he said against her hair. "Stop now."

Cecily struggled to her feet. Gil met her eyes. "Are you okay?"

She stared at him, wordless. A group of onlookers formed a distant semi-circle, as though they were spectators at a particularly intense variety of street theatre. And suddenly there was Henry, thundering in, seeing them, seeing his car stranded at a precarious angle halfway across the grass. He gazed from one to the other, uncomprehending. "I'm sorry," Cecily was saying. "I'm so sorry."

Jem bridled. "About my mum? Or my dad?"

"About your mum. About you having to find out like this."

"I didn't find out." Gil could feel her shaking. She had slackened under his restraint and he loosened his grip a little. "I remembered. You were always there, on the edges of everything, lurking in the shadows. I remembered that and I understood."

Cecily nodded. "I thought maybe you knew. And then I thought you didn't want to."

"I was a child! I didn't – I would never have believed that my dad ... " She wept. "You *stole* him."

"I didn't steal him. He belonged to me too."

Jem shrieked.

Henry said, "For fuck's sake do something with her Gil, before she gets even more hysterical."

"She does have her reasons." But he reasserted his hold on her anyway.

Cecily said, "Come and talk with me."

Jem shook her head. "You're not talking to me about them."

"But maybe I can give you some answers – "

"I don't want answers from you!"

Henry said quietly to Cecily, "It's not the time."

She ignored him. "You had a brother," she told Jem. "He died a few months after Marianne did. Can you imagine what that did to your dad? If you want to think badly of him, of us, that's fine. But just imagine what that did to him."

"Come on," Henry persisted.

"He was the best of men."

Henry nudged her gently. "All right," she said under her breath, letting him edge her away. "All right."

"Now," Gil said levelly, when they were far enough away. "We are going to the pub over there and we're going to sit in a corner and we're going to talk. All right?"

"Can't we go to your room?" She looked as shaken as he felt.

"No." His instinct was to stay in public with her, where the level of self-restraint she needed as much as he did might kick in. He maintained his grip on her arm. "I want a drink."

There were, thank God, an empty table and a couple of chairs in an alcove away from the bar. He bought their drinks, sat her down. She was trembling, her eyes wet and swollen. She looked wrecked, he thought, not without sympathy.

"She killed my mum."

"It doesn't help, you know, to say stuff like that."

"If it hadn't been for her – "

"If it hadn't been for her, Alex would have been completely miserable."

She stared at him. "You're on her side."

"Jem listen. Alex and Cecily fell in love. They were filled with guilt about Marianne the whole time. But Cecily made him happy. After everything he went through with your mum, would you deny him that?"

"But he was married to her! And it wasn't her fault she was … the way she was."

"None of it was anyone's fault."

"He didn't have to have an affair. He didn't have to have a baby with someone else."

"Sometimes things just happen. We're only human you know, all of us."

She frowned. "Would you, if you'd been in his situation?"

"Probably."

She stared at him.

"Is that too honest?" he said.

She shook her head.

"He didn't leave your mum. He didn't abandon her to carers and hospitals. To being alone. He looked after her, the best he could, for years."

"Yes," she whispered.

"And that was kind of heroic, you know?"

She said nothing.

He added, "Cecily has never got over the loss of her baby. I don't suppose Alex did either. They thought they were paying the price."

"He would've been my brother."

"He was your brother."

"I remember seeing Cecily with him," she said slowly, as if reliving it, "I told my mum – 'the lady from the café has had a baby'. She cried, and she hit him, over and over again. And then … then she … "

So Marianne had known, Gil realised. She had known the baby was Alex's. She had known Alex was having an affair and maybe she'd been able to live with that, but finding out about the baby had been more than she could take. He tried to imagine the emotional turmoil which had existed in Jem's parents' house for all those years and knew he would find it unbearable. No wonder there were ghosts.

Jem said desperately, "Why can't you see this from Mum's side?"

"I can. But I need you to see it from your dad's."

"Why?"

"Because … I want to give him back to you. The father you worshipped. Because you have to forgive him. Because there's no moving on if you don't."

"There is no moving on."

He sighed. "Jem – "

She looked at him suspiciously. "Did you *know*? Have you always known?"

"No, not at all. Not until today."

"So you're shocked as well."

He gestured, helpless.

"She betrayed you too."

He paused. He couldn't talk to her about Cecily. He'd wanted to be two people out there in the square, restraining one woman, embracing the other. He had barely trusted himself to look at Cecily, to speak to her, for he had known his feelings would be clear in his voice, in his eyes. He ventured now, against his better judgement, "What she said, about giving you some answers? Maybe that's a good idea."

"What?"

"Well who else are you going to get them from?"

She shook her head. "I don't want answers any more. I don't want to hear her talk about him. It hurts too much."

He said nothing.

She swallowed. "You said I could come to Bristol with you."

"Yeah." And his heart felt so much heavier this time.

"Can we go soon?"

"How soon?"

"Now."

London had been a winter whirlwind of trips with old friends to theatres and galleries, of gusting into the bright warmth of wine bars and restaurants with dripping umbrellas, tube signs and neon lights shining in the dark. As she stepped off the train she was aware immediately of the empty platform, of the smell of the sea and the bitter cold. For years Cecily would tell people so often she almost came to believe it herself that dancing and London had given her up, that her life there had become too draining, too full of hopeless competition. She would never refer to it as a sacrifice she had chosen to make.

The tide was in, slapping against the wall of the wharfe as she wheeled her suitcase along it, sending jets of seawater in her path, splashing over her boots. From here the gallery looked as dark and deserted as everywhere else, but she knew better. A small light shone in the window of the workshop. She pressed the handle and stepped inside.

Alex turned in surprise. "But you're back tomorrow."

"I came home a day early."

He was smiling, wrapping her in her arms. "Ah, I've missed you."

"I've missed you too. That's why I came home a day early."

He held her at arms' length, surveying her as if she had been away for years instead of a fortnight. "I can't do this anymore without you," he said.

"Do what?"

"This ... living thing."

She hugged him again, aware of the breadth and muscle of his chest beneath the wool of his jersey, the threads of grey at his temples. He was thirty-nine and she often saw women look at him twice and lingeringly, but still he seemed older even than he had a year ago, as if victim to the war of attrition waged by strain. "How is everything?"

"Fine, in fact." He was reassuring but he had said before that though he clung to her when things were bad, in peacetime he didn't know whether he felt better or worse. "How was London?"

"Mad, as ever." She grinned. Upstairs in their room he opened a bottle of wine and she took off her coat and boots. He kissed her and handed her a glass.

"So what did you do? Tell me about it."

She detailed to him the musical she had been to see, the visit backstage to her friend in the chorus. He knelt before her and removed her socks, rolling them into a ball and massaging her feet as she talked. She described an exhibition at the National which she hadn't much liked and another at the V&A which she had. He unhooked her pendant and kissed the nape of her neck. She regaled him with the story of a meal at an Italian restaurant in Soho where everyone had been filled with such a combination of wine and high spirits there had been dancing and singing at the tables. He released her hair from its clip and combed it with his fingers, his hand sliding down to cup her breast. She had stopped talking.

Afterwards he said, "Why did you really come back early?"

He knew her too well. She said lightly, "I told you. I missed you too much."

"But you love going up there. I don't want to curtail your freedom."

"You don't."

He held her gaze, disbelieving.

Oh God, she thought. She hadn't wanted to tell him this yet. She'd wanted to continue to be the source of calm and peace she'd always been to him for at least a little while longer. She'd wanted time to get her own head around it first, to be sure.

She said, "My freedom might be curtailed anyway."

He continued to gaze at her.

"I'm pregnant."

His mouth slackened. He blinked. Say something! she wanted to cry. React the way I need you to.

He said, "Oh my love."

Her heart lifted. "Is it all right? If I am?"

"Of course it's all right."

"Really?"

He smiled. "Our child? It's a kind of blessing."

Soon they were going to have to consider this, as they always had to consider everything, through the prism of the family he already had. But not yet. Not just yet.

It had taken some time to persuade Henry that she was and would be fine, that what she needed most was a bath and sleep and to be alone. He had left with huge reluctance, had been kind and concerned and taken aback to learn the story of Alex. She still felt tremulous in the wake of having to explain it all, to him, to Gil. Tremulous too in the wake of Jem's attack. But what else should she have expected? What else had she deserved? The girl was young and vulnerable and still in mourning for her father, the one constant in her life. I did steal him from you, she thought. But you never lost him. He was always yours.

The café felt odd, having been closed all day. She hadn't closed it all day for Alex's funeral. Just the ceremony, after which she had returned, stripped weeping out of her black dress and into her jeans and t-shirt, tied on her apron and turned the sign on the door. The performance had helped her through the day, through the weeks. Gradually she had become able to put from her mind the thought of Alex smashed against the rocks. And then Gil had come, alive and beautiful and wanting to save people from drowning.

She stood in the bow of her window, watching the square which had been her home for all these years. She longed to stay but only in the company of people she couldn't have. And then there he was, the man she couldn't have, standing beside his car with the young woman who was Alex's daughter, saying something, his face solicitous, sombre. Jem touched his hand, said something, turned and walked away to the furthest corner of the square, to the road she would take if she were going home.

Cecily gave it ten minutes, long enough for Jem to change her mind and come back again. She didn't.

By the time she reached the foot of the iron staircase, Gil was descending it, carrying a large wooden sculpture. A tree, she saw, maybe three feet tall, its tangled limbs stretching past him and above him, the finer branches detailed with tiny leaves.

"Hi," she said, followed swiftly by, "Oh my goodness."

"It's the Tree of Life," Gil said, self-mocking.

"It really is." He loaded it into the boot of his car and they stood, regarding it silently for a moment. Even in such a prosaic setting the tree spoke of power and hope. She said so.

He half-smiled. "I don't know. I might display it from a car boot. 'Fortitude in unexpected places'. Is that too corny? It's

278

not going to survive the journey unless I wrap it in something, is it? Maybe an old blanket. I was thinking I might try the charity shops – "

"I have an old blanket you can use."

"Right." He shut up. Her heart was thudding. What journey? He said, more gently, "Are you okay?"

"I'm fine."

He cleared his throat. "I'm going to take her away for a little while, up to Bristol. Give her some breathing space, a chance to get some perspective on all this."

"Okay." Her head felt packed tight with everything she wasn't saying. Tears burned behind her eyes.

He said, "I'm so sorry. About earlier. It was horrific."

She nodded.

He lifted her chin, to make her look at him. "Oh, don't." He drew her closer. She rested her forehead against his shoulder. "Come on," he said. "We can't do this here."

In his room she stood apart from him, desperate to retain her dignity, desperate not to cry. But he was having none of it and enfolded her in his arms. "When she was hitting you … I just wanted to make her stop."

"You did make her stop."

"For then, for that moment. But what about the next time?"

She drew back to look at him. "Next time?"

He said, with difficulty, "I can't … trust her, around you."

"Is that why you're taking her away?"

"I can't think what else to do." He sat down on the bed, his head in his hands for a moment. "I don't want to leave you." He looked back at her, tears in his eyes too.

"I don't want you to leave me." She sat beside him.

"I love you."

"Gil – "

"I love you and I can't stop thinking, if we'd got back together the minute I arrived, none of this would have happened."

"Alex would still be dead."

He gazed at her. "You're still grieving for him too."

"Yes. A little. Right now I'm grieving for us."

He shook his head. "I'll come back."

"Gil, what do you think will happen? Taking Jem to Bristol with you is making a commitment to her. If you start taking responsibility for her now it might never stop. Believe me, I know about these things. Anyway, you're supposed to be going travelling with her, aren't you?"

"I don't want to go. I don't want … " He swallowed. "I look at her now and … Jesus, I can't say it. It makes me sound like a monster."

She stroked his hair. "You're not a monster. You're just trying to do your best."

"I owe her my best."

"All right, now I'm going to sound like a monster. Why do you owe her anything?"

"I don't know." He paused. "She has no one else, and she's Alex's daughter. If it were anyone but me, wouldn't you be glad, in the circumstances, that someone was taking care of her?"

"Of course I would. But it is you. And she's Marianne's daughter too."

"Meaning?"

"I'm scared."

He shook his head. "She's not like that. She's just traumatised. We all are."

She said nothing. He lifted her hand into his and kissed her knuckles. Turned it over to kiss her palm. She watched him, desire spiralling warm and involuntary inside her. She remembered exactly how it felt to make love with Gil. The thought of it sustained her through lonely winter nights. The possibility of it now, in spite of everything, almost took her breath away. He leaned in to kiss her mouth. She opened her lips to his. He slid his hands beneath her vest and she unbuttoned his shirt. Then she was beneath him and he was kissing her throat as she was reaching to unzip him, her pants around her ankles, her skirt around her waist. He groaned and she drew in her breath.

Chapter Thirty-Seven

Gil takes the phone from me. I try to read his frown as he presses the key pad. He shakes his head, shrugs.

"Was it her?" I still can't tell what's going through his mind. "Was it Cecily?"

He says levelly, "Think about that."

I think about it.

He says, "It isn't even Henry's." He tilts the phone towards me and scrolls through the contacts list, which is comprised entirely of Italian-sounding names. My mouth crumples. I look away, choking down my tears. The flat stone walls rising from the canal wobble and shimmer.

"I don't know what's real anymore."

"I know." He rubs my back between my shoulder blades. "I know, sweetheart."

He walks me along the pavement as if I have lost the ability to move by myself. Maybe I have. When my father died, I became afraid to leave the house and spent days – weeks - shaking with grief in empty rooms. It's like that now. It's worse than that now.

Gil wants to go back to the hotel but I resist. Instead we retrace our route to the vaporetto stop and wait for the bus. He stays near me, watchful, his hand on my shoulder, trailing down to the small of my back. "Are you okay?" he murmurs.

"Mm."

After a moment he says gently, "You know nothing happened, with Henry. You know he was never there." I nod, once. He takes a breath. "I don't know. Maybe you blame him, for setting things in motion, for – "

"He has been following us though."

He says nothing.

"Gil, he grabbed me at the station in Milan. We've seen his car like a zillion times." I look into his face, which is closed against me. "Are you *denying* this now?"

"Shh." He strokes my hair. "No. I'm not denying anything. I

think we both need to get some rest. Not a few hours' fitful sleep back at the hotel. Real rest."

"How do we do that?"

"Quit behaving like fugitives for a start. Find somewhere we can stay for longer than a couple of days, lie low. Try to live some kind of life."

I gaze at him, so grateful he's saying this, pretending for both of us that it might actually happen. He squeezes my shoulder. The bus whirrs and churns into view. We board and ride the shifting waters of the canal back to St Mark's Square.

I still can't face the hotel so he takes me, inevitably, to a bar. I murmur that our whole relationship has been spent in bars and he looks surprised – "Isn't everyone's?" I remember how happy he was that night in Patrick's, before Cecily turned up and everything changed. I remember us talking that first time in *bluewave*, about music and family and fate. We will never be so carefree again. We will never be in either of those places again. I shudder and knock back the brandy he's bought me in a single gulp. "We could just get hammered," he suggests. It's an appealing idea. I can't take any more of being aware, all the time. Of being conscious. He says, "Why don't you want to go back to the hotel?"

I don't know how to answer him. I don't want to tell him that I dream, nightly, of being beaten, drowned, hacked to pieces. He used to hold me when I woke screaming but I am so inured to it now I no longer scream. Instead I sit sweating and trembling on the edge of the bed, and he doesn't stir. In the end I settle for, "I don't want to be on my own."

He frowns. "I'll be there."

"Will you?"

He pauses. "Tell me," he says earnestly, "tell me you understand that I will always be there. That you are bound to me now for the rest of your life."

I like that he says I am bound to him, not that he is shackled to me. I swallow, rub my forehead. "You're being very kind."

He tries to make light of it. "I was always kind to you."

I look at him. "Except … "

"Yes," he concedes. "Except then."

"And I ... "

"Don't." He touches my wrist as if to stop my words. "Don't, Jem."

I'm crying again. For all the talk of living a life we both know this is the end. My blurry gaze travels from his face to the darkened cavern of the bar. In a distant pool of light near the door a shadow moves.

Hours later, and we are both hammered. I cannot see a yard in front of me, let alone remember the route back to the hotel. Gil, a little more steady on his feet than I am, leads us back and forth down alleyways which seemed sinister in daylight. Now, the faint lap and gleam of water every way we turn and the far distant sussurus of laughter, the night seethes malevolent around us.

"Fuck," Gil says, distinctly enough.

"Are we lost?"

"No. I just ... I could've sworn ... " We are crossing a small stone bridge between two sheer walls of shuttered windows and he strides to its end.

"Don't leave me."

"I'm not. I just need ... " And he's gone, swallowed up into the blackness.

I wait.

"Gil?" I say after a minute. My voice sounds as vulnerable as I feel. I remember when he went missing in the night at the petrol station in France, and I was as deranged with fear as I am now. He keeps slipping away. "Gil!"

She comes from nowhere, swooping down upon me, pushing me hard against the parapet of the bridge, her arm against my throat, such rage in her eyes that I cannot even cry out. I can barely breathe. Her face is inches from mine, her eyes wild, lips drawn back, a vein throbbing in her forehead. Death has transformed her beauty into something savage. "Where is he?" she hisses.

Why do they keep coming for him when he isn't here? "He was ... " I indicate the foot of the bridge. It's a strain to talk, to point. She jerks my head back.

"I could tear you apart with my bare hands."

She could. I would put up no defence. I'm crying. "You've come to take him away."

"Damn right." Her dress is still covered in blood. I stare, want to touch. I want to know if it's still wet. She shakes me hard. "He doesn't belong to you."

"I know – "

"He never did." Her fist hits me hard between my breasts and I gasp for air, her other hand ripping back my hair. I sink, my arms raised to protect my face, until I'm crouching against the stone parapet, accepting her blows as if I deserve them. Because I deserve them.

"Jem!" Gil's voice. I can't move. "Jesus Christ." He is kneeling beside me, parting my arms to see my face. "What happened?"

"Cecily was here."

He stares at me. The bridge is empty but for us.

"I can't do this anymore." I'm sobbing. "I can't do it, Gil. I want to go home."

Chapter Thirty-Eight

Jem stood knee-deep in a fast flowing stream, unsteady with the stoney bed and the hard buffeting of the water. Just beneath the surface swam shoals of minnow, brushing against her like lengths of ribbon. She was hysterical, for these fish were poisonous. As they bit into her skin when they passed they released into her bloodstream an amount of venom so deadly she would soon topple beneath the surface, the tiny killers rushing into her mouth and throat, river water filling her lungs. She could feel the pricks of their teeth in her bare shins and calves even now.

She woke, her heart racing. The bedroom clicked into reassuring focus around her: soft white bedding; a tapestry throw; wide waxed floorboards; Prussian blue walls. And, but for the muffled rumble of traffic, silence. She sat up, flipped back the sheets to pad into the bathroom, where the tiles beneath the chrome shower were wet, the glass slightly steamed. There was a single towel on the heater, in the cabinet the barest of essentials. Months since he'd lived here, but even so.

She pulled on her clothes, crept through to an olive green sitting-room, its shuttered windows overlooking the square below, a battered leather sofa opposite the fireplace, a desk in the corner on which a laptop sat with its lid shut. Near the windows a low table held a small television and a CD player but none of his technology was state-of-the-art. There was so *little* of anything, she thought. The authors on his bookshelf were an eclectic mix – Jack Kerouac and Paul Auster, Ian Rankin and Nick Hornby - but had he actually read any of them? She couldn't remember ever having seen him read anything other than a menu.

The rooms were so quiet she heard his key turn in the lock, and hastened out into the hall to greet him. "Hey." He was laden with carrier bags. "I had nothing in. Did you sleep okay?"

"Mm." She followed him into the kitchen, where he began unloading his shopping into the fridge. She watched as he unpacked cartons of juice and cans of beer, polystyrene trays of chicken fillets and bloodied steak.

"No nightmares?"

"No." She chose not to mention the paddling with piranhas.

"Good. Do you want a coffee?" He flicked on the kettle.

She gazed along the oiled wood worktop. The kettle, a toaster, a block of knives, the tins and packets he had yet to put away. No dust or grime. Nothing useless or broken, nothing that had been sitting there for twenty years. "It's not at all what I imagined," she told him. "This place."

"Yeah? What did you imagine?"

"Something less grand. How do you live like this?"

"It was in such a state I got it at a really good price, did all the work myself. My parents chipped in quite a bit – glad to finally get rid of me." He almost smiled.

"It's so tidy."

He shrugged. "I don't have much stuff."

"No wonder you hated my house."

"I didn't hate it. It just felt … claustrophobic." He said it apologetically, put her coffee mug on the oak table in front of her. He didn't join her to drink his, instead stayed leaning against the sink. "What do you want to do?"

"Now?"

"Today, tomorrow. We could stay holed up here if you like. Or I could show you around."

"And after that?"

"I don't know." His gaze was direct. "We'll do what's best for you, but I honestly don't know what that is."

She was unnerved: he had, until now, seemed to know exactly what was best for her, had at times been quite insistent upon it. But they had driven two hundred miles last night and into another world. This was his territory now. It must be weird for him. She said, "Can we just see how it goes?"

"Sure." He sipped his coffee.

She said suddenly, a cry from the heart, "It's like we're strangers."

"Well," he said after a moment, "we are."

She stared at him. The five or six feet between them had become a chasm. His face told her he knew as well as she did that he had, for the first time in as long as she'd known him, said the wrong thing. She couldn't tell whether he was going to back-pedal or hold his ground. Her throat burned. "How can you say that?"

"Listen." He pulled out a chair, a conciliation of sorts, and sat down. "I know what you've been through the last few months. That's not everything you are, is it? No more than that the person I've been with you is all that there is to me. That's all I meant. We've been through a very intense time and maybe it's time now to crawl back out into the world again. To be ... normal again. That's what you said you want." She nodded. "Okay, so normal for me here is work and this place, it's friends and family. How far you want to be a part of that is up to you."

She shook her head. "It's up to you."

He sighed. "I wouldn't have brought you if I didn't want you here."

"So it wasn't just you being heroic then?"

"What? That makes no sense."

"It makes you look good."

"You think I'm doing this for me?" She saw the flash of hurt and anger in his eyes.

"I'm sorry. I'm sorry."

"Come with me." He didn't take her hand, draw her along with him. He just stood up. She went with him into the sitting-room. "Look," he said.

The painting she hadn't noticed earlier on the alcove wall was of a surfer, balanced on his board, a great swell of tide advancing behind him. You could admire the skill with which the artist had reproduced the texture of the sand, the clarity of the sky, the sun upon the water. You could read it as a celebration of youth and freedom, of a man caught in a moment of euphoria. Or you could interpret the weight of that terrible impending wave and the darkening of the sky behind it and you would shudder. She had said this, to Alex, when he had been painting it.

"I get this," Gil told her. "That's me, the guy on that board. But that aside, your dad was a great man. He doesn't deserve to be rejected by you, even in memory, because he reached out to someone when he was in trouble. If staying here with me helps you reach some kind of peace, well … " He raised his hands in a gesture of helplessness.

She wanted to say, so it's not about us? It's not about wanting me with you? She swallowed. "Yes. Okay. I'm sorry."

"So we'll do our best?"

She nodded. The painted figure on the surfboard would haunt her dreams.

Gil sat in the dark on a bench in the communal garden, a bench which would be screened from the view from his sitting-room window by the plane trees and rhododendron bushes lining the square. He scrolled through his contacts list, tapped her name, which brought up her photo and her number. He tapped this too and closed his eyes.

"Hello," she said in his ear.

"Were you asleep?"

"No. Not yet. How are you? How're things going?"

He paused. The sound of her voice undid him.

"Gil?" she said. "Are you okay?"

The lump in his throat almost prevented speech. "Jesus, Cecily, what have I done?"

"Oh my love – "

"I can't bullshit her but I can't be truthful either. I ramble on, spouting so much crap I hate myself for it. I don't know what I'm doing. I want to be there, with you. I want to sell up here and come to you. We could do that, couldn't we? We could make it work. We've wasted so much fucking time already."

"Are you crying?"

"No." He was. "I can't stand this. I just want to hold you. I want to sleep with you, wake with you. I want to be inside you, beside you, now and for always."

"Gil, listen to me. We have to be patient. She'll get through this, she will. And when she does you'll deliver her back home and kindly, regretfully, step away."

"It's only been a few days and it feels like a lifetime. I don't know if I can keep going for as long as it takes."

"Of course you can. If I can, you can."

"I love you," he said desperately. "I love you."

"I love you too and I want you here but Gil, I can't go through this again if it's not going to come out right."

"I know." He pressed the heel of his palm against his eyes. "I know."

"Maybe I could come and talk to her, if it would help."

"It wouldn't help. Christ. I don't know what … " But his heart twisted with longing at the thought of seeing her again. "Maybe."

She was so cold. In the flat she took his jumpers from the wardrobe and tried them on, choosing one she thought would suit him, or on which the scent of his skin lingered, and wearing it to sit huddled on the sofa. She was cold and she had no energy. Sometimes she climbed into his bed and slept through the hours he spent at his workshop. Sometimes she walked listlessly through town, doing nothing, seeing nothing. Once Alex had come to sit beside her and she had willed him away. She could no longer cry. She was so cold.

Gil crouched beside the sofa to try to meet her eyes, said he was worried about her, wanted her to eat something, tried to persuade her to come out with him. She watched his mouth opening and closing as he talked, saw the mask of concern he strapped over his irritation. He didn't touch her anymore. He rarely smiled.

Weeks passed. She wanted to cling to him but he was hardly home. When he was she was so numbed by her isolation she could barely speak to him. He gave up suggesting trips to the cinema, to restaurants. He never did introduce her to his family. One evening he arrived with packets of wires and stones, exactly the same brands and styles she always used, so she could be building up her stock while she was away. He gave her his laptop to check up on her sales. She left it all in a heap on the kitchen table, untouched.

It was the final straw.

"I don't know what to do for you." Exasperation sharpened his voice. "You know, tell me, what I'm doing wrong here because I don't get it."

She was afraid when he was angry, not of him but of what it meant. "I don't know. It takes time."

"It takes a bit of bloody effort on your part!"

"That's not fair."

"It is fair. I'm trying, I'm really trying, and you're just hiding away in here like … a prisoner on hunger strike."

"I am a prisoner."

"Jesus! Feel free to leave any time, the door's wide open."

She didn't recognise him. Her voice wavered. "You weren't like this before. You were kind and loving and you supported me - "

"Yeah and being kind and loving and supporting you had you mowing down my friends in the street! I don't think it's enough, do you?"

"Stop shouting at me."

"I'm not shouting, I'm … " He stopped, made an effort to speak more calmly. "I'm scared, Jem."

"Of me?"

He sat down wearily, ran his hands through his hair. After a minute he said, "I'm not this hero who makes a habit of plucking kids out of the sea, you know. I'm just an ordinary guy who gets tired and frustrated and pissed off like anyone else. People who've been together twenty years bail when things get tough. Are you really surprised I'm struggling with this?"

"No." Her voice was very small. "But I need you to be strong."

"And I need you to try."

"All right." She paused. "It's hard."

"I know."

She wanted him to hold her. Just touch her hand. He was the most tactile, demonstrative man she had ever met.

He stood up, and walked away.

She sat at the foot of a tree beside the harbour, yellow lights reflected off the water, tall masts shifting as the boats knocked gently together. Above the rows of trees were the spires and towers of churches, around her bars and clubs not yet busy with the night ahead. She leaned against the trunk, playing with the fraying strap of her bag, and wondered how deep the water was. Her parents had both drowned.

"I didn't actually," Alex said. "My skull was smashed. Had you forgotten?"

She turned away from him.

He said sternly, "I can't see you like this."

"Then don't look."

But this time he wasn't going anywhere.

She gave in. "I thought about you all the time because it helped. It kept you with me. It doesn't help anymore. Now when I think about you all I can see is you with her."

"She was a great source of comfort to me."

"Oh for God's sake. You were fucking her."

"I loved her."

She tipped her head back against the tree, staring up into the evening sky. After a long moment she said, "I know."

"You do?"

She nodded. Swallowed. "I don't know what to do, Dad."

"Pack your bag, get on a train, go home."

"Gil ... "

"You can do without Gil."

"I love him, like you loved her."

"Puddle. Nothing else matters now. You need to go home."

Gil poured himself a generous slug of scotch, swallowed a large mouthful of it straight down. He stretched, rolled his shoulders. She said little, did nothing, yet the flat was quiet without her. Peaceful, without her. He closed his eyes. The doorbell rang. Jem had a key. He frowned, put the glass down on the kitchen table, walked into the hall and opened the door.

Cecily said anxiously, "Tell me I've done the right thing."

"Oh God." He drew her into the flat, into his arms. Held her for a long time, pressing her body the length of his, breathing her in. "Oh God. For me, absolutely the right thing."

"For her?"

"I don't know." He released her. "I don't know."

They went into the kitchen, where he poured her a drink. "I couldn't bear it," she said. "You sounded so exhausted, so down. You didn't sound like you."

"I don't feel like me. I feel depressed and guilty and ... hopeless. " He shook his head.

"That's why I came." She hung her bag over a chair. "I thought I could talk to her properly. Tell her how much Alex loved her, and Marianne. How compared to them, I was nothing to him."

"Which isn't true."

"No, but if that's what she needs to hear ... where is she, anyway?"

"She went out."

"I thought she didn't go out."

"She's not what you'd call predictable." He smiled, looking at her. "I've missed you so much." He reached for her hand and drew her close to kiss her.

"Don't," she said. "Don't, because I'll want – "

He kissed her again, lingeringly. "You'll want?"

"You."

He laughed, lifted her hair from her shoulder and kissed the skin beneath.

Jem threaded her way through the dark and unfamiliar streets, recalling a building here, an advertising hoarding there. She had often felt uneasy, out late in the city, gangs of hoodies roaming, dark alleyways cloaking who knew what. Tonight her head felt packed with explosives, the numbness dissipated, feelings cracking electrically across her brain. She reached the foot of the steps of the house, took them quickly, then in through the front door and into Gil's apartment. Immediately she heard his voice from the sitting-room, a woman's reply. She stilled, closed the door silently behind her, let her bag slip soundlessly to the floor. Glancing to her right she saw the empty kitchen, a handbag which wasn't hers slung over a chair. Twenty feet ahead of her a woman stood in the bay of the sitting-room window. A slender, very attractive woman with tousled tawny hair. She was, improbably, the woman from the café on the square. She was Cecily Ward. Her father's mistress. Gil's friend.

Jem remained rooted in the shadows of the hall.

Gil was saying something, his words having become a babble as he walked towards Cecily Ward. He was smiling. And then he did an impossible thing. He lifted Cecily's hand to his mouth and kissed her palm. Turned it over and kissed her knuckles. Leaned in to kiss her mouth.

She stared, her knees weakening. Understanding washed over her like a winter wave.

Of course.

She backed into the kitchen, gripping the worktop to prevent herself from crumpling to the floor.

Of course.

She was nauseous, her hands trembling. She heard – " … a quick wash, can I use your bathroom?"

"Sure," Gil said cheerily. "You know where it is."

Jem dropped further back into the depths of the kitchen, watched Cecily whisk past, heard the click and lock of the bathroom door. Her heart was hammering. And there was Gil, in the doorway.

"Jesus Christ! When did you … ?" He read her face, and knew instantly. "Oh God." He came towards her. "Oh Jem – "

She snatched a knife from the block and rammed it into him.

His expression froze in disbelief. She pulled the knife out again and pushed it into her pocket. He opened his mouth. Nothing came. He staggered back a step. The front of his shirt bore a wet scarlet bloom. She would remember forever the shock and confusion and hurt in his eyes.

When she left a moment later, scooping up her bag, tumbling down the steps and careering across the road into the night, he had already sunk to the floor, a widening pool of his blood seeping across the tiles.

I'm moving as fast as I can locking doors, throwing bolts, drawing curtains and all the time there's a keening, whining noise which I know at some distant rational level is me. In the bathroom I vomit again. It gets in my hair. I'm crying and shuddering now, pulling blankets from the bed because I need to sleep but not up here, not in a bed, up here there's too much space.

Downstairs I drag cushions from the sofa and stuff them under the kitchen table. Crawl inside with my blanket. Sheltering from the bombs. I pull the blanket around me for suddenly it's cold. So cold. I can make out shapes on the dresser. A pile of books, hardbacks on their sides. I can't quite read the titles but the gold lettering glints at me from their spines. Bottles, squarish ones of oil, taller ones of wine. It calms me for a minute, staring at these things, working to identify them even though they're ours and have been sitting where they are now for the best part of a decade. My heart rate begins to slow. There's a can of some-thing and a cable, an extension lead maybe or a phone charger, an old spherical CD player with its mouth open like a Pacman and a photo of me and Dad in a frame.

He's gone now.

They're all gone now.

I'm sick again into my hand. Or I would be, if there were anything left in my stomach to hurl. I jerk up to find something on which to wipe the acid from my palm, hitting my head against the table, gritting my teeth in pain and sobbing.

I want him back.

And here he is. Storming in, angry, terrified. He's breathing hard, his hair damp and wild, and his bloodshot eyes are those of a stranger. He makes me pack a bag and we flee through the night. We cross the channel, running blind. I'm falling apart and he holds me together, grim and determined, without trust, without hope. He vanishes and I panic, the demons rushing in. I can't make it right even in my head.

and it's then that it comes

the pounding on the front door
I freeze, clamp my mouth shut to stop the whimpering.
Again. A fist against the wood. Heavy with urgency. My eyes squeeze shut and I draw up my knees, bury my head against them.

Go away go away go away go away
And it does.
It's gone.
Then he shouts my name and my unravelling is complete.

*

Printed in Great Britain
by Amazon